West Oversea

A Norse Saga

Praise for Lars Walker's Novels

West Oversea is a gripping Viking saga. Lars Walker understands the unique Norse mindset at the time of the Vikings' conversion to Christianity, and he tells a tale of seafaring adventure and exploration of new worlds that will keep you on the edge of your chair – and make you think.

> **Dr. John A. Eidsmoe**, Colonel, Alabama State Defense Force
> Pastor, Assn. of Free Lutheran Congregations
> Constitutional Law Professor
> Author, *Christianity and the Constitution*

In this Erling Skjalgsson saga as told by his faithful companion, Father Aillil, Walker takes us from Norway, to Iceland, to America, to Greenland and back. This book is not only a delightful tale of adventure and bravery, but there is also an undercurrent of commentary on contemporary culture and values.

> **Rev. Paul T. McCain**, Publisher, Exec. Dir.,
> Editorial Division, Concordia Publishing House

I cannot give a high enough recommendation to Lars Walker's Norse saga. You will not be disappointed. You will be blessed.

> **Hunter Baker**, writing in *The American Spectator* online
> Author, *The End of Secularism*

It is refreshing to read popular fantasy built on a foundation of solid research and love of the medieval Icelandic sagas.... Amazing.... This reader welcomes more fiction from Walker's pen.

> **Dale Nelson**, *Touchstone: A Journal of Mere Christianity*

Action, excitement, and the sheer fun that reading can be.... Deeply, profoundly Christian...but in a bold, battling way.

> **Gene Edward Veith**, Author, *The Spirituality of the Cross*

Not for spiritual sissies.... Rowdy action and a realistic look at the human and spiritual costs of religious and cultural conversion.

> **Rita Elkins**, *Florida Today*

WEST OVERSEA

A NORSE SAGA OF MYSTERY, ADVENTURE AND FAITH

BY

LARS WALKER

Noble Novels
Ventura, California
2009

West Oversea: A Norse Saga of Mystery, Adventure, and Faith

published by  Noble Novels a division of

Nordskog Publishing Inc.

Copyright © 2009 by Lars Walker

ISBN: 978-0-9796736-8-9
Library of Congress Control Number 2009927387

Interior Design, Production, and Editing, Desta Garrett
Cover Design and Original Art, Forge Toro
Theology and Manuscript Editor, Ronald Kirk
Copy Editor, Kimberley Winters Woods

West Oversea is a work of historical fiction. Apart from the well-known actual people, events, and locales that figure in the narrative, all names, characters, places, and incidents are the products of the author's imagination or are used fictitiously. Any resemblance to current events or locales, or to living persons, is entirely coincidental.

Printed in the United States of America

NORDSKOG PUBLISHING, INC.
2716 Sailor Ave., Ventura, California 93001 USA
1-805-642-2070 • 1-805-276-5129
www.NordskogPublishing.com

Member,

Christian Small Publishers Association

For Frisomae

In memory of some pretty intrepid journeys of our own.

Publisher's Foreword

Welcome to Nordskog Publishing's inaugural fiction book in a new series of Noble Novels! As our ongoing series of "meaty, tasty, and easily digestible theological offerings" continues with excellence, we have pride and joy in now presenting, under the imprint Noble Novels, fiction books that are exciting, thrilling, enjoyable, and fun, and which ring out the admonition of the Apostle Paul, in his epistle, to think on those things that are true, *noble*, just, pure, lovely, of good report, virtuous and praiseworthy.... "And if you do, the God of peace shall be with you" (Philippians 4:8-9).

West Oversea is an ideal book to begin our new series. Lars Walker's fiction story is based upon true, historical facts at the turn of the second millennium. Many of the novel's characters are based upon real Vikings, men who were courageous and indeed *noble*. This story is about my paternal ancestors, the Vikings, during the time of much of Norway's conversion to Christianity, and it is ideal for our initial fiction offering.

My great grandparents and grandfather, Andrae (Arne) Nordskog, immigrated from Norway to America (New York) in the late nineteenth century. As a boy, I grew up in our home listening to the famous Norwegian composer Edvard Grieg's (1843-1907) *Piano Concerto in A minor (la mineur-a-Moll)*, "The Song of Norway," and I am listening to it now, even as I write this Foreword. My Italian mother, Elinor, used to say regarding my dad, Bob, "I've taken a liking to a Viking." My dad used to relate the old story of how "10,000 Swedes were chased through the weeds by one Norwegian."

American historian and my good friend Dr. Marshall Foster (founder-president of The World History Institute) gives us some quick snapshots of the Norwegians – who were traders as well as warriors – in the latter years of the first millennium after Christ's resurrection.

Guthrum, the Viking king, took almost all of England by force, but was later defeated in 878 by Alfred the Great (a Christian king of England), who became his godfather and educated him and his leaders in the Christian faith. Erik the Red was a wild Viking who was convicted of murder and exiled first to Iceland and then to Greenland. His son, Leif Eriksson, was sent back to Norway near the end of the tenth century and converted to Christianity. He later returned to Greenland to convert the settlers to Christ, and eventually made a voyage to explore new lands to the west which had previously been seen by other Norsemen. These lands, we now know, were part of North America. Norwegian king Olaf Trygvesson, who died early in the eleventh century, tore down idols in the country and forcibly converted the pagan Norwegians to Christianity.

* * *

Lars Walker's third novel about the Vikings begins in the year 1001. King Olaf Trygvesson is dead, but his sister's husband, Erling Skjalgsson, carries on his dream of a Christian Norway that preserves its traditional freedoms. Rather than do a dishonorable deed, Erling relinquishes his power and lands.

He and his household board ships and sail west to find a new life with Leif Eriksson in Greenland.

This voyage, though, will be longer and more dangerous than they ever imagined. It will take them to an unexplored country few Europeans have seen. Demonic forces will pursue them, but the greatest danger of all may be in the dark secret carried by Father Aillil, Erling's Irish priest. You won't want to put this book down. Read on!

– *Tusen Takk,* Gerald Christian Nordskog, *Easter,* 2009

Gerald Christian Nordskog
PUBLISHER

Greenland
BRATTAHLID

LEIF'S
BOOTHS

Strange Lands

THE VOYAGE

West
Oversea

"But we also have reason to believe that Erling was a prominent merchant, possibly with good connections both in Iceland and Greenland, and perhaps even in Vinland, in America.... We can assume

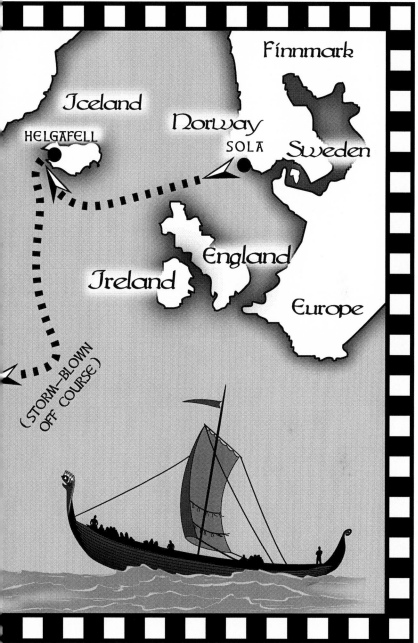

Finnmark

Iceland

Norway

HELGAFELL

SOLA

Sweden

England

Ireland

Europe

(STORM-BLOWN OFF COURSE)

that Erling Skjalgsson was personally acquainted with Leif Eriksson...."
(*Norge Blir et Rike*, by Torgrim Titlestad. Stavanger, Norway: Erling Skjalgsson-selskapet, 2000, p. 207. Trans. by Lars Walker.)

List of Characters

(with approximate pronunciations
from modern Norwegian)

GREENLANDERS

Freydis Eriksdatter (FRAY-dees AY-reeks-dotter): half-sister to Leif Eriksson, wife of Thorvard Einarsson

Leif Eriksson (LIFE AY-reek-son): The chief man of Greenland, discoverer of America

Thorhalla (TOOR-halla): Wife of Leif Eriksson

Thorkel Leifsson (TOOR-kell LIFE-son): Leif Eriksson's son (an infant)

Thorstein Eriksson (TOOR-stine AY-reek-son): Brother to Leif Eriksson

Thorvald Eriksson (TOOR-vahld AY-reek-son): Brother to Leif Eriksson

Thorvard Einarsson (TOOR-vard EYE-nar-son): A Greenlander, husband to Freydis Erikssdatter

ICELANDERS

Asdis Styrsdatter (OZ-dees STEERS-dotter): Wife to Snorri the Chieftain

Bolli Thorleiksson (BOH-lee TOOR-likes-dotter): Foster-son to Olaf Peacock, foster-brother to Kjartan Olafsson

Gunnar Valbjornsson (GOO-nar VAHL-bjoorn-son): a Norwegian chieftain

Gudrun Osvifsdatter (GOOD-roon OSE-veefs-dotter): Wife to Bolli Thorleiksson

Haldor Snorasson (HALL-door SNOO-rah-son): Snorri the Chieftain's son

Ivar Ketilsson (EE-var KAY-teel-son): Brother to Orm

Kjartan Olafsson (SHAR-tawn OO-loff-son): Son of Olaf Peacock, husband of Refna

Kjartan Thorodsson (SHAR-tawn TOOR-ode-son): officially son of Thorodd the Tax-trader; actually son of Bjorn of Breidavik

Konnall: Merchant, captain of Erling's ship

Olaf Hoskuldsson (OO-loff HOCE-koold-son) the Peacock: An important man in Iceland, father to Kjartan

Orm Ketilsson (OORM KAY-teel-son): Brother to Ivar

Refna (REFF-na): Kjartan Olafsson's wife

Snorri Thorgrimsson (SNORE-ee TOOR-grim-son) the Chieftain: An important man in Iceland, old friend of Erling

Thorarin (Toor-AR-een): Konnall's partner

Thord Snorrasson (TOORD SNORE-a-son) (the Cat): Snorri the Chieftain's son

Thorgrima (Toor-GREE-ma) Witch-face: A resident of Frodriver, wife to Thorir Wood-leg

Thorir (TOOR-eer) Woodleg: A resident of Frodriver, husband to Thorgrima Witch-face

Thorodd (TOOR-ode) the Tax-trader: Husband of Thurid Borks-datter, formally the father of Kjartan Thorodsson

Thorolf (TOOR-olf): A powerful Icelander, a kinsman of the Ketilssons

Thurid Borksdatter (TOOR-eed BOORKS-dotter): Wife of Thorodd the Tax-trader, mother of Kjartan Thoroddsson

Unn (OON) the Barren: A woman with magical powers

Vagn (VONG): Sister's son of Thorarin, Konnall's partner

NORWEGIANS

Aillil (AL-ill) (Father): Erling Skjalgsson's priest, the narrator of this book

Aslak Erlingsson (Oz-lock AIR-leeng-son): Erling Skjalgsson's first son

Astrid Trygvesdatter (Oss-treed TRIGG-vehs-dotter): Wife of Erling Skjalgsson, sister to Olaf Trygvesson, late king of Norway

Bergthor (BAIRG-toor): An old warrior in Erling's bodyguard

Brian: A freedman, husband of Copar

Copar: A freedwoman, wife of Brian

Erik Haakonsson (AIR-eek HOE-kon-son) (Jarl Erik): Ruler of western Norway under King Svein Forkbeard

Erling Skjalgsson (AIR-leeng SHAWLG-son): Chief man of west Norway

Eystein (EYE-stine): Erling's chief of defense

Fingal MacBrian: A thrall who rescues Father Aillil and goes along on the voyage

Freydis Sotisdatter (FRAY-dees SOH-tees-dotter): Niece of Lemming

Geirodd Thorbardsson (GUY-road TOOR-bard-son): A powerful Norwegian man

Helge (HELL-geh) of Klepp: An important man in West Norway, friend to Father Aillil

Kaari Skjalgsson (KOE-ree SHAWLG-son): Erling Skjalgsson's long-lost brother

Ketil (KAY-teel): A ship's captain from Norway

Lemming: A former thrall. Uncle and guardian of Freydis Sotisdatter

Oddvin Oddleifsson (ODE-veen ODE-life-son): A wealthy Norwegian man, owner of the Eye of Odin

Ogmund Bodvarsson (OAG-moond BODE-var-son): A farmer

Ragna (RAWG-na): Erling's mother

Steinulf (STINE-oolf): Erling's uncle, chief of his bodyguard

Thorbrand Gudbrandsson (TOOR-brawnd GEWD-brond-son): A young man who joins the voyage, brother to Thorlak

Thorlak Gudbrandsson (TOOR-lock GOOD-brond-son): A young man who joins the voyage, brother to Thorband

Thorliv Skjalgsdatter (TOOR-leev SHAWLGS-dotter): Erling's sister

Ulf Lodinsson (OOLF LOW-deen-son): The son of Lodin and Gyda and brother of Ragnvald, old enemies of Erling's family who were killed by Erling's father

OTHERS

Adalbert: Jarl Erik's bishop

Andrew (Father): Leif Eriksson's priest

"Finn": A Native American rescued by Erling's crew

Jon: The bishop of Iceland, an Irishman

Maeve: Father Aillil's lost sister

Oddketil (ODE-kay-teel): A merchant from Orkney

Svein (SVAIN) Forkbeard: King of Denmark

Thorgunna Thorhallsdatter (TOOR-goo-na TOOR-halls-dotter):
A widow from the Hebrides, come to Iceland to find a husband

Part One

Norway

Chapter 1

I LIKED Konnall the merchant the moment I met him. For one thing he was an Icelander with an Irish name. For another I liked his long, dour face that never smiled or spent the least effort to make itself pleasant. When you're a priest, people are forever pulling their holy faces with you, and I get weary dwelling among the masks.

"Lots of Irish in Iceland," Konnall said to me as we sat in the light summer evening outside Erling's booth. We were again at the Gula-Thing, the great regional assembly. People sat all around, on the ground or on stones or log benches, drawn like flies to honey by the promise of one of Erling Skjalgsson's feeds.

"Not just thralls either," said Konnall. "Plenty of Irish Norse from Dublin moved west in the old days, before the land filled up. A lot of them had Irish mothers; my own mother's father came from Donegal. And there was a bit of a woman-dearth at first, so many men took thralls to wife, most of them Irish."

"That would be why so many Icelanders are *skalds*, singers of songs," said I. "'Tis the music in the Irish blood."

"I don't know about that," said Konnall. "I can't sing a note myself. But I'll say this – the sweetest human voice I ever heard belonged to an Irishwoman. She was a thrall in Greenland."

"You've been to Greenland? Leif Eriksson's home?"

"Aye, the gable of the world. It's not an easy voyage, but you can name your price for meal there."

"What's it like?"

"Like Iceland, but more so. Night all day in the winter, day all night in the summer. You can't grow much of anything but grass, and the people live on meat and butter and fish for the most part."

"I'd like to see such a place, if I didn't have to cross the sea to do it."

"You're not a sailor?"

"I'll sail anywhere, so long as I can keep one foot on shore. I have to travel by ship now and then – I sailed here with Erling, for example. But the shorter the better, if I get my way."

Konnall began to recite:

> "If I had arms like the sun at dawn
> I'd stretch them o'er the sea.
> And all I loved and bid farewell
> I'd draw back home to me."

"What was that?" I asked.

"Just a snatch of a song. I heard it in Greenland, as it happens."

"Who sang it?"

"The thrall girl. The one I spoke of before."

I reached and took him by the shirt. It was an offense to touch a man so, but I cared not. "What was her name?" I asked.

He looked startled. "I don't recall. She was just a thrall. She had the sweetest voice that ever came from human throat though."

"Was her name Maeve?"

"It might have been. I think it was."

"What did she look like?"

"I'm not sure I recall. I didn't pay a lot of attention. Dark hair, I think."

"Blue eyes?"

"I couldn't say. Why do you ask?"

"My sister's name was Maeve. She was stolen by Vikings. She used to sing that song, in a voice to break a man's heart."

I excused myself and went inside the booth where Erling sat with his kinsmen and some great folk he meant to woo. I broke in on their talk.

"I'm going to Greenland," I said.

Erling looked at me for the time it took to blink thrice.

"That's very interesting, Father," he said, "and I'll be pleased to hear more about it later on. But just now I'm doing business with these men."

"Is this the famous Father Aillil?" asked one of the guests, a stout ruffian with a scar under one eye. "The one who went through the iron ordeal and rebuked Olaf Trygvesson to his face?"

"He, or his brother," said Erling with a smile.

"Much of a tale for a man without walnuts."

"This is Gunnar Valbjornsson from Saevereid," said Erling.

"Happy to meet you," I lied.

"May Father Aillil join our talk?" Erling asked the man.

"'Tis naught to me," he answered, with an unwelcoming look, so I found a place on the bench and joined them straightaway.

Gunnar looked at me through the corner of his eye as he said to Erling, "Svein Forkbeard of Denmark is the most powerful king in the north. He may take England one day."

"He killed Olaf," said Erling.

"Olaf was very pretty, and he swung a sweet sword. But he was ever a rash fool and I swore him loyalty only because I was middling sure he wouldn't last long. I was right."

"So you're content to bow to a Danish king?"

"Danish or Norse, what matters it? I've never thought of myself as a Norwegian, except when I'm overseas. I'm a Horder; a man of Hordaland. That's my country. If a king sits in Nidaros, he's an outlander to me. If I have to have an overlord, and that seems to be the way the world beats nowadays, I'd as soon have one too far off to keep a close eye on me."

"This is just my point," said Erling, eyes blazing, clenching a fist. "You want to keep your independence, your rights as a Norseman. I erred in supporting Olaf. I thought we could have a high king and still keep our rights. It doesn't work. Kings are men. Men are greedy. When you give them some power, they want more. They think it's God's will."

"That's the fault of the priests," said Gunnar with a glance my way.

"Harald Finehair had the same thought in his time, and he walked the old paths," said Erling.

"Be that as may be, kings are there. Svein Forkbeard lives. He sits in the high seat in Denmark and he's set Erik Haakonsson as jarl over west Norway. I'd like to wish it away and go back to the old days. I'd like to be twenty winters old again, too."

"Kings are not gods. Jarls are not gods. They rule because men let them. Don't you see? That's the marvel of it. All we need do is say no. If all of us say no, there's nothing Erik or Svein or the Emperor of Constantinople can do to make us fall in line. But I can't do it alone. I need you and all the others to stand with me."

"And you'll lead us?"

"Yes."

"Then how are you different from a king or a jarl? Why should I believe you aren't full as power-sick as they?"

"I call myself hersir, as you do. Not jarl. Not king. A hersir doesn't rule beyond his own fences. Anything more he does by leave of his fellows."

"So you say."

"So I say. It's the word of Erling Skjalgsson."

Gunnar took a drink from his horn and wiped his mouth. "I'll think about it," he said.

Erling and I got no chance to talk under four eyes that night. It was a feast like any other, even if most of the feasters sat under the sky, and he had host's duties. A man earns power in Norway through courage and shrewdness and luck and family ties, but he also earns it by keeping a good table and feasting his friends, and those he'd like for friends, and even his enemies if he can get them. 'Tis a noble thing, seen aright. Erling cared little for wealth in itself. Wealth only gave him the means to feed his followers and friends, and make them rich gifts. Any way of living that teaches a man to value giving over getting must have some virtue in it.

So I wearied of politicking in time (it didn't take long) and went out into the evening. I've never grown used to the Norwegian summer twilight. The silver light just lingers like an unwanted guest and, like an unwanted guest, keeps you up when you'd sooner be sleeping. In any case, the booth was full of feasters and my bed was there. Little sleep I was getting at this Thing. I wondered if I could find somebody less well-friended than Erling to take me in, Helge of Klepp, perhaps.

I wore my heavy cloak, for the air was chill, and I had on my priest's robes, which get drafty. Most days I dressed in shirt and trousers like other men with but my tonsure and the wooden crucifix on my breast to tell my office, but at a Thing, especially this one, Erling wanted every man in his best. The Gula-Thing always begins the first Thursday after Easter, which fell on St. Justin's day that year – the Year of Our Lord 1001 – so it was but a little past mid-April. From the woods I heard gray thrushes trilling, welcome law-singers sent by God Himself telling us that winter was outlawed awhile. Crusty snow still lay here and there under the trees that hedged the Thing-stead.

This Thing-stead sat on its slope like a cushion on a great, broken chair. At its foot was the fjord, where scores of long-ships, knarrs and smaller boats rode at their moorings. The mountains at the top were the chair's back. The pale light bled the bright colors out, making all gray and black, shaded in green and blue.

"Father Aillil?" said a voice.

I turned to see a tall old man approaching me. He was lean and richly dressed in a gray cloak and a blue cap.

"I am that animal," said I.

"I was in Erling's booth when you came in earlier. Is it true you mean to sail to Greenland?"

"That's my intent. I've made no arrangements."

"But you mean to go."

"If I don't I'll go mad and jump in the sea, like a lemming."

"Then will you do me a service and earn my friendship?"

"Whose friendship is that, if I may ask?"

"Pardon me, I forgot to say. I am Oddvin Oddleifsson, of Onarheim on Tysness Island. I'm the chief man of my family."

I'd reckoned that anyone invited to Erling's feast was prob-ably somebody when he was at home, and his clothing said the same.

"And what good is it a poor priest could do for a great man like yourself?"

From under his cloak he brought a casket, about the size of two fists, shaped like a house. It seemed to be made of ivory and silver.

"Take this to the far-most sea and drown it there," he said.

I looked at the thing without reaching for it. "It looks a fine piece of work, and costly."

"Costly indeed. It could cost a man his soul. That's why I'd be quit of it for good and all."

I took a step back. "If that's the way of it, I'd as soon not. There's lots of sea about – why not drop it in yourself?"

"That was my thought. But then I knew it must go west oversea. When I saw you tonight, I knew you for the man to take it."

"How?"

"Because I'd seen you take it."

"Are you drunk?"

"Of course I'm drunk. I've been feasting with Erling. But it's not the mead that speaks now."

I sighed. "Well, it's been a pleasure making your acquaintance. I'll just be leaving you –"

"Stay! I said I saw you taking the casket. I spoke truth."

"No, you didn't, friend. Here am I, and there are you with the object. You'll notice I'm not taking it. You'll notice I'm walking away from you."

"You'll be back shortly. I'll wait here."

"Have a nice time, and God bless you."

"You'll be back after the dead bird bites you."

I hastened away. God spare me from magic and madmen.

I nearly ran into three men – two big bullyboys and man in a hooded cloak the color of dried blood. He turned quickly away as I sidestepped, and I got a glimpse of a reddish beard.

They went by without a word.

I hadn't gone ten more steps when something solid, yet ticklish, smacked me on the side of the face and I slipped on some sheep berries and fell on my back (the landowner used the Thing-stead as a meadow).

I sat up and saw a dead raven lying beside me. There was shouting and the sound of feet running off.

"North-under with those boys!" said a voice. A burly man approached me. "Forgive us Father, it was my sons having a lark. They killed a raven and were playing catch with it. You walked straight between them, I'm afraid. I'd told them to take their game someplace where it wouldn't bother folks."

"'Tis no matter," said I, getting up and putting my hand to my cheek. I felt something wet. It was red on my hand. I took it for the raven's blood.

"Begging your pardon, Father, but you're cut a bit. You must have caught the bird's beak." The man tore a strip of linen from his undershirt for me to hold against it. "Good luck for you it didn't catch you in the eye."

I thanked the man, who apologized again, and turned and went back to Oddvin Oddleifsson.

"How'd you do that?" I asked. "Are you some kind of warlock?"

"I didn't make it happen," he said. His bush-browed eyes were sad. "I but saw it."

"How can that be?"

"'Tis the casket. Or rather, 'tis what's in it."

"And what's in it?"

"There are rocks here that look sittable. Let's rest and I'll tell you all."

We sat on some large, rounded rocks and he said, "Do you know the tale of how Odin got his wisdom?"

"I care little for your Norse-god stories. We've better ones in Ireland."

"The tale goes that Odin went to the well of Mimir the giant to get a drink of the water of wisdom."

"And?"

"He got his drink. It gave him the gift to see the future. But he had to pay a price."

"And this price was…."

"One of his eyes. He plucked it out with his own fingers, and it fell in the water and looked back up at him."

"And what has this to do with you and your casket?"

"Odin was not always a god. There was a time when he was a man; a man with a real body. Real hands. Real feet. Real eyes."

"Yes?"

"I'm still learning about Christianity. But I've marked that every church has a piece of a saint's body."

"A relic, yes."

"Heathens have relics, too."

I recoiled. "Are you saying this is –"

"The Eye of Odin."

"And this knowledge of things to come –"

"The eye rested in the well of wisdom many generations. A bold man found it and stole it. It passed from hand to hand over the years, until it came to my family. I had it from my father. I used it for my own purposes, as he did; but, to speak truth, it always frightened me, and I misliked the dreams it gave me. Now that I'm a Christian, I'd be rid of it."

"If what you say is true, this must be a valuable thing to have."

"I've made much profit from it. But it's cost me, too."

"Can it tell you anything you wish to know?"

"No. It tells me only what it chooses. Can an eye think; have intentions? I don't know why it tells me some things and not others."

"Does it foretell good things or evil? Or both?"

"Both. Sometimes in a dream, sometimes in a waking vision, which is a part of what I fear."

"What do you fear?"

"I fear it will tell me of my own death. Can you imagine lying in bed, fighting off sleep, worried that you'll dream your death?"

I shivered head to foot. "And you wish me to take it?"

"A Christian priest is the perfect choice. Your Christ-magic will protect you from –"

"I have no magic!" I said. "We don't work that way."

"Are you saying the White Christ is helpless against the old magic?"

"Not at all –"

"Then what do you fear?"

"See here," said I. "A thing like this should be destroyed. It should be burned in fire, or smashed with stones."

"Don't you think I've tried? This thing will not burn, even in a forge. We've rolled great boulders over it without making a dent. You can't destroy it. It's best taken away."

I shook my head. "No," I said. "I've had concourse enough with magic. I've sworn off dealing with it. Find another priest. Find another way."

"You will take it, Father. I've seen you do it."

"Have you not heard, man? The Devil is a liar. He's lied to you in this."

I left him then, chock-full of my own virtue. The feast at Erling's had broken up at last. I got a few heartbeats of sleep.

Chapter 2

I'VE explained about Things before in these chronicles. They're the heart of the Norse commonwealth; they make Norsemen what they are, for good or ill. The Things make laws and settle disputes. When a Norseman tells you, "I am a free man," what he means is, "I have a vote at the Thing. I may not be the ruler, but I have a say."

There are quarter Things and county Things all over Norway, but once each summer, chosen men are sent to one of four great regional Things. Ours was the Gula-Thing, a fair sail north along the coast.

The Gula-Thing was always a high point of the year, something a man like Erling dared not neglect. This year was no less so. It would be, perhaps, as important as the one where he'd made his compact with Olaf Trygvesson and been betrothed to Olaf's sister.

There was peace at Things by law, which was very well this year. The Thing-men had split into two camps, like armies on a field, and if any had dared to lift weapons on the holy ground, it might have come to iron-play.

The camps weren't actually divided in area, because the booths (dug-out, timbered places in the turf surrounded by turf walls, meant to be covered over with tent awnings) were passed down from generation to generation. But there were shield walls in men's minds.

One awning stood out from the others. It was a monstrous vanity, a firmament of sky-blue Eastern silk with gold edging. People made excuses to walk by and get a good look at it, and probably would have had a feel too, if a pack of well-armed bullyboys hadn't been constantly on watch.

The booth was occupied by none other than Jarl Erik Haakonsson, son of Jarl Haakon – slayer of Olaf Trygvesson and sworn man to King Svein Forkbeard of Denmark. He was here to get his rights confirmed by the Thing.

Unfortunately, they were rights on which Erling Skjalgsson already sat.

"Something's going on at that bugger's booth," said old Bergthor to me the next morning as we prepared to support Erling at the law court. We were washing from the common bowl, passed from man to man. It was a privilege of priesthood that I got to use the water next after Erling.

"What do you mean?" I asked.

"There's a strange man there. I've seen him, and others have seen him too. He wears a hooded cloak at all times, and keeps the hood up."

"Oh that one. I ran into him last night, but didn't get a good look. He might be a leper, or he may have lost his ears or something."

"He's spoken to no one outside Erik's company, and never leaves the booth without bodyguards."

"Someone important?"

"You'd think so. But Erling knows every merchant along the North Way, and nothing is secret from the merchants. They've had no news of great folk coming to Gula, other than Erik Jarl and Erling himself."

"I suppose we'll learn soon enough."

"I like to know my enemy and what his strength is before it comes to a fight. This sits ill with me."

We went to mass. I assisted, which went off a bit awkward seeing that the new bishop was part of Jarl Erik's household. But the church knows no politics (all right, it does, but it shouldn't) and neither of us would grant the other the satisfaction of casting the first insult.

After mass, we had a breakfast of ale, porridge and fish and made our way in company up to the meeting place. Erling led the way with me following, then Erling's uncle Steinulf, the marshal, and Bergthor and all Erling's men. We'd brought ninety, and Erling had outfitted each with a costly *brynje* of mail. They didn't wear the mail shirts that day, out of respect for the Thing-peace, as courts of law were the only places where Norsemen bore no arms (except in church, and that only of late). But Erling had given each one new clothing and gold or silver arm-rings, and they were as handsome a pack of cutthroats as I'd seen in Norway, even in King Olaf's household.

Up we climbed to the court of law where there was a ring-shaped area bordered by a rope strung on upright sticks of peeled hazel. Inside the ring were three circular log benches, one inside the other, for the thirty-six judges to sit on. Erling, as a lord, had a seat on the court, and he took it.

We men of Erling's stood nearby, watching. Across the court we could see Jarl Erik and his household. Erik must have favored his mother, for he looked nothing like his stocky, brown-haired late father. He was tall and fair and if you'd told me he was kin to Olaf Trygvesson instead of being his slayer, I'd have believed you. Beside him stood his mysterious friend in the clot-colored cloak.

It was the first day for men to bring their cases for judgment. Many had such cases, but Erling would go first. No one had questioned this, even Jarl Erik.

The lawspeaker, in a booming voice, called all to attention and asked if any man had business to bring to the court.

All eyes turned on Erling, and he stood and said, "I have a matter for the Thing."

"Come forward, Erling Skjalgsson of Sola, and state your case."

Erling stepped to the center and addressed the judges. "I have a claim of inheritance to make."

"Is this the place to make an inheritance claim?" asked the lawspeaker.

"When the property is contested, yes," said Erling. "I make my claim on behalf of my wife, Astrid Trygvesdatter. Another would seize her rights, and I will have them for her."

"What rights are those?"

"Her brother, the late King Olaf, held lordship over all Norway, including our Westland. I was Olaf's man to rule for him from Stad to Lindesness. Now Erik Haakonsson has slain Olaf and claimed lordship. On behalf of Astrid, I lay claim to the steerage of the lands Olaf entrusted to me. Olaf left no male heir, so his rights pass to his sister. As those rights covered the whole land, I think this a small enough claim."

"Lordship is not a thing to be inherited like a sword," said the lawspeaker. "It must be granted by the Thing."

"The Thing has yet to choose a lord," said Erling. "I know Erik Haakonsson is come to claim it by right of conquest. I claim the same by right of inheritance, through Astrid."

"Then," said the lawspeaker, "we'd best give the jarl his say. Erik Haakonsson, enter the circle."

Erik came. He wore a fur-trimmed cloak of blue, I remember, and a Russian hat of sable. I saw gray streaks in his fair beard.

"Greetings, Erling Skjalgsson," said Erik. "'Tis long since we faced the Jomsvikings together at Hjorungavaag." He held out his hand.

Erling did not move. "I cannot take the hand of Olaf's slayer," he said.

"Then let men know it was you who refused peace with a fellow Christian."

"I am willing to make peace, on lawful grounds, if you will pay *mansbot.*"

"And what blood money would you demand?"

"All the lands and rights I had from Olaf."

"You price Olaf high."

"I claim these things as blood payment. I claim them as inheritance. And I claim them by right of possession, for I have not yielded them."

"We have heard your claims," said the lawspeaker. "Erik Haakonsson, what is your claim?"

"Mine is very like Erling's," said Erik, "only older and better. My father Jarl Haakon was overlord of the West in his day, and Erling and his father Thorolf paid him tax. My father was shamefully slain at Olaf's bidding and his lands and rights stolen, a wrong I have avenged. I claim these lands and rights by inheritance; I claim them by victory in lawful battle. They are mine under every law of the land, and of God."

Erling answered loudly then, turning as he spoke to face all the judges in turn. "My friends, this man claims rights in the Westland. You'd think he was a Westlander himself to hear him talk, but he is not. He is a Tronder from Nidaros. Even that might be no great harm, but this Tronder has spent his last years with Svein of Denmark, eating Svein's meat and learning Danish ways. And what do we know of Svein of Denmark?

"We know that Svein is sick for power. Denmark is not enough for him, he must have Norway too. It's said he even lusts to be king of England. What friendship, what protection, can we look for from a king for whom all the cows in Denmark and Norway and England do not make roast enough? We've learned about high kings in Norway. Our fathers saw Harald Finehair in his time step on their rights; we've seen Olaf Trygvesson do the same. Yes, I was Olaf's man, but you all know how we parted from one another.

"I tell you this, brothers of Westland, I do not trust Svein Forkbeard. And I do not trust his dog, Erik Haakonsson.

"In these last years, who has been your friend? Who has protected you, not from foreign enemies alone but from the king himself? Who has feasted you all at his table and given you gifts? I could say that man's name, but it would sound boastful. I shall leave that name for others to speak."

Someone cried, "Erling Skjalgsson!" and soon many took up the shout, again and again.

"SILENCE!" shouted the lawspeaker.

One of the judges stood when the noise died down. "I see no cause to drag this word-dance out," he said. "We all know Erling Skjalgsson. We know him for a man of honor, wisdom and good luck. Possession weighs heavy in law, and Erling has possession of the overlordship today. Without good reason to turn him out, I see no cause to bring in a new lord."

"We may hear from Svein Forkbeard about this," said someone. "And Svein will speak with ships and steel."

"Let him!" cried someone else. "Fighting together, with Erling to lead us, we've naught to fear from the Danes!"

"YES! YES! YES!" cried the assembly. If anyone spoke against the proposal now, I could not hear him.

The lawspeaker called for silence again.

"What say you to this?" he asked Erik.

"You spoke of a reason to turn Erling out. I offer you one," Erik said.

He pointed in the direction of his band of followers, and the stranger in the blood-colored cloak stepped forward, throwing back his hood.

The gathering went silent.

The man was as like Erling as your left hand is like your right.

For the time it takes to say the "Ave Maria" there was no sound.

"May I present Kaari Skjalgsson," said Erik with a smile.

A roaring came up from the assembly as men crowded forward to see.

Erling stood motionless, his face bleached the color of old bone. It was one of the few times I ever saw him taken aback.

When the lawspeaker had quieted the crowd, Erling said, "I beg a day's time to think on this new matter." The lawspeaker granted it and called for the next case. Erling summoned a kinsman to take his seat on the benches and we all headed down to our booth.

"What's this about?" I asked Bergthor.

"Hush," said the old man. "We'll speak of it later."

Halfway down, we met a man standing in our path. He stood face-to-face with Erling and looked no more like to give way than an oak tree. He was a tall man, dark of face and hair, dressed in new clothing. One of his blue eyes was roofed by a startling white eyebrow.

"Well met, old friend," said he without a smile.

"Do I know you, stranger?" asked Erling, brought up short.

"I am Ulf Lodinsson. We were playmates once."

Erling peered at him. "I remember you now, Ulf."

"And my brother Ragnvald? And my mother Gyda?"

"One does not forget such."

"I hoped to see you here," said Ulf. "I've joined Jarl Erik's household, for the enemy of my enemy must be friend to me. This has been a good day. But better days than this are coming." He turned to go, then looked back and said, "I got this white brow when my eye was burned in that fire. Each time I see my reflection in water, I think of you, Erling."

Then as we watched, before we had time to be surprised, he changed into a wolf and loped away into the trees. I gasped.

"Let us run for spears and hunt him down," said Steinulf, the marshal.

"Remember the Thing-peace," said Erling. "Let him be for now. I've other cuds to chew."

We reached our booth and Erling called Bergthor, Steinulf and me inside with him.

"Before you start brewing plots and strategies," said I, "explain to me what's going on here. Who is this Kaari? Is he kin to you, Erling?"

"You might say so," said Erling with a thin smile.

"Kaari's his brother," Steinulf said, plumping down on a bearskin. "I've told you Skjalg and Ragna had other sons."

"I know of Aslak, who died the day I came to Sola," said I.

"There were two more. One drowned off the Hebrides. The other – that was Kaari – took the east-road to Russia and was not heard of again. All men thought him dead."

"Until today," said Bergthor.

"And, so, your brother who was lost, is found," said I. "What harm is that to you, to drain the blood from your face?"

"Kaari is my *elder* brother," said Erling.

"Ah." I began to see.

"'Tis not five years since Skjalg died," said Steinulf. "Kaari has birthright to the greater part of the estate. Sola will be his."

"A setback, no doubt," said I. "But Erling's hersirship comes by the voice of the Thing, not inheritance. Kaari can't take that."

"No, nor can I hold it," said Erling. "A hersirship comes dear. You must keep up a bodyguard and good warships. You must hold feasts and give gifts to bind men to you. How many men will follow a smallholder with one or two farms?"

"You're still Erling Skjalgsson. The name is worth something."

"I'd hope so. But a great name will not feed a hall-full of hungry bonders."

"And left unfed, they'll find a new hersir soon enough," said Bergthor into his beard.

"It can't be so bad as that," I insisted. "There's more to leadership than keeping men fat. You have friends. You have tenants. You have kinsmen. I'll swear there's a way to work it out."

"No doubt there would be," said Erling, "on another day, in another place. If I'd had some warning of this, I might have fended it off. But I was caught dozing, like Haakon the Good at Fitjar, and here is Jarl Erik to finish me off.

"If only I'd had warning! If only I'd had time to prepare!"

I had thoughts about that, but they would wait.

"What of this man Ulf?" I asked. "The one who called himself your playmate?"

"The fruits of Skjalg's madness," said Steinulf, when Erling hesitated to answer. "You've heard the tale of Gyda the thrall woman; how Erling's father Skjalg killed her husband Lodin, took her as leman and made her two sons his thralls."

"There comes a time when a man goes mad for a bit, if he lives long enough," said Bergthor. "It happened to me as well, but without so dismal an upshot. You find one day you're no longer young, and you make a fool of yourself trying to prove you're a man still."

"Ragnvald Lodinsson tried to burn my father and his household in the hall," said Erling. "Father broke out and slew him, but his brother Ulf got free."

"Yes, I remember," said I. "Your mother told me. She said Gyda walked back into the burning hall to die."

"They've made a song about it," said Bergthor. "You won't have heard it, Erling, but the thralls and the bonders sing it sometimes."

"Ulf is the least of my worries," said Erling. "I wish all I had against me was a shape-shifter."

Erling tired of the talk toward evening and left the booth. "Come with me, Father," he said.

He led the way across the slope.

"Where are we going?" I asked.

"To Jarl Erik's booth."

I sighed. "That's your way, isn't it? Wherever the danger is, you go toward it."

"That is the warrior's way. Nobodies run and hide."

"A short life, but a shining one?"

"I could spend the night worrying or I can face the thing."

"A man could get killed being your friend."

"A man could choke on a fishbone eating breakfast. It's all in God's hand; isn't that what you say?"

"I talk too much."

We neared the booth of many colors. About five of the bullyboys who served to keep the turf from blowing off stepped to block us.

"Who are you and what do you want?" one of them asked.

"You know who I am. I want to see my brother Kaari."

"He's sleeping."

"He must be a sound sleeper if he's in that booth, noisy as it is."

"Sleeps like a baby, our Kaari."

"Tell him I want to see him."

The man stood for a moment staring at Erling, and I could see behind his eyes how he took counsel with himself how insolent he dared be. He decided he'd pushed it far enough, and turned and ducked inside.

Kaari came out in a moment. Even up close, his likeness to Erling startled me. He had the same long head and the same fair hair with the red beard below. His nose was a bit thicker and his eyes a paler blue, but Thorolf Skjalg's sons were not hard to know.

"You had words to say," said Kaari without expression.

"Wonderful to see you, too, brother," said Erling. "Welcome home."

"The joy in your face when you first saw a fellow was welcome enough."

"Why did you go to Jarl Erik, Kaari?" asked Erling. "Why not come home to your own people? Mother still lives. She'll be overjoyed to see you."

"Time is coming for Mother. One had to cross Svein's waters to get home. He was kind enough to offer passage."

"And you did not balk to take up his cause against me?"

"A fellow but asks for his rights."

"Why come as an enemy?"

"There is no need for enmity if men do their duties. All that is asked of you, Erling, is to do your duty. You have a name as a man who does what is right. Now all men will see whether that is true or not."

"We'll speak again tomorrow," said Erling.

"True."

We went back to our booth. Erling went in to bed. I wanted to sleep but knew I would not.

Instead I went out to walk.

One phrase of Erling's kept singing in my ears:

"If only I'd had warning!"

I asked about until someone directed me to the booth of Oddvin Oddleifsson.

I took the accursed casket from him. My hands shook as I fumbled with the catch and opened it to look inside.

A gray eye looked up at me. I felt a shock like a whip-crack when its gaze met mine, as when you catch someone's eye across a room.

A picture came into my mind, like another man's memory. I stood at the rail of a ship, gazing as mists burned away to disclose an unknown shore.

Chapter 3

A HAND shook me awake. I rose through the tatters of sleep to see Erling's face, just visible in the booth by the light of the night-sun.

"Let us walk and talk," he said softly.

I wrapped my cloak about me and followed him outside. We went among the booths, speaking low.

"I've made many uneasy choices in my life," Erling said. "But none as hard as this."

"I'll help you if I can," said I, "but I know so little of your law...."

"With law I need little help. I know a hundred ways to make the law serve me.

"My concern is to do right. That is a harder thing."

"Always." I began to understand, and my understanding frightened me.

He stopped and spread his hands. "For years I've worked for one thing—to fulfill the destiny I believed God made me for—to be the best lord I could be. Not just a rich lord. Not just a powerful lord. A good lord. A lord men would be proud to follow. A lord known to do justice and protect the weak. The kind of lord who is loved more than feared."

"You have done this, more than not."

"And for what? To pass it all off to Kaari? To stand back and say, 'I wash my hands of it; here's what I've built; husband it or break it as you will?'"

"What kind of lord would Kaari be?"

"I cannot guess. I barely know him. Father fostered him out to a household in Agder. A small boy always thinks a half-grown brother much older than he, but I swear Kaari should be older than he looks. He was ten years my elder. You'd think he hadn't aged a day since he took ship for the East."

"What's he been about all these years?" I asked.

"God knows. I suppose he was in the thrall trade or the fur trade. That's what men do in the East."

"So what will you do?"

"It seems to me there are two kinds of right. Most times they sit in the same seat, so a man can bow to both at once. But sometimes they move to contrary ends of the hall, and then a man must choose.

"One kind of right is simple. You do what the law says. You keep your vows though it beggars you.

"The other kind of right is knottier. It means asking what action will bring the best fruit. Might my keeping my word bring suffering? Might it put folk in danger? Might it break some greater good I'm trying to work? Looking at it that way, a man might persuade himself it was right to break the law; right to break his vows."

"And what do you think?"

Erling wrapped his arms around himself and sat on the sod with a sudden movement, his cloak tented around him. He sat mute for a long time, staring at the red sun-ball in the south as the mist burned away. I waited for his word.

At last he said, "I think the second way gives a man an excuse to betray himself. I think any kind of crime and dishonor might be justified that second way.

"I will do my duty. I will lay down my power."

He added, very softly, "I think it may kill me."

* * *

In the monastery, each monk or novice has a soul-friend, a brother whose duty it is to listen to him, encourage him, and kick him in the trews when he needs it. My particular soul-friend had been a friend in name only; a wispy, unworldly, fasting-besotted stripling who touched me more than I thought strictly necessary. He did little to keep me on the narrow path, and I doubt I was much use to him either.

But I had a soul-friend here. His name was Helge of Klepp, and he lived a little south of us in Jaeder. He was old and blind, and he kept a freedman in his household who carved stone crosses and set them up here and there to the glory of God.

Helge had come to the Thing with his brother, and I could think of nothing to do this night but to go and talk to him. Chances were he'd be sleeping, and I'd not wake him if he was, but it would be foolish not to seek him out when I was in such particular need of a friend.

I found him sitting on a stone outside his tent.

"Still up?" I asked.

"Up already," he said. "I've had my sleep."

"It's still yesterday to me," said I.

"And to judge by your voice, you yet bear yesterday's burdens."

"They're heavy ones." I told him of Erling's decision. We went together down to the fjord-edge, to the pool where once Olaf Trygvesson had christened the men of the West.

"He'll step aside?" Helge asked me.

"Yes."

"He'd do that?"

"So he said. He doesn't lie."

"No. This is a large thing."

"It scares me."

"As well it should. Men for the most part, even the great ones, float through life like twigs in a stream. But now and then one stands stone-solid and makes the stream run around him. That makes for eddies and currents and white water. It can even turn the stream. I cannot see the end of these rapids."

"Will there be evil?"

"There will be evil and there will be good."

"Is it God's will?"

"It's always God's will. The question is whether God's will is anything like ours in this case."

I'd meant to tell him about Odin's Eye, but I didn't.

Chapter 4

ERLING spoke his submission that day before the Thing, his beard bright red against his white face. Kaari took his place in the court.

We boarded our ship when all was done and sailed south to Sola, a joyless company.

We sailed into Hafjrsfjord, disembarked at Somme and rode our ponies south up the hill to the steading of Sola.

Erling stopped his pony at the summit, before we turned up the walled path into the yard. He took a long time looking south over the low, treeless Jaeder coast that had been his heritage, his treasure, and his burden.

Erling sent everyone out of the new hall except his mother Ragna, his wife Astrid, big Steinulf, dark Eystein (his chief of defense) and old Bergthor.

"I am glad past telling that Kaari lives," said Ragna, "but you should not have yielded to him."

"What was I to do? Call out my own brother to a duel?"

"Certainly not. But your kin have the right to choose between you."

"I acted according to law. I've hanged men for defying the law; I can hardly short-weight it myself."

"The law is a tool. A wise man makes it serve him."

"Enough, mother. I've done what I thought right. I've given my word. The matter is settled."

"What's to become of the bodyguard?" asked Steinulf.

"Perhaps Kaari will take you on," said Erling. "He'd no men of his own that I saw. He'll need followers who know the land and the people. He'll need wise counsel."

"We sworn men did not swear to serve Sola, or whatever man they call hersir. We swore to serve you."

"The freedmen's company feel the same way," said Eystein.

"And many times I've been grateful for both. But I cannot feed you any longer. I must loose you from your oaths."

"Perhaps we'd rather follow where you go," said Eystein. "I think you'll always be a lucky man to follow."

"That's your choice. But I can promise nothing. I can scarcely guess where I'll go; whether I'll settle on whatever farms Kaari leaves me, or take the Viking road, or some other road. I just don't know."

"What of the thralls?" asked Astrid. "Will Kaari help them buy their freedom, as you do?"

"I cannot tell. I never knew Kaari well. Mother, what's he like?"

"I never knew him well either, to speak truth. Thorolf fostered him out young. No mother likes to see her sons fostered, but Thorolf would have it so. 'It turns friends into kinsmen,' he'd say. I suppose it does.

"Kaari was a strange child. He slept badly, and cried when held, except when sucking. Leave him by himself and he was best pleased. I never saw a babe like him. To be honest, I missed him least of all of you when we fostered him. Now it seems he's to be the prop of my old age."

"He'll treat you well, Mother, if only for the sake of his good name," said Erling.

There was silence a moment.

"And what of me?" asked Astrid in a low voice.

"That is for you to say," said Erling. "When Olaf first spoke of betrothing us you bridled at being wed to a bonder, a mere farmer. I worked and fought to be more than that. But here I am again, just a free man among others. I would not blame you if you turned your back on me."

"I cannot believe you'll ever be a mere bonder," said Astrid. "I bear your child in my belly. The old laws allowed a woman to divorce her husband. I stand by the Christian law, which says that marriage is for life. Where you lay your head at night, on land or sea, there will my head lie."

"Is something wrong with the fire?" asked Ragna. I realized as she spoke that the air was indeed thickening.

"It *is* getting smoky," said Bergthor, coughing.

"I think the hall's on fire," said Erling.

"Enemies?" asked Eystein.

"Very likely. The women should go out first. Enemies won't harm them."

"And we can find out who wants us dead this time," said Steinulf.

Erling and the others drew their swords and picked up shields, and we walked out into the entry room, coughing, the women in front. They went out. We stayed within. But Erling looked through the door, open just a crack, while the rest of us stood by, ready to close it in a second if someone should try to push through.

"What do you see?" Erling called out.

"Nothing. There's no one here," said Astrid. "There's no fire."

"No fire?"

We stepped out into the night.

It was a night like any other. The northern lights danced among the stars.

"It was like a fire!" said Bergthor.

"Yes!" cried Ragna. "It was just like –"
She bit the words off short.

"Like what?" asked Erling.

"Like the night Ragnvald burned us in the hall."
We heard a sound of laughing then. It seemed to come from
the north, then from the west, and from the south.
It sounded to me like the voice of Ulf Lodinsson, the shape-
changer.

* * *

The next days and weeks hang in my mind like paintings on
a church wall, seen motionless and one at a time.

There are the ships of Jarl Erik's fleet sailing into Hafrsfjord
and filling it like apples in a bowl. Danish ships, for the most
part. It was as if we'd been conquered. As if? We *had* been
conquered.

There were the endless meetings in the new hall – Jarl Erik
seated in Erling's high seat, midway down the north wall, Kaari
in the guest seat across from him, and Erling to his right. There
was room for only a few of our own people in the hall; most had
to eat in the old hall. But I was at Erling's right, and Astrid and
Ragna held their places on the women's bench at the north end.

Names of farms were brought out and haggled over like trinkets in a merchant's booth, matched and weighted one against
the other.

The upshot: five farms for Erling, one to live on and four to
have the rents from. Tjora was the largest, and had a harbor of
its own, so we'd be moving north a bit.

Kaari must have Fishhawk, Erling's great warship, for the
younger brother must not outshine the lord. Erling would have
another ship, smaller but not an insult. He would have three
knarrs – the wide-bellied cargo ships suited to ocean voyages.
There was little glory in a knarr, but money to be made.

It was all decent and civilized. No voice was raised, no weapon drawn.

It was like watching Erling eaten by ants. He was a man to be struck down, when the time came, with a clean blow, not a thousand nibbles of tiny mouths. I spent hours in prayer for him.

There was much discussion of the thralls and their freedom. It ended with Erling getting possession of all those who'd begun buying themselves. The others would be Kaari's, and he meant to give them no special help beyond the letter of the law.

At last all was settled. Kaari, lord of Sola, held a great feast in honor of the event, attended by Danes and Norwegians in uneasy fellowship.

When Erling left his seat and did not return the first evening, I had an idea where to find him.

I took the old path down to the sea-strand and there he was, in the silver light staring out into the silver surf.

"We'll have to find a new place to walk," I said to him.

"There's a strand at Tjora. It's the same sea."

"And God is everywhere."

"Is He? I suppose it's so. I mustn't think that there is no God, just because He's turned His back on me."

"He's not turned His back on you. You aren't the first man to face disappointment. You are more than your inheritance. You made yourself great."

"And this is the reward I get. It's the kind of treatment I'd have expected from Odin. I'll tell you truth. I'm not much pleased with God these days."

"I'll give you truth back. Neither am I. But we yet live, the both of us. We can hope."

"I don't know who I am anymore, Father! I was Skjalg's son, and then I was hersir, and then I was the king's brother-in-law and second man in the land. Now who am I?"

"You're the man you always were. And you're free."

"That's true. I am a free man, Father. I've no duties beyond those to my family. My duty to God is done. I can go where I like, as I could when my father was hersir. Shall we go somewhere?"

"Why not?" said I.

"Where shall we go?"

"Greenland. Let's visit your friend Leif Eriksson."

"Greenland again? What is it about Greenland for you?"

"Konnall the Icelander told me of a thrall girl there. I think she's my sister Maeve."

Erling laughed. "I've mulled it over for days and could think of no reason to do one thing more than another. This is the best reason for doing anything I've heard.

"To Greenland we go then."

As easily as that the thing was settled.

Chapter 5

"I'd not thought of a Greenland trip this year," said Konnall the Icelander, pretending indecision. "'Tis a long voyage, Greenland."

"But a profitable one," said Erling. We were in our new, smaller house at Tjora. It was strange not to have Ragna with us, but Erling's sister Thorliv was there. Her sister Sigrid was gone north, wed to Sigurd Thorisson. They had sailed back to Halogaland along with Sigurd's brother Thorir, the boys' time of hostaging with us over.

"If you make it through," said Konnall. "When Red Erik sailed from Iceland to Greenland with his first settlers, he put out with twenty-five ships. Only fourteen of them came through. It can be a bad sea."

"What happened to the rest of the ships?" asked Thorliv.

"Some had to turn back to Iceland. Others went missing in the storm."

"But people do make the trip, not only from Iceland but from Norway," said Erling. "It's not the same as putting your head in a noose."

"No, men make the trip all the time," Konnall granted. "But it's not a thing to take on lightly."

"How do we sail?" asked Erling.

"There's the old route and the new route. The old route runs first from Stad, west to Iceland, then from Snaefelsness in Iceland to Midjokull on the east coast of Greenland, where men cannot live. Then you have to sail south, around the point of Greenland and on to the settlements westward.

"But Leif Eriksson made a new road a couple years back, on the same trip where he met you. He set off from Hernar and made straight oversea to Greenland. Well, he was lucky. It worked for him."

"And which road will you take?" asked Erling.

"The old road. The one I know. You've naught against a stopover in Iceland, have you?"

"I've an old friend in Iceland, Snorri Thorgrimsson the Chieftain. He guested with us in my father's time."

"Good. I know Snorri. Everyone knows Snorri. We'll do business in both places. The gods – pardon me, God – granting fair weather, we can be in Greenland in time to winter with Leif, then return the following autumn."

"Autumn?" asked Astrid.

"That's when you get the fair winds for eastering."

"So we're talking of a long time from home."

"We?" asked Konnall.

"I'm coming too," said Astrid. "I won't be the first woman to make the Greenland voyage."

"Begging your pardon, Lady, but it's not a pleasure cruise."

Erling said, "You don't know my wife, Konnall. Best veer off before you run onto that lee shore."

"I'm coming too," said Thorliv.

We all looked at her.

"I'm unmarried and under my brother's care," she said. "This is the only chance I may get to have an adventure before I wed."

"Every body aboard displaces saleable cargo," frowned Konnall.

"Perhaps," said Thorliv, "but our ship doubles the wares you can carry. Instead of a skipper's interest in one ship's cargo, you'll now share in two ships." "True," said Erling with a smile. "It's my share that'll suffer more."

Konnall shrugged. "Not for me to say," he said. "If we were going in one ship, I'd say there wasn't room, but it's no business of mine whom you may carry in your own vessel."

"We'll talk more of this," said Erling to Thorliv.

"What is Greenland exactly? An island?" asked Thorliv.

"The sea is like a great bowl," said Konnall. "'Tis closed by land all around. If you go north along the coast of Norway, the land gets colder and colder until you reach stretches where no man has ever sailed. But up there in the unknown reaches, the land curves back westward again and turns like the rim of a bowl, holding the sea in."

"If you go far enough north, the land turns east and you come to Bjarmaland," said Erling.

"Yes it does," said Konnall, "but it turns back west further on. It has to. Otherwise all the seawater would run out.

"Greenland is an outcrop of this rim of the world, but very far north and west."

"So we could get there by land," said Thorliv.

"A long journey and cold, and far out of your way. Always sail when you can. It's the best way to travel."

Erling smiled. "Father Aillil might argue about that."

"I'll manage," said I.

I took the Eye of Odin from its chest that night. "What manner of journey will this be?" I asked it before I slept.

I dreamed I was on a ship in a stormy sea, hanging my face over the side and vomiting.

As if I needed magic to foretell that.

* * *

"Meal and timber," said Konnall. "Those are the things for Iceland, and Greenland, even more. They can never get enough meal or timber. We'll bring other things, too – ale will bring a good price, and pitch's always welcome."

"With two ships we can bring anything you like," said Erling.

"Yes. Two ships. The more I think about it, the more I like the idea. Whom will you bring as crew?"

"Bergthor is one of the best sailors I know. He's old, but he's keen to make the trip; to see the gable of the world. Steinulf won't hear of staying behind. And Lemming wants to go. That means Freydis his niece must go, too, though she can hardly be called crew."

"More profitless weight."

"Eystein would like to go, but his wife is with child again. For the rest, I'll find good men. Thirty or so is enough for a knarr."

"I'll sail in your ship," said Konnall.

"You?"

"You'll need a pilot who knows the far seas. We can't count on keeping together in storms and fogs. My partner Thorarin can pilot my ship. I'll pilot yours, unless you've aught against it."

"Nothing could be better."

"There's me, too," said I.

"Yes, you're a great sailor," said Erling with a smile.

"The Irish are a seafaring folk. I'm not that kind of Irishman, but let's not forget that this trip was my idea."

"Fear not, Father Aillil," said Erling. "You'll sail with us, crewman or cargo as you wish."

"You're not profitless weight, at least," said Konnall. "A priest is as rare and costly as meal in Iceland."

I suppose it was a sort of compliment.

* * *

The day was rainy, as so many are in Westland. I could think of nothing profitable to do so I poked about the new farm, slogging through the yard, making a nuisance of myself.

I found Astrid in a storehouse, rummaging through chests

of clothing, picking out the warmest things for the voyage, checking for split seams and moth-holes. She wore a brown dress and her golden hair was caught up with a comb.

"They say it's cold in Greenland," she said to me.

"It's cold in Norway. They say it's freezing in Greenland."

"And yet men live there, make lives and raise families."

"We need very little in this world, to be sure, if we only have the spirit to live."

Astrid looked at me. Her blue eyes troubled me. I had to look away from them. She raised feelings in me that a priest ought not to have – not the tender feelings I'd had for Halla, whom I'd loved and who was dead, but something headier, more perilous but fetching. I do not mean she was trying to tempt me. I've no need that a woman should tempt me; my mind strays of itself.

"What do you think of Erling's spirit these days?" she asked.

"He's taken a hard blow. He did what was right. His only reward was to lose all he'd built. He's not the first or last that's happened to, but it always feels like betrayal."

"If it's not betrayal, what is it?"

"Many have felt betrayed by God that way. Many of those turn their backs on Him. But some go on trusting. I've never met one such who regretted it."

"Have you been betrayed?"

"Oh, aye. When my family was killed and my sister and I taken as thralls."

"This is the sister we're going to seek?"

"Aye. It seems strange, all this for my sister."

"Well, there's the trade, too. What will you do if we find her?"

"I have silver. I'll buy her freedom. I'll try to make up to her for the years the locusts have eaten."

"Were you very close?"

I sighed. "Truth to tell, no. When I think back on our lives, when I was at home, before my time as a raider and before I tried to be a monk, what I remember most is my cruelties to her. I teased. I tickled. I hid her playthings and laughed at her. I was an uncommon bad brother. The memory of it plagues me in the night-time."

"I hope we find her," said Astrid.

"Hope," I said, "is sometimes the cruelest thing." She smiled, her short upper lip uncovering a crescent of even white teeth. "Now *you* speak of betrayal."

"I never said 'twas easy."

A terrible thing for a priest to say. I hoped that Odin's Eye would show me Maeve and assure me that this trip was not in vain.

But no such message came to me.

* * *

There's an art to loading a ship, Konnall told me. You have to balance weight against weight, and know what items are likely to shift, and which have to be stored on top to avoid the bilge-water (even when stuffed in casks), and which should be stored on the bottom for stability. There's a right place for the barley meal and the salt, and a right place for the pitch, and a right place for the ingots of iron and the linen cloth, and a proper way to stack and secure the wood planks, and a right way to tie down the two long beams you're bringing, so they'll lie nice and quiet next to the mast, one on either side. And you can never load as much as you'd like, because you know your damned passengers will want space for their profitless baggage.

Erling and I were watching him cursing the thralls one drizzly morning. It was beyond him how anyone could be so stupid as to mistake his plain instructions. I hadn't understood them myself.

We heard footsteps behind us on the jetty and turned to see two young men approaching at a brisk walk. They were like enough to be brothers, which they were, as it turned out. They had darkish-fair hair, and brown eyes in square faces. Their clothing and rings bespoke neither wealth nor want.

"Erling Skjalgsson," they said. It wasn't a question.

"I am Erling. This is Father Aillil. Who speaks to me?"

"We are Thorbrand and Thorlak Gudbrandsson, from Tinn in Telemark," said the taller of the two. He cocked his head to one side as he spoke. "I'm Thorbrand; he's Thorlak. We'd be grateful if you'd take us with you to Greenland."

"And why should I take strangers, when I've men of my own household who've asked to come?"

"Because we're outlaw and may not stay in the land."

"And how came you to be outlaw?"

"We killed two of Jarl Erik's men."

Erling raised his eyebrows. "You interest me of a sudden. Tell me how that came to pass."

"Well, we heard of your journey, and we thought it would be a fine thing to sail to the end of the world with Erling Skjalgsson," said Thorbrand.

"But we knew it wouldn't be a light matter to earn the right to sail with you," said Thorlak, the less tall one. "We knew there'd be men you knew well who'd have a better right to go."

"We thought we'd need to get your attention," said Thorbrand. "So we went to Jarl Erik at Sola and asked him to take us on. They say he's looking for men with iron in their hands."

"And he wouldn't have you?"

"He welcomed us." Thorlak smiled grimly. "We feasted with his household last night."

"And?"

"And some of the men began to speak insults about you. We thought they might."

"Did you now? What did they say?"

"No need to go into that. It was something about you and Olaf Trygvesson. You can imagine."

"Indeed I can."

"Thorbrand and I took offense," said Thorlak. He had freckles and his nose turned up a bit; I liked his looks. "You'd not
remember our father, my lord, but you did him a good turn
once. He always spoke well of you."

"There was little we could do in the hall with Erik's men
all around us," said Thorbrand. "But we marked the two who
spoke loudest, and this morning, when they went out to relieve
themselves, we cut them down on the privy path."

Erling frowned. "And then?"

"Then we shouted that we had done the killings, to make it
legal, you know, and came here."

"And they just let you go?"

"We had horses waiting, just in case. But you can expect
company soon."

And, indeed, as we looked to the south we saw a party of
armed men, about twenty of them, approaching on horseback.

"Get on board," said Erling to the brothers. He took up a
shield that lay nearby. "Father Aillil, come with me."

We walked together to the land-end of the jetty. Erling drew
his sword and stood before me, blocking the men's way.

They reined up when they saw him and got off their horses.

"Who comes to my ship?" Erling cried.

"Men of the jarl's," said their leader, a beanpole of a man
with pale eyes.

"And do you mean to board my ship without leave?"

The man paused a moment. "Have we leave to board?" he
asked.

"No."

"Then we must board in the jarl's name."

"Only by passing through me. I'm no easy man to kill, and
though I'm no longer hersir I still have kin and friends in this
land."

"So you deny us these men who've done manslaughter?"

"They'll be outlawed in the land; we both know that. I'll do you a favor. I'll take them out of the land and spare you a prosecution."

"The jarl wants them dead."

"We all want things we can't have."

The beanpole drew his sword suddenly and rushed forward, crying, "You're not a lord anymore, Erling Skjalgsson! It's time someone taught you that!"

Erling leaped to meet him. As the beanpole slashed, Erling swung his shield to meet the weapon, striking it hard enough to sweep it aside, the force of the blow actually turning the man around. Erling let the same force spin him about as well, but as he did not fight the movement he spun faster. When he came round, the beanpole's back was still to him, and it was easy work to strike him in the neck, above the brynje and below the helmet, all but taking his head off. The man dropped to the ground and spouted out his life's blood.

It was an audacious blow, one too risky for anyone but a man carrying a great store of pent-up fury inside him.

Erling stood and pointed his dripping sword-point at the other men. "Who else wants to teach Erling Skjalgsson *who he is*?" he roared.

The warriors took up their leader and rode away. So we got two more crew members.

Chapter 6

"THORLIV, settle down," said Astrid. "You're like five-year-old at Jul-eve."

We were in the hall at Tjora, the day before embarkation. We were at loose ends, looking for tasks still to be done and finding none. Everything was packed, the ship was loaded, all the arrangements had been made with Eystein and Deirdre for running the farm in our absence. We would sail with the tide in the morning, and we knew that we'd need sleep and that we wouldn't be able to sleep. We were all more or less testy.

I grew tired of the smudgy air and took the path to the strand. I resented this strand a bit. It was gentler than the one at Sola, a harbor strand, and I missed the great angry surf.

I found that Erling had joined me. We stared at the arched back of Haastein Island across the water.

"How many times have we talked by the sea?" he asked.

"The saints know. The sea's a wondrous confessor."

"We should be in a state of grace for some time then, for we'll be in that confessional at least a couple weeks."

"It will be some time before we walk on this shore again though."

"If ever."

I looked at Erling. He was staring past the horizon, west-ward, the way we were going.

"Do you think we might not return? Are you afraid of the journey?"

"No. Life or death is in God's hands. But it comes to my mind that if there were a place for me in Iceland, or even in Greenland, perhaps it would be best to stay there."

"You? Out of Jaeder forever? Out of Norway forever?"

"I dreamed great dreams, but God knocked them down. I'll never be the man I hoped I'd be in this land. Perhaps a sharp break is best."

"Have you spoken of this to Astrid?"

"Aye."

"What does she say?"

"She says she'll do what I do."

"Would you feel right taking her away for all time?"

"Her kin is gone. Her mother's dead now. All her other family, except for her sister in Sweden, died at Svold. She has naught to keep her."

"Still, she's lived in king's households. How would a farm in Greenland suit her, do you think?"

"I don't know. Perhaps Greenland's a gentler place than we fancy. She's carrying my son. I'd hoped to leave my son a great place in Norway. Perhaps I can still be a great man in Iceland or Greenland, rather than a smallholder here."

"I don't think you'll be a smallholder long."

"Two ships on the Greenland sea are a risky way to make your fortune."

"As if you'd choose a safe way."

"Let's go back to the house," said Erling. "Astrid and Thorliv are likely scratching each other's eyes out by now."

We headed up the path to the steading.

As we went Erling said, "Who are those?"

I looked up to see a company of horsemen coming on between the fields to meet us.

"Armed men," said I.

"Not all armed," said Erling. "There are three priests in the lead. With a spare horse in tow."

"Then they come from the jarl."

"No question."

"Priests likely means they're not here for a fight."

"They'll overtake us before we reach the steading, so there's naught to do but face it out."

And so we did. I'd met these priests before, at the Thing. I remembered they were German (most of Erik's priests were Germans), but nothing more. Two of them were fat, one thin.

The senior priest (one of the fat ones) spoke to me. "Greetings, Brother," he said in Latin.

"Greetings as well, Brothers," said I. "I'd thank you to speak Norse. Erling has no Latin."

"We have no errand to Erling. Only to you."

"They're being rude," I said in Norse. "They'll only speak to me." Erling nodded.

"So what's your errand?" I asked them.

"Bishop Adalbert has summoned you."

"To what do I owe that honor?"

"His Eminence did not confide in us. You will come, of course."

I had no choice in the matter. "The bishop has summoned me," I told Erling.

"I'll come with you."

"No. It'll all be in Latin. I'll let you know what he says when I return."

So I set off with my escort. The extra horse was for me. I was unmerry. I didn't like the new bishop greatly, and my Latin, never of the best, was rusty.

'Twas strange to ride up the lane into Sola and see it peopled with strangers. It brought to mind a beggar in a lord's cast-offs.

They took me to the old hall. I could hear the sounds of feasting from the new hall, but here was quiet, and it was dark inside but for the light from the smoke-holes, the long-fire and a couple fish-oil lamps spiked in the pillars. The three priests moved into the shadows. Bishop Adalbert sat in the high seat, like a king. He was a middling sort of man, neither short nor tall, neither fat nor thin. Around his tonsure his hair grew dark, with not a gray hair despite his age. I wondered if he painted it.

"Greetings, my son," he said, extending his ring to be kissed.

"How may I serve you, Your Eminence?" I asked.

"How long have you been in Norway?" He did not look at me as he spoke, as if I were some theoretical person he addressed in fancy.

"About four years."

"They say your ordination is irregular."

"I was specially ordained by Bishop Sigurd."

"One of Olaf's Canterbury men. You understand, of course, that Norway properly belongs to the See of Hamburg."

"I understand little of such matters."

"No, of course not. You're Irish, are you not?"

"From head to toe."

"It took you Irish long to learn the proper date for Easter, and how to shave a decent tonsure. One can hardly expect an Irishman to understand ecclesiastical protocol."

I might have replied that the Irish *brought* the faith to the Germans, but I thought it wiser to hold my tongue.

"I have decided to take you with me to Nidaros," the bishop said.

I had trouble getting my breath. "Nidaros?" I asked.

"Yes. You may make a decent priest in time, but you need seasoning. We'll find a place for you at Nidaros."

"But I'm going to Greenland with Erling Skjalgsson!"

For the first time the bishop looked me in the eye.

"Is Erling a bishop?" he asked shortly.

"No...."

"Then it does not fall to him to determine your calling."

"I'm – I'm Erling's freedman."

"You're saying you're a slave? One of those house-priests who's the property of a chieftain?"

This, to be frank, had always been a touchy point with me. There were such priests in Norway, poorly educated, bound to some lord. I did not like to think I was one of those, but my standing had always been a tad equivocal.

"I'm... bound to Erling by friendship and obligation."

"Greater than your obligation to Mother Church?"

"No, of course not. But I'm going to Iceland and Greenland. They've great need of priests in those lands."

"So you take it on yourself to decide your mission? The Church has no say in your comings and goings?"

I sighed. "Your Excellency," I said, "I was kidnapped from Connaught with my sister. We were parted in the slave market at Visby. I believe she may be alive in Greenland. I must go there and try to set her free. By the mercy of Christ, you must grant me leave to do this!"

"The Church is your family, Father Aillil. Your fellow priests are your brothers. The nuns are your sisters. God's poor are your children. It is not for you to put your personal ties before those you assumed when you vowed yourself to God."

I knelt in the rushes. "Your Excellency, have pity," I said. "My sister has no one but me in the world."

"She has God. The Greenlanders are learning the Faith. She will be well treated, if she is among them."

"Have pity," I begged.

"I am having pity. I am rescuing you from the folly of your

pride and self-will. A priest grows by denying himself, Father Aillil. This will be to your good.

"Father Augustine! Father Martin! Father Phillip! Conduct Father Aillil to his old house. Bar the door and set men to guard it. I do not trust his self-mastery."

And so they took me away. I hung my head as on the day the Vikings marched Maeve and me in line from our burned home to their ship.

My old house held no comfort for me. Someone had left a blanket on the bench. I wrapped myself in it and sat in the dark, unable even to pray.

I sat there for some hours wretched as a weaned calf. I could have sat in that dark until I died. What did it matter?

You live as a priest among men who honor naught but killing and getting wealth and bedding women. And you try to convince them, and convince yourself, that there are other things that make a man a man.

Then some bishop comes along to put you in your place and let you know, straight from God, that your enemies were right about you all along.

At last I heard someone working the door's bar. The door opened and, for one glad moment, I thought it was Erling come to deliver me.

But it was Kaari, his brother.

"Welcome home, Father," he said.

"My home is with your brother," said I.

"Most touching. Erling seems to inspire such loyalty. Can you tell one how he does it?"

"By keeping his word and helping others."

"No, how does he really do it?"

"If you can't understand, there's no point repeating myself."

"All right, keep your secret. So Erling goes to Greenland, does he?"

"That is his plan."

"But you must stay."

"So it appears."

"They call such things as that *sad*, don't they?"

"I call it *sad*."

"Have you wept?"

"Not yet."

"But you will?"

"Very likely."

"So that is what sadness means, not to get what you want?"

"Don't play games with me. No man ever born needed sadness explained to him."

"How did you learn sadness?"

"By having all that was dear to me murdered or stolen."

"Ah. Losing what you prize is sad as well. This is useful." He turned to go and walked straight into the gable wall. "Doors, doors," he said to himself, as if it were some difficult lesson he was having trouble remembering.

He went to the door. "If I don't lock this, I suppose you'll run away," he said, looking back at me.

"Yes."

"I see." He nodded and went out, barring it behind him.

Something was amiss with Kaari. I feared the kind of a hersir he'd be.

The true night came at last, short as it was at that time of year. The scant light from the smokeholes faded.

I wept, as Kaari had expected.

I slept, sitting against the wall. I dreamed of fog (which is almost like not dreaming at all) and of a woman with a comb and men with red skin.

I was wakened by a hand on my shoulder.

I could not see who had wakened me. He clapped a hand over my mouth and whispered, "Quiet! I'm taking you to Erling!"

The door was open, hanging crooked. We went out into the night. I was as much at sea as St. Peter, the night the angel led him out of Herod's prison.

We took the lane to the gate, then northward through the hills toward Tjora. We stumbled on rocks we could not see and bumped against stone fences. But we put Sola farther and farther behind us.

"Who are you?" I asked when we'd gone far enough not to fear being heard.

"I'm Fingal MacBrian," said the voice.

Fingal was a thrall, one of those Erling had lost to Kaari. He was a red-haired brute, tall and strong as a river at flood.

"They'll flay you alive for this!" I said.

"Only if they catch me. And I'll be on my way to Greenland with you."

"Erling sent you?"

"Aye."

"How did he know what happened?"

"Erling knows what the slaves know, and the slaves know everything."

I shook my head, then tripped in a badger hole. Why had I ever doubted?

"How did you handle the guards?" I asked.

"I killed them."

We reached the harbor near sunrise. We boarded Erling's knarr straightaway, and a moment later the gangplank was pulled in and our crew rowed us out with the other knarr just behind. We put out on oar power and caught the wind at the harbor's mouth, bellying our sail and heading westward.

Erling stood beside me as I watched Jaeder fall below the horizon. "We've spoiled Konnall's sailing plan," he said. "We'll have to bear north of west to get the heading he wants. But there's no way Kaari can get ships out of Hafrsfjord in time to catch us. Thank God for a fair wind."

I looked at him. He was beaming like a boy who'd won a ball-game.

"You've twisted Kaari's beard, and Erik's, and the bishop's," I said. "If the bishop had a beard, that is."

"Aye."

"You've harbored men who killed men of the jarl's, and you killed one yourself."

"Aye."

"You've abducted a priest."

"Aye."

"You've stolen another man's thrall."

"My brother's. It's all in the family. And the man was my own thrall not long since."

"It'll be a hard thing for you to come back to Norway now," I said. "Not while Erik rules and Kaari lives."

Erling's smile did not change. "I felt like a spanked boy when I had to yield to Kaari," he said. "Now it's all right. I may never see Norway again, but I've left it on my own terms."

He offered me a bit of cheese. "Hungry?" he asked. "You weren't with us for breakfast."

A raven swooped from somewhere and snatched the cheese from his fingers, flapping between us. It had a queer white mark over one of its eyes, and I could swear it carried something like a leather pouch, strung around its neck.

Part Two

Iceland

Chapter 7

There's a certain good-fellowship in the first days of a sea voyage. Most of the landlubbers are sick together, and even the sailors are like to be a tad green at the edges. But as time goes on even the worst sufferers get their sea legs. All except for a few chosen, like me.

Worse than the retching was the privy, or rather the lack of one. At sea you just hang your bottom over the side, grab a stay for support, and do what God intended in front of everybody, the ladies included. It will have been worse for them, though we all looked away – or I hope we did; I know I did. My heart went out to Astrid most of all, heavy with child as she was.

At sea, you sleep in a two-man bag of sealskin to share warmth. I'd noted on earlier voyages that nobody was eager to share a bag with me. I couldn't really blame them; there's a common idea that a man who wears a robe (on Sundays anyway), shaves his face and never sleeps with a woman must have something lacking, or something extra. So Fingal the thrall ended up my mate. I could have done worse; it gave me someone to speak Irish with.

We lay back-to-back the first night, wet without and queasy within, too miserable to sleep.

"I'm going to grow my hair out," Fingal said. All Norse thralls are made to keep their hair short-cropped, as well as to wear undyed clothes.

"Will they accept you as a freedman in Iceland?" I asked.

"Who gives a damn about Iceland? Ships go from Iceland to Ireland. I'm for home."

"To never see a Norseman again, if you're lucky, eh?"

"I've naught against the Norse. 'Tis being a slave I hate."

"Naught against the Norse?"

"The Norse are great folk."

"You think so?"

"Of course. We Irish've been fighting the Norse for generations. Sometimes we win, sometimes they win. We're about matched. If the Norse were worthless, what would that say of us, who get beaten by them off and on? A man is known by the greatness of his foes."

"That's one way to look at it," said I. "What do you think of sailing to the west?"

"Gives a fellow pause, doesn't it?"

"Of course we're not likely to go anywhere near the Blessed Isles."

"They say St. Brendan went there," said Fingal.

"It did him no harm."

"He was a great saint. Such folk as dwell in the Blessed Isles might be harder for ordinary men to handle. Of course you're a priest. You might be in no danger."

"I wouldn't count on it."

Sea-dreams are strange dreams, the magpies of the mind. That night I dreamed I entered an unfamiliar house, a lamp in my hand, and found a woman lying on a bench under a blanket.

I put my hand on her shoulder, and she turned and looked up at me.

It was my sister Maeve. She smiled at me – such a look of joy I've never seen – and we clamped one another in a hug like a noose.

"It's deathly important you be where you can find me, Brother," she said to me. *"I think we'll get no more than one chance."*

I woke and had to apologize to Fingal for embracing him.

What does it mean to sail the seas? It means to risk your life. It means to be sick. It means to sleep badly or not at all, and to eat your food cold, only to cast it up again. And it means to be wet – wet with rain, which is icy, and wet with spray, which is icier.

The Book of Revelation says that when God's Kingdom comes, the sea will be no more. No man yearns for the Kingdom more than I.

Konnall was near as unhappy. He knew nothing about my arrest and escape until we'd sailed, and he cursed Erling as only a ship's master would dare.

"Do you know what you've done to me?" he roared. "You've closed Norway to me forever!"

"There's more to the world than Norway," said Erling with a smile.

"You've also closed Denmark to me. And England, too, if Svein should chance to conquer it. That's poor return for my friendship and skill."

"We'll make a profit if we live. And kings come and go."

"So do merchants, and heroes," said Konnall darkly, and he dressed down the unlucky man on bailing duty and went back to watching the sea.

The spring winds, they say, tend to be easterly. Like most things they say, it's only true when God pleases. The wind is a creature, like a bear, and like a bear, you can't always count on it.

Four days at sea we ran head-on into a sail-shredder out of the west. Konnall had no choice but to down sail and drive before it, back more or less the way we'd come. I was in misery, sick and wet and cold, knowing each hour made our journey longer, not shorter.

Thorlak Gudbrandsson, the younger of the two manslayer brothers, showed special concern for Thorliv's comfort and protection during the storm, so much so that Erling took him up into the bow and had a serious talk with him, his hand gripping the boy's arm like a vise.

After a day and a half the storm died and God sent a fair wind again. The problem now was that Konnall could only guess where we were.

"What do you think?" Erling asked him.

"My guess is further south and west than before, somewhere east and north of the Faeroes. We're not sea-bewildered – the wind was westerly at the start and it's still westerly, so I'm tolerably sure we were blown east. God knows where my own ship is. I pray we're only separated, and we'll meet in Iceland."

"So we could be near back to Norway."

"It's possible. I can set a course northwest, but if we've gone north of east instead of south of east, it could put us off our way."

"Do you think you're wrong?"

"No. I know these seas. But since we've passed midday I won't be sure until tonight, if I can get a look at the polestar."

"You're the master. I took you on for your sea-lore. Use it."

So he set a course northwest by the sun, and we sailed through the afternoon and into the night. And when the sky grew dark at last the height of the polestar told him he'd been right. It was just a matter of finding our northering and running west again. Konnall reckoned by the polestar each night, if we were lucky enough to have a clear view of it.

I was at my post at the rail one afternoon when Thorbrand Gudbrandsson joined me there. "Tell me about Freydis Sotisdatter," he said. "Is she promised to anyone?"

I glanced forward, where Freydis sat chatting with Thorliv, Lemming hovering nearby as always. She got fairer every year, plump but not too plump, buxom ("ship-breasted" as the Norse say) with great, wide-set blue eyes.

"You're thinking of asking for her?" I asked.

"Not for a wife, no. But she's a pretty, lively, willing girl," he said. "And she's not so well-born as the girls some fellows fancy." He looked at his brother Thorlak.

"Freydis is trouble," said I. "I don't speak so in enmity. I do like her. But she was raised by her mother and stepfather to be a sacrifice to the old gods. They let her have her way in all things. I fear she'll never learn that other folk have needs and rights."

"Her guardian is a thrall."

"He's a freedman and her uncle. And go carefully with him. He's the strongest man I've ever seen, freedman or not, and if he thinks you're trifling with her he'll reach in through your navel and break your back."

It was an unfortunate choice of words. The picture made me sick again, and I ran to the rail and retched. Nothing came up; I was empty.

I looked up into an eye the size of a shield boss. I shuddered from head to foot, thinking for a moment that I'd met a giant rising from the sea floor.

"A whale," said Thorbrand. "Big things, aren't they?" The gray body, what I could see of it, was as large as our ship.

"It's like looking into a man's eye. As if he was interested in me and would know me again."

"Whales are wise fish. They have meat like cattle. 'Tis a pity to kill them, but men must eat."

"We'll let this one live though."

"No point spearing it here, where we've nowhere to butcher it."

Then there were more whales. The further we sailed the more whales we saw, and porpoises as well.

"We're nearing Iceland," said Konnall, joining us. "The whales swarm here."

"And kittiwakes," I said, looking at the small gray gulls that swooped over the waves all around us.

"Puffins too," said Thorbrand. I heard Thorliv and Freydis shriek in delight as a flock of the black-and-white birds with the painted beaks whirred down the length of our ship just above deck level.

"Good eating," said Thorbrand who viewed the world, wolf-wise, as a well-stocked larder.

When night came we found ourselves in the sea-glow, the whole ocean sparkling around us like the Milky Way. Porpoises swam in the glow, their shapes like moving constellations.

When I thought I saw men and women swimming with the starry dolphins, I looked away and went to my bed.

The next morning we spied a great white mountain peeking its head over the sea-rim.

"What's that smell?" I asked.

"The earth spits up fire in Iceland," said Konnall. "That's burning rock you smell."

"Brimstone," I said. "We've sailed to Hell."

Chapter 8

THE mountain became a mountain range, then a gray mass of land that loomed ever larger when the mists cleared to let us see it.

We skirted the land along the south (a dangerous coast, Konnall had said) and made north up the western shore. Our progress was unsteady, as the wind varied. We had to tack much of the way and spent a fair time becalmed, drifting with the current (going our way, fortunately), watching the rocky shore where seals basked on the rocks.

"My child will be born in Iceland," said Astrid to me, "or in Greenland, perhaps. I never thought my child would not be Norse."

"Where you're born doesn't make you one thing or another," I said. "I was born and raised in Ireland, but I'm no longer truly Irish, I fear. God knows what I am. I'm not a Norseman; I suppose I'm just a priest."

"Seals are strange beasts," said Astrid, changing the subject. "I could swear that one there was looking me straight in the eye."

"Which one?"

"That one there, on the three-sided rock. The one with the white spot over his eye."

I felt chill of a sudden. I drew my wooden crucifix on its thong off over my head and reached it to her. "I'd thank you to take this," I said.

"I have a crucifix."

"And I have others. But this one is special. 'Tis no holy relic or anything of that sort – Ulf the idiot, who's dead, carved it for me. But my prayers go with it."

"But why?"

"I'd feel better about the child if I knew you had it about you."

She hung it around her neck. "You shouldn't put fear in a woman with child," she said.

"'Tis just a whim of mine. Think no more of it." She looked at me and then went to talk with Thorliv. I stayed and watched the seals.

"Some say seals are the ghosts of drowned men," said a voice beside me. I turned my head and saw Konnall.

"They say wrong," I answered. "Men go to Heaven or Hell, or maybe Purgatory, according to some."

"You priests. You think you know every tree and all its roots. Do you know how seals mate?"

"There are many things I don't know, and that's among them."

"See those big, ugly seals? Those are the bulls. Each of them has a score or so of cows, and he mates with them all. If any other males try to get near them, he chases them off."

"I think I saw that happen, a few minutes since. But there's always a stronger, younger one in time, I'm sure."

"And when a young male gets strong enough, he finds an old bull who's grown weak and takes his cows away."

"So every male gets his turn?"

"Not at all. Most of the young males never get near a cow. Their only job in life is to make meat for the killer whales."

I was silent a moment. "I don't think I like seals as well as I thought I did," I said.

Konnall went off to inspect the bilge for the hundredth time that day, and I stayed where I was and called the seals bad names.

We made our labored way up the coast. Outside the Hvalfjord I asked what was on fire and was told that it was Reykjavik, the smoky bay, where Ingolf Arnarsson, the first settler, had made his home. The smoke, Konnall told me, was steam from hot springs.

We passed the broad Borgarfjord where Konnall said his home was. He wouldn't put in there though, because we'd have had to pay landing tolls. His own ship would dock there if she came through. We'd sail on to Snorri the Chieftain's home.

"What's this Snorri like?" I asked Erling.

Erling pondered. "It's been years since we were together, and we were young then. But most men change little however many years they put behind them."

He thought a moment. "What would you say matters most to Norsemen? What would you say we value in a man?"

"Strength, and skill at arms."

"That's true, as far as it goes. But all men are not strong and keen. That does not mean they cannot have wealth and power among us."

"I thought it did."

"One other thing we value. That is cunning. If a man can be cunning and get what he wants by trickery, we esteem him, too. Not so much as we esteem a great warrior, but we do esteem him.

"There were two great gods in the old faith. One was Thor, the mighty one.

"But the other was Odin, the trickster. No man loved Odin as some men loved Thor. But all feared Odin more.

"Snorri is a man of Odin, or he was until the true faith came."

In case you'd care to know what Iceland's like, it's a great heap of wrinkled gray rock, with strips of green here and there on the mountain slopes and in the valleys where men can live and pasture their stock. The mountains are almost exactly the shape and color of great dumpings of fine wood ash, and they have thickets of dwarf birch running partway up their sides. Some of them are white with snow at the tops, summer and winter.

Which makes it quite a lot like Norway, only Norway has real forests and its mountains don't fart.

We rounded Snaefelsness, with its shining white mountain like a beacon in daylight, and had to make our way up the Breidafjord on oar power. A knarr has only six pairs of oars, so the shifts were short. Not that I had to row. The priesthood has its privileges. I enjoyed the same status and general respect as a woman.

Mountains hemmed the fjord on both sides. The mountains in Iceland offered an even unfriendlier face than their Norwegian cousins. They seemed rawer, newer, colder and less tame. And who could say when one of them wouldn't take umbrage at us and blow itself to pieces, sinking us in a shower of sulfur?

Snorri the Chieftain lived at Helgafell, a farm that sits beneath a rounded hill all by itself on a broad ness poking up into the Breidafjord. We anchored in a good harbor near the ness-tip and sent greetings to Snorri by way of some thralls who met us at the jetty. Then we waited, swatting at the blackflies and midges that besieged us.

I looked at Helgafell, Snorri's Holy Mountain, in the distance and misliked it from the start. It didn't deserve the name mountain, being only a knob of earth sticking up out of a marshy plain, but I somehow got the thought in my head that it was a proud hill; that it reckoned itself greater than other hills. As if a heap of earth can commit the sin of Superbia.

There were seabirds everywhere – gulls and shags and swans and those black-and-white puffins. I've a particular memory of a man standing on a low cliff on a nearby island, looking black against the sky, swinging a net on a pole into the air again and again, sky-fishing for puffins.

We waited politely for an invitation to disembark and went ashore when Snorri's chief thrall came to greet us. There was much gushing about what an honor it was to welcome us, but what mattered to me was the feeling of solid earth beneath my feet, already unaccustomed it's true, but grateful nonetheless.

We trudged to the farmstead, skirting the west end of a narrow inlet. The farm stood in a hollow on the eastern slope below the hill, above a little lake. We brought some casks stuffed with meal and linen cloth, gifts for our host. I carried a kind of burden of my own. I helped old Bergthor. The thanks I got was to hear him say a dozen times that he could manage for himself. I thought, not for the first time, that he'd have been wiser to stay home.

I used one arm to help him. Under the other I carried my little ivory casket, the casket with Odin's Eye. I had a sudden vision, like a waking dream, of Bergthor lying in blood on a bed of rocks.

I saw no good in telling him of it.

Freydis Sotisdatter came up beside me as we walked and said in a low voice so that the others could not hear, "You're doing it wrong."

"What am I doing wrong?"

"You have the Sight, have you not?"

"What makes you think that?"

"You don't deny it. I've the Sight myself; I can easily tell another. You didn't have it before, but you have it now. I suppose you've picked up some talisman or other that brings the Sight with it."

"What if I have?"

"You use it amiss, as I said. You try to make it serve you, to do what you call right and help folks."

"What's wrong with that?"

"The Sight's not a tool to use as you please. You do not possess the Sight. It possesses you. To get the good out of it, you must let it have its way; tell you what it will.

"Try to show it who's master and it will show *you* who's master. Submit to its wisdom and it will give you power of another kind, as a gift."

"What if I don't wish such power?"

"Then 'tis not the Sight you want; 'tis something else. You'll only wear yourself out trying to milk a serpent."

"Fortunately this is all idle talk, since I don't have the Sight," said I.

"One other thing you should know," she said, before she left my side. "'Tis not only the future you'll see with your new eye –"

I clutched the casket to me tighter. Did she know about the Eye?

"– in time you'll be able to see spirits as well; the Old Ones and the undeparted dead. Try not to be too frightened, and for the gods' sakes, don't lie to them, too."

Houses and buildings and yards in Iceland are much the same as in Norway, except that, having little wood, they build in turf and stone, saving the precious timber for gables, pillars, rafters and doors. This makes for marvelous thick walls, which they need, as the wind blows hard in Iceland, and it can be a cold wind indeed. I thought it would knock us over once or twice as we trudged the path over the rocks and through the mires.

We were met in the yard on the hill-slope by several house-folk and Asdis Styrsdatter, Snorri's wife. She was a smallish, auburn-haired woman who'd clearly been a great beauty once but had borne a lot of children. She greeted us politely and asked us to come inside, giving Astrid, who'd donned an embroidered blue-silk overdress, a greenish look.

We went into Snorri's home through a door in the gable-end of the house, between two side-closets where, I was to learn, the Icelanders store food. Inside the house, a large one even by homeland standards, divided into a greater and a smaller room, we met the master of the place, Snorri the Chieftain. He rose to embrace Erling and bid him sit in the guest seat across the hearth-way from him. "Erling Skjalgsson," he said, "you're welcome in my house. I'd thought never to see you again."

"Nor I you," said Erling, taking his place. The women sat on the cross-bench at the end, and I sat on Erling's right.

Snorri was a man of middling height, neither powerful nor puny. Like Erling, he had fair hair and a reddish beard, but his hair was less fair and his beard redder. What I remember best about him was his eyes. In most men, feeling comes first, then reasoning. But Snorri began with the thinking, then whatever feeling he'd decided on came in afterward and sat where it was told.

The drink started going around (not ale but sour whey, what they call *skyr*; ale is scarce in Iceland) and Snorri said, "Erling, tell me what brings you to Hel's threshold. What could uproot you from the rich soil of Jaeder to sail out here?"

So Erling told the story. And ever as he spoke, I saw those merchant's-balance eyes of Snorri's working, working, trying to make out a way to feel about what he was hearing.

When Erling was done, Snorri said, "I'm not sure I follow. You left Sola because...because Jarl Erik was too powerful for you?"

Erling pulled himself up in his seat, chin tucked in. "Not at all. I was itching to measure myself against Erik."

"Then you left…because you were losing support from the bonders?"

"No. Most of them asked me to stay."

"Then you turned your back on wealth and power…. I beg your pardon. Why?"

"Because it was the right thing to do."

"You cast away your place in the world in order to do right?"

"What use is power if you lose your soul?"

Snorri's eyes went dull and I could no longer read behind them. "Most noble," he said. "I drink to your honor."

"I heard a tale that you're all Christians here in Iceland now," said Erling.

"Yes," said Snorri. "Just as Olaf Trygvesson was getting himself drowned at Svold, we Icelanders were humbling ourselves and being baptized at his command. If we'd known what was going on in the Baltic, we could have saved ourselves a deal of trouble."

"Don't let Father fool you," said Haldor, Snorri's oldest son. "He did as much as any man to push the matter through."

"Were you already a Christian?" Erling asked.

"Not at all," said Snorri. "I had business at the Thing. I couldn't do my business if it all broke down in fighting."

"It came near to a fight?" I asked.

"We've no king in Iceland," said Snorri. "We've only the law. We like it that way. Laws don't have hung-over mornings or hold grudges. They're always the same, or if they change it's because we've all agreed to it. It works for us. We keep the peace among ourselves as well as other men, which is to say now well and now badly."

"No king but the law," said Erling. "I like that."

"But the Christians had decided to live under no law but Christian law. What would follow then? How could we keep the peace if there was one law for some and another for the rest?

The Christians came in force to the Althing—"

"Althing?" I asked.

"We have a Thing for the whole land, above the Quarter Things," said Snorri. "That's what I meant when I said we have no king but the law.

"As I was saying, the Christians came in force. They brought Hjalti Skeggjasson with them, and that was a slap in the law's face. Hjalti had been outlawed for blasphemy when he wrote a lampoon about Freya. He'd gone to Norway and met King Olaf, then come home before his outlawry had run out."

"I remember hearing about Hjalti at the time," said Erling. "Olaf was furious when Thangbrand the priest came back from Iceland and told how you'd all received him here. He arrested all the Icelanders in Nidaros, Hjalti among them, and meant to hang them."

Snorri said, "Thangbrand was an ass."

"You'll get no argument from us on that point," said I.

"Hjalti and his friend, Gizur the White, had been freed on the promise that they'd come home and convert the land by one means or another," said Snorri. "And that was how they came to be riding to the Althing with their kinsmen and supporters, like an army. The heathen men were ready to do battle to stop them."

"That's when Father made peace," said Haldor.

"No more than for the day," said Snorri.

"He spoke to the heathen men and talked them into letting the Christians alone," said Haldor.

"My thought," said Snorri, "was to keep the Thing-stead from becoming a battleground. The next day, both heathens and Christians met at the Law Rock. The Christians said they meant to have a Lawspeaker of their own; they chose Hall of Sida. It came near to blows again, but we staved off battle."

"Tell them what you said about the volcano," said Thord the

Cat, another of Snorri's sons. He was a lean boy with eyes, as you'd guess, like a cat's.

"Volcano?" asked Erling.

Snorri waved a hand in a show of modesty. I wondered if it was true, or if this was a litany he'd worked out with his sons and celebrated before. "News came that a volcano had blown out near Thorodd Oyvindsson's farm, and the rockflow was threatening his home. Someone said this meant the gods were offended. I pointed to the rock all around us, which any fool could see had come from a volcano long since. I said, 'I wonder whom the gods were angry at when this rock flowed.'"

Everyone laughed at this. I personally thought it a pretty weak argument, but said nothing out of politeness.

Snorri went on.

"Hall of Sida went to see Thorgeir of Ljosawater, the true Lawspeaker under the old law. It's said that Hall gave him silver; I don't know about that. But Thorgeir went into his booth, pulled his cloak over his head and stayed that way all day."

"He was a heathen?" asked Erling.

"Aye."

"Hall took a great risk."

"There was one thing on his mind, just as there was on Thorgeir's and mine. To keep the peace. To have one peace we must have one law. Otherwise, the land is laid waste.

"The next day Thorgeir came out of his booth and gathered everyone at the law rock. I hoped for peace, but I had my sword loose in its sheath. I thought the air was going thin; I felt as if I was choking. Then I realized I'd forgotten to breathe.

"Thorgeir asked all men to swear an oath to abide by the law he would now proclaim. I thought no one would buy a swine in a sack that way, but perhaps heads were cooling. All swore. Then Thorgeir recited the new law. To be honest, it was much like the old law; right and wrong are not far different whether you're Christian or heathen. But there were these changes:

"All men must be baptized Christians. They may sacrifice to the old gods in secret; there is no penalty, unless they do it openly.

"Babies may still be exposed and men may eat horseflesh; in these things the heathens got their way.

"All men must observe the Christian feasts such as Christmas, Easter, and so on."

"How did the heathens take this, coming from their own Lawspeaker?" asked Erling.

"Many felt betrayed. But they kept their oath and submitted to the law. Which says much for them, I think."

"You still set babies out to die," said I.

"No one ever did it lightly, and when they did it was mostly thralls' children. But there's a growing feeling that we must outlaw that as well, and the eating of horseflesh, which I for one would miss. Given time, as the older men die off, we'll have the kind of laws you like, Father."

"You're not going to serve us horse, are you?" I asked.

"That would be poor hospitality when Christians have come to visit."

"Are you baptized yourself?" asked Erling.

"Aye. I have the name of priest, but no longer the right. I've built a church – I'll show it to you tomorrow – but I'll need to find a priest for it."

I should explain here that up to now I've always used the word "lord" or "chieftain" for the Norse word *godi*. I did it to save confusion, but now the confusion has come in regardless. The word *godi* properly means priest, which was what a chieftain was under the old religion. When Christianity came, the chieftains stopped being priests. They kept the name, though.

"We even have a bishop of our own now, Bishop Jon from Ireland," said Snorri.

"An Irish bishop?" I asked.

"Would you care to sell me your priest?" Snorri asked Erling, ignoring my question.

Erling put a hand out to keep me from jumping up and striking the man, and said, "Father Aillil is not a thrall."

"One can but ask," said Snorri, smiling. "No doubt you've brought many fine goods to trade in Iceland, but you've brought nothing we covet more than that priest."

"You must understand about our goods," said Erling. "I'll be pleased to buy and sell with you and your neighbors, but I mean to go to Greenland and trade the most part of my cargo with Leif Eriksson."

"I can well understand it. We pay well in Iceland, there's so much we can't grow or find here. But they pay even better in Greenland. Still, I'll see if I can't talk you out of a few hands-full of meal and stick or two of lumber."

"You can be sure of that," said Erling.

"By the way, Lady Astrid," said Snorri. "We've a man in the neighborhood you'd remember."

Astrid said, "Who would that be?"

"Kjartan Olafsson, my cousin."

"The Kjartan Olafsson who served my brother in Norway?"

"The same."

"How...interesting," said Astrid.

Chapter 9

E slept in Snorri's hall. I was no longer partnered with Fingal, who bunked with Snorri's thralls, but with Bergthor, who snored beside me on the bench and got up noisily two or three times a night to go out and relieve himself.

Snorri sent invitations to all his friends to come and meet Erling Skjalgsson, and come they did. In many ways Iceland is a length of west Norway, snipped off and replanted like a willow shoot. Talk to any Icelander and in time he'll probably mention his grandfather (or both grandfathers) who came from Sogn or Hordaland.

Among the first to arrive was Olaf Peacock, a kinsman of Snorri's. He brought his wife Thorgerd and several sons, including the aforementioned Kjartan, a good-looking young man, fair and tall, who went straight up to greet Astrid. Kjartan had a wife named Refna, a small lovely girl with honey-colored hair wandering out from under her head-cloth, and great sad eyes. She reminded me somewhat of Halla Asmundsdatter, Erling's one-time leman, and I took to her at once.

Olaf Peacock was a tall man with darkish hair going gray and dressed in a scarlet shirt. He carried himself like one accustomed to being thought handsome, though the years had thickened his nose and hung a paunch out over his silver belt buckle.

He sat down beside me and said, "Good day to you, Father," in perfect Irish.

I must have gawked. Everyone laughed at me.

"My second sight warns me that Olaf will soon be telling you about his mother, the Irish princess," said Snorri with a smile.

Olaf's handsome face went serious. "My mother was a great woman," he said. "Everything I have I owe to her." Someone passed him a horn of mead (the mead and ale we enjoyed now came from Norway, Erling's gift) and he drank deeply.

"Her name was Melkorka," he said. "She was the daughter of King Muircetach; the Norse call him Myrkjartan. I named my son Kjartan for him."

"Which King Muircetach was that?" I asked.

Olaf ignored the question and carried on with a story he'd clearly told many times. He said, "My father Hoskuld was the son of Dala-Kol, son of Thorstein the Red, son of Olaf the White and Aud the Deep-minded." (He carried on with the genealogy long enough to dry his throat and need another drink.) "Father sailed from Iceland to Norway in the time of King Haakon the Good. He visited a market in the Brenn Isles and found a Russian there, selling slaves. He saw that one of the slave women was very beautiful, but the merchant had dressed her in rags and pushed her back into a corner. This raised his interest. They haggled, and the more they haggled, the more Father wanted the girl.

"'I can't lie to you,' the merchant said, 'she has a defect. She's dumb. She cannot speak.'

"Father thought that no great fault in a woman, and in the end he paid three times the market price for the girl.

"He brought her back with him to Iceland, and I was born to them.

"One day, Father was walking in his fields and he heard a

strange, musical voice. He went to see who it was and found my mother, speaking Irish to me. Father told her she'd best come clean with the whole story.

"She said her name and whose daughter she was. She said she'd been taken as a slave when she was fifteen. All these years she'd kept silent so no one would know about her family."

"Why did she do that?" I asked. "Did she not wish to be ransomed?"

Olaf went on without a pause. "After this, my stepmother Jorunn grew jealous. Rather than let her misuse Mother, Father settled us on a farm further up the river, and that was where I lived until he fostered me with Thord the Chieftain at Goddastad.

"When I was grown, I took it into my head to go abroad as Father had. I got passage on a Norwegian ship and spent the winter with King Harald Graycloak in Norway. The king and his mother Gunnhild took to me, and when I told them I needed to go to Ireland they gave me a ship.

"We sailed out and the weather was bad – foggy and calm. After drifting blind a long time, we found ourselves suddenly approaching an unknown shore. We downed sail and dropped anchor, and when the tide ebbed we found ourselves beached in the shallows. But the bottom was soft, and our ship took no harm. There was an estuary nearby, and we managed to put out our boat and tow the ship there. The Irish came riding and told us that we were salvage now by their law, and we must surrender our ship. I think they were surprised when I answered them in their own tongue, and when we made it clear they'd have to fight us, they drew back and sent word to the king. The king came, and I was able to tell him that I was his grandson."

"That was lucky," said I, "as many kings as there are in Ireland, to sail straight to your grandfather."

"He gave us safe conduct and I was able to show him my mother's teething ring, which she'd given me as a token. This proved my claim, and I spent the summer with him, helping him to fight his enemies."

I thought it strange that a thrall had been permitted to keep a bit of jewelry, but by now I knew there was no point asking about it.

"In the spring I told him I had to return to Norway, and he let me go, though he would have liked me to stay. He even mentioned making me his heir. I spent the following winter in Norway with Harald and Gunnhild, and they too wished me to remain with them. But I'd done what I needed to do. I was now heir to my foster-father Thord, who was childless, and I'd proven myself in the wide world. I'd done all that a man could do to raise his head in Iceland."

It was a tale as full of holes as a peat digger's socks, but I was too polite to press the man more. It was pleasant to speak Irish with anyone, and Olaf was a fount of many stories, which he told in between the singing of songs from one or another of the guests. The Icelanders have more skalds – poets – even than the Norse. Almost as many as the Irish.

"Your son Kjartan seems to have much to say to my lady Astrid," I said to Olaf later on.

"He's an old acquaintance."

Indeed he was. It had been something of a scandal at the time. Princess Ingebjorg, Astrid's sister, had taken a shine to the handsome young man, who'd been one of the Icelanders Olaf had taken hostage. King Olaf, when he'd gotten his way with the Icelanders, had sent the boy home with a kick in the pants and rich gifts, so as to make his views known without causing unnecessary offense.

"I note there's another boy called Kjartan here," I said. "King Myrkjartan is well namesaked in Iceland."

"That's Kjartan Thorodsson, son of Snorri's sister Thurid, who's married to Thorodd the tax-trader. What can I say? They liked the name. Most folk prefer not to have the same name twice in one kinship while the first yet lives, but we're not so very closely related."

"It seems a fortunate name. Both Kjartans are tall and handsome."

"It's said that Kjartan Thorodsson takes after his father," said a red-faced man from the other side of the table and a little further down.

There was low laughter and Olaf made as if he'd not heard it.

"That's Thurid and Thorodd down there with Snorri," said Olaf. "I don't know who that woman with them is." He was talking about a tall, brown-haired woman who wore a rich green overdress that looked to be embroidered in gold. I thought she must have been striking once, but she'd grown wide with the years and was no longer young.

"That's Thorgunna Thorhallsdatter from the Hebrides," said somebody. "She's been staying with Thorodd and Thurid. The two women were friends and then they were not. Now they barely speak. Or so my wife tells me. Something about bedclothes."

"More than one widow has sailed to Iceland looking for a husband," said Olaf. "I reckon Thorgunna is no different. We have the name of a place where women are few and men are hungry for them. It's no longer true, but folk learn slowly."

We got to see Thorgunna's famed bedclothes that night, and they were remarkable indeed – richer even than Erling's and Astrid's at home. She strung ropes between the wall and the rafters and hung embroidered curtains of red and blue over them, and within one could glimpse butter-colored cushions and quilts. Thurid watched the process with ill-concealed envy.

Thorodd the Tax-trader stood watching, too, frowning but saying nothing. I did not get to know him well, but he seemed to be of an even sourer disposition than Konnall. Konnall at least was good company when you got to know him. Thorodd said nothing to anyone more than hello, goodbye, please and thank you.

"Ill manners," sniffed Bergthor, watching Thorgunna hang her curtains, "to sleep more richly than your host. I never set much store by Hebrideans."

The next day (when Bergthor himself had to fend off Thorgunna, after which she tipped a wing to me) there were other guests. I can't remember all of them, but two I'll never forget.

"Ivar Ketilsson and his brother Orm," said Snorri. "They live at Haug near Bjornarhaven."

They were brown-haired men, neither of them over-tall, but well built. One was nearly old enough to be the other's father, or looked to be at any rate. That one was Ivar, and the moment I saw him I thought, *This is a dangerous man.*

The world is full of dangerous men, not least where Northmen dwell. Why, I wondered, would I have such a strong feeling about this fellow?

Then I thought a mist filled the room, and in that mist I saw Ivar Ketilsson cutting a man down with an axe.

I almost cried out. The mist cleared. Ivar stood talking with Snorri as before. It had been my Sight at work. Ivar would kill, but not just now.

I ought to do something about it.

What?

The power to see the future is less useful than one might think.

Another day brought Bishop Jon and his household. Bishop Jon had a face as Irish as a shamrock, horsey and freckled, with a short nose, a long upper lip and a big chin. His tonsured hair was white. His face lit up when we were introduced.

"A proper Irish priest!" he cried, embracing me like a wet cloak. "Saints Patrick and Bridget be praised!" As soon as he could politely do so he asked me to accompany him to Snorri's church. He'd promised to consecrate the building the next day, so his excuse was that we needed to make preparations.

The church was of turf like all houses in Iceland, except that it had a single wooden gable at the west end. Earthen benches ran along the side walls. The afternoon light came in through the smokehole sufficient to let us look around. It was a passable church for a mission field.

Bishop Jon sat on a bench and folded his hands in his lap. "Did you see their eyes on me?" he asked.

"Whose eyes?" I asked. "May I sit, Your Eminence?"

"Yes, of course. Whose eyes? The women's of course."

"The women's?"

"I know what they're all thinking."

"You do?"

"It's the question on all their minds."

"What question?"

"They want me to marry. Did you see that giantess from the Hebrides, that Thorgunna? I had to peel her off my arm like half-cooled candle wax."

I shook my head. "What?"

"Surely it's come up with you in Norway, too. Everywhere those benighted English priests set their feet."

"Oh. I follow you now. The married priests from England."

"Yes. And Frankland. Taking wives; taking concubines even. Wallowing in the flesh when they should be devoting themselves to God. Setting their minds on the needs of wives and children instead of the flocks the Lord has entrusted to them. Dragging the priesthood down to the level of common life. Surely you've felt the nudging; everyone wants you to go along."

I'd felt the nudging indeed, but it had mostly come from within. I did not tell the good old man that I'd contemplated marriage on two occasions. Both had turned out badly; I'd no wish to go through it again, and certainly none to discuss it.

"'Tis like bringing up children," I said. "You can't expect them to understand all at once. We have to raise them in stages."

"Aye, I know it," said Bishop Jon. "But I feel the weight of those constant eyes. I'm an old man. I'd barely given thought to women in years. Now – I say this in confidence, my son – I think about them all the time. I think they'd give me any woman in the land – the richest and most respected widow; the youngest and fairest virgin – just to get me to change my views."

"Is there anything I can do to help you?"

"Pray for me, my son. Pray that I'll be the man I vowed God I'd be; not the man I have the power to be."

"God grant that to us all," said I.

We got the church consecrated in a service ornamented by three priests, a very splendid business for Iceland in those days. Years after, Icelanders I met would tell me how they remembered that day.

I remember even better the day that followed, when Olaf Peacock's foster-son, Bolli Thorleiksson, came with his household and his wife Gudrun. Bolli was a well-favored, brown-haired young man, not quite as tall as his foster-brother Kjartan, but maybe stronger. Gudrun was one of the fairest women I'd ever seen (though my taste ran more to Refna, Kjartan's wife; pardon me, Bishop). Gudrun was tall and graceful, with a queenly carriage. The hair tied in her headcloth was palest gold. The only thing that saved her from looking cold as a statue of stone was her dimples, which peeked out sweet as a child's when she smiled. But she did not smile often.

She joined the other great ladies at the women's cross-table, and it was not long before she and Refna were shouting at one another. Refna rose in tears and fled outside. Her husband Kjartan gave Gudrun one look, then went out after his wife.

"Refna and Gudrun," said Olaf Peacock. "I fear where it will end between them."

"It will end in blood," said I, *"with each taking the other's dearest treasure."*

"What's that?" asked Olaf, swinging about to stare at me.

"I don't know where it came from," I said, frightened at myself.

In fact I knew where it came from. It came from Odin's Eye, packed away in my chest, my possession and so a part of me.

"Pray God you haven't the Sight," said Olaf. "I love those two boys. Kjartan is a son any man would give an arm for, and I couldn't love Bolli more if he were my own flesh. The two of them were like twins growing up."

"What happened?"

Olaf took a deep breath. "There was a man called Ketil Flatnose, son of Bjorn Buna, a hersir in Romsdal in the days of King Harald Finehair—"

"Wait," said I. "I don't need to hear the history of Iceland back to the land-taking. Just tell me about the young people."

"You can't understand unless you know the roots of the thing. Ketil's sons were Bjorn the Easterner and Helge Bjolan. One of his daughters married Helge the Lean. Another daughter was Aud the Deep-minded, and a third was Jorunn Wisdomslope. These are all renowned among the first generation of land-takers. Aud was the wife of Olaf the White who was king of Ireland...."

Another king of Ireland in the family. But I'd actually heard of this one, a Norse crown-thief.

"All right," I said, "I note that you come of important stock. Tell me about the young people."

"Well Aud and Olaf had a son named Thorstein the Red, who married Thurid Eyvindsdatter...."

It went on in that vein for some time. Icelanders are unable to tell a tale without making sure you know everybody's ancestors back to Noah, and there's no way to persuade them to do otherwise. By the time Olaf had gotten to the meat of the thing I'd almost lost Kjartan and Bolli in the branches and shoots of relations.

So I'll give you the summer-night version. Bolli was the son of Thorleik Hoskuldsson, Olaf Peacock's half-brother. Thorleik had always resented Olaf, the thrall-bastard, and his grand ways. After Olaf returned from Ireland with his riches and tales of being a king's grandson, Thorleik had come near to calling him a liar to his face and starting a feud between brothers. But Olaf, who if not humble was no fool, had stretched out an olive branch by offering to foster Thorleik's son Bolli – the man who fosters a child is held to be lower in rank than the foster-son's father.

The boys had grown up together and Kjartan had cared for Bolli more than for his own brothers. They had been fierce friends.

Kjartan and Gudrun had been sweethearts. They'd meant to marry. Kjartan had promised her he'd be back from a voyage to Norway in three years, and then he'd wed her.

But Kjartan had not seen that his foster-brother Bolli also harbored feelings for Gudrun. And when they'd gone to Norway together, Bolli had watched Kjartan paying court to Princess Ingebjorg. He'd seen it as a betrayal of the woman he himself cherished. Then King Olaf had made Kjartan a hostage, and Bolli had gone home on another ship.

The three years Kjartan had promised Gudrun ran out, and Gudrun was enraged. Bolli saw his chance and made his own proposal. Gudrun accepted.

"So Kjartan came home to find his betrothed wed to his best friend," said Olaf. "I tried to talk Bolli and Gudrun out of wedding, but Bolli was in love and Gudrun felt scorned. The two of them are in fact well matched and fond of each other, but they've built their house on the graves of old hurts and I fear what the end will be.

"It's a fault of young people nowadays that they lean toward pridefulness. I can't think where they learn it," he said.

In the evening, a woman appeared and stood before Snorri's high seat. She was neither young nor fair nor well-garbed, and she probably would not have caught my attention except that she carried an owl on her shoulder and spoke in so high, grating a voice that all in the hall turned to see who talked so shrilly.

"Snorri Chieftain, I am Unn the Barren," she said. "Do you welcome the honest poor in this house?"

"I hope I'm not behind other men in hospitality," said Snorri, looking none too pleased with his guest. "You may dine with my housefolk in the old hall."

"I thank you, my lord," said Unn. "And I in turn shall repay you with what coin I have."

"And what coin would that be?"

"I have the gift to comb the lies out of people's hair."

Snorri frowned. "Forgive my speaking plain, old woman, but I think it likely that you'd give as many lice as you removed."

"I did not say *lice*; I said *lies*. Do you know the tale of Aud the Deep-minded, how when she came to land in Iceland she lost a comb at the place called Kambsness?"

"Aud was an ancestor of mine; of course I know the tale."

"But did you know why she cared so much for that comb?"

"Combs are valuable. They take hard work to make."

"This comb was special. It had been made by dwarfs for Queen Aasa hundreds of years before. It had this virtue, that when it was run through a person's hair, it would comb the very lies from his mind and bring them out to speak their names."

"Vile pagan stories," said Bishop Jon. "Send the woman away."

Snorri rested his chin on a hand. "Why would anyone want a comb of that sort?" he asked Unn.

"There are people, even of your own kin, who value the truth." Unn put a hand in a bag she wore at her waist and drew out a comb of ivory, carved in runes and riveted with silver. The owl on her shoulder flapped its broad gray wings at the movement.

"I valued the truth once," said Snorri. "I found it a food that could not be eaten and a garment that did not warm me. I would not care for a thousand combs such as that."

Unn turned about to look at the guests. "Perhaps there are others here who do not fear the truth. I see great men here; men esteemed for their honor. Do they have the courage to let their secrets come to light before the faces of others?"

She crossed the hearth-way to Erling's guest seat. "Erling Skjalgsson," she said. "You are the most famous man among us; the most powerful man in Norway once. All esteem you for your honor; you turned your back on wealth and power rather than do a shameful deed. Surely you do not fear to be combed by me?"

"I know you not," said Erling. "Why should I trust you to handle my head?"

"I am an old woman; you are a warrior. If you fear magic, you have a bishop and priests here. Are you afraid, Erling Skjalgsson? And if you are, what do you fear? Magic, or the truth within you?"

"Comb away then, and the trolls take you," said Erling, leaning forward over the table.

Unn reached in with the ivory comb and ran it through Erling's fair hair.

A few small specks flew out of Erling's hair and landed on the table. I doubt many could see them who were not close by as I was. The specks leaped up and swarmed like gnats in a small cloud.

A sound rose like tiny, shrill voices. The voices made a chorus.

The chorus said, *"I want men to think I would not like to kill my brother. I want them to think I am not angry with God. I do not want them to know that I fear for the future—how I'll live and whether I'll ever be a great man again."*

And that was all. Erling looked pale as he sat back. *"You came out well,"* I whispered to him. *"There's naught there that would be untrue of any man striving to do right. Naught to be ashamed of."*

"No man should be ashamed to have bowels either," said Erling to me. "Yet he'd rather not show them to the world."

"There are other men of reputation here," said Unn. "Kjartan Olafsson, they call you the spear-tip of honor in Iceland. Do you fear to be combed by me?"

Kjartan sat in his seat looking white as bleached linen. "I fear nothing you can do to me," he said, and leaned forward to be combed.

The comb passed through his long fair locks. Many specks leaped forth and swarmed before him. *"I fear that I cannot be all men expect of me. I fear that I am the great-grandson of a thrall, not of an Irish king. I fear that Refna will know that I yet care for Gudrun. I fear that Gudrun will know that I would have cast her off for Ingebjorg Trygvesdatter—"*

Kjartan swatted at the swarm and dispersed it. "Lies!" he cried. "Lies from the devil!" He rose from his seat and stalked out of the hall.

"Bolli Thorleiksson!" said Unn. "Are you less brave than your foster-brother Kjartan?"

Without a word Bolli bowed his head and Unn combed him.

"I fear that Kjartan is a greater man that I. I fear that Gudrun will know that I lied to her about Kjartan to win her hand. I fear that I will live my life in bitterness and die at the hands of kinsmen."

Without a word Bolli left the table and went out from among us.

"Olaf Peacock," said Unn. "You are admired above all men in Iceland. Are you willing to show your admirers what is truly in your heart?"

Olaf rose. "I know not what trickery this witch is using, Snorri," he said in a loud voice, "but I did not come to this feast to see my kinsmen slandered, or to be slandered myself. I and my household will take our leaves."

"No need for that," said Snorri. "I'll not give hospitality to a beggar at the expense of my honored friends. Woman, you have abused my welcome. Be gone."

"As you wish, my lord," said Unn. "But be warned. All men have secrets; and those not spoken will come forth later, in ways even less welcome."

"I do not like this," I said to Erling as she left. "The devil take that woman, and her owl with her."

"What owl?" asked Erling.

Chapter 10

THE next day we played games, or rather the men played games. No, that's an ill way to put it. I'm a man, and I didn't play. The fighting men played, with all the outward good humor and inward blood-thirst of warlike men bringing their swords out to see whose was longest. There were wrestling and footraces and horse fights and axe throwing and stone throwing, and team games where they kicked a bladder at one another. Erling didn't win every game, but only because he chose not to play every game. Lemming didn't go in for games; nobody wanted to play with a freedman anyway. Of the games Erling did not play, Kjartan Olafsson won the most and Bolli was next after him, but Thorlak Gudbrandsson and Ivar Ketilsson did remarkably well for men built on a smaller plan. I thought each overcame larger men by sheer force of will, a refusal to admit they'd been beaten.

We all ate and drank richly that night, and the women joined the men to share ale and talk.

Freydis Sotisdatter lived for nights like this. The men's faces shone with hard work and hard drink, and they felt yeasty and keen for any chance. You could smell the musk on them and Freydis' eyes sparkled with the bubble of it all. A crowd of men coiled about her, but the ones who kept closest were Thorbrand Gudbrandsson, Thorlak's older brother from our crew, and Orm Ketilsson, Ivar's younger brother.

You might as well have set two bulls in a pen with a lone heifer.

From what I could follow of the argument, it started with Orm proposing that all Norsemen lay with sheep, and to prove it, he said that he would stand against a pillar and let any man throw an axe toward his head, as near to it as he pleased.

We'd all left our weapons in the entry room, but Thorbrand lifted a trophy axe from the wall and said he'd be glad to play that game.

"If you kill me, it will prove that Norsemen are bad warriors, and that Icelanders are braver," said Orm.

"I won't kill you," said Thorbrand. "When I kill you, it'll be because I mean to."

"You're both drunk," said Snorri from the high seat. "If you must play idiot games, do it tomorrow when you're sober."

"Even drunk I'm worth any two sober Liceanders. Icelanders," said Thorbrand.

"He's worthless," said Orm. "He'll kill me with that axe and everyone will know what a codfish he is."

"I won't kill you. Who're you to say I'll kill you, you woolwit? If you don't stop saying I'll kill you, I'll – I'll kill you."

"You haven't got the nerve to kill me."

"I'll tell you what," said Thorbrand. "After I kill you, you can kill me. You can't say thairer than fat. Fairer than that."

"I wouldn't kill you. I'm too great a warrior to kill you."

"You wouldn't kill me because you're harmless. All Hicelanders are armless. You've nobody to fight with but other Icelanders, so you don't know how to fight real men."

Orm stood up straight against the pillar. "Throw, and Northunder with you," he said.

Thorbrand threw the axe, though many hands reached out to stop him.

One of those hands brushed the axe as it flew. The weapon altered course, just a hair.

Just enough to send it into Orm Ketilsson's skull.

Orm stood with a surprised look on his face as his blood spouted like a fountain.

Then he sagged, to hang for a moment suspended by the axe, which stood with its blade in the pillar and its beard in his head. Then his weight tore him loose, and both he and the axe dropped to the floor.

There was shouting as Norwegians and Icelanders threw themselves on each other. Orm's brother Ivar was after Thorbrand with his belt knife, Ivar defending himself with his own. Lemming, huge as a bear and roaring, leaped into the fight and began to throw men left and right, for Freydis was in the midst of it all. Erling and Snorri were down in it in a moment, and they managed to get the two groups parted with only one man badly cut and another knocked senseless.

"Peace!" cried Snorri. "This is my house! I'll not have more men dying under my roof tonight!"

"My brother is dead!" shouted Ivar Ketilsson.

"And blood-money will be paid," said Erling. "We've a house full of witnesses that the death was by mischance. It was not willful murder."

"Your man spoke slanders against Icelanders!"

"Ale-talk. Both men slandered the other's folk."

"No one means to start a feud tonight," said Snorri. "Go sleep in the other house, Ivar, and let your belly cool. You'll not be cheated and your brother will not be dishonored. But let it be done for tonight."

Ivar straightened himself and sheathed his knife. "This does not end here," he said.

"Let's hope it does," said Erling.

Men carried the body outside, and thralls cleaned up the blood. We sat for some time, all talking loudly and drinking. Then, as if by agreement, everyone grew suddenly weary and wanted to sleep. The thralls took down the tables and we spread our beds on the benches.

I awoke in darkness, roused by men's voices. Someone poked a rush into the hearth coals and got a flame with which to light a lamp, and by it I could see Thorbrand Gudbrandsson. He held a spear in his hands and his shirt was torn across the skirt.

"I was out taking a piss," he said. "I had the hem of my shirt in my teeth – you know, the way a fellow does to keep it out of the way – and this spear came sailing out of the dark and snagged itself in the cloth. It knocked me over, but I'm not hurt."

I got myself untangled from my blanket and went to join the others with Thorbrand.

"This is past an insult!" cried Snorri. "Bring your weapons and come with me to the old hall. But no one strike a blow unless I call for it."

Everyone but I took a weapon and we all went out into the night, to the old hall hard by. I took the lamp to make myself useful, spreading my cloak to shield it from the wind. Most of the men stayed outside, but Erling, Snorri, Olaf Peacock, Thorbrand and Thorlak went in. I went in too. When you're a priest you're almost never told to stay outside. And I held the light.

Snorri shook Ivar Ketillsson awake.

"You tried to kill a man at night. You tried to kill a man while he took a piss. And you tried to do it at my home, during my feast. Striking out in anger, when you're drunk and your brother new-slain, is one thing. But this is a crime against hospitality. You're lucky I don't kill you where you lie. As it is, get out. Be gone now."

"What are you talking about?" asked Ivar, blinking.

"You know what I'm talking about. Get up and ride; you and your kinsmen."

"I do not know what you speak of, but my brother is dead and now you make accusations. We'll go, but you'll hear from us."

"A door-court!" cried Olaf Peacock. "We've enough men here. Let's hold a door-court and settle this thing before it goes further. We can reckon up damages here and now. What of that, Ivar? What of that, Erling? Snorri?"

"If you think I'll pay for a night-crime I never did, you'll wait long for your silver," said Ivar. He stomped out of the house.

"Can they make it home in the dark?" I asked Snorri outside, as Ivar and his men saddled their horses.

"No, they won't get far in the dark, but it'll be dawn soon."

"I don't think Ivar tried to kill Thorbrand," I said.

"Why not?"

"His eyes were full of sleep-sand. He wasn't feigning. He'd been asleep for hours."

"So he had one of his men do it."

"While he himself slept? He doesn't look to me so cold-blooded as that."

"Who else would try to kill Thorbrand? Thorbrand has no other enemies in Iceland, does he?"

"Not that I've heard."

"Then we know."

I wasn't sure, but he had a point. Who else would attack Thorbrand?

Back to bed then, but it was soon light as Snorri had promised, and I could not sleep. I saw Erling rise and go outside. I followed. We watched the sun rise over the Alftafjord and the snowy mountains.

"This is not good," said Erling to me.

"We're in a blood-feud, aren't we?"

"Aye. No way out of it. With the murder attempt and the

insult to Ivar, I don't think this will be settled with silver."

"And that means...."

"If I sailed away it would be seen as cowardice. We're stuck in Iceland until the Quarter Thing at least, and the Quarter Thing is in the spring."

It came over me in a flood – *another winter in thralldom for Maeve.*

As we turned to go inside, we found we were not the only ones who had been out and were going in. We met Lemming at the door. I did not suspect him of the attack on Thorbrand. The look on his face was one of sorrow. As if the strongest man I'd ever known had been unstrung in a single night. He looked as if he'd slept not at all.

Chapter 11

*T*HE next morning after breakfast, folks began to pack and leave. That was when we heard the voice of Refna, Kjartan's wife, high and angry.

"My brooch is gone! What happened to my brooch?"

Kjartan's thralls and several of the other women began to lift blankets and poke in the rushes on the floor looking for the thing.

"It was gold, with green stones!" cried Refna. "My husband had it from the king of Norway!"

It was gold, with green stones. It was also nowhere to be found. They looked and looked and poked and poked, but showy as it must have been, it could not be seen.

"Enough," said Refna. "I know where it's gone."

"Where?" asked Snorri's wife, Asdis.

"The same place the other treasures my husband gave me went. Gudrun has stolen them – or her kinsfolk have, which comes to the same thing."

"What are you saying?" demanded Gudrun Osvifsdatter, walking toward her.

"Oh you'll deny it, as always. It's mere chance that every

time we're together at a feast, some fine thing of mine goes missing. You think it's funny. You think these things would have been yours if Kjartan had come home when he promised. But I'm telling you, it's no game. This will end with steel – and blood. Mark my words, Gudrun."

"You speak nonsense. Is it your time of the month? You've lost your head!"

"Heads will be lost before this is done, unless you let go your bitterness."

"What cause have I to be bitter?" asked Gudrun. "I've a better man than you; one who keeps his word." When she'd spoken, she turned and went out.

It must have been the next day or soon after that a traveler rode in with a message for Konnall. He was invited into the hall and he told his tale over a bowl of skyr.

"Your ship made it into Borgarfjord, Konnall," said the messenger, "but it fell foul of a hard storm and took bad hurt. Much of your cargo's lost, and your partner Thorarin is mad with grief, for his sister's son died in the storm and he says the ghost haunts him."

Konnall stood up straightaway. "Can you lend me some horses, Snorri?" he asked. "I must see to my cargo and my friend."

"Is there a priest to help this poor man Thorarin?" I asked the traveler.

"No. There's no priest there."

"Then I must go, too, and do what I can."

"I'll come as well," said Erling. "It'll be something to do."

"Perhaps you can steer us into another blood-feud," said Bergthor dryly.

In the end it was Erling and I, along with Thorbrand and Thorlak Gudbrandsson, who traveled with Konnall southward. A couple of thralls came to cook and watch the horses but, I'm sorry to say, I've forgotten their names. Thorbrand and Thorlak

complained that men might think they were fleeing their enemies, but Erling said he wanted to keep them in sight.

We set out with the tooth-shaped mountains of the Snaefelsness peninsula to our right and the white cap of Drapuhlidar
mountain ahead to the left and a rough climb onto the high
road south. The wind worked at blowing our cloaks off and
made our horses squint. We stopped each night at farmsteads
where Konnall was known.

"It's a big land with few men," I said to Konnall as we rode.
"Are there places inland for farming?"

"Inland is no good," said Konnall. "The farmland is mostly
along the coast. The inland is wilderness – barren rock and ice –
where only outlaws go, to die, for the most part."

The road further south was easy in the sense of calling for
little climbing, the land being generally low the way we were
headed. But if there's an unfriendlier country for a rider, I don't
know of it. We forded stream after stream, wetting our trousers
to the knees; we crossed great fields of burned rock, looking
as if a giant child had made a mess of his porridge and left
it to dry, and we threaded our way through endless marshes,
swatting at blackflies. And, always, there were the gray-green
mountains before us, and to the west, with sometimes a far-off
glint of a glacier if it wasn't raining or foggy, which, as often as
not, it was.

"One thing about Iceland; if you don't like the weather, just
wait a bit," said Konnall, shouting to be heard as the rain blew
in our faces one day.

"Very droll," said I. "That's an old joke in Ireland, too."

"But here, it's true," said Erling. "In Ireland, you can wait a
lifetime and it'll still be raining."

"Which makes it just like Jaeder," said I, with satisfaction.

"I've been to both places," said Konnall. "Ireland is worse."

"But not as bad as Iceland," said I.

And he couldn't deny it.

We arrived at last in the Borgarfjord neighborhood, notable for its marshes, and came to Konnall's home at Finnsmyr.

His wife greeted us in the yard, saying, "Thank the gods you've come!" Then she saw me and said, "I mean, thank God you've come! I sent word north to his home, as well as to you, and I had the thralls put him in the storehouse. I didn't know what else to do."

"You did admirably," said Konnall. He introduced us to her and she invited us in to eat, but we thought we'd best look to the man we'd come to see. Konnall took us to the storehouse, a turf building like the others.

Konnall lit a fish-oil lamp with a rush from the hearth. In the dim light I saw two figures. One quivered in a corner and looked something like a great, gray maggot with a man's head. It was in fact the unlucky Thorarin, Konnall's partner.

Konnall's resourceful wife had sewn him up in a woolen blanket, tight enough so he couldn't wiggle out. The blanket was well soiled but he'd done himself no harm. He was a tall young man and his face, the only uncovered part of him, was notable for its long nose.

Who the other man was, I had no guess. He sat on the bench, staring at us, wordless, and Konnall did not speak to him. He was a young man and his clothing and hair were dripping wet.

"Konnall!" cried Thorarin, eyes rolling in purple sockets. "I failed. I failed you and I failed my kin. Let me go back to the sea. I belong in the sea."

"You brought the ship home," said Konnall, sitting on the bench by him. "Be at peace. You did all a man of flesh could do."

"I lost the greater part of the cargo," said Thorarin, his eyes wide. It was strangely businesslike talk for a madman. "The meal was all spoiled by seawater. Much of the timber went overboard."

"It's a loss of goods," said Konnall. "Such things happen. We're merchants. The sea will have its toll."

"Too great a toll!" cried Thorarin, his head back and his teeth bared. "My sister's son Vagn – he drowned. Ran's daughters took him!" He shook and sobbed, like a child.

Konnall took him by the shoulders. "'Twas not your fault, Thorarin!"

"Not my fault?" Thorarin cried. "Tell it to Vagn!"

"Vagn is dead," said Konnall. "He neither hears nor cares."

"How can you say that when you see him there, glowering at me?"

"See him? There's no one here but you and I, and Erling Skjalgsson and his friends and the priest," said Konnall.

I gasped. "Can't you see him?" I asked.

Konnall stared at me. "Don't say that, Father."

"I thought 'twas a living man," said I. "Do none of you see him there, on the bench, the boy in the wet clothing?"

Erling put his hand on my arm. "You never used to have the Sight."

"I see what I see," said I.

"Well you've left us small chance of convincing Thorarin he's seeing fancies, unless we can make him think *you're* not real either. Do you think you can lay this walker?"

"I'm a priest and I see him. If I can't deal with him, I don't know who can. And someone must try, for both their sakes."

"What can we do to help?"

"Let's see if I can keep the ghost here, while you take Thorarin to the house. If we can do that, I'll try to roust him out."

Erling nodded. "God be with you, Father," he said. They lifted Thorarin like a side of beef and lugged him outside.

The dead man did not move or try to stay with them. He merely sat where he was and stared at me.

"Would you like a towel?" I asked.

He only stared, with eyes like dull blue stones. Do you know how you can tell a fish is alive by the way his eyes shine? Vagn's eyes didn't.

"Why don't you go to your rest?" I asked him. "You're not alive. You don't belong here."

He answered me with a question. "How is it you see me? It should only be Thorarin."

"I have the Sight."

"Not by birth you don't."

"I have an object that gives me the Sight."

He smiled mirthlessly. "Then you're as dead as I am."

I shivered, but I said, "You're wrong."

"Trust me. I know about being dead."

"I put my trust in God. My fate is in His hand."

"Not while that thing is in your hand. That thing does not belong to your God's way. You can hold Him or hold it; not both."

"I don't go to walkers-again for lessons in obedience."

"Tell me, when you met the bishop, did you tell him about this thing that gives you the Sight?"

"You're a creature of Hell. Church business is no concern of yours."

"So I thought. You dared not name it."

"I'll not be lectured by spirits damned!"

"You dared not name it because you knew the bishop would take the thing away, and you could not bear that."

"Codswallop."

"If I'm wrong, show me." He stretched out a dripping, steaming hand. "Give me the thing and I'll take it with me back to the sea. That's what you promised to do, wasn't it? Throw it into the sea? I'll do it for you."

"I can't trust you. You're a lying spirit."

"And you're a lying priest. You won't let it go."

"You're changing the subject. The subject was not my sins.

It was you going away."

"Give me the thing and I'll go."

"You're not in a place to set terms. I adjure you, in the name of the Father, and of the Son –"

"Your heart is divided, Priest. Therefore you've no power."

"Touching, how you care for my spiritual weal. The very fact that you say these things proves that what I do is right."

"I care nothing for your spiritual weal. I tell you these things to torment you, for I know you'll not heed me, and your path leads to destruction."

Let me tell you this, in case you ever go in for putting down spirits – don't argue with them. You can never get the last word, and it just goes on and on.

At length the door opened, and Erling Skjalgsson came in and put his hand on my shoulder, pulling me to my feet. I found I'd been kneeling on the floor. I didn't remember kneeling.

"Long enough, Father," he said.

"You shouldn't have interfered." I looked about, but the dead man was gone.

"Father, it's been two days."

"What?"

"We left you in this house with the dead man two days since. You need to eat and drink."

I knew of a sudden I was desperately hungry, and my throat was like peat ready for the fire.

Erling called a thrall girl in with a bowl of water. I drank it down like grace.

"What of Thorarin?" I asked.

"He's fine. I egged him into anger and he struck me. I drew my sword but did not kill him. I told him he'd insulted Erling Skjalgsson and lived to tell of it, therefore he was not an unlucky man. He cheered up right away, and he's been eating like a horse."

"Are you sure you need a priest at all?"

Erling looked at me more nearly than I liked. "Are you bitter, Father? Have I tread on your toes?"

"Not at all," I grumped.

"I couldn't leave you in here forever. Sometimes plans fail. Sometimes a simple, blunt way works best."

"True enough. Well done. When can we go back to Helgafell?"

"Is there something you want to tell me, Father?" Erling asked.

"Yes. We need to go to Greenland. Greenland is where we're headed. We're wasting time here in Iceland."

"We're caught up in law matters. There's naught to be done."

"I know that. Doesn't mean I like it."

"We'll go to Greenland in the spring. We'll find your sister, if she's there."

"She's there."

"How can you be sure?"

"I've seen her."

"This Sight you've gained?"

"Perhaps."

"I thought you mistrusted the Sight in others."

"One lives. One grows and learns."

"One spends two days in a house with a dead man."

"I'm hungry. Can I get something to eat?"

"Come to the house."

"Can we leave this place soon?"

"Tomorrow if you like."

"Why would I want to stay?"

"I thought you might want to sleep."

"Two days without sleep is naught to me."

But, as it happened, I slept through the next day and we started home the day after.

Chapter 12

"I'M surprised to see so many folk on the road," I said to Erling as we traveled north. "I never thought Iceland so thickly peopled."

"So many people?" he answered. "We've met but two men."

We were cresting the shoulder of a ragged hill one afternoon, with a rock wall on our right, when Thorlak Gudbrandsson said, "Someone's coming."

The boy had good eyes. It took a few blinks for me to make out the mounted men approaching us across the rock-fields. Icelanders mostly wear dull clothing, as dyes are costly, and the only man with what you'd call a strong color on was the leader. He wore a dark blue cloak.

When we were nearer, Thorlak said, "Ivar Ketilsson rides at the head."

"I see ten of them," said Erling. "We're seven with the thralls, and one of us is a priest."

"I can fight," said I.

"If you had a spear."

"And the thralls don't go armed either," said Konnall.

"So we're four fighting men against ten."

"Not good odds," said Konnall.

"No," said Thorbrand with a grin. "Perhaps we should fight bare-handed to make it more even."

Konnall did not seem to enjoy the joke.

"If we make our stand here, we'll have the high ground," said Erling.

"Then by all means, let's do that," said Konnall.

We had a sort of shelf to stand on, where they'd have to climb to come to us. The chance of them going off the path and flanking us was small, rough as the rock-field was.

Closer and closer they came. Every man of them carried a spear and a shield, and they had axes at their belts. Ivar had a sword.

"We've four spears and four shields," said Erling as we formed up in a sort of shield wall with the shieldless men in between, where the shields overlapped. I was behind and between Erling and Thorlak. "Thorbrand and I have swords. Konnall and Thorlak have axes. I've an extra axe for one of the thralls."

"One of them can have my spear," said Konnall.

The Icelanders rode to just within spear-cast. They reined in their horses and dismounted.

"There need be no more bloodshed!" Erling cried to them. "We can name go-betweens and make a settlement. Everyone can have his rights, and all go on living."

"Words won't save your lives," said Ivar.

"I'm trying to save yours."

"They may quail when you boast in Norway, Erling Skjalgsson, but we're tougher stock in Iceland. Your priest may go free."

"And you may go North-under," I said. I know a priest shouldn't speak so. I was sorry about it later, when I'd had time to meditate on it.

They rushed us, shouting and swinging steel.

I picked up a rough black stone a little larger than my fist.

"I'm going to throw this at the left ear of the tall man with the blue shield," I said to Erling in a low voice.

"All right," he said.

I've been a good stone-thrower from my youth. I sent the rock hurtling toward the man's ear as promised. It didn't hit him; I didn't expect it to. But he raised his shield to guard his head as I'd reckoned he would and when he did, Erling's spear, already in the air, took him straight through his undefended body.

He fell with a cry, and the other Icelanders closed in on us.

I had naught to do at that point but watch, being the one unarmed man in the fight. Two of the Icelanders went for Erling at once. Two against one is always a poser, because one fellow can hook your shield with his axe-beard to clear a path for his friend's weapon. But Erling rather liked fighting two at once; it gave him a challenge and made the whole business less of a chore.

Erling tilted his shield to keep it clear of an axe. At almost the same moment, he struck out with his sword, not at the man attacking him but at his friend to the right, who was waiting with axe raised and stood with his belly all uncovered. Erling slashed him across so his guts appeared, and he was no more threat to us.

This opened a hole in the Icelanders' line into which Erling leaped, cutting down the first man. Then he turned, sensing without seeing it that someone was going for his back, and he traded a few blows before splitting the boiled leather cap that the man wore for a helmet.

By now I'd picked up a spear from one of the dead men, but looking around me I saw that the fight was over. Five of the attackers were running away. Five lay dead or dying. Among the dead was Ivar Ketilsson.

One of the fleeing men stopped long enough to shout back

before mounting his horse, "Both Ivar and Orm are dead! You'll pay with everything you have!"

"I offered to pay before," grumbled Erling. He stepped to where Thorbrand Gudbrandsson lay, bleeding out through a slash in his leg that could not be stanched. He was the only dying man of our party, though one the thralls whimpered with a head wound, bleeding much but in little danger.

I knelt by Thorbrand and shrove him. "Ivar killed me, and I killed him," he said. "You warned me Freydis was bad luck." He died white as snow.

Norsemen do not weep at death. Thorlak sat beside his brother, staring off into the air, bidding his boyhood farewell.

"You go out into the world to have adventures," he said. "That's what a man does. You know that adventure means risk – but you never think it will come to this. Dying is for your enemies."

"He died like a man," said Erling.

"They'll pay," said Thorlak.

"They've paid already," said I. "Your fight was with Ivar and Orm. Both brothers are dead. Any court will call that more than even. They'll probably want *mansbot* from our side."

"A man's death is the end of a world. You can't balance men's lives against each other like hack-silver in a scale."

"Thorlak, there's no reason to kill anymore."

"There's reason for *them* to kill," said Erling. "This is not over yet."

We bore Thorbrand's body back to Helgafell on horseback, to lay in holy ground at Snorri's church. Thorlak got his brother's sword as an inheritance.

There was another sword, Ivar Ketilsson's, left behind at the fighting-ground and brought home by us. Erling made a gift of it to Snorri.

"A handsome weapon, but ill-balanced," said Snorri when

he unsheathed it. He balanced it on his hand, a hand's-breadth-and-a-half below the cross-guard. "A sword with a balance-point that low will wear its user out. I'm not sure whether a badly balanced sword is better than no sword at all."

"I've heard Father Aillil say much the same thing about the Sight, before he came to have it himself," said Bergthor.

"'Tis a pity your Sight didn't warn you of that attack," said Erling to me later.

"I don't steer the Sight."

"Does it steer you?"

That summer Erling Skjalgsson's first son was born at Helgafell.

"His name shall be Aslak," said Erling, "after my brother who was slain." He smiled as I had not seen him smile since Norway.

Erling gave the babe salt to lick off a sword-point for his first meal so that he would grow to be a warrior. I drove a knife into the wall above his crib so that the Underground Folk would not come near him. I took my crucifix back from Astrid and placed it in the crib with him. I sat up late each night beside him until everyone was gathered for the christening-feast, and I baptized him Alexander in Snorri's church.

Chapter 13

T HE year drew on to winter. Hay got made; the house-walls were tucked against the weather, thralls spread manure on the fields, and cattle and sheep were slaughtered. We men took to winding long wrappers about our legs below the knees before going out.

I've said that Iceland is like Norway, only worse. That goes twice for Icelandic winters. There's a pebbly snow that whips along on that flaying wind and tries to freeze your skin, then peel it off you in one piece, like a birch roll.

But it didn't snow every day, and some days when the wind wasn't so bad Snorri would assemble his supporters – his *Thingmen* – in the lee of his hall so we could teach them warfare in the Norwegian style. "We have the time, we have you here," he said, "I'd be a fool not to seize the salmon that swims into my hands."

Erling was happy to repay Snorri's hospitality, and it was a way to keep our men in training.

Steinulf stood in the yard with a sword and a shield in his hands.

"Do you want to be warriors?" he asked Snorri's men.

"Yes!" they cried.

"No, you don't," said Steinulf. The men in padded leather jackets and boiled leather caps peered at him and muttered under their breaths.

"What you want," said Steinulf, "is to be heroes. You want to swing your swords over mounds of fallen enemies and shout your war cries, and go home to see the girls gazing at you with bright eyes.

"But most of you will never be heroes. You can be part of winning armies – if you choose the right armies – and you can share in the victories; but only a few men are born to be heroes in war.

"You can all be warriors though. And when you're a warrior you've a better chance than most armed bonders of getting home alive, which is the best reward most warriors ever see. I can put that reward in your hands. You'll earn it by swinging your weapons again and again and hefting your shields again and again, until your arms are sore and your joints swollen and you're bored to death with the whole business. Then I'll pair you up and make you swing and parry and parry and swing until you're sick of that. Somewhere on the other side of the boredom and the pain, you'll be warriors."

Those were the good days. On the bad days, we sat in the hall breathing smoke and listening to young Aslak wail and learning where to find each other's sore points. We chafed each other and got chafed ourselves, but things were especially raw between Astrid and Snorri's wife, Asdis.

"Let me help you with that sewing," Astrid said to her, when Aslak was napping.

"Don't bother," said Asdis.

"I have my distaff. Can I help spin the wool?"

"Spinning Iceland wool is not for the likes of Astrid Trygvesdatter."

"I'm thinking of sewing her ears to her head and sticking my distaff up her—"

"Peace, daughter," said I to Astrid. We were in one of the storehouses as we spoke, she with the baby, and Erling and I, looking over some of our goods, talking alone in a rare moment apart from Icelandic ears. "The woman envies you," I said. "You're fairer than she, and she's used to being the wife of the greatest man around."

"As if I were the greatest man around," said Erling wryly. Astrid frowned at him.

"You're still rich and a famous warrior," said I. "You've played in the great game; Snorri's but an Iceland lord. The word 'Norway' means much here; more than it does in Norway. It's like a Norseman making his name in England or Constantinople."

"Perhaps I should go to England when all this is done," said Erling. "King Ethelred and I have this in common, that we both have Svein for an enemy. I could take service in England and play in the truly great game."

Astrid shook her head. "I know Ethelred from my days in exile," she said. "You'd never stick having a weathervane like him for a master. You'd be stitching his ears back too."

I started to say something about Erling needing a larger horse to ride than an Iceland pony, when a man I didn't know walked in the door. Neither Erling nor Astrid paid him heed, so I said, "What do you want, friend?"

He was a pale man with a long starved face and he spoke no word but only stared at me.

"To whom are you speaking?" Astrid asked.

I'd never thought her stupid, but my voice must have been sharp as I said, "I'm talking to this fellow here."

Erling and Astrid looked at each other.

"There's no one there," said Erling.

"Are you blind?" I snapped.

"We're not blind," said Astrid. "You're speaking to empty air."

I stared at them, fury rising in me like red in forged iron. What right had they to tell me that a man I saw with my own eyes wasn't there?

You can't argue about a thing like that. I walked out the door. The man had gone.

I went into the wind and on into the hall. I pushed past Bergthor, who was arguing with somebody, and opened my personal chest where it sat on the bench. I drew out the ivory casket, keeping it hidden under my cloak, and went out into the wind again.

I looked about me to try to find a sheltered place that wouldn't be crawling with people. I finally settled on the stables.

I ducked into the door and found two thralls there, playing a dice game by lamplight.

"I'd like to be alone," I told them. "Please go elsewhere."

One advantage of being a priest is that people generally do what you say. They wrapped their cloaks about them and jammed their caps on their heads and hurried out.

There were little walls of flat slab dividing the horses' stalls. I set the casket on top of one of them and opened it.

"This must stop," I said, looking at the Eye. It looked back up at me, gray and dull.

"You were supposed to show me the future. You've done that, but you've done it ill. And no one said aught about seeing spirits. I'm a priest. There's one Spirit I'm supposed to traffic with; no more. This must stop."

There was no reply. No voice, no vision in my head.

"Answer me, or I'll throw you in the sea now. I'll feed you to the seagulls."

Nothing.

I plunged my hand in the casket and drew out the Eye.

"You're just an eye. I can crush you with one hand," I said. I squeezed the thing.

It tightened on itself, like ice melting, only faster. A wave of agony ran up my arm, as if I'd seized hot iron. I made to drop the thing. I could not. I opened my fingers.

I had an eyeball in the palm of my hand. I mean to say, it was *in* the palm of my hand as your eyes are in your head, with blinking eyelids to protect it.

I'd acquired a third eye, where no eye ought to be.

The next moment such a flood of light, and darkness, and sound, and silence rushed in on me that I felt I'd plunged into an ocean of color and noise, knowing not how to swim but sinking, sinking, spinning, and tumbling under a world of things that are, and were, and will be, and will not be. I sucked them into me as a drowning man sucks water into his lungs.

I twisted in the maelstrom for a time, borne away on the wave, lost like a small boat.

I came to myself at last. I'd dreamed, I thought. I had shadowed memories of speaking to someone who'd given me good advice I'd forgotten.

I was confused no longer. I felt a peace such as I'd never known, the peace of certain knowledge; the peace of power.

I smiled and went to the hall. I held my right hand fisted so as to hide what was in it, though I thought no one would notice the Eye amid all the scarring from my iron ordeal years back.

Erling and Astrid were there, along with Asdis and others.

"I've a thing to show you," I said to Asdis. I walked to a certain place on the floor and bent to dig with my hand in the rushes and trash. I quickly found what I sought. It as good as leaped into my hand.

I brought it up into the light and shook it off. It was a woman's brooch, a heavy thing of gold with silver ornaments and green jewels in the shape of beasts and snakes twined together in an all but Irish pattern. The firelight glinted and sparked about it so that it seemed to dance, and it cast around the walls spatters of light that moved as it moved.

"Refna's brooch," I said. "Nobody stole it. 'Twas but lost."

Everyone stared at me. Their eyes showed amazement, and not a little fear.

It felt good to me.

"Father Aillil, come with me," said Erling, heading out the doorway uncloaked.

I followed him. All around me there were beings – things in the shapes of men and women, things in the shapes of beasts, and things in shapes never seen by mortal eyes. They did not frighten me. I knew them. I was their master.

Erling led me to the storehouse where we'd been with Astrid.

"When I was a lad in my father's house," he said, "there were always seers about, diviners and wise women. These were the things we knew and had faith in.

"But the Christian priests said not to trust the Sight; not to listen to the whispering spirits. And since you've been with me, you've said the same again and again."

"I believe all I believed before," said I. "But I believe more now. I see that there were truths we did not know."

"And you've learned these truths?"

"Yes."

"Are you certain? Are you iron-sure?"

"If you'd seen what I've seen, you'd not doubt."

"I've never known a man who walked closer to God than you, Father."

"Thank you."

"But you've been wrong before. Satan can appear as an angel of light; you told me that."

"Be easy. There's naught to fear, my son. In fact there's every thing to hope."

"What do you mean?"

"Great things are coming. You and I will do deeds here in the west. I don't see it all yet, but I see more and more."

Erling peered at me doubtfully, shook his head and went back to the hall.

Why do people always look at you sideways when you give them good news?

I followed Erling back to the hall and spoke to Konnall the merchant.

"Do you know a man named Arnulf the Easterner?" I asked him.

"Aye. He's a merchant from the Myr neighborhood."

"He's just died and his family will decide not to keep his ship. You can get it at a good price if you go quickly and make your offer."

"Snorri," I said. "You were going to buy a horse from a man."

"I don't recall telling you that but, yes. There's a stallion I saw at the last Althing that I want."

"Don't buy him if you want him to ride. He's wind-broken."

People began to come to me then. If you knew how many of the folks you bump elbows with every day have mysteries in their lives, you'd be a lot more interested in them than you likely are.

I told an old woman that her husband who'd disappeared years since had died a-viking in Ireland. I did not tell her that he'd been enslaved by his foes and had died as property. I told her that his last thought had been of her and their children, and that was the truth.

I told a thrall man that his parents in the Orkneys were dead. Strangely, it seemed to give him comfort.

I told a young woman that her betrothed, who was in Norway, still cared for her and meant to come home to marry her. Her eyes lit up, then she thanked me and kissed my hand.

Everyone praised me. Everyone called me a prophet and a seer.

I wondered if it was a good thing for me to receive so much honor.

A voice in my ear whispered, *Your glory and God's have become one.*

"It feels pleasant, doesn't it?" Freydis asked me that evening after supper, as we all sat staring at the hearth, talking of this and that. When she came near me, Lemming moved with her and sat close to us, watching, silent as the moon. I wondered what danger he thought I might be to her.

"What feels good?"

"To have something that people sorely need."

"I've always had something people sorely need. I'm a priest."

She smiled. "Perhaps. But now you have something they want as well."

"I'm always happy to help people. 'Tis a duty and a pleasure."

"Duties should always be pleasures."

"If they were, there'd be no need for duty."

"And would that be a bad thing?"

"Yes. I think it would."

"I disagree."

"If doing right were always pleasant, everyone would do right."

"Wouldn't that be good? Everyone doing right?" she asked.

"I think the idea is for men to *be* right, not just *do* right. And you can never tell why you're doing right unless it hurts to do it."

"Like when Erling gave up his power."

"Exactly."

"I call it a selfish and wicked deed. I'm not saying I don't admire it, but I've admired many wicked things."

"What are you saying?"

"Look what came of it. The Westland lost a good lord and got Jarl Erik instead, and who knows whether he's worth his feed or not? Jaeder lost Erling and got Kaari instead, and any codfish could tell Kaari's no Erling; no man at all perhaps. The thralls lost their best friend. All of us, his friends and followers, lost the lives we'd grown used to. Erling robbed Astrid and his unborn son of their futures.

"And for what? To do right? If doing right means doing ill to so many, I think I'd as well carry on doing evil – maybe it will bring good."

"You're just baiting me now."

She rolled her eyes up. "The most disappointing thing is… Do you know what a woman wants most in a man?"

"Love? Faithfulness?"

She smiled. "Power, Father. Power is what makes women's bellies shiver. You have power now – more than Erling. Think on that."

I frowned. "Is that why you wept no tears for Thorbrand?"

"Thorbrand?"

"He loved you. You knew it. You led him on. But he's dead and it seems to touch you not at all. Was that because he had no power?"

"He was just a boy."

"A boy who cared for you."

"Boys care for me all the time. If I let myself fret over every boy who loves me and dies, I'd have no time for things that matter."

I got up and moved to another bench.

But I did think about what she'd said.

When we lay on the benches at last and slept, I beside the snoring Bergthor, I dreamed that I stood outside Snorri's hall.

The sun had set, but I could see in the dark.

I saw a black wolf moving in the fast, smooth way of wolves, padding around and around the hall. I thought, *This beast means harm to us.* I ran toward him to chase him off.

But instead of running as most wolves would, he turned to face me.

He had a white mark over one eye.

I woke, soaked in sweat and frightened.

I slept again, and I thought I was alone in the hall. A man came into the hearth-light and spoke to me. He was dressed like no man I ever saw, in a short, sleeved coat over a white shirt, and a neckcloth that hung down in front. He wore long trousers of the same material as his coat. His hair was short like a thrall's, and he had no beard.

"Greetings, Father Aillil," he said to me. "It is an honor to meet you."

"Who are you," I asked, "and what people do you come of?"

. He sat on the bench across from me. "I come from a great nation that does not yet exist, but will, in the time to come."

"Where is this nation?"

"West from here."

Greenland, I thought.

"Erling Skjalgsson and Father Aillil are the fathers of our nation. We owe our greatness and our freedom to you."

"That's pleasant to hear," I said.

Do you know how in a dream you can be doing one thing with one person at one moment, and then in the next moment you are doing something else with someone else entirely?

Suddenly I was not with the man but with my sister Maeve. She spoke no word, but looked at me with reproachful eyes.

"I'm coming to you as fast as I can," I said to her. *"Next summer for certain."*

Chapter 14

T HE next morning Astrid and the child were gone.
    It was as always when someone goes missing. You
reckon they're using the privy or in one of the other houses,
and after a while someone asks where they've gotten to, and
someone else says, "I thought they were with you," and that
person says, "Well, I thought they were with you," and then
there's a deal of asking about; and the upshot is that no one has
seen them since the night before.

"They were gone when I woke," said Erling. "But that's not
uncommon. Astrid's always getting up early to get a start on
some task or other – more at home than since we've been here,
but it's not rare here either." He gazed around him, looking
unwonted feckless, as if he thought she was hiding somewhere
in the hall and he'd overlooked her. He leaned down and picked
an object up off the bench where they slept. It was my crucifix,
the one I'd given Astrid to wear and that we'd placed in the
cradle. Since the christening, Astrid had worn it again at my
bidding.

"She likely decided she was too high and mighty to breakfast
with Icelanders," said Asdis.

"Hush," said Snorri, and he sent the thralls to look for Astrid. They sought everywhere, and found her nowhere.

There was reason for concern. There were places in the neighborhood, mires especially, where the unwary could disappear forever. Why she would have wandered alone far enough for that to happen we could only guess.

Erling was helpless. Snorri was helpless. Everyone was helpless but me.

I saw before me again the beardless man in the strange, dull clothing with the neck cloth. *"Tell them you can find the woman and the child,"* he said to me.

"Where are they?" I asked.

"She is in Helgafell, the holy mountain." When he'd said this, he was gone.

I turned to Snorri. "Tell me about Helgafell. Why do you call it the holy mountain?"

Snorri looked at me a moment, then said, "There was a chieftain in Norway called Ketil Flat-Nose. He was the son of Bjorn Buna, son of Grim, a great man in Sogn. Ketil was married to –"

"Can you just tell me about the mountain?" I asked.

"I am. Ketil was married to Yngvild, daughter of Ketil Wether, a chieftain in Romerike. Their sons were Bjorn and Helge, and their daughters were Aud the Deep-Minded, Thorunn Hyrna and Jorunn Wisdom-Slope…."

It went on like that. There's no way to skip ahead with an Icelander any more than you can bypass the first mile of a journey. But I'm not Icelandic, so I'll take you directly to the part that mattered.

"My great-grandfather, Thorolf Mosterbeard, settled this Thorsness area during the landtaking," Snorri said at last. "He built this farm under Helgafell, and held the mountain so sacred that he wouldn't allow anyone to look at it with an unwashed face –"

"How do you not look at a mountain?" I asked.

"There's looking, and there's looking. If a man or a beast wandered onto it they might not be harmed until they walked off of their own accord. He believed that folk of our family went into it when they died."

"Do the...Old Ones live in the mountain?"

"It's been said that some men have looked at the mountain at certain times, and seen it open up, and there were folk feasting inside. I've not seen this myself."

"Just as I thought," said I. "Astrid and Aslak are inside the mountain."

Erling stepped forward. "We must go in after them."

"I'll go alone," I said.

"She's my wife!" He took my arm in a grip like a bear's bite.

"You cannot see the way. You haven't the eyes. You couldn't help me, and you'd be in danger yourself."

He stared at me. "And there's no danger for you?"

"Some danger, as in anything. But I have the Sight. I can find the way in, and the way out. I can see the enemy."

"I must do something."

"Then pray."

"You're the one who's supposed to pray. I'm the one who's supposed to rescue people."

I had no reply to that.

"Is this the crucifix you gave her?" Erling asked, holding it up.

"Yes. I wonder why she didn't wear it."

"The thong broke last night, while we prepared for bed. I was going to cut her another today."

"I'll take it with me now. Perhaps it will help," I said. I took it, wrapped my cloak about me and headed for the door.

"Do you need anything?" asked Snorri. "Weapons? Food?"

"Iron is good and a crucifix is good. I have my eating knife and I have this," I said. "I can't think of anything else. If I stay long enough to need food I likely won't be back at all."

I got away finally, and went over the stone fence and up the hill, the wind whipping my cloak about my ankles. There was an Icelandic sky above me; thick clouds to one side, thicker clouds roiling in from the east.

Helgafell is just a hill, as I've told you, not large enough to note if it didn't sit all by itself in the midst of a flatness. It's shaped like a shield boss, just a great haystack of a thing. It wasn't far to walk. I stood on the slope and cried, "Someone show me the way in!"

A man appeared, walking out of the hillside as if out of a mist. He wore strange garments – a short jacket with the waist pinched in, bloused breeches tucked into tall boots, and a hat with a wide brim and a feather. But his face I knew. He was Ulf Lodinsson, dark of hair and beard with the one white eyebrow. He swept the hat off his head and made a deep bow.

"Good day, priest!" he said. "You are welcome inside the mountain."

"Is there no one else to show me the way?" I asked.

"These Old Ones are shy of holy men with iron and crosses. So, if you wish to enter, it's me or none."

"Very well," I said. "I don't fear such as you."

"No, certainly not. You are the great Father Aillil, famed in the world above and the world below. Come with me, and add to the roll of your triumphs." He turned and walked into the mountain, vanishing from sight.

I misliked the sound of that. Ulf had no cause to flatter me except to cozen me. But I needed to get in, so I followed him where he went. I half expected to stub my nose on the hill-face where he went through, but I passed without hindrance and found myself, for the second time in my life, "inside the mountain," as they say.

Why was I surprised to find it different from the first time? I knew already that all you think you see in that place is only a seeming. Why should today's seeming match yesterday's? Instead of the lush meadows and woods of my last visit, this was a more Icelandic underground. I found myself in a cave, a high stone passage with walls that looked like bundles of upright staves, lit by flames that licked the veinous rock.

I was alone in that cave. Ulf had let me in and let me be; no more in love with my company, I supposed, than I with his. I wondered what I'd be walking into that he didn't want to be part of.

There were two ways to go in the passage – forward or back. I thought it as well to keep on the way I was pointed. As I made my way by the glow of the pulsing, red firelight, it seemed to me, as it had my first time in the mountain, that only the things I looked at directly had character. When I looked away from them and saw them through the corner of my eye, I thought they lost their qualities and fell into simple shapes – squares and circles and so on. But I could never be sure, because when I looked back at them to check, they were themselves again.

Anyway, it was just rock. Nothing more to see.

I almost thought I was in a dream, but not one of my own. Some meddler was dreaming it for me; deciding for me what I ought to see.

Which, for the moment, was flaming rock. Oddly, I did not feel warm. It was, in fact, somewhat chill inside the mountain.

I hadn't gone far when the passage before me was blocked of a sudden by a great, looming shadow. The shadow clotted into a form, the form of something like a huge, misshapen man.

The man had the legs and underparts of a goat. His upper body was naked and red-colored and muscular, and he had horns, pointed ears and a short beard.

"COME NO FURTHER!" he cried in a voice too great to fit in

the passage, "I AM SATAN, AND THIS IS THE GATE OF HELL!"

"You're not Satan," said I, fishing the crucifix out of my bosom and holding it up to him. "I forget what you're called, but you belong south, in Italy or somewhere. This is Iceland, and trolls and elves and dwarfs belong here."

He faded into a shadow again and went away.

I carried on the way I'd come. I reckoned there'd be further apparitions, and I got what I expected.

The next thing I saw was an old man, a thin, wizened, beardless fellow who leaned on a stick as he walked. He was dressed somewhat as Ulf had been, except that instead of tall boots, he wore ankle high shoes with buckles on them and fine white stockings covered his legs below his knee breeches.

"We have no need of God," he said to me with a smile as warm as an axehead in January. "We have learned that the cosmos is run by immutable laws. These laws account for all things that occur in any place or time. We have no further reason to take God into our calculations."

Straightaway a second man appeared. He was younger and stouter and his clothing was not far different except that he wore long trousers.

"We have no need of God," he said. "We have learned that the cosmos is chaotic and run by no laws, only the means of numbers. Since there is no design, clearly there is no God."

Then another man came and pushed his way between them. He was dressed like the last man and wore a beard. "We have no need of God," he said. "We have learned that men are weak and driven by needs within themselves of which they are not aware. One of those needs is to have a father to take care of them. Because their real fathers never live up to their dreams, they invent a Father in Heaven, and call him God. Once we understand these things, we can cast aside such false wishes and imaginings."

Then came a man with a smaller beard. "We have no need of God," he said. "We know that rich men press down poor men and make them do their bidding. They tell the poor men that God will give them justice in Heaven, and the poor men believe because they have no other hope. Once we build an order where wealth is portioned out equally, we will be done with God."

Then there was a woman dressed like the men, except that she wore a skirt – obscenely short, above the knees in length.

"We have no need of God," she said. "People believe in God because they are comfortable and fat through robbing and cheating the poor, and people of other colors, and women, and have no idea what suffering is like. If they were poor and hungry and crushed underfoot, they'd soon realize God is a luxury they can't afford."

"Who are you people?" I asked. "Where do you come from?"

"We come from the future," said the woman.

"Then you're all mad in the future."

"Perhaps we are," said the old man with the knee-stockings, still smiling his icicle smile. "But we're all agreed on one thing – in the future there will be no faith in God."

"Why should I care what you people say? All your reasonings cross each other."

"We don't care," said the man with the small beard. "We no longer believe that truths must agree."

"Then you can't deny any truth, even the truth of God."

"No, we deny all truth, including the truth of God."

"First you abandon God, then you abandon reason. In the end you'll abandon Mankind as well."

"We have," said the woman. "We are working hard to die off as a race."

I turned from them and ran in the other direction.

Was this the future for which we built? Why bother with anything then?

A woman appeared before me and I stopped myself just short of bowling her over. Unlike the woman I'd just seen, this one was not dressed immodestly. To the contrary she was over-modest, draped in a gray robe that reached to the ground and a veil that covered her hair and her face. Only her eyes showed. They were blue.

"Are you from the future too?" I demanded.

"Yes, I am."

"Are there many futures? You don't look to come from the same future as those people."

"But I do. Do you recall the woman you just met?"

"The one with the whore's clothing?"

"Yes. I am her daughter."

"Her daughter? That's a notable change in fashion in one generation."

"I wear this garment because we're all Muslims in my generation, or ruled by Muslims."

"Muslims?"

"Mohammedans."

"Moors?"

"Something like that."

"How did this happen?"

"It happened because the men of Christendom allowed their will to fail."

I let my head fall. "Because they grew fearful as I did just now?"

"Yes. They feared that men would misuse freedom, so they gave up on freedom. They feared that men would kill for their beliefs, so they chose to believe nothing. They let people like those you just met think for them, and lost the ability to think themselves."

"And then – ?"

"Did not Christ speak of a place that was swept and garnished?"

"Yes. A demon was cast out of a man and, after a time, it returned with twelve others more evil than itself, found its old home swept and garnished, and moved back in."

"Even so. If that is what happens when an evil thing is cast out, what will happen when a good thing is cast out? There is nowhere that nothing is. Where one thing rushes out, another rushes in. If you do not believe in the true God, you will believe in some god, whatever the learned men may think. My mother thought your God a tyrant, so she threw him off. Her daughter must serve a god who makes women cover themselves in shame."

I nodded. "I understand," I said.

"Good. The future needs you."

"So I've been told."

I looked back up the tunnel. "Have you any idea where I can find Astrid Trygvesdatter?" I asked.

"Here in the mountain the ways are not as in the great world. Simply go and keep your goal in mind. You will come to it at last."

"Thank you." I started to walk and turned back. "Is the future you live in bound to come?" I asked her. "Or can it be staved off if men keep faith?"

"The future is a tree with many branches. I live in one branch. There are others. Whether one branch comes to be and all the others are cast away, or whether they all come to be somewhere, somehow, or whether some come to be and some not, I cannot tell. Those secrets are locked in the Counsels of Heaven, and are not for men to know."

"But you remember? You haven't forgotten the Beloved?"

"I remember the Beloved. If I hadn't I'd have died."

I said a blessing over her and went my way.

The tunnel was not the same, going along it a second time. It had been a single passage before. Now it had side-tunnels I'd not noticed, and branchings that I knew had not been there before. I heeded the woman's advice. I kept my goal – Astrid – in my thoughts and paid no special mind to which way I went. At first I took all the right turns; then for a change I took all the left turns. Then I took the turns in turn.

I went on for some time. I thought of Astrid. It troubled me to think of Astrid, for my thoughts of her were not always priest's thoughts. But I needs must.

And then she was there. The passage opened into a high, wide cavern lit with yellow light, and Astrid was in the cavern, seated like a queen on a high seat all of gold. She wore a gown of gold and green, and had a silver circlet on her head. Little Aslak lay on her lap, wrapped in cloth of gold.

I crossed the floor toward them. It seemed to take days and days to cross that floor. The more I walked the wider it became. I called her name, but she sat staring ahead as if watching something beyond me. I turned to see what she looked at, but there was nothing there.

Clearly she was under a *glamour*. I'd have to break it somehow; either that or bear her out on my shoulder.

At length I stood before Astrid's seat. I planted my feet and said, "Astrid!"

The glamour was not a heavy one. Her eyes lit straightaway and she said, "Father Aillil!"

"Astrid!" I said. "You must come with me. Erling and all of us are worried about you and the child."

"Why, of course," she said with a smile. I must confess that smile struck me in the face like a bathhouse full of steam on a December night. Astrid was ever a beautiful woman, and now the glamour of the land under the mountain lay over her like a glory. "But first, you must dance with me," she said.

For just a moment, under the weight of that beauty and the air within the mountain, I could not think of a reason not to dance.

Straightaway I remembered myself, but by then Astrid had

risen and had glided away from me, tracing rings alone in a great circle on the floor, rocking Aslak in her arms.

She danced graceful as a candle-flame. I went after her to stay her, but as I came near, a figure moved between us – a woman, elven-fair, dressed in a green-and-gold garment like Astrid's. I checked myself to keep from overrunning her, and when she'd passed, Astrid had danced away from me.

Again I rushed toward Astrid, and again a figure swooped between us – another elf-woman, dressed the same.

I tried again. Again there was an elf-woman in my path.

It went on like that for a very long time. At length the great chamber was filled with dancing women, swirling about each the other in a twisted pattern like one of those beast-knots the Norse carve in wood. I stopped and breathed hard, not knowing what to do.

The veiled woman's counsel came back to me – *"Think of your goal."* I'd let myself be distracted by the dancers. I must think of Astrid.

I thought of Astrid and walked toward the place where I thought she might be. I thought of her beauty. I thought of her golden hair and her jewel-blue eyes. I thought of the way her skin pinked when she blushed and the elegant line where her throat curved under her jaw. I thought of other elegant lines, glimpsed in shapes under her clothing.

I'd not allowed myself to think so of a woman in a long time. My skin burned and buzzed with the nearness of her, and of all these underground women who skipped lightly away as I bulled through their twined weavings.

I shook myself like a rat and thought of other things. I thought of Astrid's courage. I thought of her faithfulness. I thought of her devotion to her God and to her man. I remembered the day at Sola when she defied her brother the king to save the lives of heathens.

And as I'd been promised, I stood at length face-to-face with her. Her cheeks glowed with the warmth of her lovely labors. She looked like a woman in passion.

I put my hand on her arm. The flesh was hot.

"We must go," I said.

She smiled, and replied. "As you will."

I kept my hand on her arm and pushed our way out of the chamber and down the passage. I was thinking now of the entrance to the mountain. "The entrance," I said aloud. "The entrance." It was harder to think of the entrance than to think of Astrid, but I kept shepherding my thoughts back where they should go.

The passage went on and on. It was hard to believe we were not lost. I was prepared to tell Astrid, "Just stay with me!" if she asked where we were going, but she never asked.

Then at last I saw a light ahead of us – just a faint distant glow, but it was white light, not red.

I tugged at Astrid's arm and pulled her on. We made headway slowly, but the white light waxed and brightened.

It took long and long to reach that light, but when we were close enough that it hurt our eyes, it began to dim. It tightened into a single spot, and that spot was on the face of a man. It faded until it was not light but only a white line – an eyebrow. Before us stood Ulf Lodinsson in his outlandish clothing.

"Well done, god-man," he said to me. "You have come through darkness and shadow, and done the thing you came to do. I salute you. I had not thought you able."

"The door," said I. "We want to go out."

"Of course," he said, sweeping another bow with his hat. "You've only to ask."

A doorway opened before us, and we stepped out into the sunshine and the fresh cold wind.

"Where have I been?" asked Astrid, like a woman wakened.

"You've been inside the mountain," said I.

"We must go to the hall. I need to be where people are. Give me your arm, I fear I'm not steady."

So we headed down the slope to the farm, and into Snorri's hall, Astrid holding onto me with one arm and carrying young Aslak in the other.

Erling was off the bench the moment he saw her. He ran to meet us and fairly lifted and carried her to her seat.

He covered her face with kisses, rocked his son, then said, "Father Aillil, from this day forth you may ask anything of me – my wealth, my life, anything up to my honor. I am your debtor."

I said polite things about how it had been nothing at all, mightily pleased with myself nonetheless.

I looked about and noted that there were unknown faces in the hall, and one known face that hadn't been here before – Leif Eriksson the Greenlander, who'd visited us at Sola in the days of Olaf Trygvesson. He was a tall, good-looking young man with red hair and freckles across his nose.

"You see we have guests," said Snorri the Chieftain. "Great matters have been settled in the time you've been gone."

"How long have we been gone?" I asked.

"About four months."

I shook my head. "I hate going into the mountain. A man could miss half his life, like coins from a torn purse."

"We've used the time to build," said Snorri.

"To build what?"

"Our commonwealth."

"Commonwealth?"

"My dream," said Erling, looking up from his reunion with Astrid and Aslak.

"What dream was that?"

"*No king but the Law*," said Erling. "A Christian land with the freedoms of Northmen."

"I thought they had that already."

"They want a leader. Not a king, but a chosen leader such as Norsemen used to acclaim."

"A hersir," I said.

"Yes," said Erling. "I am a hersir again. They have made me hersir of Iceland and Greenland."

"Greenland, too?"

"That's why Leif Eriksson came. They've all sworn me loyalty."

"Then let me congratulate you."

"You should congratulate yourself as well."

"Why is that?"

"Iceland needs a bishop."

"It has a bishop."

"Bishop Jon has returned to Ireland. He couldn't stick the married priests."

"A bishop must be consecrated."

"We'll find a way. Until then, you'll act as bishop."

Bishop! Who'd have thought it? I wished my mother were alive to know I was to be bishop—

"Leif Eriksson!" I cried of a sudden. "Is there a thrall in Greenland, a dark-haired, blue-eyed girl named Maeve who sings—"

"We've seen to that," said Leif. "Bring the girl."

A man went out and came back in a few minutes with a small, dark-haired woman. I could not see her face at first, but she came closer and moved into the light—

"Father Aillil, it's time to go home," said a voice.

I looked about me. I was in the cave in the mountain. Astrid was beside me, and facing us was Freydis Sotisdatter.

"Wait!" I said. "We were outside already. We were in Snorri's hall. Leif Eriksson was there and my sister—"

"It was a seeming," said Freydis. "You never left the mountain. You were lost. I told Erling I could find you and bring you home, and he sent me. Uncle tried to come along, but could not get in."

"Then Erling is not hersir? I'm not bishop? They didn't bring my sister?"

"You've been gone a day. All is as it was when you left. Come with me now."

She turned and led the way. I bowed my head and followed, holding Astrid by the hand.

We followed the red corridors. Though the rock looked to be afire, there'd been no smoke before. But now as we walked, the air grew dense and we found it harder to see our way. We fumbled and we groped. Finally we stumped up short against a stone wall.

"We're lost now," said Freydis.

"We can't give up!" said Astrid.

"It's grayness all around. I thought I could find the way out, but I'm bewildered in all this gray."

"You came in without knowing whether you could get out?" I asked.

"Inside the mountain or outside the mountain, it's the same to me. I'm a stranger in every place."

"Well, we must get out. We must find the way."

"When all the world is gray, there is no way."

"You're wrong," said Astrid. I could not see her, but she took a firm grip on my shoulder and she pushed me close by Freydis, side by side. Astrid stood behind us.

"Look this way," she said. "It's dark."

We looked, and it was indeed dark in that direction.

"Now look the other way. It looks lighter to me."

"Perhaps," said Freydis.

"No, you're right," said I. "It's lighter this way."

"We may not know the way. The world may be gray to us. But we can turn our backs to the dark and walk toward the light."

"Maybe the light's the wrong way."

"Not often. Not for honest folk."

"Let's go to the light," I said.

"Why not?" said Freydis.

So we went toward the light, feeling our way along the wall. And, in time, we found the door and came out into the sun.

Chapter 15

THE year wore on without further upheaval at Helgafell. That does not mean there were no troubles that fall, but the troubles were not ours; they were those of Snorri's kin. I've spoken of Snorri's sister (or half-sister), Thurid Borksdatter, mother to the younger Kjartan. They lived to the west out on the Snaefelsness peninsula, at a place called Frodriver.

You'll recall that they had a guest, a woman of the Hebrides named Thorgunna, a showy slab of mutton possessed of fancy gowns and bright bedclothes, hunting a husband and casting her net at layman and priest alike.

Thorgunna died at Frodriver that fall. We received the news without great distress. The woman had been kin to no one and hadn't wakened great fondness in those who'd met her. Nevertheless, when the news came, I felt my right hand itching where the Eye lay buried.

Just before *Jul* – Christmas, you know – came news that Thurid's husband Thorodd the Tax-trader was dead, also, drowned in the fjord. We all rode with Snorri to Frodriver for the funeral. I conducted the service. It was a memorable journey along the shoreline, on a road under the cliff-face that sometimes hugged the edge, hanging our seaward legs out over the drop and the rock-surf far below.

With Jul came Thurid and her son Kjartan to feast with us. They told us a story – much overblown, I'm sure – about Thorodd and others taking Thorgunna's corpse south to Skalholt for burial, because she'd insisted on lying there for some reason I've forgotten. To hear them tell it, Thorgunna's ghost (stark naked – that must have been a sight) had appeared to serve supper at a house where they'd been shown poor hospitality on the way.

At Helgafell that night, Thurid hung Thorgunna's bright bed-curtains up over her place on the bench.

My hand took to itching again.

It was only a few weeks after Jul that Kjartan Thorodsson came riding again to Helgafell companioned only by a pair of thralls. He'd grown thinner and paler since we'd seen him last.

Seated in the hall, after a long, deep drink of skyr, he said to Snorri, "I come to beg a favor, Uncle, but not of you."

"Of whom then?" asked Snorri.

"I'd ask it of Erling Skjalgsson, and of Father Aillil."

We all leaned forward on our benches.

"We've walkers-again at Frodriver," said Kjartan. "We need a priest to lay them, or we'll all be dead soon. Thorir Wood-leg and his wife Thorgrima Witch-face are dead already. They come into our hall every night, and sit with us on the benches." He paused a moment. "My father comes with them," he said.

"I saw my own father walk again," said Erling. "'Tis not a thing I care to remember."

"We need a priest."

"I'll go," said I.

Snorri asked, "When did the hauntings start?"

"After Thorgunna's death," said Kjartan, after a moment's thought. "Everything started going foul after her death."

"Did she curse anyone? Anything?"

"She wanted us to burn her bedclothes. Mother always coveted her bedclothes. Thorgunna left her some of her finery, but she told Father to burn the bedclothes. Mother wouldn't let him do it. She said it would be a sin to destroy things so fine."

"Well, there you are," said Snorri. "The bedclothes must be burned."

"I've never put much stock in curses," said I. "Only God has that kind of power."

"We're simple folk in Iceland," said Snorri. "We're not privy like you to the ways of God. But we know the ways of men, and we've seen curses at work.

"Nevertheless, let us humor the priest and take another tack against the ghosts as well. All Icelanders respect the law. Why not summon the ghosts?"

"To the Thing?" asked Kjartan.

Snorri smiled. "That would be a long cast. But you could hold a door-court."

"A door-court?" I asked. "Olaf Peacock spoke of them, but I'd never heard of one."

"A thing we do in Iceland. We call a local jury and summon a man at his door, then hold court and pass judgment on the spot."

"We do it sometimes in Norway, too," said Erling. "You just haven't seen it, Father."

We were nine who went at last, on pony-back. Besides me and Kjartan there were Snorri's son, Thord the Cat, Steinulf, and five thralls. Erling stayed at Helgafell with his little family, and I did not press him to come. Who would willingly travel a dangerous road in a snowstorm for the pleasure of dealing with the dead?

The road to Frodriver was less easy than ever at that time of year. The first day took us over a stretch of burned rock, churned up into peaks and waves as if an army of trolls, fighting amongst itself, had been blasted from heaven with fire and brimstone, the burnt stony hulks left lying where they died.

"God bless the man who built the road through this waste," I said.

"It was a job of work," Kjartan said to me. I haven't described him closely yet. He was big and strong, as I told you, with reddish hair of the pale kind that makes a person seem to have no eyebrows. His young face was freckled like a salmon and he had an Irish chin under his sparse beard.

"The labor of thralls, I suppose," said I.

"Not thralls. Berserkers."

"Berserkers?"

"Has no one told you the story?"

"I'm sure I'd remember that."

"Strange they didn't tell you. It's how Uncle Snorri came to marry Asdis."

"What have they to do with berserkers?"

The boy laughed, and for a novelty he skipped the family tree part of the story. "Styr, Mother's father – we're crossing his land now – got a couple berserkers as a gift from his brother Vermund, who'd gotten them in Norway from Jarl Haakon. Vermund had had the mad thought that keeping berserkers would make him a great man in Iceland. Instead they ate him out of house and home, made enemies of friends, and kept goading him to find them respectable wives."

"Small chance of that," said I.

"Indeed. So he talked Grandfather into taking them off his hands. And the first thing that happened was that one of them – his name was Halli – decided he had to marry Asdis."

"A touchy matter, saying no to a berserker."

"Grandfather found a way. He told Halli that a poor man such as he couldn't expect to marry a rich man's daughter without doing some great deed to prove his worth. The task he set before him was to cut this road through the burnt rock-field. He also bade him build a dyke across the lava to mark the boundary between his farm and the next, and a sheep-shed on this side of the dyke."

"And Halli accepted that?"

"Grandfather made it a matter of pride. The berserkers called themselves the strongest men in Iceland. They could not refuse and keep their boast. Uncle Snorri once said to me, 'Don't bother killing a man who's proud and stupid. You can get him to destroy himself when you like.'

"Halli and his friend set about clearing the road. Halli was burning to have Asdis, so he worked like a troll and he pushed his friend to do the same. And Grandfather made certain Asdis paraded herself before them now and again as they worked, to egg them on."

"And they finished the job?"

"They did. And when they were done, Grandfather rewarded them with a nice bath in a bathhouse he'd just built. A man can't go to his bridal sweating and stinking, after all."

"Of course not."

"The bathhouse was dug into the earth, with a round turf roof and hole in the top to pour the water through onto the hot rocks. He made sure the rocks were very hot."

"I'll wager he did."

"And when they were inside the bathhouse he piled stones in front of the door and poured the water in through the hole. It got so hot they tried to break down the door to get out."

"And?"

"They managed to smash it and crawl out. Grandfather had laid a wet oxhide in front of the door and as each of them slipped on it, Grandfather killed them there, with axe and spear. He dumped the bodies in a deep pit in the burnt rock-field.

"And very soon after, Asdis was betrothed to Snorri."

"Let me guess. Had Styr been to see Snorri before he formed this plan?"

"So they say."

"I think I would not like Snorri for an enemy."

"I've always tried to stay on his sunward side."

We rode on, uphill mostly, with the tooth-shaped mountains before us and, far ahead, glimpsed now and again when the weather cleared or a mountain was not in the way, the length of the Snaefelsness glacier, lying like a white pelt on its peaks far along the way we were going.

The land-way along the Snaefelsness peninsula passes through fjord country, and whether in Norway or Iceland, fjord country is the very mischief to travel across the grain. It was all hills and mountains, uphill and downhill. Where it was flat it was like as not boggy, and whether it was flat or steep it was likely to be burnt rock. It took us three hard days, meager as the light is that time of year, to get from Helgafell to Frodriver, the wind in our faces all the way, mostly blowing snow at us.

We slept two nights in houses where Kjartan was welcome. Friends and kinsmen and Thingmen of Snorri's, I seem to recall. I shared a bed with Kjartan, as we were the big barleycorns in our party.

I thought the lad lay awake beside me on our first night, when all were snoring but me.

"'Tis hard to lose a father," I said to him quietly.

He was still for some time, so that I thought perhaps he slept after all.

"I lost my father long ago," he said at last.

"You'd become unfriends?"

"No. I got along with Thorodd as well as could be looked for. He treated me fairly enough; I'll give him that. But he was not my father. All men know this."

"My apologies. It seems I've dropped the eggs."

"None needed. You weren't to know."

"Is it a thing you'd care to talk of?"

"There's naught of shame in it. My mother was married before she wed Thorodd. Her first husband had been married before also, to a sister of Bjorn Asbrandsson of Breidavik. Have you heard of him?"

"Not that I recall."

"He's a great warrior. He fought in the Baltic with the Jomsvikings."

"Them I know."

"He's the greatest warrior in Iceland. Greater even than Kjartan Olafsson. Greater than Gunnar of Hlidarand was."

I got the drift. "And he's your father."

"He and Mother were ever good friends. She wanted to wed him when she was widowed, but Uncle Snorri preferred to give her to Thorodd because Thorodd was *rich*." Kjartan spit the word "rich" out like a bad mussel.

"Do you know how Thorodd got his wealth?" he asked. "He was sailing home from a trading voyage to Ireland when he passed a barren island where he saw men waving and calling to him from the shore. He put out in a boat and spoke to them. They were men of the Jarl of Orkney's who'd been headed home with a boatload of tribute from the Hebrides and Man when their ship was wrecked. They offered him silver to take them back to their lord. Thorodd didn't want to make the extra journey, so he ended by selling them his towboat for a fat share of their wealth, and they took the offer, having no better choice. Men have called him Thorolf the Tax-trader ever since. I ask you, what kind of a way is that for an Icelander to get rich?"

"I've heard of worse. Erling told me the Norse esteem clever men, as well as good fighters."

"And Thorodd was neither. He fell into his wealth, and took advantage of needy men doing it. Great men are supposed to be givers of gifts, not robbers of the desperate."

"He was lucky at least. All men of the north respect luck. Even I know that."

"Thorodd was lucky, but he took his luck meanly, and no man respected him. Bjorn, my true father, hasn't much in the way of land or silver, but he is feared and honored."

"Have you always known Thorodd was not your father?"

"I never felt him for a father, even when I was small. But I was twelve or so before I began to think I might be Bjorn's son."

"Do you think your mother might marry Bjorn now?"

"Bjorn left the country some time since. He could not stay in Iceland and keep away from our house, so all felt it best he go."

In other words, he fled to save his life, but the boy would never see it so. We said no more that night, and at last we slept – or I did.

My most particular memory of that journey must always be Buland's Head, where a mountain pokes out into the Breidafjord and the only way around it is a narrow path over a straight drop to pitiless rocks and surf far below. We took that bit on foot, our horses tied together head to tail as we'd done on our first trip for Thorodd's funeral. I hadn't liked it then and I liked it less now with a faceful of snow.

But just at the worst moment, where the path was narrowest and the cliff steepest, the weather cleared for a space and I saw the Snaefelsness snowcap again, blazing like the sun, and I had to shut my eyes not to be blinded with it, and near lost my footing. When I looked again, the weather had closed back in and I could see less and was the safer for it.

The final day of the journey was clear and bright, with the daylight glinting off the icy mountain slopes, and Snaefel looming like the sun in our eyes, making us squint.

At each farmstead we passed on the last day, we called the men to join us. One by one and by twos and fours they saddled their ponies and joined our train. A large party came from Mavahlid, the great farm in the next dale to Frodriver.

At last, as the sun set, we rode into a valley whose length ran along the seashore, separated from it by a stony sandbank. At the bottom of this valley lay a backwater, fed by a stream that rushed from the mountains. At the valley's far end were several mounded hills, and by the hill farthest from the sea sat the farm of Frodriver.

We rode into the steading as shadows stretched across it. We dismounted outside the hall. We could hear voices inside, wailing like Rachel in Ramah.

"They'll be in there now," said Kjartan. "Who'll come in with me?"

Everyone looked at me.

"I suppose I'd best have a look," I said.

Houses in Iceland are thick-walled, and the screaming I'd heard from outside was as silence to the calamity of shrieks that outraged my ears as I passed through the entry and into the hall. Judging by the sound, I looked to see swarms of spirits damned being savaged by spear-wielding Azazels. What I saw was at once commoner and stranger.

The house was walled into two rooms, besides the entry. The first room we entered (the smaller of the two) was filled with the members of the household, those who yet lived. There were only a handful, and they looked as if they'd eaten little and slept not at all for days.

"Where's my mother?" Kjartan asked an old woman, yelling to make himself heard.

"She took to her bed," said the woman. "Sir, you must do something! We can't bear this any longer, but we've nowhere to go!"

"I've brought a priest," said Kjartan. "Be easy. 'Twill all soon be done."

The larger room had a side door. Though crowded it was strangely peaceful (barring the noise). It was as if a bonder hosted a very dull feast. All along the benches, staring into the fire, sat men and women. The clothes of several dripped water. They may have been making the screams that battered our ears – I believe they were – but not with their mouths. They sat and they stared and they dripped. That was all.

They looked like living men and women, except that their skin had turned a dark red, like dried blood.

Kjartan led me down the hearth-way between them, headed for the bedchamber at the rear. I shuddered to be near the dead, and the mud they'd made of the floor tugged at my shoe-soles as I walked.

With Kjartan I entered the bedchamber. An oil lamp was spiked in the wall and its light showed me Thurid, his mother, lying abed. She looked twenty years older than when last I'd seen her. She'd been thin – now she was gaunt. I thought her not long for the green side of the sod.

"Greetings, mother," said Kjartan. And as he spoke, he lifted her from the bed and sat her on the bench across the way. Then he began to gather Thorgunna's rich bedclothes, ripping the curtains free where they'd been carefully hung on hooks and cords.

"What are you doing?" Thurid cried.

"The evil began when you took these," said Kjartan. "They must be burned."

"But they're so beautiful!" Thurid wailed, almost louder than the ghosts.

"They're cursed, Mother. Would you die to keep them?" Kjartan had them in a bundle now, clutched against his chest.

"I don't ask for much," said Thurid, weeping now. "I've little enough in this world –"

"And you stand to lose all. I do this for you, Mother." Kjartan began to go out.

"Troll-whelp!" Thurid shouted at him. "Bastard! Straw-brat!" I followed the young man as fast as I could.

"Bring a lamp," said Kjartan, and I took a burning one from one of the pillars.

Outside, some of the men had mounded dead weeds and sticks of driftwood and a few turves of peat for a bonfire. Kjartan threw the bedclothes on the pile, and I set fire to the weeds with the lamp.

"Say a prayer, Father," said Thord Snorrisson, and I did that while we watched the blue curtains blacken in blue flame. It did not take long, with the wind slapping them like a washerwoman.

Kjartan then stood by the door and cried, "I summons Thorir Wood-leg for trespassing, for theft of life, and for theft of health!"

Thord the Cat Snorrisson took his place by him and said, "I summons Thorodd the Tax-trader for trespassing, for theft of life, and for theft of health!"

Then Kjartan summonsed Thorgrima Witch-face, Thorir's wife, and one by one they summonsed each of the ghosts in the same way.

"I call the door-court to order," said Kjartan.

"Will the ghosts come out to answer the charges?" I wondered aloud.

"Hard to say what ghosts will do," said Steinulf.

"Perhaps somebody should keep an eye on them, inside," said Thord. "In case they try something."

"And what could anyone do to stop them?" asked Kjartan.

"Well, if it was Father Aillil, he could...pray or something." Kjartan turned to me. "Do you mind, Father?"

It's strange to say, but one of my worst sins – and one that's caused me no little discomfort – has done much to get me the name I seem to have acquired, that of a redoubtable man of God. That sin is pride. When a man afraid of the dark asks me to go into the dark in his place, I haven't the humility to refuse.

So in I went, through the entryway and the outer room, to the hall where the ghosts sat, sodden and unmoving as before. My knees wanted to buckle beneath me and the room seemed to list like a ship's deck. My face burned, though no one saw but the dead.

I had no strength to stand, so I sat, and Thorodd the Tax-trader was across from me.

It's not proper for Christians to speak to the dead – though I've done it – and Thorodd had never been much of a talker, so it was an awkward moment.

Then he surprised me by addressing me.

"All my life I've waited to speak," he said. "If I wait now, I never will."

"I don't know what use a confession is to a man already dead," said I, "but it can't do any harm, I think. I'll hear what you have to say."

"I've no confession to make. I've an indictment."

"Against whom?"

"God and the world. My parents, my neighbors, my wife and that bastard they call my son."

"My son," I said, "these are not the words with which to enter eternity."

"They're the truth! Is God afraid to hear truth from me, even once?"

"I've learned that it's not God who fears the truth, but we."

He leaned forward. I could not help pulling back from his dark face.

"Don't speak to me of truth," he said. "There are men who know the truth sooner than other men. We know we will die, and live our lives in that knowledge. Do you think the truth makes a man strong? It makes him weak. When you know early on the truth that you can die, you can never match the men who think they'll live forever. The strength they draw from their ignorance gives them a leg up you can never overcome. That was the way with me all my life. I knew too much. I never had a chance."

He went quiet a moment and stared with dead eyes.

"I was never any good with a sword," he said at last.

I had no reply to that.

"I tried," he went on. "I practiced arms like every other boy. I worked hard. But I was ever that eye-blink slower than the others. I could never raise muscle like the other boys. I tired before they did.

"I always thought, someday it will be my turn. Like in the tales, where the widow's son picks up some castoff axe or wooden bowl, and it turns out to be just what he needs to do the deed that earns him the hand of the princess.

"But there is no day for men like me."

"You became rich," I said. "You have a famous name."

"*Thorodd the Tax-trader.* That was the name I earned. Whatever I did, I could never get a better one. Men sneered when they said that name. They could as well have said 'Thorodd the Sod.'"

"'Twasn't so bad as that, I think."

"It never is when it's someone else's name. You've no idea what it's like to be thought less than a man."

"You're wrong in that. What do you think it's like being a priest?"

He went on, not interested in what I had to say.

"We struggle, we fight against fate. We try to be more than we are," he said. "But, in the end, we are what we are and no more."

"Tell me about the day you got your name. What was in your mind?" I asked. "Why did you not help those men on the island?"

"I helped them. I likely saved their lives."

"You sold them a chance for life at a high price."

"'Twas late in the season. I'd have been putting my ship and crew at risk to make a side-trip to the Orkneys."

"Did you think the jarl there wouldn't reward you? Did you think he wouldn't put you up for the winter?"

"I did not wish to winter in Orkney."

"Was there some special reason for that?"

"If I tell you, you'll think me a fool."

"I thought you wanted to tell the truth. You said the truth would be your defense."

"I'm not ashamed of my reasons. But they'll seem petty to you. I meant to get back to Iceland that summer because I'd set my heart on Thurid Borksdatter. I thought that with riches enough I could make her forget Bjorn of Breidavik. I understood nothing of women in those days. I did not know that they love a dangerous man who can give them nothing better than a quiet man who'd die for them.

"You're a priest, Father. How can you understand what it means to love a woman more than your own honor and to come to know, with time, that she despises you, and will ever despise you, whatever you do or do not?"

"There's no sin in loving your wife," said I. "Husbands are commanded to do so —"

"He never loved me." I looked up at the voice. It was Thurid, in her bedclothes with a blanket wrapped around her, barefoot. She'd been bold enough to come out and have a last word with her husband.

There was no change of expression on the dead man's face, but his voice was anguished. "You cannot say that! What more could I have done to show my love than I did?"

"You might just once have asked what I wanted, rather than what you thought I ought to want! When you stepped in to part me from the only man I ever loved, you might have asked whether I wouldn't have been happier with him; even poor. Even in outlawry."

"When you love someone you want to be with them."

"When you love someone you want their happiness. You never wanted my happiness. You wanted your happiness in me."

"Did Bjorn love you thus, when he crept into our house in my absence, to give you the name of an adulteress?"

"Yes. Because to be an adulteress with Bjorn was better than to be the most honored woman in the land with you."

I put my oar in then. "You seem well matched to me, the both of you. You both want your way more than aught else. So far as I can tell, you neither of you thought much of the good of anyone else. Not each other, not your son... even Bjorn, you've done little for *his* happiness, Thurid."

"Me!" she shot me a hot, blue-eyed look. "I sacrificed all I might for him."

"No woman of the Norse may be wed against her will. Why did you not refuse Thorodd and wait for Bjorn? It seems to me you were unjust to both of them."

"Snorri never liked Bjorn. He'd never have given me to him so long as he lived."

"I thought you said you'd have borne any shame to be with Bjorn. Why did you not run off with him?"

"A priest asks me this?"

"I don't counsel it. I only ask why you, who say your passion knew no law, did not do according to your own words."

She looked down. "'Tis not easy to be a hero," she said, and she turned her back and went to her bed.

"I do not think she ever despised you so much as you believed," I said to Thorodd. "I think she despised herself."

"What a merry lot we were," said Thorodd. He stood then.

"I see no reason to linger now." He walked out through the door by the high seat.

After that, Thorir Wood-leg (I'd never actually met him, but he wasn't difficult to put a name on) said, "I stayed as long as they let me," rose and stumped out the same door. After a few minutes, an ugly woman said the same and left. And one by one the other ghosts went out into the night…back to their graves, I suppose, and their souls to the mercy and justice of God.

When no one was left but I in the room, the silence was strange to me. The living men came in from their court. They brought the cruse of holy water I'd carried with me, and I sprinkled the house all over with it, praying prayers of exorcism.

Then we made our beds on the benches and slept as if dead ourselves. I felt no fear. I felt nothing. I was only very, very weary.

In the morning I said mass in the ghost-room over a makeshift altar. If there was anything more to be done, I could not think of it.

"'Tis well now," said Kjartan to me. "I can feel it. And mother says she feels better already." They prepared a feast for us and the revelry was loud, almost frightening, like the guilty glee you sometimes feel after a battle, when your friends are dead and you're not. I did not judge them for it. In point of fact, I set about getting grimly fish-faced, something I rarely did lest I make a bad example. The ale was left over from a Jul feast that had never happened – a little sour, but drinkable.

And finally I slept again, my belly full of food and my veins a-boil with the cup of fury.

I was wakened in the night. I looked up, squinting, and saw my sister Maeve, veiled like the Blessed Virgin, with a lamp in her hand. The other men snored around me, insensible.

"I wait, but still you do not come," said Maeve.

"I'll come in spring," I whispered.

"Why not now?"

"There's a sea to cross."

"Not if you take the secret way."

"Secret way?"

"Under the mountain."

"I've been under Helgafell. I was lost utterly."

"Not that mountain. The snowy one."

"Snaefel?"

"Yes."

"There's a way to Greenland from Snaefel?"

"It goes deep under the earth, under the sea."

I sat up. "Show me the way," I said. "I'll come now."

"Follow me," and she turned to leave the house. I put on my shoes, leaving behind my leg-wrappers (I'd lain down fully clothed otherwise), wrapped my cloak about me and went out after her.

It was an Iceland night, gusty and freezing and not a star in the sky for the clouds. But Maeve's lamp never flickered and I followed it like a beacon. We trudged along the margin of the Breidafjord, over the foothills and the valleys and along the beaches with the smooth, round, black stones. I could tell they were black because the sun rose at last, which meant we must have been walking long at that long-nighted time of year.

With sunlight came clearing skies and a view of the blazing white brow of the Snaefell, bright enough to half-blind me with my eyes clenched. At some point Maeve must have disappeared, because I don't think I saw her anymore. I was watching the mountain.

The mountain, bright and distant.

The mountain, cold and tall, with spindrifts of white whisking its shoulders.

You have to have something you're going toward, every day of your life. Otherwise you won't go anywhere; you'll just stay in one place and die.

But most men don't know what they're going toward. They just go, they don't know why.

I hadn't known why I'd gone on. Through slavery. Through pain and trial. Over land and sea.

Now I knew. I'd been going toward the white mountain.

I could not take my eyes off it. Night came on, but this night was clearer, and the light of the half-moon reflected on the glacier.

I stumbled and fell over things. I splashed in waves of the surf.

I kept going, toward the mountain-brow.

I grew aware that someone was calling my name. When I grasped that I was being called I knew the voice had been in my ears for some time.

It came from behind me. I needed to stop and see who called.

I did not want to stop. I had to get to the mountain.

"Father Aillil!" came the voice.

I ought to turn and answer. A priest must pay attention when people call. Someone could be sick, or dying, or have an abscess in their soul.

But if I turned around, I might not reach the mountain. And what would be the point of it all – of my whole life – if I didn't reach the mountain?

"Father Aillil!"

I stopped. I sighed. I turned around.

"Thank God you stopped, Father!"

I looked about me and my vision cleared. I stood on a wind-swept ridge. A surf beat on rocks a mast's height below me. Looking down, I saw that my shoes had gone to pieces and where my toes stuck out, they were shredded like sausage-meat. The very sight of them made me light-headed and I all but swooned then and there, which would have tipped me off the edge.

But hands reached out and caught me before I lost my senses. I thought I recognized Kjartan and Steinulf, and then I recognized nothing for a time.

I awoke in bed in the hall at Frodriver. Steinulf stood over me.

"You're awake. Good," he said.

"How long have I slept?"

"A full day and night. But it'll be longer yet before your feet are healed well enough to let you leave that bed. You weren't hard to track, leaving a trail of blood behind."

"I seem to remember you were there. I owe you thanks."

Steinulf settled his bottom on the bench across from me.

"I've never meddled in your affairs, Father," he said.

"I suppose not."

"But I have to ask you one question, with all due respect. What in the name of all that's unholy were you doing out there almost barefoot?"

I hadn't had time to prepare for that question, and I was silent for a space. My feet burned and throbbed cruelly.

"My father used to say, 'An honest man seldom need ponder an answer,'" said Steinulf.

I frowned. "It's to do with the Sight," I said.

"The Sight led you out there where we found you?"

"Aye."

"Far be it from me to tell you your business, but if someone led me out to a place like that and set me on a cliff-edge to fall, I'd not trust them a second time."

"I only came near falling because I was wakened."

"You wouldn't have made it much further. Not on those feet."

"I don't know how it would have ended. I have to trust my vision."

Steinulf clasped his hands. "I must warn you beforehand. When I see Erling next, I'll counsel him not to follow your leading. Not in matters of our journey."

"You must say what you please."

"It's not my place to teach you the Faith, Father, but I think you've taken your bearings from the wrong star."

"Leave me now. I'm sleepy," I said.

Chapter 16

W E started back to Helgafell about a week later, I with my feet bandaged. Someone had to help me down from my pony when we stopped nights.

It took me some time to heal. They put me in a corner of Snorri's house, in a place of my own on the bench where I just stayed. My meals and a slop bucket were brought to me.

The small toe on my right foot wouldn't grow over. It puffed up twice its proper size and wept and bled and gave me hurt enough for a whole man. In the end, it mortified, and they brought in an old woman from a nearby farm to look at it. She frowned and called for a knife. I bit on a leather strap and the pain put me out of the world for a time, but after the new wound was bound up, it healed clean and I was able to walk at last. I've limped slightly ever since, when it's cold.

Spring flew in like a kittiwake on the wind, and kinsfolk of Orm Ketilsson came on summonsing day to summons Thorlak Gudbrandsson for manslaughter, along with Erling Skjalgsson and every man who'd been in the battle, myself included. Thorlak as well, for the killing of Orm.

And so we found ourselves riding to the Western Quarter

Thing on a bright, cool day as flights of swans thronged the skies over the Alftafjord.

We thronged a bit ourselves, the entire crew of Erling's ship along with the women and Snorri's household. We merged like a brook with a stream of men and women, free and unfree, that flowed to the Thing-stead by the strand on a lesser ness on the east side of Thorsness.

We set up our tent near Snorri's booth, and then we all went to hear the Lawspeaker and one of Bishop Jon's priests proclaim the peace.

As we approached the law rock, I observed by littles a change in the crowd around us. A man here, a man there began to move into our path, strolling ahead of us as if by chance. None of them looked at us beyond a backward glance now and then, but they all carried weapons and shields, and I glimpsed mail peeking from under some of their garments. Carrying weapons was expected, but shields were unusual – they were a sign the bearer expected a fight. And mail was a brazen slap at the Thing-peace. Erling gave a whistle, and the men of our company silently shifted, moving ever so casually into an order they'd practiced time and again. The crowd ahead of us grew denser as we went and suddenly someone gave a cry and they turned to face us, weapons and shields at the ready.

Erling gave a cry of his own, and it was well that our men and Snorri's had been drilling over the winter. Few of our men carried shields, not expecting trouble, but they formed their practiced shield wall nevertheless. They grouped on either side of Erling, who *had* brought his shield. They'd not chosen their places by happenstance. They stood where they'd been told off to stand, during all those winter training days.

I was as unweaponed as a thrall, and had to take my place behind them, with the women.

Our enemies struck hard.

Just as they'd practiced a hundred times, each of our men took hold with his left hand of the shield of the enemy facing him, pulled it aside, and struck with his own weapon, *not at the man in front of him but at the unprotected man just to that man's left – his own right.*

It was as Steinulf had promised. Icelanders are good fighting men – none better – but they don't drill as armies and they don't know how to fight as a body.

The shields on which our foes had placed their hope were useless, and their surprised owners found themselves naked to the steel of men they hadn't even been thinking of.

We took harm on our side too, and bad harm. But we'd stood better than they'd expected, and hurt them when they'd looked for a cheap victory. The fact that we stood and fought, capturing their shields as well, surprised and unbalanced them.

I saw one of those surprised men, spouting blood from a throat wound that meant his death in a few seconds, fall back and, with his last desperate strength, cast his spear at Erling.

It was not a good cast. It went badly astray.

I watched in horror as it sped over our men's heads, back toward the women's line where I stood.

It was headed directly for our women.

I let out a bellow and leaped in its direction, for no hopeful reason but only to do something.

In one of those stretched moments that occur when your blood is up, I watched one man of our force look up to see where the spear was going, crouch, and make a leap that, if you'd asked me, I'd have said could not be made by mortal man.

Thorlak Gudbrandsson grasped the shaft of that spear as it flew overhead and stopped its flight. It seemed to pull him along with it for a second, but then he and it tumbled to the ground.

He had made himself a target with his leap, and someone cast another spear that passed through the meaty part of his thigh. He fell on his face and tried to get up, not understanding for the moment what had happened.

Meanwhile, our men were chasing the fleeing Icelanders. Erling shouted for them to halt. It was the Thing, after all.

He told the men to hold their formation, then went back himself to see Thorlak. He knelt beside the young man, who lay pale and sweating while Lemming cut the spearhead off and withdrew the shaft, and Thorliv tore the hem of her kirtle to make him a bandage.

"You may ask anything of me," Erling said to Thorlak. "Anything at all, save my honor."

Snorri the Chieftain came to join him, shaking blood off his sword. "A terrible thing to happen," he said. "And at the Thing of all places. The Ketilssons and their kin will pay for this."

"We will indeed," said a voice, and we looked up to see a red-faced, white-haired man whom I did not know.

"Did you know they would do this sacrilege, Thorolf?" asked Snorri.

"'Twasn't strictly a sacrilege. The peace hadn't been proclaimed yet."

Snorri looked at him. "How would you like it if I told your neighbors you'd said that?"

The man looked at his feet. "Not much."

"Then let's talk sense. Erling has a case against you for unprovoked attack, and there's everyone here for witnesses. Had it happened anywhere else, there'd be the injuries your party sustained to balance it, but this deed, here and now, comes near to sacrilege and puts every man against you. I'd not be surprised if the court called for outlawry, over and above whatever's owed to Erling."

"Will you speak to Erling and to the judges for us?" asked Thorolf.

"I might…" said Snorri. "But I'd have to have your word you'll drop your support for Thorfinn Erlendsson's suit against me."

Thorolf thought a moment. "I can promise that," he said at last.

"Then I'll speak to Erling, and to the judges."

And so he did. When the haggling was done, the kinsman of the Ketilssons (I don't recall his name) who led the attack was sentenced to the Lesser Outlawry (that's three years out of the land), the various deaths and woundings were balanced against one another (we made a small profit on that) and Snorri won his lawsuit (a suit I didn't recall having heard about earlier).

And so we went home, bloody and sore but victorious and free to sail for Greenland at last.

We had to lay up for a bit to get our crew healed well enough for even a short voyage. Thorlak healed quickly and was on his feet, leaning on a stick, in a few days.

The first thing he did when he could walk was to go to Erling. Erling sat on the bench with Astrid, both of them playing with little Aslak.

"Erling Skjalgsson," Thorlak said. "You promised me any reward I might name for stopping that spear."

"You saved a life, perhap's Astrid's," said Erling with a smile. "I'm deeply in your debt."

"The reward I ask may seem to you past my deserving."

"I'd call that unlikely in view of your service."

"I'll name my request then. I wish to wed your sister Thorliv."

Erling stopped smiling and handed the baby over to Astrid.

"It's customary to send kinsmen to bid for a wife," said Erling.

"I have no kinsmen in Iceland. I had a brother."

"A woman is not a sword or a ring. I do not barter my sisters like horses."

"And I would not bid for her as for a horse. I've Thorliv's consent in this."

Erling sat and looked at Thorlak for a minute. Thorlak gave him his look back.

"I married my other sister to a high-born man from Halogaland," he said. "What advantage could you bring to our kinsmen, if I made you an in-law?"

"He'd be taking me off your hands," said a new voice, and Thorliv walked out of the shadows. "I give you my word, Brother. I will wed no other man while Thorlak lives. So it's marry me to him or maintain me as a spinster."

"What bride-price and morning gift can you offer?" Erling asked Thorlak.

"Her bride-price is her life, which I've given already. The morning gift must be from my profit on this trip. I've something coming for my brother's death, I think."

"You'll have silver for him, when the voyage is done. But it'll be no fortune. I'll feed my sister myself all her life if necessary, before I'll see her live in poverty."

"I would not keep her in poverty. Let our betrothal last while I make my name."

"I should properly consult my kinsfolk on this."

"But they're in Norway, and you gave me your word."

"Then take her promise. But we'll wait, as you said, for a decent morning gift before we'll talk of a wedding day."

The betrothal called for a feast. The feast served a double use, being our farewell to Iceland.

I celebrated mass each morning during the feast.

The night before the final day I was in the church, setting things in order.

I heard a footstep behind me and turned to see Snorri the Chieftain. I was surprised. He'd never much sought my society.

"So, when all's done, what think you of Iceland, Father?" he asked.

"'Tis a land of skalds and lawyers, fair in its ugliness. Like an enchanting woman I'd sooner die than wed."

"You've a skald's tongue, Father."

"And you've a lawyer's."

"You don't much like me, do you?"

"I don't much trust you, but that's another matter."

"I've done you all no harm, I think. You've lost but a little time."

"There's a trifling matter of men's lives."

"Seafaring men share a sleeping bag with death each night. They know that before they ship out. I think a man dies when the gods – pardon me, God – dooms him to die, whether on sea or land."

"That's a comforting thought for men with bloody hands."

"We are men, not angels. We've all bloody hands."

I bowed my head. "You speak truth there."

Snorri sat on the bench and looked up at the smokehole, where the twilight came in.

"Do you think Erling knows what I did?" he asked.

"That you threw the spear – or had one of your men throw it – at Thorbrand that night at the feast? To draw us into a feud with the Ketilssons so you could use the weight of our arms against your own enemies? I think he suspects, but he's too high-minded to bring the thought to light."

"'Twasn't so evil, was it? To keep my old friend with me for the winter? Do you think Erling would have minded greatly had he known?"

"You didn't ask him."

"I've found the best way to get a favor is to put a man in a place where he's angry if you don't take it from his hands."

I shook my head. "I have the Sight, you know," I said.

"Not enough to see my plans and thwart them, it seems."

"Be that as may be. I have visions of the future. I see much of you in the future, Snorri. You will be father in spirit to many nations."

"Is that a good thing, or a bad?"

"Very, very bad."

"Why?"

"Because of the way you use the law."

"By law the land stands or falls. That's a proverb in Iceland."

"Quite so. And it is men like you who kill the law."

"I've given my life to the law!"

"Did you ever have an ill-balanced sword?"

"Erling gave me one."

"The law is like a sword. It can be balanced or ill-balanced. When men use the law skillfully, but without its spirit, they make the sword blade-heavy and set it out of balance."

"I'm not clever enough for this parable, Father."

"I doubt that very much. Let me say it plain. When you use the letter of the law to get your way contrary to the spirit of the law – the intent of the lawmakers – you destroy the law, and thereby destroy the land.

"Think of a land where you can leave your house and valuables and not lock them up or set armed men to guard them. That is the spirit of the law, when decent folk live together and would be ashamed to steal.

"The letter of the law means a land where every man must lock his house, and keep a guard, too. It means that the law, meant for a last resort when plain decency has failed, becomes the sole protection remaining. Such a protection as that is almost the same as no protection at all. In the end, it means the tyranny of the sons of Snorri, the men who wield the law like a sword.

"If you want to be free, you must strive to be good. If you won't be good, you can't be free for long.

"You've great freedom here in Iceland. That's what Erling likes about this place. But I think your freedom will not last, and it will be the sons of Snorri who bury it."

I saw his eyes shine in the twilight. I told him it was time to go. He locked the church door behind us.

* * *

As we made our way down to the ship on our sailing-day, I noticed that Fingal the thrall was among us, carrying his possessions in a sack over his shoulder.

"I thought you meant to stay and take passage for Ireland," I said to him.

"Ah, well, there's no hurry with that. I'd like to see this Greenland men speak of. I'm sure ships go Ireland-ward from there, too."

Part Three

The Gable
of the World

Chapter 17

E had a fair wind out of the Breidafjord the first day, and it seemed no time at all before we looked our last on the ice-blink of the Snaefel sinking out of sight.

Every one of us thought it a good omen – all but Konnall. He stood to the tiller scowling, like a swampy black cloud.

"What's plaguing you now?" I asked. "Even such a day as this doesn't suit you?"

"Too good," he grumped. "Two omens forebode a bad voyage. One is fair weather at the start."

"And the other?"

"Foul weather at the start."

I smiled. "You're a hard man to please, Konnall."

"Not so hard. I mistrust what's too good or too bad. Most things in life drop someplace in between, and I'm tolerably easy with that."

The most teeth-grinding thing about Konnall was that he was right more often than not.

I began to have my own misgivings ere long. I'd grown used to seeing things hidden to others. I'd learned not to speak to strangers unless I was sure others saw them, too. Often I saw beasts as well, mostly knowable by some strangeness of color or shape – a golden raven, for instance, or a pony with antlers.

I had less trouble knowing the spirits of the sea. When you see a woman or an ox walking on the waves, it's a fair guess they're not the workaday sort.

At first the creatures keeping us company were like the ones I saw on land – ordinary or deformed, morose as a rule for some reason I never understood but could guess. But, by stages, they were joined by uglier creatures, grimmer ones, who watched us with hot, hungry eyes. I looked away at last only to glance up and spy a small, hairy beast with a long nose peering down at me from the masthead.

I care nothing for spirit-beasts, I thought in my heart. *This is the sea that will take me to Maeve. That's all that matters.*

As evening came on the crewmen began to look darkly at the sky, muttering.

"What's the matter?" I asked Bergthor.

"It's the smell of the air; the chop of the sea," he answered. "Can't you tell?"

I sniffed. "It smells like rain," I said.

"Rain and more than rain. This is storm weather. Any seaman knows it. Konnall knew it before the rest of us, but then he always does."

"What can we do?"

As if in answer, Konnall's voice sounded, "Reef the sail!"

Quickly the crewmen loosed the backstay to let the sail down. Others tied the reefs up and the sail was quickly raised again, the stay secured again in its cleat.

And none too soon. The sun winked out as if God had plucked it from the sky, and suddenly the clouds were among us and the world shrunk to a space half the length of the ship. The wind that carried the fog bellied the sail out and bent the mast like a bow, and somebody yelled to me "Bailing time!" and

I hopped down into the hold and started passing up leather buckets-full.

I cannot tell you how long that storm lasted. None of us ever knew. Day and night were one in that tempest, illumined only by the lightning at intervals. I plied my bucket until I was spent, and a while longer, and only left the hold when I found myself lying face-down in the bilge and somebody hauled me out and dumped me like a load of wet wash back near the stern where I'd be out of the way. I shook my head and looked up to see that the sail had been reefed at least twice again, and the men were struggling with the backstay to do it once more.

"Get her down! Down! She won't hold!" shouted Konnall, and the men strained at the walrus-hide rope to free it from its cleat. I could see blood on some of their hands when the lightning let me.

"Down sail!" Konnall shouted again. "I said down sail!"

"She won't let loose!" someone shouted back. "She's drawn too tight!"

"Well put more men on it!"

More men took a hand, but it didn't come free until Lemming himself added his strength to theirs, and it was he who got the knot loose.

As it came free he raised his hands in triumph. Just at that moment the ship pitched and a wave caught him and he was gone overboard.

Weary as I was I clawed my way up the side and peered back in our wake. There was nothing to see, not even water, only scudding rain and fog. Freydis stood at the rail and screamed, and Thorliv spread her cloak around her.

Erling was at my shoulder. "Is there nothing we can do?" I shouted to him.

"There's no way to turn back. And in water this cold a man can't last long."

I looked back, feeling as helpless as ever I had.

I saw Lemming's face looming out of the spray.

That's his fetch, I thought. *He's already dead, the poor heathen.*

"Haul him in!" shouted Erling! "Get him out of the water!"

Then I knew that I'd seen not a spirit but the man himself. He'd caught hold of our towboat's painter and was pulling himself up hand over hand.

A dozen hands pulled him in and lugged him over the rail. Steinulf had already fetched the roll of spare greased wool we kept aboard for sail repairs. He immediately began to wrap it around the man, shivering and blue.

Freydis wrapped her arms around the bundle of him and wept.

But we'd no time to enjoy that victory, because the wind was stiffening still. They got the sail raised again, and the next thing we knew Konnall was yelling "Down sail! Down sail!"

The knot must have been kinked the last time, because now they freed it without Lemming's help. The sail was splitting at its seams and would soon need some of that patching that was wrapped around him.

We ran under a bare pole then, and let the wind drive us.

"Somebody get to work on that sail!" Konnall shouted, straining at the tiller. "If it blows up any more we may have to hoist it to turn her head into the wind!"

But it did not come to that. We just ran before it throughout the night, or what seemed like the night. It was night to us, days and days of it perhaps.

The strain on the hull-strakes was more than they could bear without deforming. Their joins loosened and we began to leak badly. Every free hand was in the hold now or emptying over the rail, bailing with buckets, bowls, helmets. The water came in faster than we could pour it out. We could only pray that the storm would run out before too much water ran in.

And at last it did. Slowly, slowly the sky cleared. It didn't lighten, because it was night, but the quarter moon gradually appeared and the wind slackened.

Then, as suddenly as it had come, it seemed the storm was gone. We rocked on a calm sea under a wind from – who knew where?

We had survived. The leakage slowed and we began to make some headway emptying the hold.

"The caulking's failed, though," said Konnall. "We must careen her when we find land. Until then, it's bailing in shifts through the day and night."

"And where are we?" Erling asked.

"God knows."

"This is what they call the sea-bewilderment," said Bergthor to me as we bailed side by side. "You're blown off course with no guess where you are. You can reckon how far north or south by the sun or the polestar, but how far east or west? That's any man's guess."

But some men's guesses are worth more than others. Konnall sighted the polestar – which gave us our bearings at last – and said, "We're far south from our course. So we make northwest."

Erling nodded.

"Why northwest?" I asked Bergthor. "Why not northeast?"

"There's only one way to make our destination," said Bergthor. "We must work as far north as Greenland, then sail straight east or west to it. If we make northwest to the proper northing, we can be tolerably sure we'll get there sailing east."

"We could do the same sailing northeast and working west."

"Aye, but that would be to retrace our steps. A waste of time, and bad for the spirit. Also, the prevailing winds this time of year are westerly, as is the current."

So Konnall set a course northwest. The hastily repaired sail was set to catch the breeze, and on we went.

"Suppose we've been blown far west?" I asked Bergthor as we bailed together. "Won't that be a waste, too, to overshoot our mark so far?"

"Ah, but going west we'll see new things. If you must be sea-bewildered, you might as well take the opportunity to see new sights."

"Not all new sights are pleasant."

Bergthor paused in his bailing to straighten his stiffened back. "You're thinking of the Blessed Isles," he said with a smile (Bergthor was never really happy except when there was trouble).

"How do you know of the Blessed Isles?"

"I spent that year in Ireland with Erling and his father. I heard plenty of Irish tales then."

"The Blessed Isles are naught to grin about. A man goes ashore there and spends what he thinks is a year, and when he goes home one hundred years have passed and he falls to dust the moment he touches the soil."

"I made up my mind to die in the western lands, in any case. A one-hundred-year addition wouldn't break my heart."

I looked at him. "You made up your mind to die?"

"I'm an old man. I must die ere long, in any case. In my family it's not uncommon to get a hint beforehand, and I've had the feeling for some time this will be my last voyage."

I remembered the vision I'd had of Bergthor lying in blood. I did not tell him of it, but asked, "Have you any inkling of the manner your death?"

"What does that avail? Few deaths are altogether pleasant. As for me, I say let the Norns do their worst. There's no death or pain they can lay on Bergthor Svertingsson that will make him play the coward."

We had two days' good sailing before we sighted land. A

dark strip along the western horizon slowly thickened into a coastline of low, wooded hills.

"Greenland!" cried Thorlak. "We're not so far off course as we thought!"

"That's never Greenland," said Konnall with a snort. "The first sight of Greenland is the ice-blink off the mountains. And we're too far south unless the sun and the stars have changed course."

"What land is it then?"

"No land I know."

"Are we going to explore it?"

"We must find somewhere to tighten our seams at least."

I stared at the unknown land.

A voice began to scream. "STAY AWAY! FOR GOD'S SAKE STAY CLEAR OF THAT TREACHEROUS PLACE!"

It was the voice of Fingal the thrall, my sleeping-bag mate. As he shouted he scrambled toward the stern, where he curled himself up like a hedgehog, behind the steersman's place where Konnall stood.

The Blessed Isles, I thought. *We seem to be going everywhere in the world – and out of the world – everywhere but Greenland, where Maeve is.*

Chapter 18

OR all Fingal's moaning, we needs must lay up for repairs, so Konnall took us northward along the coast until he found a likely-looking inlet. We dropped anchor and Konnall himself took a few men in the towboat to scout the place out. He came back with word that there was sufficient draft for our vessel and a decent place to beach her.

"No!" cried Fingal. "ARE YOU ALL MAD? NONE OF YOU WOULD WILLINGLY GO INTO THE MOUNTAIN! THIS PLACE IS A THOUSAND TIMES MORE DANGEROUS THAN THE MOUNTAIN!"

Konnall and his party climbed up the side and Konnall said, "Will somebody please shut that thrall up?" Steinulf was there before he'd finished speaking, stuffing a sock in Fingal's mouth and tying a towel around his face. One of the other men tied Fingal's hands with a belt.

Konnall nodded his approval. "There could be people in this land, and I'd rather not draw their notice."

He set a man in the prow with a sounding line and started some of the others rowing us into the inlet.

"It's a rich land for wood," said Erling. "We must take some on to replace the goods we used up in Iceland. We may not be able to bring them meal, but we can bring them wood. By all accounts the Greenlanders are hungry for it."

"If Greenland is anything like Iceland that's surely true," said I. "What I don't understand is why nobody's paying heed to Fingal. You all believe in magic. You know as well as I do that it's dangerous inside the mountain. Why would you doubt that these might be the Blessed Isles?"

Erling smiled. "Not a man of the crew isn't writhing in his bowels, whatever face he puts on. But the careening must be done. This is the only land we have to do it on. When a thing has to be done, you don't whine about it. You do it, and live with the upshot."

"I don't like thinking the Norse are braver than the Irish."

"We're not. An Irish warrior would act the same. Fingal's no warrior, is all."

"Like me."

"You're the one who's been inside the mountain."

"Yes, and for that reason I'll tell you plain; if we took a vote, I'd vote to bail our way to Greenland, be it never so far."

The trees grew right down to the stony shoreline here and walled us on either side as we passed into the inlet. I might have called it a fair land if I'd been friendlier disposed to it. Strangely, the spirits of the place kept shy of me. I glimpsed them flitting behind the trees but did not get a good look at them. My memory is of men with birds' or wolves' heads – that sort of thing.

We rowed on as the water widened into something like a small lake. Konnall set our course to port, toward a broad beach on the southern shore. The men loosed the rigging and we all put our hands to the job of unstepping the mast. Konnall ordered the men to slow their stroke as we neared the sand and at last we heard the grating from below, and stumbled as our ship lurched to a stop, beached in shallow water.

Then it was every man out of his shoes and rolling up his

trousers for the wade to land. There was a notable pause, though, before anyone actually leaped over the side. It seemed no one wanted to be the first to touch the doubtful land.

"These are the times when a lord earns his rich food and fancy clothes," said Erling, pushing his way forward and vaulting the rail. He called for the mooring rope and began to reel it out as he waded up to the beach and beyond it, to knot the rope neatly to a stout oak tree.

Steinulf and Konnall came next, and then all the men except for six or so Konnall told off to stay aboard and offload cargo.

I could have stayed with the women and watched, but if this business was to be done then 'twas best done with dispatch, so I shed my shoes and rolled my trousers up too, then leaped into the water.

Rolling my trousers up was a meaningless act since I was wet to the waist right off. But so was everyone else. The men aboard began to hand down bundles and casks, and we made an ant line receiving them and carrying them up above the high tide mark. From time to time, the lightened vessel would float free and then we'd all tug on the mooring line to bring her closer in.

"I don't mind a little work, but I hate the mosquitoes," said Thorlak. He only spoke what we'd all been thinking. The mosquitoes were here in clouds, and shooing them off was a vain exercise.

"We were free of mosquitoes in Iceland," said Steinulf with a laugh.

"Aye," said Thorlak. "Instead we had those miserable black-flies. I thought I'd never complain of mosquitoes again after the blackflies. But the mosquitoes back home were nothing like this."

"You get used to anything with time," said Bergthor.

Thorlak replied with action, jumping fully clad into the

water to escape his tormentors for a little. But he had to come up in time, and the insects were waiting.

Finally there was naught left on board except the offloaders, the women and poor, trussed-up Fingal. The women were carried ashore by gallant men, and Fingal was carried ashore less respectfully, wriggling like a worm on a hook. The ship rode higher on the water now. Konnall set some men to cutting young trees to be stripped of their branches and used as rollers.

It was coming on to evening when we got her beached at last, rolling her on her keel and her belly on the port side. That was hard work but we got it done, and Konnall grudgingly granted that he'd seen the job done worse.

We were too weary to hunt or fish, so we ate sea rations and raised our tent and crowded into it. Erling set men to keep watch, and the rest of us slept the sleep of honest folk in spite of the mosquitoes.

We rose with the dawn, stiff and itchy but refreshed, and Erling took pity on Fingal and set him free. Fingal was done with his antics. He just sat in the grass, rubbing his numb wrists and ankles, swatting mosquitoes and muttering, "By now twenty years will have passed in the Christian world."

"Do you really think the Blessed Isles would have biting bugs like this?" I asked him.

"Perhaps it isn't the Blessed Isles then. Perhaps it's Hell."

Someone had risen early to go fishing, and we had fish for breakfast.

"This land seems to me neither fair enough nor foul enough to be enchanted," said Bergthor to me. "It's a good land—I've seldom seen better. But I think it's not your Blessed Isles."

"I'm inclined to agree with you," said I.

Parties of men gathered dry wood from the forest for the fires we needed to boil pitch.

"First the pitch we brought to over-winter in Greenland is used in Iceland," said Erling. "Now the pitch we meant to sell in Greenland goes for repairs. If we're to winter there we'll have to buy pitch at Greenland prices."

"That may be so," said I, "but the smoke of boiling pitch won't come amiss for keeping the insects away."

Once the pitch was hot and liquid, thick ropes of loose wool, prepared by the women, were dipped into it and worked in between the ship's strakes with knives. Finally we gave the whole lower hull a new coat of pitch. I helped with a will, feeling eyes on my back all the time.

The job took two days. We ate well, as our fishermen were busy and a hunting party brought down a fat deer. When the port hull was tight, we had to oh so carefully shift her over, so we could work on her starboard side.

Eventually it was done, and Konnall said he allowed we might possibly make it to Greenland now if the sea was gentle.

On the third day we began the difficult task of rolling the ship down to the water again, a job which Konnall timed with the tide so that the water rose to meet us and at last began to raise our stern, righting the ship and easing the job considerably. Then came stepping the mast, a touchy task, but finished at last with the help of many men and some long poles and tackle. Finally we were able to begin reloading our cargo.

It was while we were at this that the stranger appeared.

He was a man unlike any I'd seen before. The closest match would be one or two Arab merchants I'd observed in markets, but they were bearded men and this one was clean-shaven. Also he wore fewer clothes.

He was of middle height, very strong and lithe looking. His skin was the color of copper, his eyes black as jet. His hair, too, was black, and he wore it in a sort of tonsure, most of his head shaved, leaving only a strip of hair that ran along the top of his head from brow to nape, stiffened somehow to make it stand upright. He wore no shirt. His trousers were of leather and did not cover his groin. Instead he had a sort of loincloth that ran under his belt front and back and hung down at both ends. His feet were covered with leather shoes. In his hands he bore some kind of bowl.

"One of the Fair Folk!" cried Fingal.

"He doesn't look like any Fair Folk I've ever seen," said I.

Erling, who'd just finished passing up a cask, wiped his hands on his shirt and said, "Steinulf, bring some men and keep me company. This fellow may not be alone."

Erling waded to shore and went unarmed, but Steinulf and his men belted their swords and axes and took spears and shields. They marched up the beach to the place where the copper man stood.

After a moment's dithering, I decided my place was with Erling and followed in their tracks. On closer view I wondered if the man might not be one of the Fair Folk after all, for he bore one of their marks – peculiar ears. Then I decided that they had been intentionally deformed. Someone had cut them inside the ridges, allowing them to heal open.

He did not smell like one of the Fair Folk either. He smelled like a beast some days dead.

He smiled and spoke rapidly in a tongue I'd never heard before. He proffered the bowl, which Erling took, and then pointed to it, and into the forest the way he'd come. He repeated the motions several times.

"This is food, I think," Erling said, not turning to look at us as he spoke. "My guess is he's inviting us to supper."

Erling made motions as if to wash his face. "I'm trying to tell him we need time to get ready," he said.

"You're not thinking of going with him?" asked Steinulf.

"I'd not think of offending him. This is his land. We don't

know what manner of folk he comes of. They may be strong. They may be numerous and well armed."

"A fine way for a Norseman to talk," said Steinulf. "In my day we raided first and feasted after."

The stranger seemed to comprehend Erling's meaning. He smiled and nodded and sat cross-legged in the grass to wait for us. The group of us marched back to our company, who stood in a bunch near the waterline. Erling explained the situation as best he understood it.

"We're not leaving the ship unguarded, I hope?" asked Konnall.

"Never. Let's take half our men, well armed. The women will stay here. Let the men who stay finish loading and watch on shore, but let the women be aboard ship."

"Not me," said Freydis. "I want to see these people."

"We don't know what their idea of a feast is," said Erling.

"That's the fun of it, isn't it?"

Erling forebore arguing with her. "I supposed Lemming must come too then," he said. Thorliv wanted to come as well, but Erling and Thorlak talked her out of it.

In the end Erling and I went, with Steinulf and Bergthor and Thorlak, Freydis and Lemming, and several others of the men. We washed and donned our best clothes. I got my priest's robes from my chest, thinking a little divine protection would not come amiss just here.

"Wear your armor, men," said Erling, pulling his mail *brynje* over his head. Most of the men had mail, and those who didn't had leather jackets with iron plates riveted on.

At last the troop of us trudged up the sand to the copper man, who turned lightly and led us into the forest. It was late afternoon and the mosquitoes were descending like the Assyrians on Jerusalem.

The man led us among the trees in the familiar fashion of a bonder crossing his home-field. Although we saw no track, he never hesitated. I noticed that Steinulf, who carried a hand-axe, was cutting blazes in trees at intervals along the way, just in case we had no guide coming back. A prudent man, was Steinulf.

At last we reached a clearing by a stream, and within the clearing we saw a large palisade built of tree-trunks, set side by side and sharpened at the top.

"We know one thing," said Steinulf. "These are folk who know the ways of war."

Outside the walls some women were working in cultivated fields. Their crops I did not recognize.

Our guide led us through a gate and we entered the village, for such it was. Within the palisade were several large long-houses not unlike Norse houses in shape, though they were covered with skins and their roofs rounded at the top. Smoke drifted from smokeholes in each roof.

The men of the village looked and dressed much like our guide, so I dropped the idea I'd entertained that the tonsured man might have been some kind of priest. The women wore their hair braided and sported long dresses or shirts and skirts, all of leather, decorated in patterns worked in what proved to be, on close inspection, quills of some beast like a hedgehog. They were not in the least standoffish, but crowded around us, both men and women, to chatter loudly and touch us. They touched the men in mail especially, exclaiming as they poked their fingers in the links.

"These folk know almost nothing of metal," said Steinulf. "Look around. Not an iron tool. A few copper trinkets. For the most part, bark and stone and wood."

"Nor soap, either, from the smell of them," said Bergthor. It was a harsh saying, but a true one.

"I was right about the warfare," said Steinulf. "See how many of the men have bound-up wounds. They've been in a battle not long since."

A number of them gathered around Freydis, whom they seemed to regard as a singular marvel. They touched all our hair, so much lighter than theirs, but Freydis' especially seemed to fascinate them.

"Easy, Lemming," said Erling to the big man, who had his hand on his sword and clearly did not like this handling of his little girl. "We're guests here. They may not have steel, but there are a lot of them. Unless they show us violence, let's keep the peace."

Lemming frowned, but let go the hilt. Instead he reached to pull a copper man's hand off Freydis' breast, giving it a friendly squeeze as he did so. The man went pale under his dark skin and trotted quickly away.

At that point, I noticed a handsome woman who stood before Erling, proffering an earthen bowl. Erling was shaking his head and trying to push the bowl away, and as I edged over I discovered why. Whatever was in it seemed to be the source of the rotten smell they all gave off. Our guide stepped up beside the woman and made rubbing motions over his face and arms.

"They seem to think we wish to reek as they do," said Erling.

Our guide began to point all around him, at what I couldn't tell. Then he slapped his arm with his hand a few times.

"Mosquitoes!" I said. "He's talking about mosquitoes!"

"What has that to do with anything?" asked Erling.

"I think he's telling us that this grease will keep the mosquitoes from biting."

Erling's eyes went wide. "Ah," he said. "That's another matter." He dipped his fingers in the bowl, brought out a dollop of the stuff and wrinkled his nose. "It smells like rotten meat," he said, but he tentatively rubbed some on his face. Our guide broke into a big white-toothed smile.

"I think it works," said Erling. He rubbed some on his hands. "It does work! The mosquitoes stopped biting right off."

Soon we were all reaching for the pot, holding our breaths and anointing our exposed skin. The relief was immediate and blessed, and we got used to the stink before long. Our esteem for our hosts soared.

We were approached at last by a group of older men whose clothing was richly quilled and who wore many ornaments of copper, seashells and feathers. One of them began to speak, gesturing broadly, and then extended his arm toward a place where a number of fur robes had been laid in a large circle around an open fire. He walked that way and waved us to follow.

There was no caution left in us as we went after him. No man who delivers you from an earthly Purgatory is likely to be your enemy.

We sat on the robes around the fire, cross-legged like our hosts, and the man who seemed most important spoke words that sounded, and probably were, eloquent.

Then the food came, and that was something we all understood. These were folk who liked to eat. It was good food, too – venison and duck and shellfish, and garden stuff that was only somewhat familiar. There was a kind of bean, and a kind of gourd, I think, and a peculiar sort of grain – yellow and black, large-corned, with an unfamiliar but pleasant sweetish taste. They served those three mixed together, making a dish that I, for one, enjoyed.

"I think these people may be Christians," said Bergthor. "They're friendly to strangers and they're generous, just what you tell us Christians ought to be. I'd thought never to see a real Christian country in my life – Christian in your meaning of the word, I mean, Father – but this may be it."

"They seem to be good people," said I, "but that doesn't make them Christian. I haven't seen any priests or crosses about."

"Perhaps real Christians don't need a lot of priests," said Bergthor with a smile.

"Or maybe they're the Fair Folk as we thought," said Thorlak. "Maybe this food is that forbidden food we hear of in tales, that enthralls you so you can never go home again."

"I've been inside the mountain," said I. "It's nothing like this."

"You've been there twice," said Thorlak. "Were both times the same?"

"No, but each was more like the other than either was like this."

"I agree with Father Aillil," said Steinulf. "But for a different reason. Splendid as these people are, they have no ale. The Fair Folk would have ale. Christians would, too."

No one could argue with his reasoning.

We ate and we laughed with the copper people, and none of us had the faintest idea what the others thought or said.

"This is a good land," said Erling to me as we ate. "I wonder if there's room for Norsemen here."

"A strange thing to say," said I. "You Norse never wondered if there was room for you anywhere else you've fared. You just moved in and took land."

"Those places were but a short sail from home. We're far from friends and kin here – very far south by the sun, and who knows how far west? There'd be little help from Norway for a colony in this land, I think. We'd need to be at peace with the locals."

"A colony?"

"Aye, a new colony like Greenland. But Greenland, by all accounts, is a cold, treeless place. This land is warm and wooded. Think of the trade we could do, just shipping timber to Greenland!"

"If we ever find Greenland."

"Oh we'll find it. I've great faith in Konnall. But what think you of living in a fine place like this? We could have a true

Norse land – no king but the law. How'd you like to be bishop of a whole new land?"

I thought of my vision inside Helgafell, but said only, "I'm not sure I'd care to wear stink-grease all the time."

"Doubtless they have winter here."

The sky was beginning to darken to evening when drums began to beat and our hosts to shout and wave their arms.

"I'd say it's time for the entertainment," said Erling. "I wonder what sort of merriment these good folk enjoy."

We got the answer quickly. Two big men brought another man into the firelight, carrying him between them, as he could not easily walk. He was a man of the same copper color as they, only he wore his hair full and long. He was completely naked and his hands were bound behind him. He bore the plain marks of ill-usage.

To the sound of drum-beats and shrieks, the man was bound to an upright pole set in the earth.

Then the women of the tribe gathered around him and began to go at him with stone knives and the red-hot ends of sticks from the fire. The men watched and laughed. The victim showed more than human strength of mind, never screaming or groaning, and barely changing expression whatever his tormenters did.

Erling rocked as if struck in the face.

"You were right, Bergthor," said Freydis. "They *are* Christians."

Erling spoke loud enough for the men to hear, but in an even voice. "Men, I mean to free that wretch. I'll need you to cover me with your shields. Then we'll have to make our escape as quickly as we can. We're badly outnumbered, but we have the advantage of iron and armor and shields. Even so I'm not sure we can make it, but we're going to try."

"It seems a poor return for their hospitality," said Steinulf.

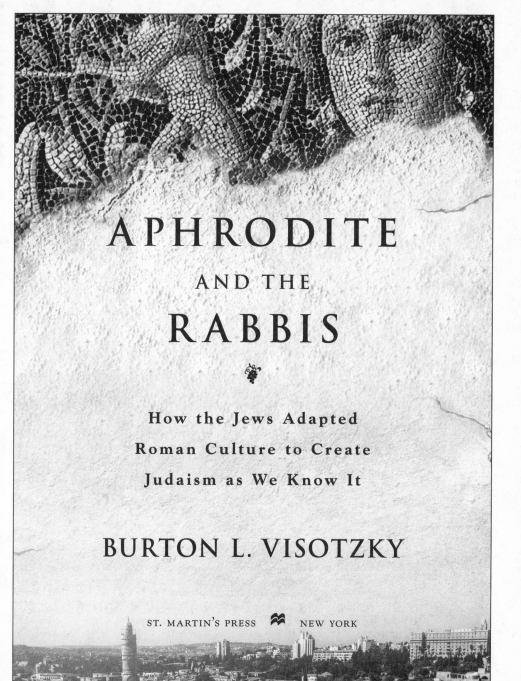

APHRODITE
AND THE
RABBIS

How the Jews Adapted
Roman Culture to Create
Judaism as We Know It

BURTON L. VISOTZKY

ST. MARTIN'S PRESS ⚬ NEW YORK

www.stmartins.com

Design by Meryl Sussman Levavi

Library of Congress Cataloging-in-Publication Data

Names: Visotzky, Burton L.
Title: Aphrodite and the rabbis : how the Jews adapted Roman culture
      to create Judaism as we know it / Burton L. Visotzky.
Description: First edition. | New York : St. Martin's Press, 2016.
Identifiers: LCCN 2016024623| ISBN 9781250085764
      (hardback) | ISBN 9781250085771 (e-book)
Subjects: LCSH: Judaism—Relations—Roman religion. | Judaism—History—
      Talmudic period, 10–425. | Judaism—Relations—Greek religion.
      | Jews—Civilization—Greek influences. | Jews—Civilization—
      Roman influences. | Civilization, Classical—Influence. |
      Rabbinical literature—History and criticism. | BISAC: RELIGION
      / Judaism / History. | ART / History / Ancient & Classical.
Classification: LCC BM536.R66 V57 2016 | DDC 296.3/992—dc23
LC record available at https://lccn.loc.gov/2016024623

First edition: September 2016

1   3   5   7   9   10   8   6   4   2

For Asher:
a book with pictures

CONTENTS

APHRODITE

AND THE

RABBIS

—

CHAPTER I

GREEK, ROMAN, HELLENIST, JEW

Beneath the streets of Rome, below even the subterranean layer of buildings still awaiting the kiss of the archeologist's spade, lies a silent city of the dead. Its web extends in a collection of catacombs that served as Christian and Jewish burial grounds in the late second through fourth centuries. The Christian catacombs are the more famous; they have long been open to visitors who are willing to travel a bit beyond the walls of the ancient city to the sites on the famous Appian Way. Church authorities supported the cleansing of their catacombs, removal of corpses, ventilation of the tunnels, lighting, buttressing, and other safety measures that make a trip there as tourist friendly as a visit to an underground tomb can be.

Alas, this is not the case with the Jewish catacombs, which are generally closed to the public. I visited the Jewish catacomb of Villa Torlonia by special arrangement in 2007. A fistful of euros having changed hands, I am led through the catacomb, its entrance curiously located on the grounds of a villa once inhabited by Mussolini. My tour guide for the day is the city electrician who checks monthly on the exposed wiring, left over from earlier failed attempts to improve the site. We wear miners' caps, beams of light wobbling before us. In one hand we each carry a lantern. Our other hands alternately follow the wire or gently mark a path along the porous tufa walls. The soft stone made it easy for the ancients to dig the tunnels and rooms that made up the warren of catacombs. But it is moist to the touch and leaves the humid air with a taste of rot that does not improve my sense of otherworldly claustrophobia. Nor, to be frank, do the bones and skeletons that still lie dormant upon their shallow platform graves dug into the walls.

Furtively, I summon my courage and touch, ever so gently, the remains of the dead. I am more than startled when the bone yields to my finger, spongy rather than ossified. Deep breathing ensues on my part, but the fetid air does not exactly help matters. I finally calm myself by reading, which almost always positively affects my emotions. What am I reading in the murky confines of the catacombs? Beside nearly every body, either grafittied onto the tufa stone or mounted as a marble inscription, are the epitaphs of the departed. Not surprisingly, given that we are in Rome, the names of the Jewish dead are recorded mostly in Latin, sometimes in Greek. But unlike on the headstones we might find in Europe or even in an American Jewish cemetery, there is nary a word of Hebrew. The only way we know that we are in a Jewish catacomb is that some of the names are biblical, and the frescoes that decorate the Villa Torlonia catacombs are replete with Jewish symbols, including ubiquitous menorahs—the seven-branched candelabrum of the Jerusalem Temple destroyed in 70 CE. I read a name aloud and walk to the next set of bones, where I pause and read again. Slowly it comes to me that I am making a cemetery pilgrimage to Jews who perhaps have not had such a visit in 1,700 years. As I turn to the next skeleton with a name beside it, from some place deep in my soul burble up the words to the Jewish memorial prayer, *El Malei Rahamim,* "God full of mercy."

"God," I pray in Hebrew, "give proper rest to the soul of Simonides beneath the wings of your divine Presence. May he rest in the Garden of Eden. May his soul be bound up in the bundle of eternal life. And let us say, 'Amen.'" I have been blessed with a pleasant baritone singing voice, so as I walk I gain confidence, offering prayers of condolence for the long, long departed. Soon I realize that the moisture on my cheeks is not just the humidity of the catacombs, but the steady welling of tears from my eyes as I mourn for those so long unvisited by loved ones. Eventually, I notice that the electrician, too, has tears in his eyes, although I am sure he does not understand a word of Hebrew. I knew at that moment, even as I know now, that the inspiration to recite the memorial prayer would count as one of the few truly religious experiences of my life.

They say that Jews have been in the city of Rome since the century before Christianity. Even so, they took their time arriving. The Jewish Diaspora, the dispersion of the Israelite peoples from their land, took place first in the eighth century BCE (Before the Common Era, what Christians call BC) and again in 586 BCE. Both the Assyrian and Babylonian conquests sent the Israelites into exile eastward. It wasn't until the Greek era, during the fourth to third centuries BCE, that Jews migrated west and settled around the Mediterranean basin. By the time Jews came to Rome, there were Jewish communities in North Africa and Asia Minor, as well. The Five Books of Moses were translated from Hebrew into Greek by the third century BCE for the community in Alexandria, Egypt. Of course, there were Jews who much earlier had returned from exile to their ancestral homeland in what was then called Roman Palestine. Those Jews spoke Hebrew and also Aramaic (the language of their Assyrian captors of centuries earlier). But the Jews of the western exile spoke the local languages of Hellenism, which is how I came to be reading Latin and Greek grave inscriptions beneath the modern city of Rome.

As I look back years later, I still feel a connection with those who were buried in the catacombs so many centuries ago. But I do wonder about them. Would they have understood my pious gesture? Might there have been a chance—despite the absence of the language among all of the inscriptions—that they could have understood the Hebrew I intoned? Would they even have approved of the sentiment? Did Roman Jews share the outlook of the rabbis of the Land of Israel that the soul would eternally survive? It was, after all, an idea that pagan Greek philosophers shared.

As a scholar, I know that by the time the Jews in that catacomb were buried, the Judaism of the rabbis, Judaism as we still know it today, already had begun to develop. And yet, aside from pictorial fealty to the menorah, would their Roman Judaism have been recognizable to me? And what might they have thought of my Judaism, visitor from a distant future as I was? Is then like now? Were those cosmopolitan urban Jews of Rome comparable to the Jewish community today, say, in New York City? Can asking questions like these about them teach anything about us now? Or is this just so much naïve wishful thinking? I will return to this question a bit later, but for now, allow me to pay homage to the dead.

The Jews buried in the catacombs were Romans who spoke mostly Latin. Those whose families hailed from the Eastern Mediterranean probably spoke Greek. By culture, those Jews would be described as Greco-Roman Hellenists. That is, they were part of a millennium that started with Alexander the Great, who was born about 350 BCE, and ended at the fall of the Roman Empire, approximately 650 CE. That adds up to a thousand years of Hellenistic/Greco-Roman culture.

The father of Hellenism, Alexander the Great, was tutored by none less than Aristotle, the quintessential standard bearer of Greek philosophy and culture. The Greek Empire founded by Alexander ruled for only two hundred of this thousand-year reign; the Greeks were conquered by Rome in the mid-second century BCE. From that point onward Rome ruled militarily—but the majority culture nevertheless remained Hellenistic. So, we call it Greco-Roman.

The Roman Empire as a pagan enterprise persisted into the fourth century CE, when the emperor Constantine converted to Christianity and declared it a legal religion. The inhabitants of the empire soon followed his lead, and over the next hundred years, the Roman Empire became Christian. The term "pagan" refers, rather intolerantly if you ask me, to all non-monotheistic religions. Yet for all of the shifting to Christian forms of monotheism and the decline of paganism, Greco-Roman *culture* persisted. Judaism post-Temple, after 70 CE, coincides with the

ALEXANDER THE GREAT MOSAIC,
NAPLES NATIONAL ARCHEOLOGICAL MUSEUM

heyday of Roman culture, which spread as far west as what is England today and as far eastward as Armenia and the Caspian Sea. Although the Romans spoke Latin, the *lingua franca* in the west (modern Europe), Greek was very much the norm throughout the eastern empire, particularly along the Eastern Mediterranean shores, including the Land of Israel.

Geographically, the Land of Israel is smack-dab in the middle of the empire, although you have already seen that Judaism was not limited to the Holy Land. Chronologically, most of what I will be discussing dates from the second through the sixth and seventh centuries CE—from the middle of the Greco-Roman era until its end.

During the earlier part of the Roman period, in the years designated as BCE, what I am calling biblical or Israelite religion was focused on the Temple in Jerusalem. There, according to the dictates of Leviticus,

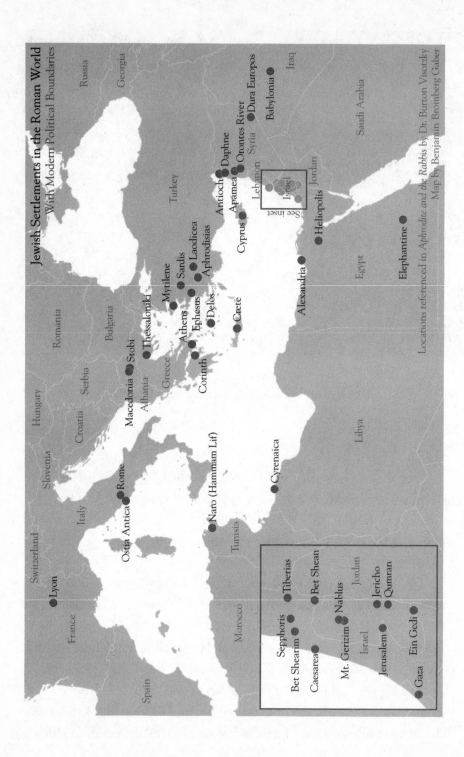

Jewish Settlements in the Roman World
With Modern Political Boundaries

Locations referenced in *Aphrodite and the Rabbis* by Dr. Burton Visotzky
Map by Benjamin Bromberg Gaber

Russia

Georgia

Iraq

Babylonia

Dura Europos

Syria

Saudi Arabia

Orontes River

Apamea

Daphne

Antioch

Lebanon

Jordan

Israel

See inset

Heliopolis

Cyprus

Turkey

Aphrodisias

Laodicea

Sardis

Mytilene

Ephesus

Athens

Delos

Corinth

Crete

Alexandria

Egypt

Elephantine

Greece

Thessaloniki

Stobi

Macedonia

Albania

Bulgaria

Romania

Serbia

Croatia

Hungary

Slovenia

Switzerland

Italy

Rome

Ostia Antica

Naro (Hammam Lif)

Tunisia

Libya

Cyrenaica

Lyon

France

Spain

Morocco

Sepphoris

Bet Shearim

Tiberias

Bet Shean

Caesarea

Nablus

Jordan

Mt. Gerizim

Jericho

Qumran

Israel

Jerusalem

Ein Gedi

Gaza

the central book of the Torah, priests offered sacrifices to the One God. Some of these offerings were made in thanksgiving, some in atonement; almost all involved the spilling of animal blood on the Jerusalem altar. I sometimes nostalgically, sometimes mischievously, yearn for those days of yore. How satisfying it is to think that offering an animal for sacrifice could wipe clean the slate of my sins. And how interesting it would be if, instead of painfully chanting a prophetic portion in broken Hebrew, a bar mitzvah boy were called upon to prove his Jewish manhood by slaughtering an ox on the synagogue stage.

Oh well, those days are long past. In that time, before there were rabbis, the hereditary priests (kohanim) were the leaders of religious life, and there was a dynastic Jewish king who led political life in the Land, even as he was a vassal to the Roman emperor.

The watershed took place beginning in the year 66 CE, infamously known in Roman history as the year of the four emperors. That's right, four different men served as emperor of Rome, and as you might guess, none of the first three died of natural causes. You might also guess that the fourth, the last man standing, was the general who controlled Rome's armies. It was in this shaky political climate that Jewish zealots (that is actually the Greek term ancient historians used to describe those armed rebels) decided to rebel against Rome. War consumed the Judean province from 66 to 70, at which point the walls of Jerusalem were breached, its citizenry starved into submission, and the rebels crucified. The year 70 CE was not a good one for the Jews, although, in sorry retrospect, inevitable from the moment the rebellion broke out.

There is a genuine break in the flow of Jewish history before and after 70 CE. It took longer for Rome to end the insurrection than the empire had anticipated; its victory came not only at great cost to the Romans but with the stunning destruction of the Jewish centers that inspired the rebellion. The beautiful Herodian Temple, a wonder of the ancient world, lay in smoldering ruins. No longer would the biblical priesthood offer sacrifices to God upon its altar. Indeed, most of the hereditary Jewish priests were killed or scattered. Jews were partially banned from the Holy City of Jerusalem, the arable land for miles around was destroyed, and the forests were denuded of the trees that were felled to feed the Roman war machine. Never again would the dictates of the biblical book of Leviticus be performed. If Judaism were to survive, something new had to arise from the remains of fallen Jerusalem.

There is a great deal of debate about what Judaism looked like in that post-Temple period of the first centuries of the Common Era, and I vacillate on whether I should even call it Judaism or, perhaps better: Judaisms. If I use the singular, I betray a bias that there was one, possibly orthodox form of Judaism that characterized Jewish practice and belief in the Roman Empire. As we will see, there were broad varieties of Judaism, both pre- and postdestruction—enough, perhaps, even to speak in the plural of Judaisms. But to do that ignores what might be a common denominator of all of the varieties of Judaism across the empire, sometimes called "common-Judaism," which had its expression in the catacombs in the depiction of the seven-branched menorah. The menorah was a symbol by which Jews worldwide united in remembrance of, if not mourning for, the Jerusalem sanctuary.

It took quite a few more centuries for Judaism to find a singular expression as "rabbinic Judaism." In what follows, I speak of Judaism and the Jewish practices of those fellows we call "the rabbis" as though they were one and the same thing. When I refer to Judaism, I am referring to "rabbinic Judaism." This form of Judaism, so overwhelmingly prevalent today, did not become the normative flavor of Judaism until a mere eight hundred or so years ago. I will refer to other forms of Judaism; but the literature of the rabbis and their practices have stuck with us, and that very stickiness, along with the fact that I am a rabbi, leads me to speak of rabbinic Judaism as "Judaism" in the pages that follow, without further qualification. Reader, I lay my bias before you.

Who were those rabbis, and what was their Judaism? When the Jerusalem Temple and its priesthood came tumbling to the ground, it could not be put together again. What I have called the Israelite religion of pre-70 CE, when those Temple and cultic institutions still existed, was replaced after 70 by other religious phenomena: what is called today

Judaism. It has long been a given that Christianity arose from the Roman Empire, assimilated its culture, and became Western Civilization. In this book I will show that Judaism had a similar arc. When the Israelite Temple cult ended, it was replaced by Judaism—ultimately a religion that was shaped and defined by rabbis, who themselves were comfortable denizens of the Roman world.

Those ancient rabbis are the forebears of the modern rabbis of all varieties and denominations who still lead Jewish institutions to this very day. At the outset, the rabbis confronted the loss of the Jerusalem Temple with determination, originality, courage, and panache. In the face of the loss of the sacrificial cult and exile from Jerusalem, this small group of sages and their disciples in each generation built Judaism—a Roman religion that fit comfortably in the broader culture and so was able to survive for the ages.

The earliest leaders of the "rabbinic" Jewish community are portrayed in later texts as having come to leadership roles while the Second Temple still stood, around the turn of the millennium. Hillel the Elder, his colleague Shammai, and Gamaliel are names we associate with the beginnings of Judaism. Hillel and Shammai are not called rabbis, but each is given the title "elder." When we refer to Hillel the Elder, it is not because there was some younger guy also named Hillel running around at the same time. "Elder" was Hillel's title, as it was the title for Shammai and Gamaliel. In the religious community, the title "elder" persists in the church in its Greek usage: *presbyter*.

When the rabbis look back at Hillel, they note that he was originally a Babylonian. Yet the earliest generations of rabbis lived and taught in Roman Palestine. The rabbinic movement expanded eastward into Iraq, or Jewish Babylonia, only from around 220 CE. I emphasize that the Judaism of the rabbis was a product of the Land of Israel in its beginnings and was only later exported to the Diaspora. When the rabbis themselves narrate their origins, they always recall that Hillel—one of their founding fathers—was Babylonian, as though it were foreordained that rabbinic Judaism would flourish there, too. It didn't have to be that way, especially since what became a major center of Judaism, Babylonia, flourished under a different political empire and different culture than either the Jerusalem Temple or the earliest rabbis.

If I tell you again and again in this book that the rabbis were Greco-Roman Hellenists, I should also disclose that the rabbis of Babylonia certainly inherited aspects of Hellenism from their rabbinic forebears but lived in the Sasanian Empire, where the dominant culture was Zoroastrian. Jews are nothing if not complicated folks.

Although Hillel the Babylonian is not called rabbi, he is nevertheless seen as the rabbis' George Washington, as it were. Ironically, the earliest person given the actual title *rabbi* also received it anachronistically, as his story was written just after the destruction of the Jerusalem Temple, in 70. Looking back, the Christian Gospels refer to Jesus of Nazareth as "rabbi," going so far as to transliterate the Hebrew term into Greek letters and then define it as "teacher." In fact, the rabbis as a movement came to the fore only after 70 CE, once the priesthood had been scattered and the Jerusalem Temple burnt. The Hebrew term *rabbi* literally means "my master," and in the Hebrew Bible refers to the captain of a ship (Jonah 1:6) or other officer. In the Mishnah, the earliest compilation we have of rabbinic literature (ca. 200 CE), *rabbi* can refer to a slave owner; but most regularly it is a title for a master who teaches disciples. By the second or third century, the title *rabbi* was retrojected not only onto Jesus but even onto Moses and Elijah. The "rabbanization" of biblical figures is part of the way in which the rabbis reinforced their ideology by retelling biblical history through a decidedly rabbinic lens.

Yet for all that, from 70 CE to approximately 200 CE, the rabbis remained a fairly small group of men with no more than a dozen or so leaders in any given generation. I like to remind my own rabbinical students that on any given day there are more rabbis in-house at the Jewish Theological Seminary than there were in any given *generation* of the early centuries of rabbinic Judaism. Each rabbi back then had a circle of disciples, and some of these students traveled from rabbi to rabbi in order to master the oral traditions they transmitted. The traditions of the elders combined with their biblical commentaries to form what the rabbis called their "Oral Torah," which they insisted was the appropriate companion to the Written Torah, or Five Books of Moses. While the Temple still stood, Israelite religion had been centered on the priesthood and the Jerusalem sacrificial cult. Once it was destroyed and rabbis began to emerge, they established disciple circles that mimicked those of Greek and Roman philosophers. In those philosophical schools, oral transmission of the traditions of the earlier teachers (in Greek: *paradosis*) was the common mode of teaching and learning.

The disciples' zeal for their rabbis' teaching was boundless. One rabbinic source tells of the early third-century Rabbi Kahana, who once slid beneath the bed of his teacher and eavesdropped while the teacher "conversed, and played, and met his needs" with his wife. Kahana let slip aloud this thought: "You would think that my master had never tasted this dish before!" The teacher hauled him out from under the bed and said, "Kahana! Get out of here. This is really not done!" Kahana blithely replied, "But this is Torah and I must learn." Torah, indeed.

Beyond the oral tradition, the rabbis were also deeply invested in the interpretation of Scripture. The rabbis struggled to interpret the Torah text for continued relevance. This almost obsessive rabbinic focus on the interpretation of the Hebrew Bible as the source of authority to replace the Temple was, oddly, yet another reflex of their broader Roman culture. Much as the Greeks and Romans wrote commentary and endlessly quoted from the twenty-four books of "the divine Homer," so the rabbis quoted and commented on the twenty-four books of the Hebrew Bible. That the number of books is the same is not a coincidence; it required the rabbis to do some creative accounting in order to show that the rabbinic canon and the Greco-Roman "canon" were libraries with the same number of volumes.

Despite this apparent affinity, in the first seventy years of the rabbis, beginning with the revolt against Rome in 66 CE, there were an astonishing three Jewish military clashes against the empire. The war of 66–70, and then what is called the Bar Kokhba rebellion, from 132 to 135 CE, both took place in the Land of Israel. In between there was a series of pogroms, if you will, in the Mediterranean and North Africa from 115 to 117 CE, which decimated the Jewish communities there. In every case of misguided rebellion or mismatched rioting, the outcome was clear. The only question was how much the Jews might suffer. And yet like a phoenix rising out of the ashes, to invoke a Hellenistic simile, from the remnants surviving those three wars, rabbinic Judaism arose, a Roman religion.

In short, what is now called "Judaism" was invented in the matrix of Roman culture. Even as some rabbinic texts depicted Rome as the enemy, there is overwhelming evidence that Judaism took root in Roman soil, imbibed its nourishment, and grafted the good and pruned the bad from the Roman Empire, until a vibrant new religion—Judaism—arose from the wreckage of Israelite religion and the Temple cult, nurtured by the very empire that had destroyed it.

CHAPTER II

——

LIKE A FISH OUT OF WATER? STORIES OF JUDAISM IN HISTORICAL CONTEXT

About two decades ago I appeared at New York's 92nd Street Y on a panel about reading the Bible. My conversation partner was my friend Tom Cahill, author of the bestseller *The Gifts of the Jews*. We each spoke about Judaism as a religion of the book, how it was necessary to see the biblical canon as an anthology of Jewish religious writings, and the potential perils of using sacred Scripture as the sole source for history of the biblical period. The evening seemed to be going very well until the question-and-answer period following our presentation. The proverbial little old lady stood up and asked, "How much of the Bible is true?" Given the cautions we had just sounded, Tom answered glibly, "Fifty-six point four percent," or some such number. Imagine our astonishment as that woman took a small pad and pencil out of her pocketbook and carefully wrote down "56.4%."

Tom shot me a look that said, "Now what do we do?" I stepped up to the podium and extemporized. I explained that we needed to make a distinction between what had occurred historically and what was considered "true." Both were somewhat slippery categories. I relied on an old truism and pronounced, "History is written by the victors. It displays a bias, a point of view." But then I blithely contradicted myself by asserting that if history is a record of what happened, if it is "just one damn thing after another," then truth was something else entirely. I warmed to my theme. "The most important truths we learn in life," I suggested, "we often learn through reading fiction." I was proud of that distinction and remain so.

In this book I am trying to offer some historical insight from stories that may be true but may not have happened exactly as they were told and then retold. The rabbinic texts I share here, often composed as commentaries on the Bible, are particularly difficult to read as straightforward historical accounts. It is important that we keep sight of the contexts in which these stories were told. Every tale the rabbis tell has a religious purpose and may be a well-crafted piece of didactic fiction. To offer you an analogy from Americana, I referred to George Washington in the last chapter. But do you believe he actually chopped down a cherry tree as a young man? Or was that story told to teach a lesson about the values our Founding Fathers held dear, and so to teach what we should aspire to be like as Americans? The stories we tell reveal who we are, even as they shape our own identities.

In the world of Late Antiquity, from the first through sixth centuries of the Common Era, Greek and Roman pagans told stories of the gods, stories of historical characters, stories of their political leaders and philosophers. The Jews of that period told similar stories—sometimes even the exact same stories. What these stories and many other shards of evidence teach is just how thoroughly the Jews saw themselves as Romans, even as they shaped an identity somewhat apart. The Greeks and Romans were people of the book before even the Jews were. The difference was that for Hellenists the book was Homer, while for Jews, the book was the Bible.

In the centuries following the destruction of the Temple in Jerusalem, once the canon of the Bible was fixed, other Jewish books and stories developed as well. I quote from these throughout this book. The

Jews and Romans also shared a common stock of tales. To teach simple lessons, raconteurs both Roman and rabbinic loved to relate family-friendly fox fables. Tales of animals were apt for those wags who wished to express human dilemmas, morals, and received truths. No one could think these fox stories actually occurred as historical fact. These fables were a staple of Greek and Roman grammar schools, where the collections of Aesop and the moral lessons derived from them were studied. This well-known fox fable—recounted by the rabbis—tells us much about Jews, Romans, and the world they shared:

> A story is told about a fox that was walking by the riverside. He saw fish darting from place to place and asked them, "Why do you take flight?"
>
> They replied, "We flee the nets that men bring to catch us."
>
> That wily fox said, "Why don't you come up onto the dry ground where you and I can dwell together, just as my ancestors dwelt with your ancestors?"
>
> They said to him, "They call you the smartest of the animals? You are an idiot. If we fear in the place where we live, how much the more so shall we fear the place of our certain death!"

This Aesop-like fable is told in the Babylonian Talmud (Berakhot 61b). It has no direct parallel in the Greek fable collections, so, lacking the traditional ending we would find in such anthologies, I ask: What is the truth taught by our fox fable? Perhaps the moral to the story is: Stay with the familiar. Your home is your safety. But if I take a step back, a different moral can suggest itself: Context is everything. Live within your context and although you may fear, you will be safe. But if you are unaware of your context, you will be like a fish out of water, assured of death.

With that moral in mind, let's consider the fox fable in its sixth-century Talmudic context. Why was it told? Reading the broader passage from the Babylonian Talmud, we will see that the fable was offered as an analogy, placed in the mouth of a famous second-century sage who was offering a biblical commentary.

> Rabbi Aqiba commented, "'And you shall love the Lord your God with all your heart, with all your soul, and with all your might' (Deut. 6:5). 'With all your soul' means even if they take your soul."
>
> It was taught by the early rabbis that once upon a time the Evil Empire decreed that Jews should not study Torah. When Pappus ben Yehudah came and found Rabbi Aqiba gathering crowds to study Torah in public, he asked, "Aqiba, are you not afraid of the empire?"
>
> Rabbi Aqiba replied, "Let me give you an analogy: The story is told about a fox that was walking by the riverside. He saw fish darting from place to place and asked them, 'Why do you take flight?'
>
> "They replied, 'We flee the nets that men bring to catch us.'
>
> "That wily fox said, 'Why don't you come up onto the dry ground, where you and I can dwell together just as my ancestors dwelt with your ancestors?'
>
> "They said to him, 'They call you the smartest of the animals? You are an idiot. If we fear in the place where we live, how much the more so shall we fear the place of our certain death!'"
>
> Aqiba continued, "So it is for us, too. Now we sit and study Torah, of which it is written, 'It is your life and the length of your days' (Deut. 30:20). If we were to cease from it, how much the more so would we forfeit our lives?"

In this context, instead of a warning to stick close to home and abide by the familiar, the fox fable becomes a call to defiance, even as it explains a verse in Deuteronomy. The fish of the fable offer the voice of an embattled minority against the dominant majority culture. Our hero Rabbi Aqiba invokes the fable to explain his resistance to Rome, even if he is fearful. For all that Aqiba's fox fable encourages the study of Torah, when we read even further, it becomes ironically clear that Rabbi Aqiba does forfeit his life.

They say that not many days passed before Rabbi Aqiba was arrested and imprisoned. And then they arrested Pappus ben Yehuda and imprisoned him, too. Aqiba asked him, "Pappus, what brought you here?"

Pappus replied, "Blessed are you Rabbi Aqiba. At least you were arrested for teaching Torah. Oy to me, for I, Pappus, was arrested for trivial matters."

When they took Rabbi Aqiba to be executed it was the time of day to recite the *Shema* (Deut. 6). As they combed his flesh from his body with combs of iron, Rabbi Aqiba accepted the yoke of God's kingdom upon him by reciting the verses of the *Shema*. His disciples asked, "Rabbi, shall you go even this far in your devotion?"

He replied, "All my life I was troubled by the meaning of this phrase, 'with all your soul' (Deut. 6:5). I knew it meant 'even if they take your soul,' and I wondered when might I have the opportunity to fulfill this commandment. Now that the opportunity is upon me, shall I not fulfill it?"

Aqiba pronounced "the Lord our God the Lord is one" (Deut. 6:4) and drew out the final word until his soul left him at "one." A voice came from Heaven and declared, "Blessed are you Rabbi Aqiba who departed at 'one.'"

The ministering angels said to God, "This is his Torah and this is his reward?!" . . . A voice came from Heaven and declared, "Blessed are you Rabbi Aqiba, for you are invited to Life Eternal in the World to Come!"

Wow! Context really *is* everything. According to the sixth-century Babylonian Talmud, Aqiba still swims in the waters of Torah, and though he might forfeit his life in this cruel world, he is granted life in the hereafter. Rome, the Evil Empire, cannot destroy his soul, even as they torture his body. Rabbi Aqiba's martyrdom becomes exemplary for all Jews for all time. It is enshrined still today in the prayers recited on Yom Kippur, the holiest day of the Jewish year. Aqiba is granted the immortality of a tale we tell almost two millennia after his gruesome death.

But what happens if we look beyond the legend on the page of the Talmud? The Rabbi Aqiba martyrdom story is disconcerting for many reasons, not only to those praying on Yom Kippur, but also to the historian. Whether you focus on Jewish history or on Roman history, the facts don't add up. Of course, the martyr's tale has a place in mythic memory—it moves us to tears as we recall Aqiba's cruel death at the hand of his oppressor. It sets the stage on Yom Kippur for remorse and devotion. But still you have to ask, *sotto voce:* did it actually happen?

How likely is it that Rabbi Aqiba turned his torture session into a Torah lesson for his disciples? As our story begins, Pappus speaks with Rabbi Aqiba. Pappus is a Roman, not a Hebrew, name. I wonder if our narrator chose him as a warning against assimilation to the culture of "the Man." Pappus contrasts Aqiba's noble adherence to Torah study with his own trivial deeds. But Pappus vanishes from the narrative as Aqiba turns to teach his students. Aqiba's comment, "All my life I was troubled by the meaning of this phrase," is a commonplace in the Talmud to introduce a new interpretation of a verse or phrase of Scripture. It could easily have been put into Aqiba's mouth by a narrator or editor who wished to offer an interpretation for the biblical text. Further, there is no other historical evidence that Rome prohibited teaching Torah in this period. Even Aqiba's death by such cruel torture is suspect, because another rabbinic text (*The Midrash on Proverbs,* ch. 9) also tells the story of Rabbi Aqiba's imprisonment but recounts a quiet death with no mention of such torments.

The version of the story that recounts the gruesome torture is first told in the Babylonian Talmud, compiled over four hundred years after Aqiba's death. To make matters worse, it was compiled in Sasanian Babylonia, which was not only five hundred miles east of Roman Palestine, where Aqiba lived, but was the Roman Empire's chief rival. Maybe there's more to casting Rome as the Evil Empire than meets the eye? Knowing this makes me doubt the historical accuracy of our tale. Dare I suggest that the famous story of the martyrdom of Aqiba is as much a fictional fable as the one he himself tells about the fox and the fish? And the emphatic opposition between Rome and the Jews is more than overstated. Is this Aqiba story a rabbinic equivalent of George Washington and his cherry tree?

I do not relish playing the curmudgeon and bursting the bubble of the too-easy narrative of Us versus Them—foxes v. fish. But martyr stories are simple, even simplistic, while history is messy and complex. It's bad enough that we tell a tale of a martyrdom that may not have happened; it is made worse when the tale is taken utterly out of context and the Talmud then pretends that Rome was the implacable enemy of Judaism everywhere in the empire and for all of its lengthy history. Indeed, I do you a disservice simply contrasting Jews v. Romans, for the Jews *were* Romans. Let me give you a different analogy, one that does not involve chatting animals—after all, are we really meant to learn Jewish cultural history from talking fish?

In a twentieth-century analogy, I might say that Germany was the implacable enemy of Judaism for all time, throughout the reaches of all Germanic-speaking countries, as many Jews today, in fact, do say. But while this proposition certainly strikes a post-Holocaust chord, it also denies so much of the richness of German and of German-Jewish culture throughout the nineteenth and twentieth centuries. It might be emotionally satisfying to condemn all things German as simply being Nazi; but to deny German influence on the development of modern Jewish culture cripples our ability to understand Judaism in the twenty-first century.

I ask you the same questions about the latter half of the first century that we ask about the second half of the twentieth century: What does it mean to be a Jew in the decades following the destruction of the center of Jewish life? How did they recover from the deaths of immense numbers of fellow Jews? Is it possible to go on and regroup? Can we conceive of a new type of Judaism rising from the ruins of the devastation?

Could we imagine a revival of Judaism in the Land of Israel itself? Could a powerful Jewish community live comfortably in the Diaspora? Is it possible that the new Judaism that grew, nourished on the ruins of what came before, might reflect the values of the very culture that destroyed its earlier center?

For almost a century, modern historians have debated these questions about the (re)birth of Judaism in the wake of the destruction of Jerusalem and the Temple cult by the Romans two millennia earlier, in 70 CE. The Greco-Roman culture in which rabbinic Judaism grew in the first five centuries of the Common Era nurtured the development of Judaism as we still know and celebrate it today. It is not coincidental that the Judaism of now, particularly American Judaism, which flourishes as a minority religion within the Christian empire that is America, sees itself reflected in the development of the religion of the rabbis of the Roman world.

We can look back on those leaders of the Jewish community and all too often see a version of ourselves. They, as we have done post-Holocaust, adapted to their surroundings, at first to ensure their survival. Eventually they flourished. Just as we bear witness to the horrors of the Holocaust and it shapes our idea of what it means to be Jewish, so the rabbis held firm to the memory of destroyed Jerusalem even as they built a very different Jewish life—no longer one of animal sacrifice, priests, and kings. Rather, the rabbis made Jews and Judaism into the people of the Book, a religion based upon the study and interpretation of the Torah—a Judaism that was Western, essentially Roman. Using the rabbis' tales and other evidence, I retell their stories, which is their history.

Because I want to learn the lessons of history, I must ask: Do those ancient Jews look like me because they *were* like me? Do I see the rabbis on their rounds as unique and particular to their own day and age—mediating between the Roman overlords and the remnants of their Israelite religion and culture? Or do I see them as being like so many American Jews, getting along, assimilating as much as necessary and then some, running a risk of disappearing into the larger culture? Or can I try to see them as they perhaps saw themselves, making their way in a world where it seemed that God might have abandoned them and their Holy City, yet nevertheless desperately trying to find a way to hold on and keep the faith?

If this book places the rabbis and the Judaism they invented into their own historic Roman context, it is worth a moment to set this book itself in context as a product of twenty-first-century American Judaism. This modern perspective of American Judaism as a flourishing minority religion in the broader Christian culture is what makes the ancient story seem so familiar. But it runs the risk of our misunderstanding the milieu of the rabbis in the Roman Empire. Allow me to explain by means of another fox fable. This one is from Aesop:

> There once was a fox walking by the riverside. That fox had caught a fish and was preparing to eat it when he gazed into the river and caught a glimpse of his reflection. Thinking he had seen another fox with a fish in its mouth, he opened his jaws to snatch away that fox's prize. Of course, no sooner had he opened his jaws than the fish he had already caught leapt back into the water and swam away.
>
> The moral to the story is that what he wanted in his greed he could not have, and further; he lost what he already had.

The moral to Aesop's fox fable also is found in the Babylonian Talmud (Sota 9a), and it offers a lesson to heed. Writing the story of the invention of Judaism during the Roman Empire, I run the danger of seeing only my own reflection as an American Jew. So, *caveat lector*, as the Romans used to say—"read with care" and with the knowledge that my biases as writer and yours as reader may cause us to see things in the rabbis and the Romans that reflect us all only too well. We may marvel at how much they were just like us. How readily the rabbis invented a Judaism that allowed Jews to have the best of both worlds—the Judaism of their ancestors, albeit somewhat transformed, and the best of Roman (read: Western) culture, with but slight adjustment. This should give us a few moments' pause. Has my presentation simply reinforced what we all already think about our own circumstance?

I hope to tell the story straightforwardly. Yet I am limited not only by my current situation and the confines of my limited vision, but also by the reliability of my sources. As for methods, I seek to narrate the moments of Judaism's birth, as though it were the goddess Venus rising from the sea, or the divine Athena leaping from the head of Zeus. You see my problem—it is fairly easy to turn to Roman myths to narrate Jewish events, which underscores the point I am trying to make. I already read the history of the early rabbis through the lens of Greco-Roman culture.

Most of the stories I discuss were composed orally in the rabbinic circles of the first five centuries CE in Roman Palestine. Of course, all of these texts understandably have a decidedly pro-rabbi bias. These traditions are the very ingredients that helped to bake the cake of Judaism. But it is precisely the religious bias of these texts that makes them unreliable as historical documents. To state it as baldly as possible: None of the narratives of the rabbis in this period are about history. They are about law, lore, folk cures, religious practice, ethics, belief—each of which all but precludes us from knowing "what really happened." Yet the very legal and literary qualities of the rabbinic library allow us to compare these works to Roman literature and see the strong affinities between them.

Still other stories I quote are pagan Roman, Greek, and Christian. Each of these may have its own prejudiced view of Judaism. For many, their biases will be self-evident. It is sufficient to remember that they view Judaism as "them," not "us." But in all of these cases, my ability to compare rabbinic texts to non-Jewish texts allows me to show the broader context of Roman culture.

I make use of some nontextual materials as well. Here, folks often get excited because art and archeology, artifacts, seem to be historical facts. But art and architecture are also a form of text that need to be read and analyzed, and often are subject to heated debate and interpretation. The past is a cipher and I do not necessarily hold the decoder. So I gather provisional information, array the pieces of the puzzle, rejoice when they seem to fit together, and try my best to get a view of the broader Roman context and hope that it is "true."

As we look at that big picture, we note that there in the corner, concealed in the details, sits our much-fabled fox. That sly animal is a potent symbol for the nexus of Roman and early Jewish culture. Just as Roman moralists trotted out the fox, as it were, for a rhetorical flourish or to make their point, so too did rabbis know when to deploy that sly fellow for maximum effect. A marvelous example of the power of the fox fable may be found in the fifth-century Midrash on Leviticus, where we are told (in folksy Aramaic):

> Shimeon son of Rabbi [Judah the Patriarch] made a wedding feast for his son. He invited all of the rabbis, but neglected to invite Bar Kappara; who went and wrote [graffiti?] on the gate of the banquet hall: "After rejoicing comes death; so what's the point of rejoicing?"
>
> Shimeon asked, "Who did this to me? Is there someone we didn't invite?" They told him that he had neglected Bar Kappara. He said, "We'd better invite him now, lest he become an enemy." So he threw a second banquet, inviting all of the rabbis, this time including Bar Kappara.
>
> When each course of the banquet was brought out to the guests, Bar Kappara stood and entertained them with three hundred fox fables. The guests were so entranced that they didn't touch their food and it grew cold—until each dish was returned to the kitchen untouched. (Lev. Rabbah 28:2)

Too bad we no longer have the obviously compelling fables Bar Kappara told to distract the wedding guests from their dinners. This delicious example of rabbinic cattiness (or should I say foxiness?) hinges on the popularity of Hellenistic fox fables. The moral of this story could well be: revenge is a dish best served cold. If I may add two tasting notes to this tale: First, Bar Kappara is the son of an early rabbi, Rabbi Elazar HaKappar. Elazar has the distinction of being one of the very few rabbis whose name is preserved in an ancient inscription. Second, the groom in this story is the grandson of Rabbi Judah the Patriarch, editor of the Mishnah. The rabbis lived in a cozy world where they all went to the same schools and lived, as it were, in the same zip codes.

This tale of fox fables makes it clear that the rabbis were comfortable in both Hebrew and Aramaic. But the story also uses the Greek and Latin term for banquet dishes, neatly transliterated into Hebrew characters. In fact, there are thousands of loanwords from Greek and Latin found in the literature of the rabbis. That is a huge penetration of culture, on a par with the ubiquity of American English terms found throughout the world today.

I conclude with one final fox fable about Jacob and Esau, the eponymous ancestors of the Jews and Romans. In the biblical book of Genesis (ch. 32–33), when Jacob confronted his brother, Esau, after having cheated and then fled from him two decades earlier, he feared the reunion. In his panic, Jacob divided his sons into camps, fore and aft, in anticipation of a violent reception. Yet when he finally met his brother, he was greeted with a kiss and a forgiving welcome. Still, Esau is the rabbis' symbol of all that is bad about Rome, so they cannot even read his reception of Jacob positively. The rabbis say if Esau kisses you, you should count your teeth afterward. Yet even the rabbis cannot ignore the fact that Esau is Jacob/Israel's twin brother. Perhaps that is why, above all else, they chose Esau as the symbol of Rome.

In the commentary to the passage in Genesis 33:1, which recounts the reunion of the brothers, Midrash Genesis Rabbah (78:7) teaches,

> Once the lion was angry with all the animals. They asked one another, "Who will go and reconcile with him?"
>
> The fox said, "I will lead the way, for I know three hundred fox fables which can assuage him."
>
> All the animals said, "Let's go [agomen]!"
>
> They walked a bit and he stopped. The animals asked the fox, "Why have you halted?" He confessed, "I have forgotten a hundred fables."

They said, "No matter, two hundred fables are a blessing." They walked a bit and the fox stopped again. The animals asked the fox, "Why have you halted?" He confessed, "I have forgotten another hundred fables."

They said, "No matter, even one hundred fables are a blessing."

When they arrived at the lion's lair the fox cried, "I've forgotten them all! Every man for himself!"

I should note that when the animals in the fable say "let's go," they do so in Greek, neatly transliterated into Hebrew letters. In the Hebrew Bible's narrative, Jacob begins with bravado, yet by the time he reaches Esau he has essentially told his sons, "Every man for himself!"

In the rabbis' own story, they are Jacob. They approach Esau, Rome, with caution. They understand very well that the fox fable, or, if you will, Roman rhetoric, is the way to approach the Roman other and to show that we are one and the same, twin brothers who share a lineage. Over time, we have forgotten some, even much, of the common language of Greco-Roman culture that marked Judaism as part of the Hellenistic household. In the immediate centuries following the destruction of Jerusalem, as again today, it seemed that Judaism resembled the fox's "every man for himself."

And in a way, it is also "every man for himself" as we evaluate the stories in this book and how I present them as evidence of how the Jews adapted Roman culture to create Judaism. Then and now, our shared heritage of Hellenism remains a source of self-identity. Looking back, we can discern the path by which the rabbis chose to take the best that the Roman world offered them and see how they reshaped it so that Judaism could survive. Knowing that this synthesis between the Temple cult and Hellenism created a vibrant Judaism that survived two millennia is heartening. Reflecting on that dual history reveals who we are. At this inflection point in Jewish history, it may also help us discern the truth of who we yet might become.

———

CHAPTER III

JUDAISMS OF THE *OIKOUMENE*: WHO WERE THE JEWS IN THE ROMAN WORLD?

J udaisms of the OY what?" *Oikoumene* is a Greek word, but one that has currency in English in the term "ecumenical." In Late Antiquity, the *oikoumene* was the Hellenistic world, the lands of the Greco-Roman Empire. In the Jewish-Roman world, this included all of the varieties of Judaism found throughout the Roman Empire—what Solomon Schechter a century ago quaintly called "catholic Israel"—hence Judaisms. While it is true that in this book I essentially equate "Judaism" with the Judaism of the rabbis, I want to put that particular Judaism into the context of the many other, more or less Hellenized varieties of nonrabbinic Judaisms throughout the empire in our period.

This penchant for equating all "Judaism" with the Judaism of the rabbis is due to the success of rabbinic Judaism as the dominant mode of Jewish expression, perhaps as early as the end of Late Antiquity and onward through modernity. In recent decades, thanks in part to archeological and manuscript discoveries, other Judaisms have begun to be recovered by historians, so that rabbinic Judaism can now be placed in a much broader context. In America, declining synagogue membership has been complemented by a rise in other expressions of Jewish culture, resulting in a greater interest and ease in speaking of Judaism in multiple forms.

In truth, there have always been varieties of Judaism, even when the Jerusalem Temple dominated Israelite religious practice in the Ancient Near East. Jews nostalgically recall a time when the priests served God in Jerusalem and, encouraged by the exclusivist strictures of the biblical book of Deuteronomy, recall that Temple as the *omphalos tēs gēs*. This Greek phrase implies that the Temple was the center of the universe, but literally translated it means "belly button of the world." In the rabbinic imagination, if one were to unhinge that belly button, primordial chaos would engulf the world.

But the Hebrew Bible reluctantly acknowledges that even when the Jerusalem Temple was first built, there were rival altars and sanctuaries. When King Solomon's Temple was destroyed, in 586 BCE, and Jews were exiled to Babylonia (modern Iraq), some remnant of the Judean community remained in the Holy Land. They called themselves Samaritans, which means "the preservers or guardians," and they built a sanctuary to replace the destroyed First Temple. Their own Temple was built in Samaria (modern Nablus), on Mt. Gerizim. This mountain is mentioned in the biblical book of Deuteronomy as the site of the blessings and imprecations that Moses commanded the Levites to offer at the Israelites' entrance into the Promised Land. The Samaritans persisted as a distinct group throughout the Israelite exile and became a rival form of Jewish presence in the Land of Israel. Even when the Second Temple was built, they persisted. In fact, the Samaritans remain on Mt. Gerizim to this very day, still performing biblically enjoined sacrifices!

There were yet other sanctuaries that sought to rival the Jerusalem Temple. Egypt was one place where non-Jerusalem practices flourished. There was a Temple on the Nile Island of Elephantine that dates back to the biblical period. There are small archeological traces at the site, as well as records preserved on papyrus. The Elephantine papyri offer evidence of a community living as part of the military outpost on that

Nubian island as early as the fifth century BCE. There also was a Jewish Temple complex at Leontopolis in the Nile delta region of Heliopolis, the site of the biblical city of On. That Temple persisted for two to three hundred years and seems to have been destroyed about the same time as the Second Temple in Jerusalem, which is to say ca. 70 CE. In other words, throughout the "Second Temple period," there were Egyptian Jewish centers to rival Jerusalem and its priesthood.

Alexandria was also home to a large community of Jews. The Egyptian city was founded in the fourth century BCE by Alexander the Great, and the Jews there thrived under Hellenistic rule. The most famous product of that community may well have been the third-century BCE Greek translation of the Torah, called the Septuagint. The mythic story of that translation says that the Jewish residents of Alexandria reached out to the Jerusalem Temple authorities for assistance in the translation project. By the first century BCE, Alexandria had a highly Hellenized Jewish population, though they maintained their own separate Jewish political structure. The city produced the famous turn-of-the-millennium Jewish philosopher Philo, who wrote an allegorical commentary on the Torah, attempting to reconcile it with Hellenism. The multivolume work is a fascinating peek into the mind of a highly educated Jewish leader. Philo relied wholly on the Septuagint Greek translation, as he apparently had poor command of Hebrew.

Philo's nephew, Tiberius Julius Alexander (love that nice Jewish name), was sufficiently assimilated to Hellenism that he abandoned his roots in the Jewish community entirely. Perhaps he found his uncle's writings and disquisitions, or the Alexandrian community itself, just too boring—some things never change. In any case, the first-century CE Jewish historian Josephus reports that Tiberius Julius Alexander demonstrated his loyalty to *Rome* by commanding army troops who first acted against the Alexandrian Jewish community and then besieged Jerusalem in the years 66–70 CE! While Uncle Philo saw the relationship between Judaism and Hellenism as a "both/and," his nephew saw it as a stark "either/or," in which Judaism lost the battle.

The Jewish community of Alexandria persisted into the second century, when it suffered severely in the anti-Jewish rioting of 115–117 CE, sometimes referred to as the Great War of the Diaspora. In that period, riots broke out throughout many of the Mediterranean and North African Jewish communities. Pagan locals' resentment of the special privileges that many of the Jewish communities received from Rome resulted in vicious pogroms that decimated the Jewish-Roman world. This may have been a mortal blow to the existence of a separate Jewish community in Alexandria. Nevertheless, the reputation of that ancient Jewish community persisted, so that in the early third century the rabbis could imagine nostalgically:

> Rabbi Yehudah said, "Anyone who did not behold the double-columned [diplostaton] synagogue of Alexandria of Egypt never really appreciated the greatness of the Jews. It was a basilica that had columns [stoa] within columns. There were times when it held double the number that left Egypt [=1,200,000!]. There were seventy-one golden thrones [kathedra], one for each of the elders . . . and there was a dais [bema] of wood in the center and the director of the congregation stood there with a cloth [soudarion] in hand. When they prayed he would wave the cloth so they could reply "amen" to each and every blessing, and then the next one further down would wave his cloth so the rest could respond, "amen."
>
> They did not sit mixed, but by guilds: the goldsmiths sat together, as did the silversmiths, the weavers, the bronze workers and iron workers. Why? So that strangers [ksenoi] who came could be accepted by those who shared their craft, and they would thus find employment. (Tosefta Sukkah 4:6)

This is a rabbinic fantasy; but the story they tell of the synagogue of Alexandria is instructive. To begin with, they use seven Greek loanwords (in italics above) in two short paragraphs. The rabbis contemplate a synagogue so large that it could hold over a million Jews, or, as they put it, "double the number that left Egypt." There is a delicious irony here: the rabbis imagine such huge numbers in Egypt, all those centuries after the biblical Exodus. The synagogue architecture they project onto Alexandria, a basilica building with diplo-stoa, or two sets of columns, was exactly the kind of Greco-Roman architecture that the rabbis saw in synagogues throughout the Land of Israel in their own times. And, like modern Orthodox synagogues of today, they apparently did not use microphones on Shabbat.

Were there other Hellenistic Jewish communities in the predestruction period? Yes, indeed. In the very epicenter of Hellenism, Athens, there is evidence of an ancient synagogue. St. Paul visited and preached there, as is mentioned in Acts 17:16–17. By the way, the New Testament is often a good source for information about early Jewish communities, especially because Paul worked and wrote his famous Epistles in the 50s, a generation before Jerusalem's destruction. Five centuries later, the rabbis took notice of the Athenians, making them the butt of rabbinic humor. Here is an example:

> An Athenian came to Jerusalem where he met a child. He gave him some coins and said to him, "Go bring me figs and grapes." The child bought the fruits and replied to the Athenian, "Thank you, you with your money and I with my legs."
>
> So the man said to him, "Take and share it." The child took the bruised fruit for himself and set the good before the stranger.
>
> The man exclaimed, "Well done! Rightly do they say that the people of Jerusalem are very clever. Since this child was aware that the money was mine, he gave me the better and took the bad."
>
> The child thereupon replied, "Come, now, let's throw dice. If I throw and win, then I take your share; but if you win you take my share." And so it happened that the child took the best fruit for himself. (Lam. Rabbah 1:6)

Clearly the rabbis were tired of hearing about the wise men of Athens. Fellows like Plato and Socrates were smart but, in rabbinic eyes, were no match for a savvy Jewish kid from Jerusalem. If the church father Tertullian asked, "What has Athens to do with Jerusalem?"—the rabbis of this story have a witty riposte.

The other axis of the Greco-Roman world was the great city of Rome herself. Jews were certainly there from the first century BCE. They are mentioned in the New Testament, and there are historical texts speaking of expulsions of Jews from Rome under the emperor Tiberius (14–37 CE) and again under Claudius (41–54 CE). Between their reigns, the Jewish philosopher Philo of Alexandria traveled to Rome in 39–40 CE on an embassy to the crazy emperor Gaius Caligula. Philo describes the Jewish community across the River Tiber in Rome as "citizens who had been emancipated . . . liberated by their owners and not forced to violate their native institutions." Philo goes on to remark that the Jews of Rome have "houses of prayer" where they "meet on sacred Sabbaths to receive training in their ancestral philosophy." Further, he reports, "they collect money for sacred purposes from their first fruits and send them to Jerusalem to offer sacrifices." A decade or so later, St. Paul wrote his famous Epistle to the Romans, addressing it to portions of the Jewish community.

Although there have been no archaeological remains of synagogue buildings found in Rome proper, there are ruins of a synagogue at the old port of Rome: Ostia Antica. What survives is minimal, but enough for scholars to guess that the synagogue was there from the first through the fourth or fifth centuries. The most notable Jewish feature is a column—technically an architrave—with an incised menorah, a ram's horn (*shofar*), and the biblically enjoined palm frond and citron (*lulav* and *etrog*—used for the holiday of Sukkot). These symbols are regularly found in synagogues across the Roman Empire from this period.

Among the vast array of funerary inscriptions (approximately six hundred) in the Jewish catacombs underneath Rome itself, there are references to a dozen other synagogues. These may not all have existed simultaneously, as the catacombs date from the second through the

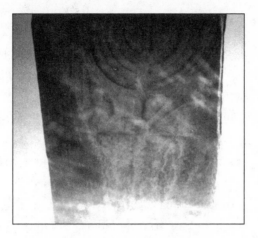

OSTIA ANTICA SYNAGOGUE

CATACOMB INSCRIPTION WITH MENORAH, RAM'S
HORN, PALM FROND, AND CITRON

fourth or fifth centuries CE. In addition to inscriptions, the Roman Jewish catacombs have yielded wall frescos, sarcophagi, lamps, gold glass-
ware, and other artifacts.

The catacombs, not surprisingly, produce a rich picture of at least
one essential aspect of the Roman Jewish community: their attitudes
toward death, burial, and life in the hereafter (or lack thereof). The inscriptions also list names of the deceased and, in many cases, their ages
at death. Virtually all of the inscriptions are in Latin and Greek.

In the pre-70 era, when the Temple still stood, there were already a fair variety of expressions of Judaism. The Greek works of Philo and Josephus teach us in particular about three differing sects of Judaism, enumerated by them as Sadducees, Pharisees, and Essenes. I have spoken a bit about Philo of Alexandria already. Josephus was a different kind of bird entirely. All of the works by Josephus are preserved in Greek, but it is clear that he himself was a native Hebrew and Aramaic speaker; and his own Greek was less than polished. He had a secretary to style edit for him. Josephus has left us a kind of commentary on the Torah (as did Philo, but his was allegorical). Josephus called his work *archeology* in Greek—probably best translated as "Antiquities." Josephus also left an account of the War against Rome from 66 to 70. He began the war as a priest in Jerusalem, then abandoned his Jewish brethren to side with Rome and ended his days as a hanger-on in the palace of Titus, the emperor who destroyed the Temple. That such a man left a self-serving autobiography comes as no shock. Yet historians of the period must make do with what contemporaneous sources as there are, no matter how tendentious.

A close reading of these two Jewish, first-century Greek writers, combined with some other literary records, shows us that the Essenes are probably more than one group, depending upon location and era. Philo distinguishes between the Essenes and the Therapeutae. These latter seem to have been a group of Jewish ascetics in the Alexandria region. Philo notes that the Essenes were an exclusively male community, while the Therapeutae admitted women; yet both sects practiced forms of sexual abstinence. I note that these guys were Jews. Josephus and Philo each describe the Essenes as dining exclusively within the confines and purity strictures of their own community. They also practiced other forms of asceticism as well as fervid devotion to their leadership. To the extent that the Essenes are identified with the Jewish separatists from Qumran described in the Dead Sea Scrolls (a point still debated among scholars), these Jews also actively rejected the Jerusalem Temple and declared its priesthood corrupt and unacceptable. What is common among all three of these subgroupings—Essenes, Therapeutae, and the

Dead Sea covenanters—is their membership in an "outsider" community by individual choice rather than by birth.

The Dead Sea Scroll community lived in isolation for a number of generations. Although they were but a short journey from Jerusalem, they rejected urban life and Temple ritual; but they may have performed their own sacrifices at one time. They adopted a very rigorous set of purity and food laws, and their Sabbath observances were most stringent. The surviving manuscripts reveal an apocalyptic mentality that imagined the end of days upon them and the war of the sons of Light (them) v. the sons of Darkness (everyone else, but especially Romans and other Jews) already begun. In short, these pre-70 CE anti-Temple groups saw themselves as the sole possessors of truth and the only authentic Jews of their day.

The Sadducees were depicted across ancient sources in a very different light. Hailing from priestly family backgrounds, they wielded power in part by cooperating with the Roman authorities. They are often described as the Jerusalem Temple establishment. Josephus and the New Testament draw sharp theological contrasts between the Sadducees and the Pharisees. The Sadducees are described as rejecting the notion of bodily resurrection—a tenet embraced by early Christianity as well as Pharisaic and, later, rabbinic Jews. Further, the Sadducees are depicted as rejecting the validity of received tradition in favor of the written Torah law. Historians even today describe the Sadducees as the "patrician" upper class of Jewish society. Whether this is a fact of late Second Temple history or a fancy of twentieth-century Marxist historiography, it does have support from New Testament descriptions of the Sadducean sect. The Sadducees are also described as arguing with the Pharisees over the minutiae of purity rules, even as they sat together on the ruling council of the Jerusalem Sanhedrin. That term *Sanhedrin* is used in the New Testament and throughout rabbinic sources (transliterated into Hebrew characters), and it is borrowed from the name of a Greco-Roman ruling council.

Not all of the Temple priests were necessarily Sadducees. The historian Josephus, himself from a priestly family, writes in his autobiography that after trying out each of the major sects, he chose to affiliate with the Pharisees. Perhaps we should understand the New Testament's claim that the Pharisees were eager to seek converts in this light: that they sought other *Jews* to join their sect (like certain Hasidic groups do today). In addition, it seems clear that in the Late Second Temple period there were priests who remained unaffiliated with any of the variously identified sects. Following the destruction of the Jerusalem Temple, certain priests or priestly groups may have even continued to hold sway over some segments of the Jewish population in the South of Palestine, as well as in the Galilee.

The Pharisees for their part are described by Josephus as urban, yet maintaining the loyalties of the villagers. They promoted fidelity to the teachings their ancestors handed down, in addition to those laws actually written in the Torah. Josephus explicitly likens Pharisees to the Greco-Roman Stoic philosophers. Most modern historians see the Pharisees as the forebears of the rabbinic movement. But recently, some Jewish historians have exercised caution at too easily identifying the Pharisees as the spiritual ancestors of the rabbis.

In the New Testament, the Pharisees are depicted as the opposition to Jesus. As such, the name *Pharisee* continued to be used as a term of opprobrium into the twentieth century. Later Jewish sources offer a view of the Pharisees as a liberal and inclusive group of Jews who claimed access to nonscriptural traditions, yet were nonetheless punctilious regarding food and Sabbath laws, purities, and tithing. I emphasize these various groups in order to display the bewildering varieties of Judaism that existed even before the central Jerusalem shrine was destroyed.

One final group of Jews in the Land of Israel were the revolutionaries who fueled the insurrection of 66–70 CE. Not all of those who arose in opposition to Rome can be collapsed into one general category. As is common even today among such revolutionary groups, the narcissism of petty differences loomed large. The various revolutionary groups included Zealots, *Sicarii*, and *Biryoni*, but we have no clear information regarding them. As the rabbis of the Palestinian Talmud (j. Sanhedrin

10:5) later noted, "The Jews were not exiled from Jerusalem until there were twenty-four sects" dividing one Jew from another.

When the Roman legions destroyed the Jerusalem Temple and razed the city in 70 CE, Judaism in the Land of Israel, as well as throughout the Diaspora, changed in profound and lasting ways. During the years of the rebellion (66–70 CE), groups such as the Zealots and *Sicarii* were killed off by the Roman armies. The separatists at Qumran on the shore of the Dead Sea vanished from the historical record. The neat division Josephus had offered of Pharisees, Sadducees, and Essenes ceased to be meaningful. The priesthood could no longer serve in Jerusalem. Those Mediterranean communities that had sent funds and offerings to Jerusalem could no longer do so. A long process of rebuilding—even reinventing—Judaism ensued, renegotiating relationships with Gentile neighbors, the Roman Empire, and the nascent Christian community.

It was precisely at this moment in time that something new came to the fore: Judaism. This was a Hellenistic religion in which canon—the formation of a community around a shared work of literature (itself a Hellenistic concept)—became the basis for a common Judaism across the Empire. It is not coincidence that Philo and Josephus, each publishing his work in Greek, felt the need to explicate the Greek translation of the Jewish Scripture. Indeed, the translation and their very commentaries helped shape that canon and fix it into the form it retains today: the Bible.

A common core of Jewish practice was more or less shared by Jewish communities across the vast breadth of the Roman world; yet it may have been no more than a patina. It seems that almost all groups that identified as Jewish shared Greek as one of the languages they employed. They each had particular food laws (although not necessarily all the same ones), they lit lamps for a Sabbath meal on Friday nights, they refrained from labors of various sorts on Saturdays and on various holidays already mentioned in the Bible, and they had some physical communal institution where they gathered. This amalgam is a fair amount of the common Judaism by which non-Jews across the Roman Empire might identify Jews as "other." But if these few rituals and customs separated the Jews, it was their shared Hellenism that united them with one another, as well as with the pagans of the empire.

What made Judaism into what it continues to be to this very day were the rabbis' interpretations of the Jewish written canon, as well as the oral laws and customs that they claimed had been part of God's revelation to the Jews since Moses stood at Sinai. Indeed, the very emphasis on the revelation at Sinai as the signal event forming Jewish identity was itself a Roman-era novelty. During the biblical era the exodus from Egypt was the seminal event of Israelite history. Only after the Temple was destroyed and Judaism reconstituted around the Book did it become necessary to shift emphasis to Sinai.

Before I discuss the rabbis and their affinities for things Greco-Roman, I want to survey what we know of the emerging Jewish world after the destruction of the Temple in 70, as I promised at the outset of this chapter. At the western edge of what is now Europe, the church father St. Irenaeus lived in the Roman town of Lugdunum, Gaul (now Lyon, France), during the late second century. In his writing against Christian heresies, Irenaeus kvetches about the Jews of western Europe, decrying their interpretations as false and their refusal to recognize Christ as the very essence of heretical behavior. But whether these were actual Jews he was railing against, or merely Jews who served him as straw men in his rhetoric against Christian heresies, is unclear. We do not know much else about these Jews, so it is instructive to read what later rabbinic works say about them and their imagined love-hate relationship with the priesthood of the Jerusalem Temple back when it still stood. It is equally unclear to me whether the rabbis themselves knew actual Jews from Spain and France or whether they, too, mention them symbolically as Jews at the far end of the known world. The rabbis of fifth-century Galilee may, in fact, be projecting onto their Western European brethren their own ambivalences about the long-destroyed Temple.

> "When a person offers a grain offering to God, it shall be of
> fine flour . . . that he shall bring to Aaron's sons, the priests;
> who shall take a handful of the fine flour. . . ." (Lev. 2:1–2)

> Rabbi Hiyya taught. . . . See them come all the way from Gaul [France] and Spain and other lands nearby. Then they see the priest [*kohen*] grab a mere handful of the grain-flour offering for the altar and eat the rest himself. They will say, "Oy for me who took all this trouble to make pilgrimage so that this guy gets to eat!"
>
> They assuage him by saying, "If the priest who took but two steps between the courtyard and the altar merited to eat—you who took all this trouble to come so far, how much the more so will you be rewarded!" (Lev. Rabbah 3:6)

It's as though the pilgrims express their pique: "I came all this way and that fat *kohen* waddles over and eats my offering!?" I don't know whether the rabbis' consolation is any solace, but it doesn't matter. They are speaking of these pious pilgrims as an act of biblical interpretation that reflects their own concerns about how the sacrificial system worked. They look back four hundred years to a Temple long gone. The narrator of this tale speculates on what the pilgrims may have felt. As a result, we cannot learn about the actual history of the Jews of France and Spain then.

Sardis, on the other hand, was a major city of Asia Minor, and there is no doubting that Jews flourished there. Today, the site contains only the archeological dig. When my wife and I visited there a few years ago, we found that the synagogue was the largest building in town, smack in the center of the city next to the gymnasium. It is about the size of a football field, with a decorated niche for the Torah, and has a double entryway, so there is a huge main room and a smaller courtyard. The synagogue boasts mosaic pavement floors, a huge urn in the courtyard (perhaps for ritual washing?), and plaques on the walls with geometric decorations.

Geometric decorations often are found in pre-70 synagogues, which scholars attribute to reluctance on the part of synagogue officials or donors to depict living beings. This is taken to be an interpretation of the second of the Ten Commandments, against graven images. Later in this

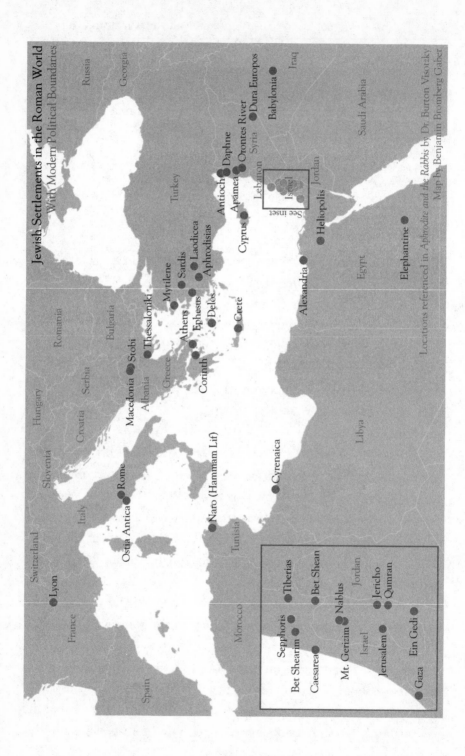

Jewish Settlements in the Roman World
With Modern Political Boundaries

Locations referenced in *Aphrodite and the Rabbis* by Dr. Burton Visotzky
Map by Benjamin Bromberg Gaber

book we'll look at post-70 synagogue art and see that there was little to no hesitation about pictorial representation of animals, humans, even God. The Jews of Sardis certainly did not seem to worry about the strictures of the Second Commandment. The synagogue at Sardis is replete with animal designs on the mosaic floors, which probably date from the third to the fourth centuries. Here, too, we find an elaborately carved menorah, but this one has an inscription with the name Socrates in Greek—likely the name of the donor, not the philosopher. There are other menorahs in evidence at the Sardis synagogue. At the front of the synagogue there is a large carved marble table—perhaps for public reading of the Torah. Curiously, the legs of the table are carved with bas reliefs of Roman eagles. These may be original to the synagogue, or perhaps they were reused from some other building project. Statues of lions flank both sides of the table.

SARDIS SYNAGOGUE

The inscriptions recovered from Sardis Jewry have been little discussed. One, in Hebrew, is limited to the word "Shalom." Another, set in mosaic, refers in Greek to a "priest and teacher of wisdom." This may have been the congregation's religious leader, but he was not a rabbi we know of from the Talmud. Elsewhere in town, biblical Hebrew names are found written in Greek in inscriptions, which often identify the one named simply as "citizen of Sardis." It is tempting to interpret the accoutrements of the synagogue, such as the table and the urn, or amphora, through the rabbinic lens of Torah reading and ritual purity. But as the Gershwin brothers taught us, "It ain't necessarily so."

Another ancient city of Asia Minor, Aphrodisias, also is located in modern Turkey not far from Sardis. The extensive archeological site at Aphrodisias yielded a long Greek synagogue inscription among the many now piled up there. Listed alongside the row of names of the Jewish supporters of that synagogue are a group of townsfolk styled as "God-fearers," which possibly refers to Gentiles who have adopted some Jewish customs or who have other affinities with the Jewish community, while not formally converting. This category of God-fearers or semi-converts is referred to in both rabbinic literature and church literature. But if I try *not* to read through rabbinic lenses, the only thing I can really say about the archeological remains at Aphrodisias is that the Jewish community had friends in the Gentile community. Perhaps they simply donated sufficient funds to the synagogue to have their names inscribed as "God-fearing." Or perhaps they were non-Jews who were married to Jewish members of the Aphrodisias congregation. But in both of these possible scenarios, I run the danger of anachronizing from the customs of the current American Jewish community.

Antioch on the Orontes, also located in current-day Turkey, was a major center of the Roman East. Back in the day, Antioch's Jews were wealthy enough to have influence beyond their own city. Rabbinic literature contains references to rabbis traveling from Roman Palestine north to Antioch to collect charitable funds for their students and poor. They tell of the time that

Rabbi Eliezer and Rabbi Yehoshua and Rabbi Aqiba went to the suburbs of Antioch to collect charity for the sages. There was a man there nicknamed "Father of the Jews" because he gave charity so generously. But then he lost his fortune. When he saw the rabbis coming to his house he felt sick. His wife asked him what was the matter and he explained that the rabbis had arrived and he had nothing to contribute. His righteous wife asked, "Don't we still have one field? Go sell half and give them the proceeds."

He did so and when he gave them that small contribution they said, "May the Omnipresent restore your losses."

The rabbis went their way and he went to plow his remaining half field. While plowing, his ox stumbled and the ground cracked open. There he found a treasure!

When the sages returned the next time they asked after him. They were told, "Who can even get in to see the Father of the Jews? He who has sheep, goats, oxen, donkeys, camels!"

When they came to him he said, "Your prayer has borne fruit, and then interest on the fruit!" (Lev. Rabbah 5:4)

Whether or not there actually was a man called "Father of the Jews" is incidental. The rabbis of fifth-century Galilee who wrote this little story about earlier rabbis imagined their Jewish neighbors to the north as quite well-off. Further, there is literary evidence that the Palestinian Jewish patriarch in the years ca. 364–396 CE carried on a correspondence with the great Antiochene pagan teacher of rhetoric, Libanius, who was supposed to be instructing his son (the boy took the money and spent it on a road trip).

In the same period, the fiery church father John Chrysostom railed against the Jews and the synagogue they attended in the Antioch suburb of Daphne, which was famous for its shrine to the Greek god Apollo. The synagogue in Daphne was called the Matrona, and according to Chrysostom, Jews there celebrated "Trumpets, Booths, and Fasts"—most likely the autumn festivals of Rosh HaShannah, Yom Kippur, and Sukkot. Bishop Chrysostom also complains that pagans and Christians used that synagogue for the administration of vows, which they imagined to be especially effective there. He characterizes the Jewish fast as being accompanied by the ritual of taking off one's sandals and going barefoot in the marketplace. He knows his own congregants admire the synagogue as a place of books, and he excoriates his flock for going to the Jews of Daphne for healing remedies, spells, amulets tied on their arms, and potions.

All of this comports with the textual traditions about rabbinic Judaism of that era. In other words, there is both church and rabbinic evidence of a major Jewish community whose Judaism was not all that different from rabbinic Judaism. Rabbinic Jews took off their sandals when they fasted on Yom Kippur. They also tied "amulets" on their arms, in the form of phylacteries (tefillin). They said Hebrew prayers that would have sounded like spells to a Greek listener. And there were rabbis who were famous as healers. But the name of the synagogue, "the Matrona," or Roman matron, doesn't sit all that well as a name for a rabbinic locale. On the other hand, rabbinic literature does refer to a matrona. Scholars debate whether this word is a generic reference or a proper name. Here's a tale of a matron or Matrona:

> A matron [Matrona] asked Rabbi Yosé ben Halfota, "How many days did it take God to create the world?"
>
> He replied, "Six days, as it is written (Ex. 31:17), 'In six days God made the heaven and the earth.'"
>
> She asked, "And what's he been doing since?" . . .
>
> Rabbi Berechiah said, this is what Rabbi Yosé ben Halfota answered her: "God is sitting and making ladders. Some folks get brought down, while others are raised up. As it is written (Psalm 75:8), 'God judges, bringing one down and uplifting another.'" (Lev. Rabbah 8:1)

It is fairly clear from elsewhere in the story that this matron is not Jewish. But still, she would have liked Rabbi Yosé's clever answer, for already in the second century a pagan writer had written that "Pittacus made a ladder for the temples in Mytilene, not for any purpose other than as an offering. His intention was to hint that fortune moves up and down, with the lucky, as it were, climbing up and the unlucky climbing down."

Rabbis and pagans employed similar metaphors, perhaps particularly when speaking with one another. The Jews of Daphne lived and worked in a suburb of Antioch famous for its pagan shrines. Indeed, some of those Jews probably worked in the tourist industry serving the pagan pilgrims. Others commuted into Antioch proper to work in the Roman government or to study. It is not very likely that the Matrona synagogue was named for a pagan, unless she was a donor, as at Aphrodisias. But what kind of synagogue might be named for a non-Jewish donor? And how much of a donation would *that* take? I think we are better off not trying to over-read the evidence one way or another. I am content to know that there was a large Jewish community in Antioch that attracted the attention of rabbis (for contributions) and church fathers (for censure).

Turning south, we come to the port town of Tyre in modern southern Lebanon. It is mentioned as a Jewish community by the New Testament, in Matthew 15. The later rabbis also know about it and what might be its very peculiar Jewish practices. In the fifth century they tell the story of a certain rabbinical student who perhaps got his Jewish law all mixed up:

> Jacob of the village of Nevorayah once taught in Tyre that fish require kosher slaughter. Rabbi Haggai heard about this and sent him the message: "Come, be whipped!"
>
> The student demurred, "Would you whip me for that which is taught in the Torah?" The rabbi patiently inquired, "And where in the Torah do you think it says that fish must be slaughtered according to rabbinic law [and not merely hauled out of the water]?"
>
> Jacob offered, "It is written in Genesis 1:20, 'Let the waters swarm with living creatures and birds that fly.' Just as birds

require kosher slaughter, so fish must require kosher slaughter," he proclaimed.

Rabbi Haggai said, "You did not reason correctly."

Jacob impudently asked, "Where will you prove this from?"

The teacher replied, "Bend over to be whipped while I prove it to you! It says in Numbers 11:22, "The cattle and beasts will ye slaughter . . . and the fish of the sea will ye gather.' It doesn't say slaughter, but gather."

Jacob conceded, "Whip away, I guess I need the lesson." (Gen. Rabbah 7:2)

Perhaps the Jews of Tyre had a different notion of what was kosher than did the rabbis to their south. This would be of some interest, as it might indicate a community that was actually more stringent than rabbinic laws dictate, at least when it came to eating fish. This is no small thing, as fish were undoubtedly a mainstay of the port community. But perhaps I should not jump to conclusions, as the stringency is laid at the feet of a zealous, if foolish, fellow. Later in the passage quoted, he offers his opinion that a child born of a non-Jewish mother can be circumcised on Shabbat. This is tantamount to saying that Jewish lineage follows the father's religion, an opinion diametrically opposed by the rabbis, who support the matrilineal principle. In fairness to poor Jacob of Nevorayah, in the Bible itself Israelite lineage is determined by patrimony, as he had ruled. But once again, Jacob was whipped by his rabbinic mentor.

Is this, then, a case of an outlier who simply does not know his stuff? Or might this indicate a very different custom in the Jewish community of Tyre? In one instance they would be zealous about preparation of fish. In the other they might follow what was biblical custom and prefer patrilineal descent as an indicator of Jewishness. Again, we simply cannot know.

To return to Roman Palestine, I remind you that the disastrous Bar Kokhba rebellion against Rome from 132 to 135 CE was fueled by zealotry and misplaced messianism. The extreme Roman repression of this rebellion, which centered in the Judean South, caused Jewry in the Land of Israel to become more concentrated in the Galilee. As a punishment for two successive revolts, from 66 to 70 CE and again from 132 to 135 CE, Rome banned Jews from Jerusalem, which was refounded as the pagan city Aelia Capitolina. Despite the ban, other Jewish centers did flourish in Judea, scattered from Gaza to Ein Gedi and Jericho. On the Mediterranean coast and in the Galilee, large Roman urban centers such as Caesarea, Tiberias, and Sepphoris anchored Jewish settlement. Each of these cities was thoroughly Hellenized, with pagan art prominent among the archeological materials that remain. These same motifs are also found in the Byzantine-era synagogues of the Galilee. With very few exceptions, these synagogue buildings resemble the churches and Roman broad-house and basilica structures found locally. They are identified as synagogues primarily by details such as mosaics depicting biblical scenes (similar to those found in churches) and bas reliefs displaying menorahs, shofars, and the like. Of course these synagogues also display the ubiquitous donor inscriptions in Hebrew (rarely), Aramaic (often), and, in very significant measure, Greek.

Synagogues across the *oikoumene* served as places for many functions—praying, studying, having meals—and they often served as hostels for travelers or, possibly, as housing for officers of the Jewish community. They appear to have been places to deposit communal funds, hold communal gatherings (hence the Greek name: *synagogue*, whose literal meaning is "gather together"), administer oaths, and hold sessions of local Jewish tribunals. In virtually none of these functions did the synagogues of the Land of Israel differ appreciably from those of the Diaspora. Synagogues in the Holy Land and throughout the remainder of the Roman world also seemingly have in common their apparent ignorance of rabbinic law. I use the term "ignorance" consciously, for we cannot know whether they did not know about rabbinic law or whether they knew but simply ignored it. Very few of the synagogues' physical remains thus far discovered follow rabbinic ordinances regarding the physical layout of the building and its entrances. If I were to rely only on archeological remains of synagogues and the inscriptions found there, I would be hard-pressed to know that rabbinic Judaism existed (let alone was founded) in Roman Palestine.

The one apparent exception to the rule among synagogues unearthed thus far is in the Beth Shean valley in northern Israel, a crossroads for travel both east to west and north to south. The Rehov synagogue there has a large mosaic floor that quotes from a range of still-extant rabbinic literature regarding the permissibility of Sabbatical-year agricultural produce that might otherwise be prohibited by biblical law (see Lev. 25). This mosaic text is the earliest physical quotation of rabbinic literature and the only mosaic discovered thus far that attests to the Judaism of the rabbis. Other physical evidence for the rabbis of classical rabbinic literature comes from the Golan, east of the Jordan River, in the village of Dabbura. There, archeologists found a lintel that identifies the academy of Rabbi Eliezer Hakkapar, who is regularly mentioned in early rabbinic literature. Complicating matters, though, the lintel postdates the rabbi by a couple of centuries. Maybe the academy was named for him posthumously.

There is one other archeological site where rabbis are mentioned. In Beth Shearim, in the lower Galilee, the burial chambers of well-known Talmudic and political leaders, along with the family of the Palestinian Jewish patriarchs, were excavated in the late 1930s and again following World War II. Dozens of figures of menorahs are found in the catacombs there, as well as over two hundred Greek inscriptions. The very few Hebrew inscriptions consist of names, and repeatedly, the word *shalom*. There is even a dual-language inscription, first in Hebrew and then in Greek, of the name Rabbi Gamaliel, possibly the same rabbi who was patriarch of the Jewish community. Artistic motifs on the Beth Shearim sarcophagi include the ark or desert tabernacle, palm fronds, and lions (of Judah?)—all commensurate with rabbinic religion. But there are also eagles, bulls, Nike (the goddess of victory), Leda and the swan (aka Zeus), a theater mask, a spear-carrying warrior fragment, and yet other fragments of busts, statues, and bas reliefs of humans, none of which might be considered very "Jewish" by the rabbis of the Talmud. It's hard to know what to make of this mishmash of pagan and Jewish burial symbols.

Even more confusing, perhaps, is the fact that in a number of synagogues from the Byzantine period that have been unearthed across the Galilee, the mosaics on the floors, most often in the central panels, display a zodiac with the twelve months, depicted in a circle enclosed in a square frame. At each corner of the square is a personification of the season of the year in that quadrant—except for the one mosaic, where the floor guy got the order of the seasons confused and laid them in the wrong corners. I suppose a zodiac is conceivably within the pale, except it has a whiff of paganism about it. But what is truly astonishing about these mosaics is that in the center of the circle in each of these synagogues, there is Zeus-Helios, riding his quadriga (a chariot drawn by four horses) across the floor-bound sky!

BEIT ALPHA SYNAGOGUE MOSAIC, HELIOS

BERLIN BRANDENBURG GATE

To say the least, the god Zeus is unexpected on a synagogue floor, and there is no scholarly consensus whatsoever as to what this possibly can mean about Judaism in Roman Palestine. The quadriga is, however, a fairly popular and perhaps even universal symbol of strength. Above is the famous quadriga atop Berlin's Brandenburg Gate.

But really, Zeus-Helios riding across the floor of Holy Land synagogues? We'll discuss this more later. But if we add to this artistic record the Samaritan's Temple on Mt. Gerizim (near modern Nablus), we must conclude that the overwhelming physical evidence of Judaism, even in Roman and Byzantine Palestine, is decidedly *not* the Judaism of the Talmudic rabbis.

At some point in the 220s CE, emerging rabbinic Judaism, now represented by a compendium of its teachings called the Mishnah, found its way from Roman Palestine eastward into the Sasanian Empire. In

224 the Sasanian army—which professed the religion of Zoroastrianism—conquered the Parthian Empire to Rome's east. Their laissez-faire treatment of non-Zoroastrians allowed for new expressions in the Jewish community. It helps us to recall that Jews had been part of that region, which they called Babylonia and we call Mesopotamia or Iraq, since the Babylonian exile in 586 BCE. This adds up to eight hundred years by 220 CE! Aside from what the Bible says—and that isn't very much— what is known about that region has been learned from the singular lens of the Babylonian Talmud, the quintessentially rabbinic Jewish document. But were there forms of Judaism situated somewhere between the Bible and the Talmud? Is there any evidence of Hellenistic influence on that Judaism, too?

By and large, I prefer to think of the Talmud as imbibing its Hellenism from the rabbinic traditions it imported from the rabbis of the Land of Israel, rather than to imagine Hellenistic influences in the severe Zoroastrian society of the Sasanian Empire. But Rome's empire stretched east while the Sasanians' stretched west, and just at the point where their borders met, at a town called Dura-Europos, was a treasure trove of evidence about Jewish life in the first half of the third century CE. The town had served as a Roman garrison for approximately a century, from 166 to 256 CE, when it was destroyed by the conquering Sasanians. Following its destruction, it lay desolate, covered by sand until its rediscovery, beginning in the 1920s. Among the buildings that were excavated then were several temples to Roman and Eastern gods, as well as a church. The synagogue that was discovered on the street adjacent to the wall of Dura revealed floor-to-ceiling wall paintings of biblical scenes, neatly arrayed in three registers, surrounding a so-called "seat of Moses" and a shell-arched Torah niche. The paintings are captioned in Aramaic, Greek, and Persian. It is a spectacular archeological discovery with a clear date for the synagogue in the mid-third century, at the very moment when rabbinic Judaism first finds expression in Babylonia. The archeologists brought their finds to the Damascus Museum, where they are now largely inaccessible, except for a few images on the museum website. I fear for the survival of this archeological treasure and worry

DURA SYNAGOGUE, LONG WALL

that it, too, may be destroyed in the seemingly endless battle that is consuming Syria.

The wall paintings are a mix of Roman and Persian styles, and the scenes of the Bible run the gamut from Jacob to Esther. Some of the scenes are not literal but are interpretive depictions of Bible stories. In these cases, the "texts" of the wall of the Dura-Europos synagogue often predate existing works of rabbinic midrashic interpretations by centuries. The ceiling of the synagogue has been reconstructed. As usual, there is a donor inscription, found on one of the tiles and preserved in Aramaic. The finds at Dura-Europos show us a distinctly Jewish community living cheek by jowl with their Christian and pagan neighbors. The artistic and building conventions of that Jewish community are of the same style, if not content, as those of their neighbors. They apparently lived in comfort with the non-Jews of that town at the very border of the Roman world and died there together with them under the siege of their Sasanian enemy.

Ultimately, the Jews flourished under the Sasanian Empire, which persisted until the advent of Islam in the seventh century CE. This gave the Babylonian Jewish community about four hundred years to come thoroughly under the sway of the Talmudic rabbis. Later in this book, we will see that the already-existing bits of Hellenistic Judaism represented in the rich wall paintings at Dura complemented the Hellenism that the rabbis brought to Jewish Babylonia from Roman Palestine. Like the synagogue walls at Dura, the Babylonian Talmud is a rich amalgam of Eastern and Western cultures. Even the Jews living in Zoroastrian country could not help but be influenced by the magnetic pull of Hellenism to its west.

The Jews in Late Antiquity interacted with virtually every other religious group in the communities that were spread throughout the Roman *oikoumene*. Across the Roman world, Judaism simultaneously stood somewhat apart and distinctive from its neighbors, no matter what its expression. There was a common core of Judaism, which made it familiar to all who practiced it, no matter what the local details of that practice may have been. While this tempts us to equate these common Jewish practices, such as lighting Sabbath lamps or observing food strictures, with the observances of the rabbis, we can discern distinct customs from one Jewish community to another. Many of those communities preexisted rabbinic Judaism, so it is clear that they were not following the dictates of a small group of men in the Galilee. Even so, the Jewish practices they shared, for all of their local differences, made Judaism somewhat "other" to the pagan non-Jews who embodied the broader Greco-Roman culture. Yet under the aegis of Hellenism, the Judaisms of Late Antiquity in all of their varieties were deeply part of the surrounding Roman culture.

───

CHAPTER IV

ESAU, EDOM, ROME: WHAT DID THE RABBIS REALLY SAY ABOUT THE ROMANS?

F or the Jews of the Roman Empire, the disastrous rebellion against Rome of 66–70 CE ended with the destruction of the Jerusalem Temple. The Bar Kokhba debacle of 132–135 CE ended with a virtual exile of Jews northward to the Galilee. In between those devastations, rioting and police actions decimated the Jewish communities of North Africa in the period from 115 to 117 CE. These wars with Rome had a profound effect on the collective and individual Jewish psyche. Whether these wars represented a last-gasp effort to regain the quasi-independence the Jews had under the Hasmonean Maccabees, or whether they manifested a messianism gone awry, or even the flexing of Eastern provincial political muscle at times when the imperial center in Rome itself was thought to be weak, can never definitively be determined. The origins and causes of each outbreak remain multifaceted and obscure. Minimally, however, the three military engagements pushed the Jewish community to a more submissive stance in which "go along to get along" became the norm and Stoic passivism expressed the communal ethos. This engendered deeply complex attitudes about how the Jews saw Rome, as well as about the construction of their own Roman-Jewish identity.

Jews who were Romans had at once a strong sense of their Judaism and pride in their Roman citizenship. They held this latter quality despite their minority status and the earlier rebelliousness of a militaristic subset of the community. In truth, during none of the three "wars" was the entirety of the Jewish community implicated. Each military disaster involved only a segment of the Jewish community, no matter how far-reaching the aftermath. So when the emperor Caracalla expanded citizenship to every potential taxpayer in 212 CE, Jews lined up to register themselves in the archives to become official citizens of the empire. When they did so, they took on Greek and Latin names: Reuven became Rufus, Joseph became Justus, Shimeon became Julianus, and Benjamin was now Alexander. At least this is the report of a fifth-century rabbinic commentary (Midrash Song of Songs 4:12), which says that the Jews of Egypt merited redemption for *not* changing *their* names—presumably unlike the Jews of the Roman Empire.

To say the least, there is a great deal of ambivalence regarding Rome lurking between the lines of the ancient rabbis' books. While the rabbis consistently kvetch about the empire, the Rome they speak of changed over time. In the earliest rabbinic literature, indeed up to about 350 CE, "Rome" meant pagan Rome. But the latest layers of rabbinic literature deal with Christian Rome. While the rabbis' relationship to Christianity is certainly very important, it is a topic for another book.

Here, I focus on the Roman Empire as the monumental representative of the Greco-Roman culture that ultimately gave rise to Judaism. The complex Jewish attitudes the rabbis express toward Rome find their origins in the Hebrew Bible. You might reasonably ask, "Where will we find the Roman Empire in the Bible?" The answer, surprisingly, lies in the book of Genesis. The trick is in knowing how to decode the text. The story begins with one of the most moving verses in the entire Bible. The matriarch Rebecca, after long being unable to conceive, finally becomes pregnant when her husband, Isaac, prays on her behalf. God responds to his prayer, and as with many modern pregnancies in which there has been an intervention, Rebecca finds herself pregnant with twins. It is a very difficult pregnancy; as the Bible puts it, "the children rumbled inside her" (Gen. 25:22). Rebecca, in despair, seeks an oracle and poignantly asks God, "Why me?" (Gen. 25:23). It's the existential question everyone asks at one time or another in life. And it is especially apposite to a woman pregnant with twins.

But these are not ordinary twins. Indeed, God tells Rebecca,

> Two nations in your belly; two nations from your womb shall part. One will be stronger than the other; the elder to the younger enslaved. (Gen. 25:23)

Esau was born first; his younger brother followed, grabbing his heel, and so was called Jacob (which has the Hebrew word for "heel" as its root). Esau was, in modern parlance, macho, while Jacob was what we might call metrosexual. In the next ten verses, we learn that Esau hunted and Jacob stayed home. Dad loved Esau for the game he brings him, while Mom just loved her Jacob. When, one day, Esau was famished, young Jacob bought his birthright for a bowl of red (in Hebrew: *adom*) lentil porridge. Therefore, we are told, Esau was called Edom—a bad pun, to be sure, but the Bible and the rabbis love puns.

In the Bible, this birth begins an epic rivalry laced with hatred and murderous intentions. Rebecca's oracle is the original self-fulfilling prophecy. The last of the classical prophets, Malachi, says it this way: "'Is Esau not Jacob's brother?' says the Lord. 'Yet Jacob I love and Esau I hate'" (Malachi 1:2–3). Jacob, who becomes Israel, seems forever destined to conflict with Esau, aka Edom. Centuries later, in the earliest rabbinic commentaries, Esau or Edom symbolizes Rome. It is the Jews and Rome who now appear to some rabbis to be locked in a struggle for primacy.

Rebecca's prophecy was interpreted as anticipating Israel's final triumph and Rome's eventual enslavement. History just has to play itself out for the Jews to rise from beneath the imperial boot. As the fifth-century Rabbi Nahman commented on the creation of the sun and moon, "So long as the great luminary shines, the lesser luminary is eclipsed. Only when the great luminary sinks from view does the lesser luminary shine forth. When Esau's sun sets, then shall Jacob shine forth" (Gen. Rabbah 6:3).

But this black-and-white view is reductive and far too simple. After all, the Torah also reports that after Jacob flees Esau's wrath, he ultimately returns home. On the very eve before he met Esau again after two long decades, Jacob wrestled through the night and was renamed Israel (Gen. 32). When Israel finally met his brother, the much stronger, much-cheated Esau "ran to greet him, he hugged him, fell on his neck and kissed him; so they wept" (Gen. 33:4). A happy reunion after all? Well, it depends on how you read it. In a Torah scroll, the Hebrew word for "kissed him" has dots over it. What do these mysterious dots mean? Some rabbis say it means that the kiss was venomous, like the kiss of the spider-woman. Others say Esau bit him. Yet others say, when Esau kisses you, count your teeth afterward, he's such a no-goodnik. One lone rabbinic voice says, "The kiss was a sincere kiss of brotherly love" (Sifre Num. #69 and Gen. Rabbah 78:9).

The reason for that final positive opinion lies in the recognition that Israel and Edom are nonetheless brothers, twins at that. When the rabbis chose a symbol for Rome it is true that they chose the one who was "set against them." But we cannot ever forget that the classic rabbinic symbol picked to represent Rome is Jacob's fraternal twin. It strikes me that in this choice of Esau as the symbol of Rome, the rabbis gave voice to the complexity of their relationship. Yes, Rome is rhetorically construed as the eternal enemy. Yes, Jews in the Land of Israel rebelled against Rome twice. Yes, Rome exercised a harsh hegemony against the Jews of Roman Palestine and elsewhere in the Empire.

But . . . but, but. But Rome behaved that way toward all its colonies, especially the rebellious ones. But Rome worked with and benefited from the Jewish populations in the empire. But Rome afforded Jews special privileges in their food distribution to its citizenry, giving the Jews separate kosher items. But Rome gave the Jews exemptions from military and other forms of government service due to Sabbath laws. But Rome recognized the Jewish patriarch in Palestine and gave him certain powers. But Rome kept the peace so long as there were no rebellions. But Rome built roads and aqueducts, regulated markets, established courts.

Once upon a time, the curiously named "Rabbi Judah son of Converts" said,

> "How admirable are the deeds of this nation. They have built markets, bridges, and bath-houses." His colleague Rabbi Yosé was silent; but Rabbi Shimeon ben Yochai retorted, "Anything they have built has been for their own needs. They build markets so their whores have a place to ply their trade. Bath-houses to pamper themselves, and bridges to collect tolls and taxes." (Babylonian Talmud Shabbat 33b)

Elsewhere Rabbi Hanina sourly notes, "Pray for the peace of the Empire; for were it not for the fear they inspire, people would swallow one another alive" (Avot 3:2). It is well to consider the ambivalence of the literature. Some rabbis sing Rome's praises. Some are scathing in their scorn. Still others are silent.

In a narrative about the coming of the Messiah, the rabbis teach:

> Rabbi Yehoshua ben Levi once asked the prophet Elijah, "When will the Messiah come?" He replied, "Go ask him. He sits among the paupers at the gates of Rome" . . .
>
> He went and greeted him, "Peace upon you, my master and my teacher."
>
> He replied, "Peace unto you, son of Levi."
>
> Rabbi Yehoshua asked, "When will you come?"
>
> To which the Messiah replied, "Today."
>
> Rabbi Yehoshua commented to Elijah, "He lied to me, for he said he would come today, yet has not come!"

Elijah explained, "He was quoting Psalm 95:7: 'Today, if you would but obey God's voice.'" (Babylonian Talmud Sanhedrin 98a)

There sits the Messiah patiently at Rome's gate, awaiting his triumph. The future king of Israel is ready, if only the Jews could just for once obey God. Here the rabbis blame their subjugation not on Rome but on themselves. God's kingship is the ultimate dominion; yet Rome will rule so long as God's sovereignty is not fully accepted. This is the notion the Bible itself adopts to explain exile. God has not been defeated. Rather, God uses the foreign conqueror as God's scourge. For the rabbis, God and Rome work hand in hand in history. It is the divine destiny of the Jews ultimately to throw off the yoke of history and succeed someday in the messianic future to kingship over Rome. As Rome conquered Greece, so the rule of earthly kingdoms eventually will end and Israel will ascend. The irony is not lost on the rabbis. Rome's culture will influence the Jews and shape them, much as Greece had done to Rome in its turn. But that is, of course, messianic speculation.

There is no better embodiment of the Greco-Roman Empire than its founding conqueror, Alexander the Great. If the rabbis can imagine the Messiah at the gate of Rome wrapped in bandages, they mischievously imagine Alexander at another gate, fully bedecked in his armor, at the far end of his kingdom. Like everyone else in the empire, the rabbis told Alexander legends. I quote this one as it illustrates the rabbis' ambivalence toward the empire that Alexander represents. The rabbis' run-up to the Alexander tale is instructive as well, so allow me to spin this story at length. It starts with the same rabbi whose chat with the Messiah we just reported.

When Rabbi Yehoshua ben Levi went to Rome he saw pillars of marble wrapped in tapestries so that they would not crack in the cold nor break in the heat. Next to the pillar he saw a pauper wrapped in a thin reed mat. Of the pillars the rabbi recited the first half of Psalm 36:7, "Your beneficence is like the mighty mountains." He commented, "When You bestow, You do so in abundance."

And of the poor man he recited the next part of the verse, "Your judgment is like the deepest depths." He said, "When You smite someone, you are punctilious in Your retribution!"

The tale is ambiguous. It would be too easy to blame Rome for showing more sympathy to the marble columns than it did to its own poor. Yet Rabbi Yehoshua chooses to frame this as a matter of God's enigmatic justice. When God chooses to reward, there is the magnificence of Rome. When God punishes, human suffering abounds.

The fifth-century Midrash continues in colloquial Aramaic:

> Alexander of Macedon went to the Far Kingdom beyond the Mountains of Darkness. There he found a city called Cartagena that was entirely of women. They came out before him and declared, "If you make war against us and conquer us, your reputation will be that you destroyed a town of ladies. And if we conquer you, the word will go out that you were beaten in war by women. Either way, you won't be able to show your face among the other kings."
>
> When he departed he inscribed on the city gate [pylae], "I, Alexander of Macedon, was a foolish king until I came to Cartagena and learned sound counsel from its women."

The storyteller is parodying Rome's pretensions to conquest. Alexander gets his comeuppance from the wise women of Cartagena. Where, pray tell, is this fabulous far-off city? It well might be Carthage, in North Africa. Alexander, of course, never got there, but that need not have stopped the rabbis from imagining him there for the sake of their satire. It is even more likely that they liked the name of the city as an amalgam of two words, the first Aramaic: *karta,* or city. The second word is

Greek: *gynae*. Females know from visits to their *gyne*cologists that this word means "women." So the town named Cartagena translates as "city of women."

The narrative continues with another Alexander legend, this one lampooning so-called Roman justice:

Alexander went on to a city called Afriki. They came out before him bearing apples, pomegranates, and loaves of bread, all made of gold. Alexander asked, "Is this what you have to eat here?"

They replied, "Do you have no food in your country that you came here?"

Alexander demurred, "I did not come to see your wealth. I came to see your laws and justice."

As they were sitting there, two gentlemen came to find justice before the king. The first said, "I bought a derelict building from this man. When I knocked it down I found a treasure. I insisted he take it, as I paid for a building and not a treasure."

The second man replied, "Master, when I sold that derelict building, I sold it and its entire contents to him."

The king asked the first, "Do you have a son?" He said, "Yes."

Then he asked the other, "Do you have a daughter?" He said, "Yes."

The king said, "Let the boy marry the girl and together they can enjoy the treasure!"

Alexander was astonished. The king asked him, "Why sir? Did I not judge well?" Alexander said, "Yes, you did." So the king asked, "Had this happened in your country, how would you have judged?"

Alexander answered, "I would cut off the head of this one and cut off the head of that one. Then, I'd keep the treasure for the royal household."

The king asked him, "Sir, does the sun shine on your country?" Alexander said, "Yes." And so the king asked, "Sir, does rain fall in your country?" Alexander said, "Yes." The king then asked, "Perhaps you have small grazing animals in your country?" Alexander said, "Yes, why?"

The king said, "This man [viz, Alexander] should drop dead! It is through the merit of those poor animals that the sun shines and the rain falls upon you. Those small animals are your salvation, as it is written, 'Man and beast do You deliver, O Lord' (Psalm 36:7). You deliver the men for the sake of their beasts." (Pesikta DeRav Kahana 9:1)

It's not very often that a verse of Psalms provides both the setup and the punch line for a joke; but the rabbis admittedly have an odd sense of humor. In the full narrative, they open with Psalm 36:7 about the pillars

ALEXANDER THE GREAT MOSAIC—NAPLES MUSEUM

of Rome and contrast them with the poor. The bada-boom comes when we learn that it is because of the lowly sheep and goats—animals otherwise reviled for their omnivorous foraging—that Alexander's kingdom thrives. If it depended upon the vaunted system of Greco-Roman justice, there would be neither a drop of rain nor a ray of sunshine. Alexander may think himself great, but he survives by dint of the little people.

Note that the rabbis do not attack Rome directly. Rather, they humorously imagine Alexander as incredulous that people might be generous to one another or that a judge might be anything but rapacious. In truth, rabbinic law also makes it clear that folks are not always as munificent as the people of Afriki (that is, Tunisia). Rather, it is the local king who indicts Alexander for the cravenness of Roman justice, much as the women of Cartagena emasculate Alexander's pretensions as a conqueror. The rabbis repeat these tales with relish, but they do not directly indict.

Another oft-told rabbinic story recounts the very cusp of Judaism's (re)invention, in the immediate aftermath of the destruction of the Jerusalem Temple in 70 CE. This Talmudic tale about the first rebellion against Rome and the siege of Jerusalem involves three emperors and also confronts the ambiguities of the relationship between rabbinic Judaism and Roman culture.

> Our House [the Temple] was destroyed; our Sanctuary was burned; we were exiled from our land. He sent Nero Caesar against them. As he came, Nero shot an arrow to the East; it landed on Jerusalem. To the West; it landed on Jerusalem. To all four points of the compass; it landed on Jerusalem.
>
> Nero asked a child, "Tell me the verse of Scripture you are studying."
>
> The child said, "I will wreak My vengeance upon Edom, through the hand of My people Israel" (Ezek. 25:14).
>
> Nero reasoned, "The Blessed Holy One seeks to destroy His house and then wipe His hands on me."

So he fled and converted to Judaism. His descendant was
Rabbi Meir. (Babylonian Talmud Gittin 56a–b)

The story opens with tragedy. The "He" of the narrative is God, using
Rome as a scourge against the Jews. Their sin? According to the Talmudic narrative preceding this passage, the sins of the Jews were the twin
transgressions of factionalism and baseless hatred of one another. The
emperor Nero comes to make war and, as he does, shoots off arrows and
quizzes a schoolchild in order to take omens on the eve of battle. All
signs point to his conquest of Jerusalem, but there's a catch. Although
Nero might win the battle, he will lose the war, as God will then hold
him culpable for Jerusalem's destruction and punish him accordingly.
The verse of Ezekiel, "I will wreak My vengeance upon Edom," tells us
that the rabbis relating this tale see Nero as a stand-in for all of Rome.

The rabbis also understand that the relationship of Rome to Judaism
is exemplified by the very omens Nero performs. The first is martial; he
shoots arrows. The second is more religiously inclined. He asks a child
to recite a verse of Scripture. This might foreshadow Nero's imagined
conversion to Judaism. But Nero's method of using a child's verse as a
predictor of things to come is found not only among Jewish texts but
also among Christian and, yes, pagan works, too.

The rabbis tell this tale while under Rome's thumb. So the verse
about God's vengeance against Rome is presumably aspirational, and
Nero is, I suppose, to be credited with a long view of history. It is entirely
irrelevant to our narrator that Nero never stepped foot in Palestine—
not to mention that he certainly never converted, nor was he the ancestor of a famous rabbi. So what, then, is the point of making claims that
are so patently false? The rabbis also take the long view of history. It is
as though they say, "Yes, Rome destroyed Jerusalem and God's Temple.
But be patient. Ultimately we will conquer them." Why does the Talmud
go so far as to imagine that Nero converts and engenders a great rabbi?
Is this a subtle recognition that Judaism underwent transformation as
a result of Rome's elimination of the Temple cult? It is as much to say

that with the Temple gone, Rome itself will help father the new entity represented by the great sage, Rabbi Meir.

Our Talmudic tale continues:

> He sent Vespasian Caesar against them. He came and besieged them for three years. . . .
>
> Now the Jews had enough provisions to feed the besieged Jerusalemites for twenty-one years; but among them were thugs who called themselves the "capital guards." The rabbis said to them, "Let us go out and make peace with the Romans." But those thugs did not permit them to do so.
>
> The "capital guards" said, "We will go out and make war upon them." The rabbis said, "The matter will not have support from Heaven." So those "capital guards" arose and burned the storehouses of wheat and barley, and famine ensued.

Now our story has taken a turn toward the historical. Vespasian actually was the general sent to besiege Jerusalem in 66 CE. Alas, the Talmud also accurately represents the internecine fighting among the various factions within the Jewish community. This sad fact is also attested to by Josephus. The famine that ensued is corroborated by his as well as pagan Roman narratives of the war.

What follows in the rabbis' telling, however, has less to do with history and more to do with how the Jewish community related to Rome in the aftermath of the war. One might even go so far as to say that the rabbis collaborated with Rome and against the Jewish rebels. I must consider the possibility that later rabbis are offering an indictment that places an act of betrayal at the very birth of the rabbinic movement. Revisionist history is never welcome, but I think it is fair to ask whether it was the rabbis or the rebels who cared more for the Jewish community and its future. The nature of the cooperation with Rome does, in any case, define the future of rabbinic Judaism—so this story may not be historically accurate but is otherwise self-defining.

Abba Sikra, the head of the "capital guards" in Jerusalem, was the nephew of Rabbi Yohanan ben Zakkai. Yohanan sent him the message, "Come to me in secret." When he arrived, Yohanan asked, "How long will you continue doing this, killing everyone with famine?"

He replied, "What can I do? If I say anything to them they will kill *me!*"

Yohanan said, "Let's see if there is a way for me to leave Jerusalem. It might be possible that I can save a small bit."

He said, "Pretend you are ill and have everyone come and ask after you. Then put something smelly nearby and have them say that your soul has gone to its rest. Let your disciples enter—and do not let anyone else do it, lest they feel that you are too light—for everyone knows that a living person feels lighter than a corpse."

We have no historical information regarding Abba Sikra. Some associate his name, Sikra, with a movement of rebels whom Josephus calls *sicarii,* so named for the stilettos (*sicarii* in Latin) they carried. With these daggers they killed their Jewish opponents. The term I have translated as "capital guards" could as well be translated simply as "thugs." Thugs, indeed; yet apparently our relatives. The story of escape from a besieged city by playing dead is an old one, found among other Greco-Roman siege accounts. Is it historically accurate? I do not know. Does it tell us that the rabbinic self-perception is one of Judaism that has died and been resurrected? I believe so. The drama of this escape comes with the recognition that the Temple and its cult are over. The afterlife comes when a rabbi encounters an emperor and a new synthesis begins. Of course, death and resurrection are not so easily achieved, so the story still has a few bumps to work out.

Rabbi Eliezer carried him from one side and Rabbi Yehoshua carried him from the other side. When they came to the gate with the "corpse," the guards sought to stab the body to be sure it was really dead. The disciples protested, "Do you want people to say that you desecrated the body of our master by stabbing him?"

They thought to just shove him. The disciples again protested, "Do you want people to say that you desecrated the body of our master by shoving him?" They relented and opened the gate. They went out.

The bluff worked! It is as though the rabbis said to the Roman besiegers, "Do you really want the media to cover this while you abuse our venerable rabbi's corpse?" With that the gates open and Rabbi Yohanan was able to carry out his secret mission to General Vespasian.

When Rabbi Yohanan got to the general's camp, he said, "Peace be upon you O King; peace be upon you, O King!"

Vespasian replied, "You have condemned yourself twice over. First, I am not emperor and you have committed *Lèse majesté* by hailing me as emperor! Further, if I were emperor, what took you so long to come?"

Rabbi Yohanan responded, "As for your saying that you are not emperor, surely you are an emperor, otherwise Jerusalem would not be given into your hands. . . . And as for your asking why I did not come sooner, those thugs would not permit it."

Vespasian said, "If you had a barrel of honey with a serpent coiled around it, would you not destroy the barrel to kill the serpent?"

Rabbi Yohanan was silent.

Rabbi Yosef, and some say it was Rabbi Aqiba, recited the verse, "'It is I, the Lord, Who turns sages back and makes nonsense of their knowledge' (Isa. 44:25). What he should have said to him was, 'Take a pair of tongs, remove the serpent, and leave the honey barrel intact.'"

This is a very popular story in rabbinic literature, repeated many times, in many versions. Until fairly recently, historians of the period treated this as an historical narrative. I assuredly do not. But I can report with delight that in one ancient version of the telling, Rabbi Yohanan greets Vespasian with the words (nicely transliterated into Hebrew characters) *Vive Domini Imperator*, exactly how the emperor was saluted in the Roman world. In our Hebrew/Aramaic version the rabbi says, "Shalom." The point of the story seems to be that when you have escaped a siege and are making a bargain with the enemy (who is about to become your new friend), you are in a "one-down" position. Vespasian has the witty reply while Rabbi Yohanan, in what is surely an unusual moment for any rabbi, is silent. Of course, it doesn't take very long for rabbis who were not there on the scene to second-guess him and tell him what he should have said.

Vespasian speaks a little Greek in his reply, for the term for *serpent*, for which there are certainly good biblical Hebrew terms (think Eve and the apple), is, instead, *drakon*. That word also supplies our English term *dragon*, but in Greek of the period the word is somewhat less dramatic. Our story continues.

> Just then a military attaché [Greek: *paristake*] arrived from Rome and said, "Arise, for Caesar has died and the nobles of Rome wish to seat you at their head."
>
> Vespasian had just put on one boot; but when he tried to put on the second, it would not go on. So he tried to remove the first boot, but could not. He asked, "What's this?"
>
> Rabbi Yohanan explained, "Don't worry, it's just the good news you've received, as it is said, 'Good tidings fatten the bone' (Prov. 15: 30). What is the remedy? Bring someone whom you are unhappy with and have him pass before you, as it is said, 'Despondency dries up the bones'" (Prov. 17:22).
>
> He did so and his boot went on.
>
> Vespasian said, "I must leave now and will send someone in my stead. But ask of me some favor that I may grant it."

He said, "Give me Yavneh and its sages; and the Gamalielite line; and a physician to heal Rabbi Tzadok."

So much for Vespasian: he's gone from being the witty general to
being Little Diddle Dumpling, "one shoe off and one shoe on." Rabbi
Yohanan's "prophecy" about Vespasian's ascent to the throne is confirmed. The rabbi is the clever one now, while the new emperor of Rome
cannot even get his boots on without a little rabbinic interpretation of
Scripture. Presumably this all took place before the invention of the
shoehorn.

In classic folk-tale fashion, Rabbi Yohanan gets three wishes. It is
through Rome that Yohanan gets the benefits of a place to study and
laissez-passer for the Jewish leadership of Gamaliel's family during rebellion. It is intriguing that Yohanan asks favor for his political opponents,
the Gamalielite dynasty. That family became the leadership of the Palestinian Jewish community immediately following Rabbi Yohanan's
triumph. Gamaliel and his offspring ruled the Jewish community in Roman Palestine into the fourth century. Among his illustrious offspring
was Rebbi Judah the Patriarch.

Rabbi Yohanan also asks Vespasian for a doctor to heal Rabbi
Tzadok, who had been fasting for forty years to prevent the destruction of Jerusalem. He apparently foresaw the coming horror through either his political savvy or his prophetic piety. Although Rabbi Tzadok,
a priest, ultimately failed in his mission to save the Holy City, he stayed
alive and became a model rabbinic disciple.

Rabbi Yohanan's first wish, for the town of Yavneh and its sages, is
anachronistic. In fact, when the rabbi met the general, the town was not
called Yavneh, but rather Jamnia—it was then the garrison town for the
Greek-speaking soldiers of the Roman legions. In other words, Yohanan
met Vespasian in the heart of the Roman army encampment and asked
for that very town to become the place where he and his disciples could
study going forward. Maybe Yohanan needed military protection from
the Jewish zealots after sneaking out of Jerusalem and breaking the siege.
Only later in rabbinic memory did Jamnia, which the rabbis called "Greek

town" after the language the troops spoke (in Hebrew: *Yevvani*), come to be called Yavneh, which in Hebrew means "to build" or, equally possibly, "to understand." The Roman military center gave way to the place where Judaism was re*built* through *understanding* of Torah. The pun is subtle, but the mythmaking is undeniable. Meanwhile, back in Jerusalem:

Vespasian left and sent Titus.

"And he said, 'Where is their God, the Rock in Whom they sought refuge?'" (Deut. 32:37). This verse refers to Titus, that evil one, who blasphemed against Heaven.

What did he do? He took a whore by the hand, entered into the Holy of Holies, spread forth a Torah scroll, and committed a transgression upon it. Then he took his sword, penetrated the veil of the Temple, and a miracle occurred and blood spurted forth. Titus thought he had killed God, as it is said, "Your foes roar in the midst of Your meeting place, they place their standards as ensigns" (Psalm 74:4). . . .

What did Titus do? He took the veil of the Temple and used it like a basket [Greek: *girguthani*] in which he put all of the vessels of the Sanctuary. He loaded them on a ship and went to have a triumph in his city of Rome. . . .

A storm arose at sea and threatened to capsize him. Titus reasoned, "It seems to me that their god only has power upon water. When Pharaoh came, he drowned him in water. When Sisera came, he drowned him in water. Now he wants to drown me in water. If the god of the Jews really has power, let him make war with me upon dry land!"

A voice came forth and said to him, "Evil one, son of an evil one, offspring of the evil Esau. I have a simple creature in My world named a gnat." *Why is it called "a simple creature?" For it has a mouth but has no rectum.* "Get up on dry land and make war with it!"

When Titus arrived at dry land, a gnat flew up his nose and drilled into his brain for seven years. . . .

When he died they opened his head and that gnat had grown to the size of a dove, two *liters* (Greek) in weight. (Babylonian Talmud Gittin 56a–b)

Titus was Vespasian's son and became Rome's emperor after him. His triumph over Jerusalem is commemorated in the (in)famous Arch of Titus in the Roman Forum, depicted below. As can be seen in the picture, Titus really did take the vessels of the Jerusalem Temple back to Rome. But let us look at how the story of Titus is spun by the rabbis. We can assume this is rabbinic fantasy by the simple expedient that much of the action takes place in the Holy of Holies, where no Jew would dare venture. So, they made it all up. Titus is "credited" with transgressing the three cardinal sins of Judaism at one fell swoop: he spills blood, he has forbidden sex, and if we count his sexual blasphemy as an act of sacral prostitution, he commits idolatry. In a medieval telling of this

ARCH OF TITUS—ROME

tale (Avot D'Rabbi Nathan 1), Titus smacks the altar with his penis and brays, "*Lykos, Lykos* You consume the flocks of the Jews and give them nothing in return." Give that storyteller credit for a memorable scene—the vulgar Titus calling God *Lykos*, Greek for a ravenous wolf (think: lycanthropy).

I cannot help but think that the tale of Titus and his whore is inspired by his real-life mistress Berenice. Titus met his girlfriend well before the revolt against Rome. She was the daughter of the Jewish client King Herod Agrippa I and sister to his successor, King Herod Agrippa II—a genuine Jewish princess. Titus was about a decade younger than Berenice, and he successfully wooed her for his own. Poor Berenice. After Titus was elevated to emperor, the Roman courtiers forced him to send her back to her Jewish community in ignominy. You really can't make this stuff up.

Back in our Talmudic tale: when God deigns to seek vengeance for Titus's blasphemies, Titus is at sea. The story imagines how the polytheist thinks. "Well," says Titus, as he dutifully recites a version of Jewish history, "God must be like Neptune, limited in his power only to the seas." It is curious that the rabbis presume the pagan emperor had some knowledge, however fractured, of Jewish history. He mentions Sisera and Pharaoh. According to the Bible, Sisera's chariots were mired in mud when rain swamped him (see Judges 4–5). And Pharaoh and his troops were drowned during the Israelite crossing of the Red Sea (Ex. 14–15). Thus did God defeat Israel's enemies.

In our story, Titus avoids drowning and makes it back to Rome for a triumphal procession celebrating his and his father's victory over the Jews. God has other plans. Instead of a triumph, God sends Titus a tumor. Here, too, we are in the realm of fantasy. The revenge the Jews imagine for the man who destroyed the Temple is cruel and follows the rabbinic rule of punishment measure for measure. Titus, that a—hole, is destroyed by a creature so lowly it does not even have a rectum. And the gnat/tumor grows to the size of a two-liter dove—exactly what used to be sacrificed to God on the altar that Titus trashed.

There is an undercurrent of irony here. Vespasian and his son, precisely because they put down the rebellion against Rome, are reviled in rabbinic memory, even as there is ambivalence about them. Among the emperors of Rome, Vespasian fared far better in history than the rabbis allow. He became emperor in the long year after Nero's reign, a year referred to by Romans as the year of the four emperors. Between Nero and Vespasian were the emperors Galba, Otho, and Vitellius, none of whom died a natural death. Is it any wonder that the man who controlled the Roman armies ascended to the royal purple? And yet, Vespasian was an old soldier, emphatically not a patrician of the Julio-Claudian emperors' family. He compensated by being the first to endow a chair of learning in Rome—the imperial chair of rhetoric. While others remember him for his contributions to Roman culture, the Jews have a more fraught recollection. In retrospect, I wonder whether Vespasian's endowment of an academic chair helped give rise to the rabbinic notion that he helped found the town of Yavneh, where the rabbis gathered to study Torah after the Temple's destruction.

In 132–135 CE, the Jews again rebelled against Rome, and they recall the depredations of the brutal quashing of the uprising with even more surprising ambiguity. Hadrian, who ruled from 117 to 138 CE, was among the most urbane of Roman emperors. Hipster that he was, Hadrian sported a beard, took a gay lover, and was fluent in Greek. The rabbis recall Hadrian with a certain degree of bemusement. Hadrian visited Roman Palestine in the years before the rebellion. In fact, in 1975, a tourist visiting Israel who was searching for ancient coins accidentally unearthed a bronze statue of him in the Beit Shean valley, in the Roman city of Scythopolis. Readers will not be surprised to learn that in addition to the nice statue of Hadrian, archeologists discovered a synagogue in the town, complete with its requisite menorah depiction and the word *shalom*.

This did not stop the messianic pretender Bar Kokhba from rebelling. Hadrian's perceived softness may have fed the revolutionaries' resolve to strike against him. In a Midrash on the Song of Songs (2:1:16), a fifth-century rabbi looks back and says simply of Hadrian: "He killed

4,000,000 Jews." By the Middle Ages the number has swollen to imagine Hadrian putting 80,000,000 Jews to death. I do not deny that the death of thousands, perhaps hundreds of thousands, of Jews was tragic. Yet I must point out how obviously, even ridiculously, these numbers have been inflated. Hadrian is recalled as having banned many Jewish practices, including Torah study, which was the background to the Rabbi Aqiba martyrdom story I recounted earlier.

Hadrian's having a bronze statue does not reflect much about the attitudes of the Jews toward him. After all, he did build the pagan city of Aelia Capitolina upon the ruins of Jerusalem. Although there is every reason to expect unremitting hatred in rabbinic recounts of Hadrian, where he is standardly referred to as "Hadrian, may his bones be ground to dust," we actually find a much more ambiguous record.

In the fifth-century Midrash on Genesis, the rabbis can imagine:

> Hadrian, may his bones be ground to dust, asked Rabbi Ye-hoshua son of Hanania (an elder contemporary of the emperor), "How did the Blessed Holy One create His world?"
>
> The rabbi replied that God had taken six packets of fire and patted them together with six packets of snow: one for each of the four cardinal directions, one for above and one more for below.
>
> Hadrian replied, "Is that really possible?"
>
> The rabbi brought him into a small room and asked him to stretch out his arms east, west, north, and south. He said, "That's how God did it."

I don't suppose this conversation really took place, despite Hadrian's advent in Roman Palestine at the time this story is set. I am not convinced, either, by the rabbi's pseudo-science. What does impress me, though, is the utterly innocuous nature of the conversation. Instead of being depicted as a murderous tyrant, Hadrian is painted as curious enough about creation to ask a rabbi. The Hadrian depicted in the story is polite, even deferential, to the Creator.

Another Hadrian story tells how he is sympathetic, even kind, to an elderly Jew.

Hadrian, may his bones be ground to dust, was strolling on the pathways of Tiberius when he saw an old man digging and hoeing. Hadrian said to him, "Grandpa, grandpa! Had you worked early you wouldn't need to be working so late!"

The old man replied, "I worked early and I work late [in my life]. I do what pleases my Master in Heaven."

Hadrian said, "By your life, old man, how old are you today?"

He said, "I am one hundred years old."

Hadrian replied, "You are one hundred and still digging and hoeing?! Do you think you will be able to eat the fruits of your labor?"

The old man said, "If I merit, I shall eat. And if not, just as my ancestors labored for me, so I labor for my offspring."

Hadrian said, "By your life, if you merit eating the fruits of the tree you are planting, let me know."

After much time, the tree bore figs. The old man said, "The time has come to tell the Emperor."

What did he do? He filled a wheelbarrow [Greek: *kartella*] with figs and went to the gate of the palace. The guards asked, "What is your business?"

He said, "To appear before the Emperor."

When he entered Hadrian asked, "What is your business?"

He replied, "I am the old man who was digging and hoeing. You said if I merited to eat the fruit of those trees I should let you know. Now I have done so, and these are those figs."

Hadrian declared, "I command [Greek: *keleunin*] to bring forth a golden divan [Greek: *sellion*] to seat him. I further command that you empty the wheelbarrow of figs and replace it with dinars."

His courtiers asked him, "Would you give such honor to this old Jew?"

Hadrian replied, "His Creator honors him; shall I not also do so?" (Lev. Rabbah 25:5)

This story is a favorite folktale that revolves around the touching line the old man utters, "Just as my ancestors labored for me, so I labor for my offspring." Its sentiment of planting for those who come after is so lovely that it was used by a national Jewish charity for its fund-raising campaign. Indeed, in many versions of the story, it is a mere passerby who asks the old man the question that invites his memorable response. The story uses a well-known Greco-Roman rhetorical form, a *chreia* in Greek (more on that later).

In our otherwise Aramaic version of the tale, when Hadrian says, "I command," he does so in Greek, transliterated into Hebrew letters.

HADRIAN EQUESTRIAN STATUE—CAPITOLINE MUSEUMS, ROME

When the old man is seated on a divan, again we have a Greek term, which is why I used the loanword "divan" for my translation. When Hadrian's courtiers mildly object to his showing honor to a Jew, Hadrian rebukes them, complimenting God along with the elderly Jew. This is hardly the portrait of a bloodthirsty tyrant. The rabbis' ambivalence about Hadrian is readily apparent. Rome may have brutally put down a rebellion against it; but the empire, embodied in the emperor, apparently has its good points, too.

When Hadrian visited Roman Palestine in 130 CE, he met with his provincial governor, Tinius Rufus. Rufus was known to the Jews of the Land of Israel. It was he who was charged with brutally putting down the Bar Kokhba rebellion in the years 132–135. So it is curious to find that rabbinic literature records imaginary conversations between Rufus and the legendary Rabbi Aqiba, who may have supported the rebellion. Among these pieces of rabbinic performance is one about the mythical Sabbath River, Sambatyon:

> The evil Tyrannis Rufus asked Rabbi Aqiba, "What is today [the Sabbath] of all days?"
>
> He replied, "What are you among all men?"
>
> Rufus asked, "What did I say to you and what did you say to me!?"
>
> Aqiba explained, "You asked how the Sabbath is distinguished from the other days; while I asked how Rufus is distinguished among all men."
>
> Rufus replied, "The Emperor has honored me!"
>
> Aqiba noted, "So, too, the Blessed Holy One has honored the Sabbath."
>
> Rufus asked, "How can you prove this to me?"
>
> Aqiba said, "The River Sambatyon proves it, as it flows all week long, but rests on Shabbat."
>
> Rufus said, "Are you kidding me?!"
>
> Rabbi Aqiba said, "Well then, let the necromancer prove it. He can bring up the dead all week long, but not on Shabbat."

Rufus went and checked by raising his father from the dead. He rose all week long, but not on Shabbat. Rufus asked him, "Dad, since you died, you've converted to Judaism?! Why won't you rise on Saturday?"

His father told him, "Whoever may not observe the Sabbath among the living surely embraces it here . . . for all week long we are tortured, but on Shabbat we are allowed respite." (Gen. Rabba 11:5)

This is a lovely rabbinic parody. Even the most credulous believer in the veracity of rabbinic accounts would probably draw the line at ghost stories. And watch how the rabbis tweak Rufus by punning on his "first name" and calling him *tyrannis* (tyrant) instead of Tinius. Rufus and Rabbi Aqiba have an exchange in which they first speak past one another (an intriguing metaphor for rabbis and Roman culture), but eventually Rufus is set straight that Aqiba is answering his question about Shabbat. When Rufus presses Aqiba for proof, he resorts to natural science: the River Sambatyon. The Roman naturalist Pliny the Elder reported on such a "Sabbath" river in his *Natural History* (xxxi:24). When that's not sufficient proof, Aqiba appeals to supernatural science, as it were, and raises Rufus's father from hell. We are not meant to overlook the insult delivered with the assumption that Rufus's father is being tortured in Hades, even if Rufus is oblivious. But the joke is still on him, as his father welcomes in the Sabbath with relief and delight—just like the Jews do. This hearkens back to the report about Nero's converting. Rabbinic storytellers like the idea of pagans becoming Jewish as a sign of ultimate victory.

All that said, I once again must attend to tone. While other rabbinic texts make Rufus out to be Aqiba's tormentor, here he is presented as simply outwitted in dialogue. The tale does not disguise the pleasure with which the fifth-century editor of Genesis Rabbah includes a tale about Shabbat that mocks Rufus and his family. But aside from a snarky narrative, it is not really very damning of the Roman governor who so brutally put down a Jewish rebellion.

The emperors who visited Roman Palestine often come in for this kind of mocking. Diocletian was emperor from 284 to 305. Early in his reign, in ca. 286 CE, Diocletian visited the city of Tiberias, in Roman Palestine. The Jerusalem Talmud (Terumot 8:10, 46b) reports that the disciples of Rabbi Judah II suggested that before he was emperor, he was a swineherd. This is a clever shot at the emperor, as his plebeian origins were impugned by association with the emphatically not-kosher and, let's face it, filthy pig. In a fifth-century commentary on Leviticus, the rabbis say of Rome:

> Why is it likened to a pig? To tell you that just like the pig, when it wallows in filth, puts forth its feet [thus showing its split hooves] as though to claim it is a pure and kosher animal; so too this evil empire is arrogantly violent and steals, yet tries to appear as though they have justice by holding a tribunal [Greek: *bema*]. (Lev. Rabbah 13:5)

The sting of the story comes when the word they use is the same Greek term the Romans use for their tribunals (*bema*). The messages the rabbis deliver on Rome are decidedly mixed.

But then, there was the emperor Antoninus. He seemingly could do no wrong. There is neither ambiguity nor ambivalence; the Rabbis ♥ Antoninus. The trouble is, we cannot be sure exactly who this Emperor Antoninus actually was. There were seven emperors of the so-called Antonine imperial line, of whom five were called "the good emperors." Of those, we can eliminate Nerva and Trajan as far too early.

We can also drop Hadrian (may his bones be ground to dust) from the list of possibilities. We are left with two really viable candidates: they are Antoninus Pius, who ruled from 138 to 161 CE, and Marcus Aurelius Antoninus, who ruled from 161 to 180. I prefer Marcus Aurelius, not only because he was a Stoic philosopher who left twelve books of *Meditations* in Greek, but also because his years in office line up better with his rabbinic buddy, Rabbi Judah, Patriarch of the Jews of Palestine.

Judah, who is affectionately called Rebbi by his colleagues, published his Mishnah around 200 CE. So he would have been a much younger contemporary of Marcus Aurelius. Despite the lack of historical accuracy, rabbinic literature is replete with tales of the great "bromance" between Antoninus and Rebbi.

The Babylonian Talmud looks back upon the two of them with great nostalgia and with none of the venom it usually reserves for Rome. It imagines Antoninus seeking political advice from Rabbi Judah:

> Antoninus asked Rebbi, "I want to have my son Severus rule as Emperor after me and I want to declare the city of Tiberias an imperial colony [*colonia*]. If I ask for one they will grant me that, but if I ask for two they will not."
> Rebbi brought a fellow and had a second man ride on his shoulders. He gave a dove to the one on top and told the one below, "Tell your fellow to release the dove."
> Antoninus inferred from this that he should appoint Severus; and once he was emperor then he could make Tiberias an imperial colony. (Babylonian Talmud Avodah Zarah 10a)

We can only admire Rebbi's cagey advice. Without committing himself verbally, he acts out in mum-show what Antoninus needs to do to have his way. What is curious about the tale is that Marcus Aurelius had no son named Severus. In fact, none of the emperors mentioned just above had such a son. But Septimius Severus reigned as emperor from 193 to 211, so he would be an excellent candidate to be the son of Rebbi's "best friend forever." The years don't all quite match up, but the choice of Severus offers historical plausibility for the story. Rebbi has yet more advice.

> Antoninus complained that the grandees of Rome were opposing him. Rebbi took him to a garden where he plucked a radish. Day after day he did this. Antoninus inferred that he

should kill off his enemies one by one, rather than attack them all at once. (ibid.)

The Talmud then goes even further in its flight of the imagination about their relationship:

> Every day Antoninus would wait upon Rebbi; serving him food and drink. When Rebbi wanted to go to bed, Antoninus would bend down and say, "Climb upon me up to your bed."
>
> Rebbi protested, "It is not appropriate to treat the emperor so disrespectfully."
>
> Antoninus replied: "Would that I could be the mat beneath your seat in the World to Come!" (Babylonian Talmud Avodah Zarah 10b)

In Roman Palestine the rabbis never went quite this far. Instead, they imagine the emperor engaging Rebbi in more appropriate philosophical discourse. So, for example,

> Antoninus asked our holy Rabbi, "At the time when a person dies and the body has decayed, will the Blessed Holy One resurrect that person for judgment?"
>
> He replied, "While you are asking me about the body, which is impure, ask me also about the soul, which is pure." (Mekilta D'Rabbi Ishmael Shirta 2)

That's a nice conversation for a Stoic philosopher king to have with our holy rabbi. In fact, the rabbinic analogy to body and soul is a famous tale about how a blind and a lame watchman collaborate. This story of cooperation between blind and lame is also found in the classical Greek Anthology, a tenth-century collection of ancient Hellenistic literature. The story also is found in the earliest rabbinic commentary on Exodus, compiled in Roman Palestine during the generation immediately following that of Rebbi and Antoninus.

Note that Rebbi is called here "our holy Rabbi." The Palestinian Talmud tells a tale about Antoninus and Rebbi that explains why, while at the same time elevating Antoninus to almost otherworldly stature.

> There are indications that Antoninus converted to Judaism; and there are indications that Antoninus did not convert:
>
> They saw him on Yom Kippur with a broken shoe [observing the rabbinic prohibition against leather footwear on the holiday].
>
> But even the "Heaven-fearers" do this. . . .
>
> When Antoninus heard the verse "No uncircumcised person may eat of [the Paschal lamb]" (Ex. 12:48), he went and was circumcised. He went to Rebbi and said to him, "Rebbi, look at my circumcision!"
>
> Rebbi demurred, saying, "I have never looked at my own circumcision, now I should look at yours?!"
>
> Why was he called "our holy Rabbi?" Because he never looked at his circumcision in his life. . . .
>
> Rabbi Abbahu quoted Rabbi Lazar, "If the [God-fearers] are counted as righteous converts in the Messianic Future, Antoninus will be at the head of the line!" (Jerusalem Talmud Megillah 1:11 72b)

I have to wonder whether Rebbi really got his nickname by never looking down! And while I am snickering about that story, I should add that it is highly doubtful that an emperor called Antoninus converted to Judaism. It is not even likely that there was a Roman emperor who could qualify as a "Heaven-fearer." To refresh our memory, there was an inscription at Aphrodisias in Asia Minor that listed the names of "God fearers." It is likely that they were donors to the synagogue of some sort and that the two terms are synonymous. Maybe they were also sympathetic to Judaism—fellow-travelers, if you will. It is said that Nero's wife Agrippina also was keen on Jewish customs; but we cannot really know. Still, how likely is this designation for a Roman emperor?

We offer one more Talmudic text that might put this discussion in perspective.

Just a couple of folios after the story we just saw from the Jerusalem Talmud, we read:

> Antoninus made a Menorah for the synagogue. Rebbi heard about it and said, "Blessed is God who put it in his heart to make a Menorah for the synagogue." (Jerusalem Talmud Megillah 3:2 74a)

This report, I think, should not be discounted. The quintessential symbol of Judaism in the Roman world, menorahs were truly ubiquitous in synagogues. Synagogues from east to west had actual menorahs, bas reliefs, and frescoes of menorahs. We have even seen that a certain Socrates "made" a menorah. It could be that he, too, was a Gentile who made a dedicatory offering. Or, he could have been a Jew with a particularly Gentile-sounding name. Either way, when we combine the Talmudic report about Antoninus with the donor listings at Aphrodisias, we understand why some thought that the emperor was a "God-fearer." This no doubt gave rise to later confusion, because in rabbinic literature the term refers to semi-converts, or those who take up Jewish religious practices.

I am not particularly concerned with the historical reality regarding whether an emperor made a donation of a menorah, or wore broken sandals on Yom Kippur, or even flashed Rabbi Judah the Patriarch. What is of interest to me here is the ease with which the rabbis retail these stories with nary an objection that a Roman emperor could have affinities for Judaism and devotion to our holy Rabbi. Part of this is, of course, attributable to Jewish chauvinism. "Whom among us does not love Jews?" they seem to say. But there has been a shift in the rhetoric about the emperors who symbolize Rome that may be attributable to the passage of time. During the rebellions against the empire and their aftermaths, rabbis told stories that were negative or, perhaps, neutral. They indulged in parody and put-down. But two generations following

Bar Kokhba, by the turn of the third century, when the Pax Romana reached even Palestine, and with Judah, the popular Jewish patriarch, having good relations with Rome, the tone shifted toward the positive. It seems that after many years, Jacob/Israel reconciled with his martial brother Esau/Edom, who was Rome.

In the Roman Empire of that period, the Second Sophistic flourished. It was a movement that celebrated Greek education and literature and had a strong impact on the East, where Greek remained the lingua franca. The rabbis recognized that Roman instruction held some distinct benefits for them and for their movement. They increasingly adopted Roman traditions—in particular, Roman rhetoric. An education in rhetoric was the key to advancement in the Roman Empire. The Jews embraced a rhetorical education then as they have embraced education ever since to open the doors to success in the broader world.

MOSES AT DURA
Dura-Europos

AHASHVEROSH AND ESTHER IN DURA

Photo courtesy Yale University Art Gallery, Dura-Europos Archives

DURA SYNAGOGUE, LONG WALL
Photo by SodaBottle

DURA-EUROPOS SYNAGOGUE,
TORAH SHRINE OR SEAT OF MOSES
Photo by Marsyas

JEWISH CATACOMBS AT VIGNA RANDANINI, ROME

Photos by Robin Jensen, top fig. Burton Visotzky, lower fig.

ALEXANDER THE GREAT MOSAIC (NAPLES MUSEUM)
Photo by Carol Raddato

HERCULANEUM
Photo by Wolfgang Rieger

JEWISH CATACOMBS AT VIGNA RANDANINI, ROME

Photos by Robin Jensen

Beit Alpha synagogue mosaic

Photo by J. Schweig

Beit Alpha synagogue

Photo by J. Schweig

MADABA MAP, JORDAN

Photo by Jean Housen

CHAPTER V

RABBIS LEARN THE THREE RS: READING, WRITING, AND ROMAN RHETORIC

T here's an old joke about the comedians' convention that took place in the Catskills back in the 1950s. All the great stand-up artists were there, eating their way to heart attacks, so long as they didn't "die" on stage. Every night a different comic would provide dinner entertainment while his colleagues *fressed*. They'd sidle up to the microphone and snap off a series of numbers, such as "seventeen, six, forty-two, twenty." Mouths full to overflowing, the house roared their appreciation. A newcomer watched the scene with confusion. "I don't get it," he said to his buddy. "These guys recite a list of numbers and everybody laughs. What? Are they all playing the numbers?"

His more experienced colleague explained, "Naw, but these guys come here every year and they've heard every joke in the book. To save time, each joke has its own number. When they hear a stand-up comic run the numbers, they all remember the jokes and laugh. That's it."

The newcomer was astonished and determined to have his turn at the microphone. He trotted on stage and practically crooned into the mic: "Two, seven, nine, forty-four." The house was absolutely silent. Panicked, he tried again, "Six, fourteen, fifty-seven, three." The audience began booing. He left the stage before they started throwing things.

"OK, I still don't get it. The first guy said a bunch of numbers and they laughed their *tuchess*es off. I get up there and die on stage. What's the difference?"

His friend patiently explained, "It's how you tell it."

This could as easily be a joke about ancient Rome as the Catskills. In antiquity, everyone who was anyone learned rhetoric. That means that everyone knew the same set of anecdotes and stories about characters from Roman history. Everyone could trot out a well-known bon mot. What made you a successful rhetor in the Roman world was how you'd tell it.

This type of Greek education had a significant place within the Jewish community. In the Roman East, rhetoric depended on knowledge of Greek language and the Greek classics. Those legends were the source of the rhetorical equivalent of Borscht-belt jokes and stories. So it is surprising to read an early rabbinic text listing Greek—and, as we will see, Greek rhetoric—among the things Jews disdained after the three disastrous wars with Rome between 65 and 135 CE. It's from the Mishnah, that compendium of Jewish laws compiled by Rebbi Judah the Patriarch in approximately 200 CE. Rebbi Judah is looking back upon Jewish reactions to these so-called wars, referred to by the Greek loanword *polemus* (think: polemics).

> During the war [*polemus*] of Vespasian they decreed a prohibition against grooms wearing wedding crowns and against using the tambourine.
>
> During the war of [the provincial governor, General Lusius] Quietus (the so-called War of the Diaspora) they decreed a prohibition against bridal crowns and that a man should not teach his son Greek.

During the last war (the Bar Kokhba rebellion against Hadrian) they decreed a prohibition that brides no longer be carried through the city on a palanquin; but our rabbis permitted a bride to be carried through the city on a palanquin. (m. Sotah 9:17, following the text of the Cambridge manuscript)

I do not wish to minimize the damage inflicted by Rome upon the Jewish people in these military engagements: thousands were killed and exiled from their homes. Jews were banned from Jerusalem. The Jewish community was essentially helpless to respond in any significant way. This is what their reaction looked like seventy years after the final of those battles: Jews "got even" with Rome by not using tambourines! No more bridal crowns! Really? And *fuggidaboud* riding on a palanquin. Of course the rabbis, those good guys, they really knew how to make a girl happy. They rescinded that prohibition and permitted brides to ride palanquins. Who was it in the Jewish community, referred to as "they," who did the forbidding until "our rabbis" came along and said the equivalent of, "Oh let the poor girl have a happy wedding day. After all, haven't we suffered enough?" I have no idea who "they" are. I am suspicious that the rabbis of this Mishnah have set up a straw man intent on prohibiting things, so that our dear rabbis can come along and once more permit them. Yay rabbis!

A palanquin is the equivalent of those open-top stretch limos from which prom goers wave their arms and torsos, all the while snapping selfies. The scandalized Jewish community of Late Antiquity apparently prohibited palanquins in the aftermath of all that death and destruction. Who knows, it could lead to mixed dancing or some other horrific form of levity. The response seems so feeble it's risible. It's as though modern Jews decided to forbid wedding caterers to serve mini-frankfurters to punish Germany for World War II. So there!

My jaundiced reading of this text is pertinent here because of the line almost hidden away in the middle section of the Mishnah, right after the business about bridal crowns: "that a man should not teach his son Greek." Oh? Did "they" really prohibit teaching Greek? How then might the eager Jewish young urban professionals find a leg up in the Roman East? Greek was essential for their career advancement. Learning Greek for the Jews of the Roman Empire was functionally equivalent to learning English for immigrants to America.

The same tractate of the Babylonian Talmud where the problematic Mishnah we just read is found also records a countertradition (Sotah 49b) attributed to Rebbi's father that says,

> There were a thousand students in my father's house, five hundred of whom learned Torah and five hundred of whom learned Greek wisdom.

A few words later, the Talmud qualifies this tradition by commenting that "the house of Rabban Gamaliel is different, because they had close relations with the [Roman] imperial government." Within rabbinic culture there was a pecking order among the members of the so-called rabbinic class of Palestine by political and socioeconomic criteria. Those who were wealthier were generally more acculturated to Greco-Roman society. Those who held political office were, of necessity, engaged in Roman politics and Greek and Latin culture. The more urbanized classes of Jews—and these surely included a significant proportion, likely the majority, of the rabbis—were more likely to see themselves as citizens of the Roman Empire and behave accordingly. What exactly did those yuppie students learn in the patriarch's house or school? The Greek wisdom referred to, in fact, meant Roman rhetoric. The rabbis and other Jews of Roman Palestine were given the basic grammar and rhetorical education that would be expected of any functionally literate citizen of the empire.

Libanius was the most famous teacher of rhetoric (after Aristotle, of course). He lived in the fourth century CE in Antioch, on the River Orontes, in what is today eastern Turkey. Libanius held forth at his school of rhetoric during the heyday of rabbinic Judaism that unfolded in the Galilee, just to his south. Among his students over the years,

Libanius could count hundreds of pagans and even some Christians who would grow up to become bishops of the church. We briefly met Libanius on our quick tour of Antioch. There, I pointed out that among his few Jewish students was the son of the Jewish patriarch of Palestine, who was either Rebbi's grandson or great-grandson. Rhetoric was what one needed to learn if one was to advance in the world. Much as parents try to send their kids to Ivy League schools today, those who were ambitious to advance them in the bureaucracy of the Roman world sent their children to study rhetoric with Libanius.

In Antioch they learned the basics: grammar, reading and writing, fluency in Greek, and the ability to quote the works of Homer and the other Greco-Roman classics by memory. This education was a *sine qua non* for anyone who wanted to work in imperial offices or as an attorney. Students studied with Libanius from one to three years, some perhaps as long as five or six years. Above all, they were trained to be sophists: young men who could speak extemporaneously, holding their audiences spellbound. They employed their skills in legal forensics; that is, interpreting and, even more importantly, arguing the law on behalf of clients. The most basic tool of their education was their ability to produce the appropriate exemplary story at the right moment and to tell it in a fresh way, at length or briefly, as their case required. "Six, fourteen, fifty-seven, three." See? Now it's funny!

These anecdotes (in Greek: *chreia*) are often called "pronouncement stories," as the main character says something memorable. They constituted the basic repertoire of every student schooled in rhetoric. We know this from ancient rhetorical texts. Students' rhetorical practice slates have survived in many places across the Mediterranean basin, including its eastern shores. These student copybooks conform to the formal training manuals that also survive. Teaching rhetoric was an art honed for almost a thousand years. All the evidence teaches us the importance of the *chreia*.

The anecdote we recounted in chapter three about Alexander the Great in Cartagena qualifies as a *chreia*, as it ends with the pronouncement, "I, Alexander of Macedon, was a foolish king until I came to Cartagena and learned sound counsel from its women." Here's a *chreia* about Alexander the Great from Libanius's textbook for his students: "Alexander, upon being asked by someone where he kept his treasures, pointed to his friends." Maybe that's why they called him "the Great." In Libanius's still-existent textbook, the rhetorical exercise is given, and then he demonstrates how to tell it first briefly, then in paraphrase, then as demonstration of a cause, in a comparison, as an example for others, as testimony from ancient authority, and, finally as a brief epilogue. The training in rhetoric was painstaking and thorough.

Another short example of a *chreia* comes from Libanius's personal correspondence. He sent a letter to his relative Aristaenetus in the year 393 CE, hand-delivered by one of his students. The letter opens, "The bearer is both Pelagius's son and mine; for the former begat him, while I taught him to love rhetoric." This saying is striking, as it makes the teacher a second father to his pupil. I compare it to a Mishnah (ca. 200 CE) that teaches, "His father brought him into this world, while his rabbi, who taught him wisdom, brings him to the world to come." In this rabbinic encomium, the rabbi is even more important than the father; for it is the rabbi who teaches wisdom or Torah, and so brings him salvation.

Around the same time as the Mishnah, early in the third century CE, a Greek philosopher named Diogenes Laertius quoted Aristotle (fourth century BCE): "Teachers who educated children deserved, he said, more honor than parents who merely gave them birth; for bare life is furnished by the one, while the other ensures a *good* life." Libanius was borrowing his rhetorical trope from Diogenes Laertius and not the Mishnah. Yet the Mishnah's rhetorical elevation of the teacher is exactly the same as that attributed to Aristotle.

Diogenes Laertius also tells us the tale of an earlier Diogenes, this one a founder of cynic philosophy, who lived at the same time as Aristotle. Among Diogenes the Cynic's observations, we are told the following *chreia*:

STUDENT BEARING LETTER—ARCHEOLOGICAL MUSEUM OF MILAN

When visiting Megara, Diogenes looked at their sheep, whose valuable wool was protected by leather jackets; yet the Megarans' children ran around naked. Diogenes remarked, "It is better to be a Megaran's lamb than his son."

This *chreia* has three notable points. First, in the story Diogenes is a foreigner, who has come from afar to comment upon what he sees. Second, he has a witty remark about the folks he sees. Finally, there are those crazy sheep dressed in leather vests.

Forty-five years ago the scholar Henry Fischel pointed out that these three motifs also can be found in a story about the renowned Jewish sage Hillel:

This law was forgotten by the elders of Betayra. Once upon a time the 14th of Nissan (when the paschal sacrifice takes place) fell on Shabbat and they did not know whether the performance of the paschal sacrifice overrode Sabbath prohibitions or not. They said, "There is a Babylonian named Hillel who served his teachers Shammaya and Avtalyon. He may know whether the paschal sacrifice overrides Sabbath prohibitions or not. Perhaps he will be of help" . . .

They asked him, "What shall we do, for people have not brought their knives with them to perform the sacrifice (and are forbidden from carrying them on Shabbat)?"

He said to them, "I heard this law but I have forgotten it. *But leave it to the Jews; if they are not prophets, they are the children of prophets.*"

Indeed, everyone whose paschal offering was a sheep tucked the knife into its wool and everyone whose paschal offering was a goat tied his knife between the goat's horns. That way the paschal offerings carried the knives themselves. When Hillel saw this he remembered the law and said, "This is what I heard from Shammaya and Avtalyon." (Palestinian Talmud Pesahim 6:1, 33a)

This very Jewish telling of the *chreia* is set in the first century, when the Temple still stood and the Jews were bringing their Passover sacrifices. A legal ruling is called for, and Hillel the Babylonian is consulted and makes a pronouncement about what he sees. He memorably plays on the words of the prophet Amos—a sheep breeder—who said, "I am not a prophet, nor am I the son of a prophet" (Amos 7:14). So we have a foreigner who comments wittily about the people he observes, while the sheep cavort. This is an impressive rabbinic retelling of an ancient *chreia*.

The rabbis had their own cycles of *chreia*, as well. Hillel is a popular character in many of the *chreia* of the rabbis. In the Midrash we read,

Hillel was once walking with his disciples. When he went to take leave they asked him, "Master, where are you going?"

Hillel replied, "I am going to do a kindness for the guest in my home."

They asked, "Do you have guests every day?"

Hillel said, "Is not my lonely soul a guest in my body? For one day it is here and on the morrow it departs." (Lev. Rabbah 34:3)

One of the most famous of all rabbinic stories is a *chreia* involving Hillel:

Once a gentile came to Shammai and said, "Convert me on the condition that you teach me the entire Torah while I stand on one foot." Shammai pushed him away with the builder's cubit that he was holding.

He came to Hillel who converted him, saying, "What is hateful to you, do not to your fellow. This is the entire Torah. The rest is commentary. Go, study." (Babylonian Talmud Shabbat 31a)

This tale is one of a series of Hillel anecdotes collected on the Talmudic folio just quoted. In each, Shammai the Elder plays the curmudgeon, a foil to the warm embrace of Hillel. The punch line of this particular *chreia* is the negative form of the Golden Rule—a platitude that was omnipresent in the Greco-Roman world, attributed to Seneca (a contemporary of Hillel) and to Jesus (another contemporary of Hillel), among others. I love the way the story makes the Golden Rule so rabbinic-sounding by insisting that there must also be commentary and that the newly minted convert now must go study. All of these details are predictable, especially in an academic setting. What seems unique to our tale is the clever challenge, "while I stand on one foot." Yet even this is a Greco-Roman commonplace. In the first century, the Greek essayist Plutarch (Sayings of the Spartans #18) reports this *chreia*:

A man who was visiting Sparta stood for a long time upon one
foot, and said to a Spartan, "I do not think that you, sir, could
stand upon one foot as long as that."

The Spartan interrupted and said, "No, but there isn't a
goose that couldn't do that."

I suppose we should be grateful that the rabbis' version of the *chreia*
resisted imagining a goose standing on one foot on its way to being
sacrificed in the Jerusalem Temple as a side dish for the paschal lamb.
The *chreia* form we are dealing with is quintessentially Greco-Roman,
as clear a staple of Greco-Roman culture as talking baseball would be
among American males. The only difference with the rabbis' examples
is local color and Jewish law. In fact, if you think about it, the joke about
the Jewish comedians in the Catskills is also a *chreia*.

One of the longest-running performances of Roman culture is found
in a type of Greco-Roman literature called the symposium. Literally, the
sym-posium is a cocktail party. *Sym* is Greek for "together," as in sympathy (having fellow feeling). *Posium* is from the Greek word meaning
"to drink." It is related to the English word *potable*. So a symposium is a
cocktail party, specifically a literary cocktail party. I have no doubt that
cocktail parties were regularly held in the ancient world, just as they are
today. But the symposium is a cocktail party where the chatter is decidedly bookish. Maybe we can still find parties like that near Columbia or
Harvard. But in the Roman world, the point was to write a story about
a bunch of famous people at a cocktail party. Whether or not they were
actually there is not important. The point was to show them drinking
a few cups of wine, nibbling crudités, and all the while cleverly quoting
the classics. Indeed, it would be fair to refer to the symposium as a literary genre, which dates as early as Plato's *Symposium* in the fourth century BCE, all the way to Macrobius's *Saturnalia* in the early fifth century
CE—contemporary with the Jerusalem Talmud. For 750 years, Greeks
and Romans reveled in the literature presumably quoted, the speeches
supposedly made, the drinks quaffed, and the scandals whispered during
the symposia.

The recipe for a successful symposium starts, of course, with wine. At least three cups, preferably more, and ideally you would need between three and five famous guests. Macrobius describes a symposium at which he imagined all the guests drinking together, even though some were already long dead. They eat hors d'oeuvres, which they dip into a briny sauce. Their appetite is whetted by sharp vegetables, radishes, or romaine lettuce. The Greek word for these veggies is *karpos*. Each food is used as a prompt to dig through one's memory to find apposite bookish quotes about it. The writer Athenaeus (who was actually born in Egypt and lived in Rome, his name notwithstanding) cites two hundred works of literature, many long lost to us except by his mention of their having been quoted during his long cocktail party. Above all, guests at a symposium love to quote Homer, the divine Homer. Quoting his work was, to them, like a Baptist preacher quoting the Bible or an English major spouting Shakespeare. It showed you were well schooled.

As the main course was brought in on platters, more wine was mixed with water. Civilized Romans considered it uncouth to drink their wine neat. Instead, they added a good splash of water, warm if the wine needed a little help in bringing out its bouquet. If you were fancy, you served the wine over ice or snow, not an easy thing to have on hand in Late Antiquity. Think of the snow cone as the epitome of classiness. If the wine was wretched, well, they added sugar (now think of Manischewitz). Alcohol in antiquity was limited to wine or beer—no one figured out how to distill hard alcohol until the high Middle Ages. To kick off a symposium, a libation was poured to Bacchus. Then the dinner guests took their places reclining on pillows, leaning on their left arms, and using their right hands to eat. Of course, they washed their fingers before eating their Mediterranean flatbreads, scooping up meats and poultry—no forks back then.

Athenaeus records a debate about dessert, a sweet paste of fruit, wine, and spices. Many think it a nice digestive, but Athenaeus quotes Heracleides of Tarentum, who argues that such a lovely dish ought to be the appetizer, eaten at the outset of the meal. After the sumptuous meal and the endless quotation of texts (recalled by mnemonic devices), the symposium diners sang their hymns of thanksgiving to the gods. Then, the burlesque show began. Scantily clad women called "flute girls" did what they did best (hint: it did not actually involve wind instruments), while vaudevillians worked the room for vulgar laughs. The signal for the descent into debauchery was intoned in Greek: *api komias*—to the comedians!

All of this should seem suspiciously familiar to anyone who has ever attended a Passover Seder. The traditional Seder begins with a cup of wine, and blessings to God are intoned. Then hands are washed in preparation for eating the dipped vegetables, called *karpos*, the Greek word faithfully transliterated into Hebrew in the Passover Haggadah. Like the symposiasts, Jews dip in brine. The traditional Haggadah recalls who was there at the earliest Seders: Rabbi Eliezer, Rabbi Yehoshua, Rabbi Elazar ben Azariah, Rabbi Aqiba, and Rabbi Tarphon (a Hebraized version of the Greek name Tryphon). The conversation is prompted by noting the foods that are served and by asking questions whose answers quote sacred Scripture.

There is more. Traditionally the Passover banquet is eaten leaning on the left side, on pillows. Appetites are whetted by bitter herbs and then sweetened by the pastelike Haroset (following the opinion of Heracleides of Tarentum?). Seder participants even scoop up food in flatbread. Following the Passover meal there are hymns to God.

But the rabbis drew the line at vaudeville: no flute girls, no comedians. Indeed, the Mishnah instructs, "We do not end the meal after eating the paschal lamb by departing *api komias*." That final phrase, thanks to the Talmud of Jewish Babylonia, where they did not know Greek, has come to be Hebraized as "*afi-komen*," the hidden piece of matzo eaten for dessert. But in Roman Palestinian they define the term quite accurately: "*Api komias* refers to comedians." As long ago as 1957, Siegfried Stein wrote the authoritative "The Influence of Symposia Literature on the Literary Form of the Pesah Haggadah." It seems that the reason this night is different from all other nights is that the rabbis adopted the structure of the Greco-Roman symposium banquet for the Jewish feast of freedom, perhaps at the end of the first century CE.

This quoting of texts and placing books at the center of the rabbinic enterprise is a reflection of the Greco-Roman culture in which the rabbis lived. In the Passover Seder, the rabbis frequently quoted from the Bible. Furthermore, the ways in which they selectively quoted and interpreted set the course for their readings of Scripture for centuries to come. The elucidations that the rabbis offered for Scripture employ the same methods of interpretation that the Alexandrian Greeks did when they read Homer and, later, as the Sophists did in construing Greco-Roman law using those rules of understanding. I have already quoted from Libanius's textbook teaching his students how to be effective lawyers and orators by using a *chreia*. The rabbis employed the same skill set to advocate for Jewish law and sway the hearts and minds of the Jews toward their interpretations of the Torah and Judaism.

My teacher Professor Saul Lieberman wrote back in the 1940s and '50s about the rabbis' regular use of Greco-Roman interpretive strategies in their Midrash (Scriptural interpretation). He lists a broad range of Greek terms and styles that the rabbis shared. In some instances Professor Lieberman even suggests that the rabbis adopted these methods directly from the Greeks and Romans. When the Alexandrians read Homer and were stumped by a difficult term, they often used another verse of the *Iliad* or *Odyssey* to unlock the opaque first verse. Lieberman calls this interpreting Scripture by Scripture. There is a lovely example in the Passover Haggadah that aptly illustrates the method.

There is a difficult phrase in Deuteronomy 26:5, which is the beginning of the story of the Exodus in the Passover ritual. In English we tend to translate the verse so that it makes sense: "We went down to Egypt . . . *few in number.*" But the Hebrew text, *b'metai m'at,* is obscure and difficult. The word for "few" is: *m'at.* The other Hebrew word in the phrase, *b'metai,* assuredly does not mean "in number," no matter how well it works in English. I lean toward translating the entire phrase more accurately, as "mortals few," guessing the word *b'metai* shares the Hebrew root *met,* which means "corpse." My translation of Deuteronomy 26:5 would read, "We went down to Egypt . . . *mortals few.*"

So how does the Haggadah interpret Scripture by Scripture? It pairs Deuteronomy 26:5 with Deuteronomy 10:22, "with seventy persons (*nefesh*) did your ancestors descend to Egypt." The explanation of the difficult term comes in the juxtaposition itself. The word "few" in Deuteronomy 26:5 is presumed to be equivalent to "seventy" of the other verse. The latter verse's word "persons" then defines the difficult term *b'metai*, which is why I translated it as "mortals."

For the Greeks, another way of "solving" difficult passages of Homer was to use that most Alexandrian of interpretive techniques: allegory. In allegory, the interpreter is essentially saying, "this means that." When my high school teacher explained Hemingway's *The Old Man and the Sea*, she pointed out that the old fisherman Santiago is allegorically understood as a Christ figure. His hands bleed, he carries the mast as Jesus carried his cross, and so on. We are able to understand Hemingway's old fisherman as Jesus, "fisher of men," so long as we can say "this means that."

We also can see the method at work in the Passover Haggadah, where verses from Deuteronomy 26:7 are read with this lens. The method of interpretation is pure Greek allegory: "This means that."

"God saw our affliction" this means that God saw the separation of husbands from their wives. . . .

. . . "and our burden" this means the sons who were thrown into the Nile. . . .

. . . "and our pressure" this means the Egyptians' oppression of us.

These methods of interpretation persist throughout rabbinic midrashic readings of the Bible. After the destruction of the Jerusalem Temple in 70 CE, rabbinic interpretation of Scripture became urgent; the absence of the sacrificial cult that figures so prominently throughout the Five Books of Moses required that these biblical passages be reinterpreted. Other passages needed explication so that observance of Torah law might continue. The rabbis established a virtual cottage industry of interpreting the Bible. Midrash—rabbinic interpretation of the

Bible—was the calling card of their movement. Masters and disciples studied the sacred text and reread it with a keen eye toward proving its eternal relevance.

The earliest rabbis compiled lists of rules for interpretation. Their debt to Roman modes of interpretation is palpable. One famous list begins with two rules that were patently taken from the world of Roman rhetoric. The first of those is reasoning from minor premise to major premise. Let me give you two examples of how it works, one from the Passover Haggadah and a second relating to Passover observance.

In the Haggadah we count and recount the many marvels God wrought during the Exodus from Egypt. We list each miracle individually, and we sing *"Dayyenu,"* which means "it would have been enough." The point is sweet: any *one* of those miracles would have been awesome and amazing, how much the more so *all* of the many miracles of the Exodus and the miracles during the years of wandering in the wilderness. The key to understanding this passage comes in the phrase "how much the more so." We have gone from the minor/weaker—one single miracle—to the major/stronger—a whole heap of miracles. If we are grateful for one, *a fortiori*, we are grateful to God for the many, many miracles God bestowed upon the Jewish people. Did you catch my use of Latin there? A *fortiori* means "to the major/stronger." You can see it relates to the rule of interpretation from minor to major, or from weak to strong, by looking at the Latin root "fort" (think: fortitude). A *fortiori* reasoning was a principle of Roman rhetoric.

Here is another example, this one about observing the detailed rules of Passover. Let us reason from minor to major. If on the Passover holiday it is permitted to cook, still, an observant Jew is not permitted to write on the holiday. *How much the more so* on Shabbat, when it is *not* permitted to cook, it is not permitted to write! A *fortiori; q.e.d. (quod erat demonstrandum* = thus it has been demonstrated).

We move on to the second rule borrowed from Greco-Roman rhetoric, called in Hebrew *gezera shavah,* "an equation of equals." You can take my word that this phrase is awkward Hebrew. It is a rather literal translation of the Greek term taught by our friend Libanius: *syngkrisis pros ison,* which means an "equation of equals." As a rule for interpretation, it is pretty sensible. If you don't know what a given word means in one context, find it elsewhere and infer from the second context what it means in the first place. The earliest rabbis are somewhat restrained in their uses of this interpretive method. Here's an example of how they interpreted the Deuteronomy 26 passage we've been quoting from the Passover Haggadah:

> "And the Egyptians **oppress**ed us" (Deut. 26:6). As it is said,
> "So they put task masters over them in order to **oppress** them
> with their burdens, that they build garrison cities for Pharaoh:
> Pithom and Raamses." (Ex. 1:11)

How do we know what it meant when Deuteronomy said that Egypt oppressed the Israelites? We look to a passage in Exodus that uses the same term for "oppression" and provides some details for interpretation. The "oppression" is understood as building garrison cities for Egypt. This is a way of interpreting Scripture with Scripture, but also specifically zeroing in on a common word the two verses share. That's the comparison of equals.

Later rabbis, bless their hearts, got absolutely slap-happy finding the same Hebrew verbal root all over the Bible and then inferring all kinds of stuff from one context to the next. So long as two verses shared a word in common, those rabbis asserted that they were actually about the same thing. You can appreciate how radical a means of interpretation this could be when the rabbis blithely say that verse A has the word "to" in it, and verse B has the word "to" in it, hence they must be talking about the same thing. Wow, using this method you can make anything mean anything you want it to. Cool, but perhaps a bit scary when we realize that the rabbis are making restrictive rulings about what Jews can and cannot do—Jewish law. By the fourth century, the rabbis themselves decided to call a halt to this type of radical interpretation; it was too slippery a slope.

The rabbis were more comfortable invoking Greek rules for interpreting Scripture when the material was nonlegal (aggadic), and so the stakes didn't seem quite so high. They were sufficiently relaxed that they called these interpretive techniques by their original Greek names. We will briefly review two: *geometria* (related to the term *geometry*) and *notarikon* (like a notary public).

In *geometria*, and this is equally true in Greek or Hebrew, each letter has a numerical value. If this worked in English, we'd say that a=1, b=2, c=3, d=4, e=5, and so on. So the word "cab" would have a value of 6 (3+1+2), while "dad" would have a value of 9 and so be "equivalent to "Ed" (you can do the math). In Greek α=1, β=2, γ=3, et cetera. In Hebrew א =1, ב =2, ג =3, so that in Hebrew the word for father, Abba (אבא), adds up to 4 (1+2+1). How does it work in Scriptural interpretation? An example from the fifth-century Genesis Rabbah (42:2) comments on the curious fact that in Genesis 14:14, Abraham hears that his nephew has been taken captive and rides out to his rescue with 318 warriors. And so, you really have to ask: where did they all come from?

> Rabbi Shim'on ben Laqish says, "It was Abraham's servant Eliezer, all by himself; for the numerical value of the name Eliezer equals 318 (א=1; ל=30; י= 10; ע=70; ז=7; ר=200)!"

Thanks to *geometria* we can now imagine Abraham and his servant Eliezer riding off to do battle, like Don Quixote and Sancho Panza.

And what about that other Greek method, *notarikon?* It presumes that each word is, in fact, shorthand, a series of acronyms forming a new amalgam, like "scuba" (=Self-Contained Underwater Breathing Apparatus) or "CentCom" (=Central Command). The *notarius* was the Greek shorthand writer who served as court reporter and recorded verbatim an ad-lib speech. If one assumes that words of Scripture can be read as such, then through *notarikon* we might assume that the first word of the Torah, *beresheet* ("In the beginning"), is a form of shorthand and may be divided into two constituent words: *bara sheet*. If we translate these Hebrew and Aramaic words, as did the rabbis, we may conclude that God created (*bara*) six (*sheet*) things before God created anything else.

Earlier, when I was describing the Passover Seder and the symposium, I mentioned that at some point during the symposium, before it descended into debauchery, the narrator summarized the evening's discussions and quotations using mnemonic or memory devices. In the Passover Haggadah, when the ten plagues are enumerated, Rabbi Yehudah recalls them by means of such a memory device. It says in Hebrew that he used *simanim*. The singular is *siman*, which is simply a transliteration of the Greek word *seimeion*, a sign or mnemonic. We use the word in English, too. English majors will recognize the word *semiotic*. Sailors will wave the flag in *semaphore*. The code succinctly delivers the longer message.

The symposium, of course, frequently quoted from what the Greeks called "the divine Homer." Indeed, Homer's *Iliad* and *Odyssey* were central to the entire Greco-Roman canon. Greeks did not, perhaps, afford the esteem to Homer that Jews show to the Torah scroll. However, Homer's poems were the texts that were used in teaching Greek reading, grammar, and spelling. Homer was memorized by students, and the myths of Homer pervaded the culture. Interpreting Homer was what gave the Alexandrian commentators something to do each day at their famous library.

The very methods the Alexandrians used for understanding Homer's works became the methods the rabbis themselves used to interpret the Bible. Yes, the rabbis adapted the reading strategies of the Greeks to read and interpret their own Hebrew canon. To say this another way: the rabbis read the Bible through the lenses of their own time. Furthermore, the division of Homer's epics the *Iliad* and *Odyssey* into twenty-four books each was the inspiration for the rabbis' creatively enumerating the Hebrew Bible as twenty-four books.

Homer and his books were the premier example that rabbis used when referring to works of Greek literature. Indeed, the rabbis grappled with Homer's status in their own community. The Mishnah refers to him explicitly in a debate they imagined taking place between the ancient Sadducees and Pharisees on the canonical status of Scripture. The Mishnah teaches:

> The Saducees say: We complain against you Pharisees, for you say that sacred Scripture renders one's hands unfit, yet the books of Homer do not! . . . Rabbi Yohanan explained that as they are revered, so is their ability to render unfit. The Bible, which is revered, renders the hands unfit; while the works of Homer are not revered, so they do not render hands unfit. (Yadayim 4:6)

This rule seems counterintuitive. I might expect that unfitness should characterize unwanted books. Yet the rabbis wished to protect Jewish sacred texts from stains, book-worms, and vermin. To do so they declared that sacred texts would henceforth "render the hands ritually unfit" if they were touched. In the rabbinic mind-set, no one whose hands were unfit would then eat food when handling books, since by merely touching the food, it also became unfit—and therefore forbidden to consume. This prohibition kept people from eating anywhere near biblical texts. The result of affording this extraordinary degree of protection means that any book that "renders the hands ritually unfit" is considered canonical or sacred to the rabbis. The Mishnah cannot resist taking a poke at Homer in the contrast they make. The Torah is sacred, which must mean then that Homer is, in essence, secular and presumably not revered. So there!

In truth, the works of Homer were revered by the Greeks much as was the Torah by the rabbis. The Palestinian Talmud (Sanhedrin 10:1, 28a) to some degree recognizes this when it declares that reading Homer is permissible. Yet the rabbis' ambivalence is apparent when they explain that one who reads Homer is not reading a forbidden document, but rather it is like "reading a secular document."

In other Jewish legal contexts, Homer's "secular" nature is contrasted by the rabbis to the sacred nature of Jewish texts. On the Sabbath, it is forbidden to carry objects from a private domain into the public domain. "But what if there is a fire on Shabbat?" the rabbis ask. Their answer is that the Bible must be saved. The Babylonian Talmud (Hullin 60b, following the manuscript readings) goes so far as to say that there are many verses of Scripture that seem random and uninspired and so might be thought appropriate "to burn as one would allow the books of Homer to burn" and not be saved on Shabbat. Yet they rule that in the end, *all* verses of Hebrew Scripture are essential Torah and must be saved, while Homer, alas, may not be saved. I think we can infer from this ruling that there were Jewish institutions that had both Torah scrolls as well as scrolls of Homer housed within them!

Finally, in a poignant short narrative, the medieval Midrash to Psalms (1:8) imagines King David, purported author of all of the Psalms, yearning that his poetry will "be studied like the Mishnah is studied, and not merely like the songs of Homer." What a lovely anachronism. David yearns for his poetry to be studied like the Mishnah, which in fact was composed twelve hundred years later than Psalms. What do all three works—Psalms, Mishnah, and the epics of Homer—have in common? They were regarded by their communities as sacred texts, each in its own fashion. And each was recited publicly, which is to say chanted aloud by memory.

I told you the story about Bar Kappara and his public recitation of three hundred fox fables to spoil the feast that was given to appease him. The rabbis used fox fables, Aesop's fables, animal narratives, motifs from the Alexander romances, snippets of Homeric narrative, whatever it took to get their point across. Of course, even while they employed well-known Greek fables, they also drew heavily on the store of fabulous animal narratives in the Bible, which includes both a talking snake (Gen. 3) and a talking donkey (Num. 22).

One of the richest means the rabbis used to explicate complex ideas in simple, concrete, oral performance was the king parable. When the rabbis spoke about God, they did not employ lofty theology. Instead, they invoked a king parable, which opens with the phrase: "Let me give you an analogy. What does this matter resemble? A king of flesh and blood who . . ." There are hundreds of these king parables found through centuries of rabbinic literature. They provide a necessary rabbinic analogy to God, because unlike the Greeks, the rabbis did not develop an abstract theological vocabulary. Instead, they compared God to a human king, saying how God was either like or unlike that human monarch. Thus they were able to explain otherwise complicated notions in a memorable form. They also invoked these king parables to explicate verses of Scripture.

Most rabbinic king parables had two parts (not unlike the fables of Aesop): first the parable (*mashal*) and then the moral to the story or analogue to the parable (*nimshal*). What is astonishing about the rabbinic composition of these king parables is that the overwhelming majority of them have fairly precise parallels in Greco-Roman literature. In 1903 a scholar named Ignaz Ziegler published an almost seven-hundred-page book laying out the rabbinic king parables and their Greco-Roman parallels. Even more amazing than the man's thoroughness and breadth of knowledge was the fact that so many of the literary parallels were from Greco-Roman historical literature. In other words, the rabbis drew analogies to God by talking about the emperors and local Roman governors of their own eras. This is a daring means of expressing their theology; and it revealed the authors of these king parables to be utterly conversant with local Roman news. It is like a rabbi or minister preaching her sermon by making an analogy from the *New York Times,* if you could imagine that.

Two examples will suffice. The first is a commentary on the first verse of Genesis (which I will translate following its original Hebrew word order, so you get what the rabbinic Midrash is driving at):

> "In the beginning / created / God / the heaven / and the earth" (Gen. 1:1). Rabbi Yudan quoted Aquila, "'This one is fitting to be called God.' In the way of the world, a king of flesh and blood is praised [*mitkales*] in a city before he has built public baths [*demosiaot*] and before he has given them waterworks [*phraktasia*]."

> Shimeon ben Azzai said "[a king of] flesh and blood mentions his name and then his works [*ktisma*]: so and so *augustali*, the most illustrious [*ho lamprotatos*]. But the Blessed Holy One is not so, rather only once God has created the needs of the world does God mention his name, 'In the beginning created,' and only then does it say 'God.'" (Gen. Rabbah 1:12)

I am fortunate that Rabbi Lieberman unpacked this story in detail. First, let us note that one of the sages quoted is named Aquila. This is not only a good Greek name, but this Aquila was a convert from a pagan religion who is reputed to have translated the Torah into Greek. All of the words above in italics are, in fact, Greek words transliterated in the Hebrew text. When the king is praised, the term used, *mitkales*, comes specifically from praise of the Roman emperor. As soon as the Roman emperor appeared in a town, folks lined the road shouting, "*Ho Kalos!*" (This one is Good!). Aquila says of God, "This one is fitting to be called God." In so doing he contrasts God with the flesh-and-blood Roman emperor—who more often than not was deified by the Roman senate. The usual public works bestowed upon a town are listed: public baths and waterworks. Imperial funds or extremely wealthy townsfolk paid for the aqueducts and the baths in most towns; they were simply too expensive to build otherwise. These public works, called *ktisma* in Greek, were uniformly praised and listed in detail on imperial statues throughout the Roman world.

When Shimeon ben Azzai talks about how the Roman grandees are listed along with their titles, he may as well be reading from monumental inscriptions or perhaps even from a synagogue donor plaque. To be called an *augustali* (minor Augustus) was not just idle praise; it was a title bestowed by the Roman emperor and noted on statues and tombs. The same is true of the title "most illustrious." In Latin this would be a *vir clarissimus*, and in Greek it would be *ho lamprotatos*, just like in our Midrash. The rabbis took note of the world around them and knew who was who. The title *lamprotatos* actually appears in the Greek donor mosaic of the Hammat Tiberias synagogue!

The rabbis not only knew who was who, they also knew what was what. The same fifth-century Midrash tells the following story to comment on Genesis 2:1, "The heaven and earth were finished."

> Rabbi Euphos expounded in Antioch, "finished" means smitten or put an end to. This is like a king [of flesh and blood] who enters a town and the townsfolk praise [*kilsu*] him, and their praises [*kilusin*] pleased him. So he increased the races and the chariots [*ayniokhos*]. Later they angered him, so he decreased the races and the chariots [*ayniokhos*].

Our Rabbi Euphos (a Greek name meaning "good light") is in the city of Antioch, which we visited earlier. There, he teaches about how God "finished off" the works of creation, much like the emperor brought an end to the imperial games and fired the charioteers. Again, the terminology is in Greek, transliterated into the Hebrew text. A fourth- to fifth-century Roman history work (*Scriptores Historiae Augustae*) reports that the citizens of Antioch supported a pretender to the throne who sought to overthrow Marcus Aurelius Antoninus and deify himself instead. It states about Antoninus (remember him?), "He nevertheless pardoned the citizens of Antioch . . . but he did abolish their races and public entertainments." It seems the rabbis' king parables were ripped from the headlines.

Greek folk sayings and tales were also among the currency of rabbinic story telling. As a case in point, many rabbinic texts tell the story of a woman who went over to her neighbor's house so they could bake bread together. Because she was leaving her house, she rolled three coins into her apron, just in case. When they went to knead the dough, however, she put the coins on the counter and accidentally rolled them into the dough. When the bread came out of the oven she took her loaves but then noted that her coins were missing. Her neighbor swore on the life of her son that she did not have the coins. The son died. When the

EQUESTRIAN MARCUS ANTONINUS—CAPITOLINE MUSEUMS, ROME

first neighbor went to console her, the foolish mourner brought up the missing coins and swore on the life of her second son. He died. The same thing happened to her third son. The moral to the story is related in Aramaic: "This is what folks say: whether right or wrong, flee from an oath!" (Lev. Rabbah 6:3). The exact same formula is invoked in a collection of Greek proverbs. Folk sayings are fungible from Greek to Aramaic.

Again and again, the rabbis employed the methods of the Roman world they lived in to deliver their Jewish message. Proverbs, rhetoric, fables, interpretation, symposia, narratives: all came directly from the Roman repertoire. Greek and Roman education and culture was as much the turf of the rabbis as the borscht belt was to Jewish comedy. As they themselves might have said, *Excelsior!*

CHAPTER VI

HOW MANY LANGUAGES DOES A JEW NEED TO KNOW?

"Ay, he spoke Greek."

—SHAKESPEARE, *Julius Caesar*, Act 1, Scene 2

A s a fifteen-year-old, I made my first visit to Israel. I wandered the streets, carefully sounding out the letters on store signs, proud of my ability to read the alphabet and, often enough, translate the words. One sign read in Hebrew, *sefarim*, and I knew that meant "books." Another sign read, *falafel*, which no longer needs translating, although it was a mystery back then. Yet another read, *bank*, which actually meant "bank." *Kafe* meant "café." And *televisia* meant "television!" That last sign was a hard nut to crack, for it had so many letters and required pronunciation out loud to reveal its meaning.

I invoke the ascendancy of English vocabulary in Israel and, while we're at it, elsewhere around the world as an example by which I can highlight the dominance of Greek in Roman Palestine. The preponderance of English usage points to the outsized influence American culture has today. Given the state of television and Hollywood, this is a decidedly mixed blessing, and I suppose the ancient rabbis might have felt the same way about the Greco-Roman influences, such as theaters and gladiator spectacles. That said, the rabbis were not shy about deploying Greek for the *mot juste* or using Latin terms when speaking of the military or court system. They achieved a certain *je ne sais quoi* when they trotted out Greek, much like we do when using French or, perhaps still, even Latin. As a lawyer might say, *res ipsa loquitur*; it speaks for itself.

But just how loudly did Greek and Latin speak within the ancient Jewish communities? Did every Jew know Greek? Or perhaps most rabbis lamented, like Shakespeare's Casca, "but, for mine own part, it was Greek to me." All told, we are talking about *thousands* of Greek words entering the rabbinic lexicon—enough to make it clear that every rabbi must have known at least some Greek, even those who were not fluent. Still other rabbis and Jews of Roman Palestine, we shall see, most probably spoke Greek as their primary language. Roman Palestine was a trilingual society in the first two centuries CE, with more Hebrew in the south, more Aramaic in the villages, and more Greek in the big cities. Over time, Hebrew usage diminished and became more academic, so that the concentration of Jews in the Galilee during the third through sixth centuries CE spoke primarily Aramaic and Greek, depending on where they lived and to whom they were speaking.

The synagogues of Roman Palestine were not exactly like the ones we attend today, even though I might argue that in our own sanctuaries there is a similar mixture of Hebrew and English, with the mix shifting in ratio from Orthodox to Reform synagogues. Not so very long ago, Yiddish was a third language in the American synagogue linguistic mix. But, as I move away from this inexact analogy, I will argue that the rabbis of the Talmud and Midrash—that is, the Jewish literature that still exists from the ancient period—had far less to do with synagogue life than do rabbis now. There is a growing consensus that the rabbis named in ancient Jewish literature were primarily academics, confined to their disciple circles. Synagogue leadership depended on others: some who were laity (like today's synagogue board members) and others who were perhaps some kind of clergy (but we do not know much more about them). These synagogue leaders spoke Aramaic and Greek. In the previous chapter alone we saw the use of Greek words like *ho kalos* (the

Good); *augustali* (most august); *ho lamprotatos* (most illustrious), and this last example came from a synagogue floor in Tiberias, a large population and rabbinic center in the Galilee.

In nearby Caesarea, the Talmud (p. Sota 7:1, 21b) reports that a congregation not only had Greek inscriptions but recited the *Shema* in Greek! This is worth notice not only because recitation of the *Shema* is central to Jewish liturgy, but also because it is made up of passages from the Torah itself, so we might have expected the synagogue members in Caesarea to know the prayer in the Hebrew original. When Rabbi Levi sought to put a stop to the practice, Rabbi Yosé rebuked him and said, "Just because they cannot read Hebrew letters you wish them to not recite at all? Rather, they should recite it in whatever language they know."

I would have expected Hebrew from the Jews at least in their prayers and their public reading of what is, after all, Hebrew Scriptures. Yet in a synagogue in the Land of Israel, in a major center of rabbinic learning, there was a congregation of Jews who prayed in Greek because they could not, in fact, read Hebrew. Nor, apparently, could the Jews of Caesarea even recite in Hebrew by memory, like a bar mitzvah boy today might, as they did not speak the language sufficiently to do so.

The same passage of the Talmud makes clear that some rabbis thought one should pray in synagogues in Greek or in whatever language they "could make known their hearts' desires." I assume that the rabbis thought God could understand Greek as well as Hebrew. But still, I find it somewhat surprising that in the heart of the Land of Israel there was such ignorance of Hebrew. While I am used to such a lament here in America, I did not expect to hear rabbis kvetching about lack of Hebrew back in the fourth century CE in the Galilee. Further, the Talmud says that Jews should recite the blessings after eating food "in whatever language they employed to acknowledge the One Whom they were blessing." If the Jews did not use Hebrew in synagogues, there was little chance they would do so when praying at home. But this rabbinic concession to Greek usage in prayers indicates just how much Greek outweighed Hebrew in the Land of Israel.

The case for using Greek during prayer goes further. As in water-parched California, the Jews of the Land of Israel were somewhat obsessive about rain. In their Hebrew prayers they prayed for "rain in its season" or for vivifying "dew" during the hot summer months, as Jews still do today in drought-stricken areas. But the mid-third century Galilean rabbi Resh Lakish noted (p. Shevuot 3:10, 34d), "One who sees it is beginning to rain and says *kyrie poly brekson*, is taking an oath in vain. . . ." You may infer from the word *kyrie* at the beginning of that short prayer that this entreaty was uttered in Greek. Resh Lakish declares it "an oath in vain" not because it is in Greek, but because once the rain has begun, the die has been cast. To pray for the nature of the rain to change from light rain, say, to abundant rain would be to take God's name in vain. Indeed, the Greek of the too-eager petitioner means: "God [*kyrie*] let much [*poly*] rain fall." You can almost hear The Band sing it: "rainmaker . . . let these crops grow tall."

In the Land of Israel in the Roman era, then, the language of prayer was often the primary spoken language of the one who was praying. This was recognized by the rabbis, who, while they preferred to pray in Hebrew—what they called The Holy Tongue—accepted that prayers should be uttered in the language of "ones heart's desire." Practically, this meant Greek for the larger urban centers.

Oddly enough, a Greek word or two has even snuck into the Hebrew prayer books that traditional Jews use to this day, whether here in America or in the modern State of Israel. When the standard prayers were being formulated, the emperor was the central a figure in the Roman world. So there are many instances of the rabbis employing the vocabulary of imperial etiquette. When the emperor visited a town, the citizens came out to greet him, shouting, *Ho Kalos!* Whether it was true or not, they were proclaiming of their ruler that he was "the Good." This same proclamation, *Ho Kalos*, has made its way into rabbinic Hebrew and appears in Greek, conjugated as though it were a Hebrew verb; it appears in Jewish prayer books as *ulekaleis*, part of a string of verbs with which Jews declare the desire to praise, extol, glorify, and proclaim the Goodness of God.

I was taught many years ago that this strangely Hebraized loanword from Greek is one of but two in the formal Hebrew liturgy. The other loanword from Greek found in the Jewish prayer book is invoked only on certain fast days. On those occasions when some historical tragedy is recalled and mourned, Jews bemoan that they were overrun by *legionot*, the Roman legions. It is an irony that even when the rabbis recall Rome as the ancient enemy, the Greek language of the majority society seeps into the otherwise Hebrew liturgy.

Prayer is a natural outpouring of the heart. I had a friend who, before he died, surprised me by admitting that he, a hard-boiled Madison Avenue executive, prayed every morning. He characterized it with the panache of a lifelong ad man, saying, "Some days it's more 'Please,' and some days it's more 'Thank You.'" I am certain that my late friend made his daily prayers in English—spontaneous Hebrew was not part of his linguistic repertoire. This captures, I think, what happens when folks just speak their hearts to God. Even in the ancient world, Jews prayed in the tongue most comfortable to them—as I suppose should be the case for all sincere prayer.

This also can be seen in a folk prayer, which in this case one might equally characterize as folk magic. The prayer I am about to show you was found half a century ago, when a scholar was researching among Hebrew fragments preserved in an ancient Jewish book depository discovered in Fustat, or Old Cairo, Egypt. Among the thousands upon thousands of personal documents uncovered in what is called the Cairo Geniza—its manuscripts and fragments are now preserved in libraries around the world—he found an incantation that begins in good rabbinic Hebrew and shares many formulae with standard rabbinic prayers. But then it veers wildly off course. This prayer is part of a work from the third or fourth century, appropriately called *Sefer HaRazim*—the Book of Mysteries. The particular prayer is recorded in Greek and carefully transcribed into Hebrew letters, but to ice the cake, the prayer is addressed to Helios! We have already seen that the Greek god Helios appears in zodiac mosaics of synagogue floors in the Galilee and elsewhere in the Holy Land. In beautiful rabbinic Hebrew, *Sefer HaRazim* offers prayers to God and to the angels. In the section of the work titled "The Fourth Heaven," it instructs the would-be mystic:

> If you wish to see the sun at night, travel north. Purify yourself for three weeks of all food and drink and everything unclean. At the third hour of the night stand watch, wrapped in white garments, and pronounce twenty-one times the name of the sun and the names of the angels that accompany it at night. And say: "I adjure you O angels who fly in the air of the firmament . . . in the name of the Holy King who travels on the wings of the wind, by the letters of the explicit divine name that were revealed to Adam in the Garden of Eden, Who reigns over all the constellations, and to Whom bow the sun and the moon like slaves to their master . . . I adjure you to make known to me this great miracle that I request, to show me the sun in its might upon its wheeled chariot . . . and tell me the deep secrets and make known to me all devices, but may he not harm me by any evil." And when you have finished speaking you will hear the sound of thunder from the north and see something like lightning illuminate the earth before you. After he has shown you thus, bow and fall on your face to the earth, and pray this prayer.

Did you catch that? The person uttering this prayer has just requested to see "the sun in its might upon its wheeled chariot," and at night, no less. What follows is the prescribed prayer for seeing the sun, or Helios. It is twenty-two words of Greek, transcribed in Hebrew letters. Professor Daniel Sperber deciphered the Hebrew script into Greek. I follow his translation into English from the decoded Greek:

> I revere you HELIOS, who rises in the east, the good sailor who keeps faith, the heavenly leader who turns the great celestial wheel, who orders the holiness [of the planets], who rules over the poles, Lord, radiant ruler, who fixes the stars.

Now that's a lot of Greek! I promise to return to this bizarre example of a Jewish prayer from fourth-century Roman Palestine. The Greek language so carefully transcribed teaches us that Jews offered their prayers in a language they hoped would be effective—Greek—and perhaps prayed to a Greek god who they thought could be effective: Helios.

Even among the thousands of works found in the old Cairo Geniza, the existence of books such as *Sefer HaRazim* was very rare. Indeed, the existence of any book was rare, given how difficult it was to actually produce a book. The wealthy hired specialists who had to know a great deal in order to manufacture a book: writing in one or more languages, the production of papyrus or parchment. If the former, you needed to know how to work the reeds. If the latter, you needed to start with an animal, strip and preserve its skin, remove the hair, whiten the hide's surface, score it with guidelines, prepare an ink that would not run, etc. This was a hugely time-consuming and extremely expensive venture. The rabbis did promote the manufacture of Torah scrolls, but the rabbis' own teachings were transmitted orally, by memory. To some very real extent this was true for Greek books, too. Homer was said to be a blind poet whose works were recited or sung. In a form of reverse snobbery, *reading* the works of Homer (or of the rabbis, I suppose) was considered a kind of cheating.

The rabbis lived in a world where books were nonetheless well known. Each synagogue shared communal books, such as a Torah scroll. Actual prayer books were less common, as Jews recited their prayers by memory or the prayer leader did so while others simply responded, "Amen." But there were other kinds of books in the Jewish community; we have read evidence of Greek books. Despite this, or perhaps in an effort to promote use of Hebrew, the rabbis only reluctantly acknowledged the existence of books written in Greek, and did so in very few instances. In the Mishnah (m. Yadaim 4:6), the rabbis refer to "the books of Homer." In a wickedly clever pun, the rabbis compare the books of Homer at first to Jewish sacred texts, and then analogize them to the bones of an ass. The Hebrew phrase for "bones of an ass," *atsamot hamor*, sounds an awful lot like the Greek phrase for the "songs of Homer," *asimat homerou*. It is a clever put-down of the sacred text of the Greeks. The bilingual pun was noted by Daniel Sperber, the same smart fellow who translated that Greek prayer to Helios.

This kind of disrespect for Homer is, alas, not uncommon among the rabbis, especially in the locker-room atmosphere of the rabbinic academy. I refer to what began as small groups of young men who attended a master, their rabbi. Like the Greek philosophers, these small disciple circles took pride in their cleverness and set themselves apart from others. Over time, as the rabbis grew in strength, the groups of rabbis' disciples formed schools. In addition to the Torah and wisdom they learned, they behaved like the boys they often were—poking fun at outsiders with juvenile wit. Scattered throughout the rabbinic literature that remains, we can find barbs directed at Gentiles, Christians, non-rabbinic Jews, and at women, too. Sigh. Would that all the rabbis were a tad more, well, rabbinic. Truly this was a case of boys being boys.

Another example of this kind of disrespect is seen in a similar Greek-to-Hebrew bilingual pun found in manuscripts of the Babylonian Talmud (Shabbat 116a—it has been removed from most printed editions by Christian censors). There, the New Testament—in Greek: *evangelium*—is punned in Hebrew as *avon gilayon*, the scroll of sin. While both of these puns are unfortunate, painful, puerile, and impertinent, they do demonstrate a command of Greek among the rabbis sufficient for bilingual wordplay—no small feat.

Given this linguistic aptitude, we are not surprised to find entire phrases, sentences, and idioms from Greek carefully preserved in Hebrew letters in rabbinic texts. This use of Greek is somewhat hard to decipher, all in all. Were the rabbis native Greek speakers who spoke Hebrew only in the rabbinic academy? To be sure, Hebrew was quite uncommon as a spoken language in the Galilee. More likely the language competition was between Greek and Aramaic. I've already noted that Greek was more urban, while Aramaic was more rural. Still, both languages were widespread, with Hebrew running a distant third as a kind of formal, scholastic language. Greek was used in rabbinic circles for a variety of purposes. At times, the Greek was exactly the right term for what was being discussed. Or Greek was trotted out for effect—displaying the cultural pretensions of the speaker. Finally, we must consider the possibility that Greek was just easier for certain speakers than were Aramaic or Hebrew, so they lapsed into Greek for a bit of linguistic relief. That's what the prayer for rain we saw above feels like to me.

The rabbis employed Greek, transcribed into Hebrew letters, in their own Hebrew and Aramaic literature. I will try to demonstrate the breadth of their range of uses. As an example, e.g. (I can't resist citing instances in which we English speakers trot out Greek or Latin, even now), we find the phrase—transliterated here into Latin characters—*para basileus ho nomos agrophos.* The Greek translates as, "For the king the law is unwritten," which the rabbis (Lev. Rabbah 35:3) correctly understand to mean that the king does not feel constrained to follow the law. The rabbis offer their contrast: God, the King of the king of kings, follows the laws of the Torah scrupulously. The phrase used is in Greek, for surely that's how they heard it in response to their protests about this or that. The reply they heard: *para basileus ho nomos agrophos*—get over it, the world isn't fair and the law is not observed by everyone. The rabbis use the Greek phrase here as a sharp rejoinder to the lack of respect for law they observed among Roman authorities.

In the Palestinian Talmud (Berakhot 9:1), we are treated to a barrage of Greek terminology about the emperor and the imperial government. It is not surprising, upon reflection, to find Greek employed in discussion of the court, where Greek was the language of discourse. The emperor is referred to as *basileus, kaisar, augustus,* with all three Greek imperial titles—king (e.g., basilica), general (Caesar), augustus (as in the adjective *august*)—written in Hebrew characters. The emperor is also repeatedly referred to as *patron,* as though he were a Mafia don or a politician who took care of his precinct workers. Elsewhere in rabbinic literature, the emperor is grandiosely styled as *kosmocrator,* ruler of the cosmos. This is said tongue in cheek in the Talmud, as not only is the emperor compared to God—Who in the rabbis' eyes is the One and Only ruler of the universe—but it is dryly noted that this term is employed much as the term *hyparch*, a local governor, is used. The emperor may think he's hot stuff, but compared to God he's a *schlepper*.

Many rabbinic sources tell a story about the Roman Caesar Vespasian and Rabbi Yohanan ben Zakkai. When Vespasian was a general besieging Jerusalem, the great rabbi escaped the city in a coffin and made his way to him. The tale was popular as mythic history, an account of how the rabbinic circle first was established in the aftermath of the destruction of the Temple. In the Talmudic version of this legend (Gittin 56a–b), Rabbi Yohanan greets Vespasian in Aramaic. In another rabbinic version, the rabbi greets the emperor in Hebrew, saying, "Long live my lord the Emperor!" But in the manuscripts of Lamentations Rabbah, which probably reflect the earliest and most authentic telling of the tale, the rabbi says the same thing in good military Latin: *Vive Domini Imperator!*

And then there is the story of the Emperor Hadrian, related back in chapter four. When Hadrian encountered the old man who was planting a fig tree, he asked him to bring him the fruit, should the elderly farmer live long enough to see the harvest. The old codger brought a cartful (Greek: *kartella*) of figs, and Hadrian declared, "I command [Greek: *keleunin*] to bring forth a golden divan [Greek: *sellion*] to seat him. I further command that you empty the wheelbarrow of figs and replace it with dinars [Greek: *denari*]." The narrative not only presents a sympathetic emperor, it displays correct knowledge of the emperor's household: the language of imperial command (*keleunin*) and the furniture appropriate for someone of senior magistrate status, the *sella curulis*.

The educated rabbinic class clearly possessed a keen awareness of Greek that reflected either the high literary culture of the Roman world (Homer) or that of the imperial court. But they were not the only Jews who were fluent in Greek. Thirty years ago a group of scholars published a papyrus from Egypt written in Hebrew characters. It included the Greek word *lamprotatos* (most illustrious), which we have seen in Greek letters on a synagogue floor and which is represented in Hebrew characters in a fifth-century rabbinic commentary on the book of Genesis. The

Egyptian papyrus in which *lamprotatos* is written dates to 1,600 years ago—the year 417 CE, to be precise. It is a marriage contract between two Egyptian Jews: Samuel son of Sampati and Metra daughter of Lazar. Mazal tov!

The Egyptian marriage contract shares many affinities with rabbinic marriage contracts, and where rabbinic-sounding technical language is used in the document, it is written in Aramaic. Given that to this day traditional Jewish marriage contracts are written in Aramaic using Hebrew characters, this is not surprising. But mixed in higgledy-piggledy with the Aramaic is Greek, also in Hebrew characters. The standard formula header for contracts, giving the date according to Roman rule, is recorded in Greek; later, when the items in the bride's modest trousseau are listed, they are described in both Greek and Aramaic, all recorded on papyrus in the Hebrew alphabet. There is no mistaking the ease with which these average Egyptian Jews spoke both languages.

Thus far, I have focused on legal and more technical documents that reflect Greek as it was used in the daily lives of the ancient Jewish community. But Greek was also used by the rabbis in fifth-century Galilee when they discussed "natural science" (Gen. Rabba 14:2). Rabbi Huna explains that some children are born after seven months of gestation, others after eight. For reasons unexplained, the "seven-month" children thrive, while the eight-month children perish. Obviously, this is not empirical obstetrics and gynecology—note my use of Greek. Huna's colleague Rabbi Abbahu offers an explanation by way of a Greek pun. Here, the entire linguistic transaction takes place in Greek. Abbahu relies on something we observed earlier: Greek letters each have numerical value. He says "*zeta hepta, eita okto.*" This could be depicted as a simple listing of the numerical value of the Greek letters, with *zeta* equaling seven and *eita* equaling eight:

zeta=ζ=7
eita=η=8

But it can also be read as: *ze ta hepta, ei ta okto*—a Greek sentence that translates as, "The seventh lives [longer] than the eighth." Clever Rabbi Abbahu displays his thorough facility with Greek language.

Rabbi Abbahu's good Greek notwithstanding, many rabbis were content to display their knowledge of Greek culture by quoting in Aramaic or Hebrew translation rather than the Greek original. We have heard the story of the foolish woman who baked bread and took a vow on her sons' lives. The moral to that story was, "Righteous or not, flee the oath," which was reported in Aramaic in the rabbinic narrative. It is a precise translation of the Greek adage, much as we today might quote Lao Tzu's "Even the thousand mile journey begins with the first step." Very few people quote this in the original language. But most who quote it know it comes from Chinese culture. In other words, you can display cultural awareness even if you do not master the original tongue.

Of course, there is culture and then there is what we might call "low culture." Think about the export of American television and movies, adored by fans worldwide—so long as the dialogue is dubbed or subtitled in the receiving culture's language. Hollywood movies often gross as much in foreign-language versions as they do in the English originals. But for the most part, people around the world are more likely to be viewing *Rambo* than a Handel opera. The same was true to some extent even in the ancient world. The trick when reading ancient Jewish literature is to recognize the Roman original behind the Hebrew or Aramaic dubbing, as it were. Here are two examples of popular culture from the world of Roman gaming: playing dice and horse racing.

It is true that Jews played dice and probably would have done so whether or not there ever was a Rome. But the idiom for the dice throws was distinctly Roman in the case at hand. The second-century Rabbi Shimeon ben Azzai critiqued the Jewish legal system by suggesting, "A Jewish dog's ear is better than Jewish judges" (Deut. Rabbah, ed. Lieberman, p. 13). This otherwise opaque statement can be understood only if we know that when Romans threw dice, a three was called a "dog's ear" (*kunotes*). Throwing a dog's ear was a winner, and so a better bet than the Jewish courts of ben Azzai's time.

Another rabbinic statement comes from the Roman racetrack: the hippodrome. Here we are in truly Roman territory, as archeological remains of these tracks abound in sites throughout the ancient Roman world. We already had occasion to refer to the races in Antioch. The circus races were incredibly popular. Charioteers were the rock stars of their day, with high earnings, and there are extant posters and graffiti supporting favorite drivers. The races were divided into four factions: red, white, blue, and green; and as with today's sports, everyone had "their" team. In the fifth-century commentary Leviticus Rabbah, the Midrash twice (13:4 and 35:6) states in Aramaic: "Poverty is as becoming to the Jews as red reins on a white horse." This sentiment is repeated in other rabbinic collections, and the comment is often interpreted in praise of poverty. Quite the contrary, however; throughout the Byzantine era, the "red" racing teams consistently lost. This rabbinic adage was an exercise in irony, disdaining poverty as a certain loser. The last thing to bet on was a red bridle.

APHRODITE AND THE RABBIS

The rabbis were monotheists living in a polytheistic environment. Everywhere they looked, they saw evidence of the pagan gods; especially idols. Jews did not entirely know what to make of this ubiquity of images, and there is a great deal of discussion among the rabbis about how to navigate their way through such an idolatrous world. The earliest document of the rabbis, the Mishnah, discusses the laws prohibiting idol worship (Avodah Zarah 3:4). The following story is offered there to explicate a shift in rabbinic legal attitudes toward pictorial art:

> Proculus son of Philosophus inquired of Rabbi Gamaliel, who was bathing in the bathhouse of Aphrodite in Acco, "It is written in your Torah, 'Let nothing that has been condemned

stick to your hand' (Deut. 13:18). So what are you doing in the bathhouse of Aphrodite?"

He replied, "One may not reply [to a question of Jewish law] in the bathhouse."

When they exited, he said, "I did not come on to her territory, rather she came on to mine. It was not the case that they said, 'Let us make a bathhouse as an adornment to Aphrodite.' Rather they said, 'Let us make an Aphrodite [statue] as an adornment for the bathhouse.' Another thing, even if they said to you, 'We will give you much wealth,' you still would not enter your pagan temple naked or polluted, nor would you urinate in it. Yet this [statue of Aphrodite] stands before the gutter and everyone pees right in front of her!"

"The prohibition is only regarding images of the gods that are venerated as gods. That which is not venerated as a god is permissible to enjoy."

Rabbi Gamaliel makes his point sharply. First, he displays his Jewish piety by refusing to engage in "Torah talk" while naked in the Roman bathhouse. Next, he disparages the behavior of those pagans in the baths toward the statue there. He demeans the questioner's own religious piety, even as the oddly named Proculus son of Philosophus, presumably meant to represent a knowledgeable pagan, invokes a verse of Jewish Scripture. Finally, Gamaliel pronounces a general principle that became the norm for accepting pictorial art in Jewish settings, despite the so-called prohibitions of the Second Commandment:

> "You shall not make a sculptured image or any likeness of what
> is in the heavens above or on the earth below . . . you shall not
> bow down to them or worship them." (Ex. 20: 4–5)

As Rabbi Gamaliel interprets it, only those images that are actually designed as objects of worship are forbidden. Sometimes a statue is just a statue.

Mosaic Aphrodite in Sepphoris/Diocaesarea

The rabbis also loved telling tales of the Roman demimonde. These stories caricatured the Romans by focusing on their seamy side. In the earliest rabbinic commentary to the biblical book of Numbers (Sifre, Shelah, #115), the rabbis gleefully narrate a heartwarming story about a happy hooker. Not surprisingly, the love goddess Aphrodite again appears.

Numbers 15:37–41 serves as the final section of the daily *Shema* prayer, and so the paragraph commanding Jews to wear fringes, *tsitsit*, on the corners of their garments was very well known. The last verse of the paragraph begins and ends with the phrase, "I am the Lord your God." This is just enough information for you to follow the story and get the punch line of this rabbinic joke.

Rabbi Nathan said, "Each and every commandment in the Torah has its reward. We can learn this from the commandment of tsitsit. It once happened that there was a man who was very careful regarding the commandment of tsitsit. He heard there was a prostitute in a harbor town who charged four hundred gold pieces as her price. He sent her four hundred gold pieces and made his appointment for her services. When the day came, he went and sat in her antechamber. Her maid came and told her that the man who had the appointment had arrived. She said, 'Let him enter.'

"When he entered she spread before him seven beds of silver and a bed of gold at the very top. Between each one was a bench [subsellium] of silver, and the topmost was gold. But when he came to do the deed, his four tsitsit arose like witnesses and slapped him in the face!

"He immediately disengaged and sat down on the ground. She, too, climbed down to the ground and sat next to him. She said, 'Agapé of Rome! I will not allow you to leave unless you tell me what flaw you saw in me!'

"He replied, 'By the Temple service! There is no one as beautiful as you in the world. But the Lord our God commanded us a simple commandment wherein it is twice written, "I am the Lord your God." The first time is to teach that God will reward us, and the second time teaches that God will also punish us.'

"She said, 'By the Temple service! I will not allow you to leave until you write down your name, your city, and the name of the rabbinic academy where you learn Torah.'

"So he wrote what she desired and went on his way. She then arose and dispersed all of her wealth: one third to the government, one third she gave to the poor, and the final third she took with her to the rabbinic academy of Rabbi Hiyya. She asked him, 'Rabbi, will you convert me?'

"He asked her, 'Have you set your eye on one of my students?'

"She handed him the note that she was holding. Rabbi Hiyya called his student and said to him, 'Rise now and take what you contracted for. When you first contracted for her it was forbidden. Now that she is converting, she shall be permitted to you.'

"If this is the reward for the commandment of *tsitsit* in this world, in the World to Come, I cannot even imagine!'"

The joke demands some commentary, for even with a clever punch line, it remains a subtle narrative about the marriage of Judaism and Hellenism, both literally and figuratively. As we have come to expect, there are Greek words dotted through the story. The first, *subsellium*, is a technical term in both Greek and Latin for a small bench or step stool—the means of ascending from one bed to the next. When the beautiful woman is rejected after the bizarre comic incident with the ritual fringes (think Three Stooges slapstick), she uses a vow formula, swearing: "*Agapé* of Rome!" *Agapé* means love, in this case, a nickname for the love goddess Aphrodite. Our pretty prostitute takes her vow on the name of her patroness/goddess, while the hapless rabbinical student takes his vow "by the Temple service." His is a remarkable vow, given the reality of the Jerusalem Temple lying in ruins. Perhaps it represents the state of his male, er, ego at that moment.

Nevertheless, following their joint witness of what they take to be the mini-miracle of the slapping *tsitsit*, the prostitute herself is moved to switch her allegiance and she, too, vows "by the Temple service." This is the first step in her conversion process. Next she depletes her great wealth by paying off the government in bribes to allow her to give up her profession—no doubt prostitution was a lucrative form of bribery income for the local officials. She spends one-third of her wealth on the poor—a benefaction common enough in the Jewish community but virtually unheard of among pagans. Finally, she comes to Rabbi Hiyya, who sagely discerns what has happened.

Every time my own rabbinical students read this story in its original Hebrew they stop at this point in the narrative and finally declare it too unbelievable. They simply cannot credit that the student who hired the prostitute would be stupid enough to give her his real name, let alone the name of the seminary where he studied! In our ancient rabbinic fantasy, however, Rabbi Hiyya not only susses out what happened, but then turns the woman over to the young man whose *tsistit* reminded him that the paragraph of Numbers says,

> "These shall be your *tsitsit*, that you may look at them and recall all of God's commandments and observe them, so that you do not go astray after your heart and eyes, lusting after them."
> (Num. 15:39)

The Hebrew word I translate in the biblical verse as "lusting" shares the same Hebrew root as the word for "prostitute" in our story. Although Rabbi Hiyya nowhere actually says his disciple may now marry the new convert, everything we know about rabbinic morality makes it clear that this must be the end of the story. The devotee to Aphrodite will come into God's house. Greco-Roman Hellenism will enter the rabbinic academy and be permitted. They will happily marry; and in the world to come, who can even imagine?!

CHAPTER VII

LOVE OF WISDOM
AND LOVE OF LAW:
IN PURSUIT OF
PHILOSOPHY AND JUSTICE

I t wasn't all love all the time among the rabbis. Their culture was based on disputation—on virtually every one of the over five thousand pages of the Babylonian Talmud* you will find rabbis arguing with one another. Theirs was—in a memorable phrase from Pirke Avot, a tractate of the Mishnah, which is the backbone of the Talmud—"an argument for Heaven's sake."

The stakes of the argument varied. Study was a form of divine service; and to the rabbis, argument in study was as much a way of sharpening the intellect God had granted them as it was of reaching a result. Rabbi Hama bar Hanina commented on the verse that reads: "'As iron sharpens iron' (Prov. 27:17)—just as one knife blade sharpens against another, so do two disciples of the sages sharpen one another" (Gen. Rabbah 69:28). For the most part, rabbis embraced dialectic—it was a path to exploring the parameters of Jewish law, while at the same time a

---

* There are 2,711 folios in the standard printed editions of the Babylonian Talmud. That yields 5,422 print pages.

path to knowing the One Who Spoke and brought the world into being. The dialectical mode of reasoning was often the end in and of itself. The rabbis reveled in what Greeks and Romans called Socratic dialogue. Argument, dispute, dialectic—these were the closest the rabbis came to philosophy, per se.

There were times when the stakes of the argument seemed very high. Early in the history of the rabbinic movement, arguments between prominent rabbis sometimes threatened to bring down the entire enterprise. It was one thing to strenuously argue a point. But there were occasions when the argument verged on the point of no return. Haven't we all found ourselves at that precipice at one time or another? Sometimes, we do not even recall what the argument was about when it is finally over. But sometimes, arguments lead to a rupture in relations—and some of these can last many years. It's hard to walk back words spoken in anger.

We also know of political arguments, in which debate is a struggle over minutiae that seem to grow larger with every second they are disputed. In the very first generation of the rabbinic movement, in the aftermath of the destruction of Jerusalem, such an argument broke out between two of the great leaders of the rabbis. The disagreement quickly escalated to become a matter of power politics, which had potentially dire consequences for the survival of Judaism. On one side of the argument was a family dynasty: old money, well-connected, led by the brash young patriarch Rabbi Gamaliel. His opponent, Rabbi Yehoshua, was elderly, wise, and well-loved by his colleagues. He earned a paltry income digging peat moss to make charcoal and was, in theory, the second in command to the patriarch. Their argument would be akin to the president and vice president of the United States having a public dispute.

The debate was about how and when to proclaim the not-yet-regulated Jewish calendar. The year's cycle of months was based on the moon. Since it could be seen in the sky, it seemed a fairly easy thing to declare the new moon every month. This declaration determined on what day any holiday in that month might occur. Once witnesses came to the court and testified that they had seen the new moon, it was duly sanctified by the courts. This ancient method is still used by Muslims to determine the Islamic calendar today. The idea of having witnesses testify to what they saw in the sky predated the ability of ancient Jewish astronomers to calculate the calendar. The trouble came when the witnesses were less than reliable about what they saw. Let's let the Mishnah tell the story:

> Once two witnesses came and said, "We saw it early morning in the East, and early evening in the West."
>
> Rabbi Yohanan ben Nuri said, "They are false witnesses." Yet when they came to Yavneh, Rabbi Gamaliel accepted their testimony.
>
> In another instance witnesses testified, "We saw it in its time, but on the night of its 'birthing' it was not seen." Rabbi Gamaliel accepted them.
>
> Dosa ben Harcinus said, "They are false witnesses! How can one testify that a woman has given birth and on the morrow her belly is still between her teeth?"
>
> Rabbi Yehoshua said to him, "I agree with you."

The quiet agreement of Rabbi Yehoshua with his colleague Dosa sets the conflict aflame. Now there is a very public power struggle between the two leading rabbis.

First, let me explain the text of this conflict, so we can see what they are arguing about so passionately. To see the new moon, you would ideally witness the thin sliver of the old moon one night, on the bottom left of the waning moon, and the thin sliver of the new moon the very next night, at the bottom right of the newly waxing moon.

The first set of witnesses said they saw the new moon in the early morning with the sunrise. Looking east, into the sun, they simply could not have seen the thin sliver of the new moon. Its narrow crescent would have been indiscernible in the glare of the rising sun. The same is true that night—they claim to be looking west into the setting sun, so they could not have seen the slight arc of the newly "born" moon.

The second set of witnesses offered even worse testimony. They said they saw the old moon but then said that on the night when they should have seen the new moon, "it was not seen" (I love their passive voice: mistakes were made). This is the worst possible testimony they could have offered! They basically said in court: we saw nothing. Therefore, one should conclude, they have no testimony. Yet Gamaliel said, "Hey, close enough. Let's call it a new moon." No wonder Rabbi Dosa not only called the witnesses false but piquantly described the birthing moon as though it were a birthing mother—you can't say it gave birth if the next day she is still carrying so high that her belly is, as it were, between her teeth. No baby, no new moon, no new month. And Yehoshua, who also had had enough of Gamaliel's shenanigans, sided with Rabbi Dosa, publicly disagreeing with Gamaliel. This was a strong challenge to his power, as it was over a potent issue—regulating the calendar and holidays.

If it were a game of poker, Gamaliel would be deemed to be holding a very bad hand. Yet Gamaliel, player that he was, turned and commanded Rabbi Yehoshua regarding the month of Tishri, when the holiday of Yom Kippur (the holiest day of the Jewish calendar) fell on the 10th of the month:

> I decree that you must appear before me with your walking staff and wallet on Yom Kippur as it falls according to your calculation.

Talk about cojones! The man had nothing but deuces, if that, and he commanded Yehoshua to show up before him on the very day Yehoshua deemed it to be Yom Kippur! It was as though Rabbi Yehoshua determined that the holy day of Yom Kippur was on Tuesday and, according to Rabbi Gamaliel, it should be on Thursday. Gamaliel commanded Yehoshua to show up on Tuesday as though it were just another work day. This was pure power politics. Gamaliel was really making Yehoshua knuckle under to his authority. But the way he did so is curious. Why did he command that Yehoshua appear with "staff and wallet" on

Yom Kippur? Why not say, "Let's have lunch together" on a day when eating was expressly forbidden? Of all the things he chose to command, why these two things? It is true that one should not handle money on Yom Kippur, but it is a minor prohibition. And there are surely rabbinic legal circumstances under which it would have been permissible for Yehoshua to carry his walking stick—for example, within a walled city or enclosure. What is the significance, then, of commanding him to show up on Yom Kippur carrying his staff and wallet?

Here, the Greek philosophers come to our assistance, for the staff and wallet were the universally recognized symbols of their calling. Diogenes Laertius, in his Greek work *Lives of Eminent Philosophers*, writes of Antisthenes, "And he was the first . . . to take up a staff and a wallet. . . ." The great Cynic philosopher Crates writes to a new mother about her baby, "Rock him in a cradle . . . dress him not with a sword . . . but with a staff and a cloak and a wallet, which can guard men better than swords." In his turn, Diogenes the Cynic writes to his own father, "Do not be upset, father, that I . . . carry a wallet over my shoulders and have a staff in my hand." Rabbi Gamaliel is commanding Rabbi Yehoshua to carry the very signs that identify him as a rabbi and sage, that is to say, a philosopher. Gamaliel forces Rabbi Yehoshua to kowtow publicly bearing the symbolic garb of his office.

Let's leave behind the new moon and even the politics of the first generation of rabbis. But just to satisfy your curiosity, know this: Gamaliel won this argument when the great yet conservative Rabbi Aqiba sided with him on this issue. Aqiba said, "We cannot question authority as we will undermine the entire edifice. We may as well question Moses' authority." Rather than risk a split in the rabbinic community just as it was gaining its voice, Aqiba counseled acquiescence. So Rabbi Yehoshua and his colleagues lost the day, and Yehoshua appeared before Gamaliel as commanded. But you should also know that when Gamaliel publicly humiliated Rabbi Yehohshua yet again, the other rabbis deposed Gamaliel from office!

Like the Stoics, Epicureans, Neo-Platonists, Cynics, and the like, the rabbis lived their philosophy and borrowed both Greco-Roman

CRATES THE PHILOSOPHER—MUSEO DELLA TERME, ROME

philosophical garb and ideas to present their ideology as one that Jews would adhere to. In the early centuries of the rabbis, they consistently presented themselves as the type of intellectual group that Romans found comfortably familiar and respectable. Philosophers not only were distinctive in their modes of living and their dress, but they proudly advertised their intellectual lineage, by listing their teachers and their teachers' teachers to all who came to hear them. Indeed, the rabbinic tractate Pirke Avot produced a similar "chain of rabbinic tradition" in order to buttress the intellectual fitness of Rabbi Yehoshua and the other disciples of Rabbi Yohanan ben Zakkai to lead the rabbinic movement, in contrast to the dynastic succession of the Gamaliel family. In trotting out this "chain of tradition," the Mishnah is actually adopting yet another Greco-Roman philosophical method.

Pirke Avot opens its "chain of tradition" by stating,

> Moses received the Torah from Sinai and transmitted it to Joshua.

Joshua to the Elders.

The Elders to the Prophets.

The Prophets transmitted it to the men of the great assembly. . . .

Simeon the Righteous was among the remnant of the great assembly. . . .

Antigonus of Sokho received it from Simeon the Righteous. . . .

Yosé ben Yoezer of Tzerida and Yosé ben Yohanan of Jerusalem received it from them. . . .

Hillel and Shammai received it from them. . . .

Rabbi Yohanan ben Zakkai received it from them. . . .

Rabbi Yohanan ben Zakkai had five disciples. These were Rabbi Eliezer ben Hyrcanus, Rabbi Yehoshua ben Hananiah, Rabbi Yosé the Priest, Rabbi Shimeon ben Netanel, and Rabbi Elazar ben Arakh. (Pirke Avot 1–2)

First, I should point out that the very notion of a meritocracy in which socioeconomic class has little bearing is itself a democratic ideal of Hellenistic philosophy. That Yehoshua, an elderly charcoal maker, could engage in debate with a patrician like Gamaliel must have seemed outrageous to the younger rabbi. Yet among the Stoics of the Roman Empire, we find philosophers who are emperors, such as Marcus Aurelius, and philosophers who are slaves, such as Epictetus. Following the destruction of the Temple in 70 CE, the Jews might have chosen to restore the power of the priesthood, a dynasty, or the power of the Davidic kingship, another dynasty. Instead, they opted for the power of Torah and intellectual endeavor—the most salient characteristic of Greco-Roman philosophy.

Many scholars think that Pirke Avot was once the capstone to the Mishnah and that this chain of tradition justified the rabbis' teaching of "Oral Torah," by tracing it back to God at Sinai. No doubt this is true, but there is much else at work in this text that might be characterized as rabbinic propaganda. I have virtually eliminated the content of what the ancients taught in favor of focusing on its form. The list above has been abbreviated—the two Yosés are actually the start of a listing of five "pairs" of pre-rabbinic leaders, culminating with the Elders, Hillel and Shammai. They, in turn, pass on the traditions to their disciple Yohanan ben Zakkai—the very rabbi who survived the siege of Jerusalem and brought his students to Yavneh. Rabbi Yohanan and his boys provided the political opposition to Gamaliel and his family. Ultimately, though, the dynasty won out—Rebbi Judah the Patriarch, editor of the Mishnah, was a direct descendant of Gamaliel. Given this battle with dynasty, it is notable that neither priests nor kings are mentioned in the chain of tradition. If anything, the priesthood is slyly co-opted by Rabbi Yohanan when he counts Rabbi Yosé the Priest among his disciples. Because the priesthood was scattered at the destruction of the Jerusalem Temple where they had once served, it was useful to claim them as among his disciples. It gave his disciple circle a certain standing and prestige.

This famous passage of Pirke Avot justifying rabbinic teaching actually displays a great deal of its Greco-Roman background. The text famously begins, "Moses received the Torah from Sinai and transmitted it to Joshua." In fact, each successive generation "receives" the tradition and "transmits" it to the next generation. The use of receive and transmit is not merely the stuff of navy radiomen plying the oceans during World War II; it is technical terminology used in both the church and in the Greco-Roman philosophical schools for passing on the authentic teachings of the previous generation. Here, too, the rabbis have quietly declared that they stand within the Greco-Roman orbit. In fact, the very notion of a "chain of tradition" has its origins in the philosophical schools. There, when a new leader of a philosophical school took his place at the head of his disciples, he would produce such a chain, tracing his intellectual lineage back to the founder of that school. So, a Stoic like Marcus Aurelius might trace his academic pedigree back to Zeno; or an Epicurean might trace his lineage back to Epicurus.

Chains of tradition buttressing the right to rule the school were commonplace among the Greek philosophers. Each of these "chains" shares an odd common trait with the others: no matter what the actual chronology may be, each chain of tradition is fourteen links from the founder to the newest head of the academy. It does not make any difference whether those fourteen generations took one hundred years or five hundred years—accuracy in counting years is not the point. Getting from the newest head of the academy back to the founder of the school in but fourteen links is what it's all about. This oddity also can be observed in the New Testament, where Jesus's lineage is traced in groups of fourteen (father to son, rather than teacher to disciple). And were we to laboriously count out the chain from Moses at Sinai to Rabbi Yohanan and his disciples, we'd get the same magic number: fourteen. No one knows why fourteen seems to be the "correct" number of links, but Pirke Avot joins with all the philosophical schools in tracing its newest leader's lineage back to the founder in fourteen generations.

Pirke Avot also has other affinities with Greco-Roman philosophy, specifically Stoicism. When Pirke Avot was formulated, around the turn of the third century CE, the ethos of the Roman Empire was broadly Stoic, much as we might characterize the American ethos today as one of liberal democracy. Stoics were famous for not showing emotion and for being content with what they had. Yohanan ben Zakkai conducted a veritable philosophical session when he instructed his disciples:

> "Go forth and see, what is the Good way a man should cling to?"
>
> Rabbi Eliezer said, "Generosity [literally: a good eye]."
> Rabbi Yehoshua said, "A good companion."
> Rabbi Yosé said, "A good neighbor."
> Rabbi Shimeon said, "One who sees that which is born."
> Rabbi Elazar said, "A good heart."
> Rabbi Yohanan ben Zakkai said, "I prefer Elazar's answer, as his words include all that you say."

My teacher Judah Goldin explained that the philosophy Rabbi Yohanan's students exhibit here is classical Stoicism. "The Good" was a mainstay of Stoic philosophy, and the search for the Good was the task of the philosopher. Rabbi Yosé opted for good neighbors. Whom you lived among determined what you were; much as his contemporary, the Stoic thinker Epictetus, taught: "The key is to keep company only with people who uplift you, whose presence calls forth your best."

In our bit of Pirke Avot, Rabbi Shimeon's maxim that the Good way is "One who sees that which is born" is usually taken to mean that one should anticipate the consequences of his actions. To do so is good. To not do so is selfish and irresponsible. Rabbi Elazar has the last word and opts for a good heart. Among Greek philosophers as well as rabbis, there is a debate as to what one might find "in the heart." For some, the heart was the seat of intellect, just as we today would locate it in our heads. For others, the heart was the place from which our emotions flowed. Whether cognitive or affective, the heart was an important organ in ancient thought. I suspect that the fact that the Midrash teaches us that Rabbi Elazar was Yohanan's chief disciple and surrogate son may have influenced the master's preference for his disciple's maxim.

In Pirke Avot, the dialectic back and forth on the Good is followed by a similar question-and-answer session on the Bad way, which must be avoided. Each disciple replies to his master with the negative of what he is recorded as saying above. Rabbi Shimeon, again the odd man out, says that the Bad is "to borrow and not repay." This is surely true of one who does not recognize the consequences of his actions, and who is selfish and irresponsible. At the end of the dialogue, Pirke Avot makes clear that it has Stoic doctrine in mind, as Rabbi Elazar teaches (Pirke Avot 2:14), "Know how to refute an Epicurean (Greek: *epikurus*)."

The Stoics and Epicureans often debated one another in the marketplace or *agora* of the towns of the Greek-speaking East. They each believed in doing the Good, but for different reasons. For the most part, the Stoics believed in divine providence, which is to say that the gods cared what one did. By and large, Stoics counseled that one should strive to do the Good. Ironically, Epicureans, who are often caricatured as believing one should "eat, drink, and be merry," also believed in striving for the Good. They differed from the Stoics in that they taught that the gods were utterly indifferent to humankind. There was neither judge nor judgment. This sharp sentiment led some to "eat, drink, and be merry," but Epicurus and his Epicureans counseled that all else being equal, one may as well do good. This is not unlike the philosophy found at the end of the biblical book Ecclesiastes (12:13): "The end of the matter when all has been said: revere God and perform God's commandments."

To the rabbis, however, it was not only the outcome that mattered. Rabbis fervently believed that there was a judge, God, and that there would be judgment; be it on the High Holidays, when one's deeds are weighed, or at the time of bodily resurrection, when all of one's deeds are reviewed by God and appropriate reward or punishment is meted out. To say there was neither judge nor judgment was the ultimate blasphemy the rabbis could imagine. And so, Rabbi Elazar counseled, "Know how to refute an Epicurean." Ultimately, the name Epicurus (Hebrew: *apikoros*) became an epithet for any Jewish heretic or blasphemer. In this passage of Pirke Avot, the rabbi's disdain for Epicurean doctrine is explicit. Avot tilts decidedly in favor of Stoicism.

Epictetus, a Stoic philosopher and slave, teaches, "Wealth consists not in having great possessions, but in having few wants." A good thought for a slave to have, that! He also taught, "He is a wise man who does not grieve for the things which he has not, but rejoices for those which he has." The rabbis teach this as a paradox in Pirke Avot (4:1): "Who is wealthy? One who is satisfied with his lot." One more Epictetus quote also deserves our notice and comparison with Pirke Avot. He taught, "Keep silence for the most part, and speak only when you must, and then briefly." Rabbi Shimeon, son of Rabbi Gamaliel and a contemporary of Epictetus, taught it this way: "All my life I was raised among the sages and I have found nothing better for myself than silence" (Pirke Avot 1:17).

The Greco-Roman Stoic philosophers also taught the value of self-control (*sophrosyne*). The late-second-century writer Philostratus, in his Greek work *The Lives of the Sophists*, says, "A prince is really superior if he controls his anger . . . if only it be kept in check by reason." The rabbis seconded this virtue, and it becomes especially apparent when they apply their worldview to their model Moses, who famously had an anger-management problem. In his youth, Moses struck and killed an Egyptian (Ex. 2:12). Even as an elder leading Israel, Moses grew impatient as he tried to produce water for the Israelites in the wilderness and struck the rock, rather than speak to it as God had commanded (Num. 20:11).

In the earliest rabbinic commentary to the book of Numbers (Sifre #157), Rabbi Elazar ben Azariah notes that in three places Moses gave in to his anger and as a result forgot his "Torah." The consequence of Moses's loss of self-control was forgetfulness and error in the law. These two phenomena are interlinked, because for the rabbis the law is Oral Torah, which is memorized. If anger causes one to forget, it causes one to err in teaching. That any rabbi might consider that Moses, the law-giver, could have erred in his teaching, is a sure sign of how highly the rabbis valued the Greek virtues of self-control (*sophrosyne*) and avoidance of anger (*a-pathia*). Rabbinic teachings conformed very closely to Stoic virtues, even to the extent that the rabbis, like the Stoics, sought to refute Epicureans.

The Stoic Epictetus also taught, "We are like travelers at an inn or guests at a stranger's table." A similar sentiment is attributed to the rabbis' "founding father" Hillel the Elder, in this *chreia* recorded in a fifth-century rabbinic commentary to Leviticus (34:3) that I quoted earlier:

> Hillel was once taking leave of his disciples and preparing to go on his way when they asked him, "Master, where are you going?"
>
> Hillel replied, "To do a good turn for the guest [Greek: *kse-nos*] who is staying at my home."
>
> They asked, "Do you then have a guest [*ksenos*] every day?"
>
> He replied, "Is not my poor soul a guest [*ksenos*] in my body? One day it is here and on the morrow it will be gone."

Epictetus might be speaking about the transitory nature of life in general. But for Hillel, as well as the rabbis who came after him, body and soul were distinct entities, with the pure soul being eternal. The earliest rabbinic commentary on Exodus (Mekilta, Beshalach 2, p. 125, restored with Leviticus Rabbah 4:5) imagines the following conversation:

> The Emperor Antoninus asked Our Holy Rabbi [Judah the Patriarch]: "When a person dies and the body decays, will the Blessed Holy One resurrect him for judgment?"
>
> He replied, "Do not ask me only about the body, which is impure, but rather ask about the soul, which is pure. It may be analogized to a king of flesh and blood who had an orchard, within which were beautiful young figs. He set two guards therein, one lame and one blind, that they might guard it.
>
> "He said to them, 'Be careful of the fruit.' Then he left them and went on his way. The lame one said to the blind one, 'I see beautiful young figs.' The other one said, 'Let's eat!'
>
> "The first one said, 'Can I walk?' The blind one said, 'And can I see?' What did they do? The lame one rode on the back of the blind one and so they took the fruits and ate them. Then they each went and sat in their original places.
>
> "Some days later the king came and asked them, 'Where are my fruits?' The blind one said to him, 'Can I see?' The lame one said to him, 'Can I walk?' The king, who was wily, what did he do? He made the lame one ride on the back of the blind one and tortured them together. He said, 'Thus did you eat them!'
>
> "So, in the Coming Future, the Holy will say to the soul, 'Why did you sin against Me?' She will say to God, 'Master of the Universe, was it I who sinned against you? It was the body that sinned, for from the day I have departed from it, have I sinned at all?'
>
> "God will ask the body, 'Why did you sin?' The body will say to God, 'Master of both worlds, it was the soul that sinned, for from the day she has departed from me, am I not tossed out like a potsherd on a garbage heap?'
>
> "What will the Blessed Holy One do? God will restore the soul to the body and judge them as one."

This story teaches us a number of aspects of rabbinic philosophy: belief in the world to come when there will be bodily resurrection of the dead, subsequent judgment, and punishment for sins committed. The body and soul are judged together for the sins they commit as one, yet the soul is deemed pure, while the body is not. That said, despite privileging the soul, the great rabbi holds the soul culpable for sin.

It is perhaps not coincidence that the metaphor of the blind and lame is found in the Byzantine collection called *The Greek Anthology*. Once again the rabbis shared an image with the Greco-Roman world. But in this instance, the narrative about the blind and lame guards is uniquely applied by the rabbis as a metaphor for the relationship of body and soul, while in the Greek text it is simply a metaphor for synergy. The tables are turned when the good rabbi instructs the philosopher emperor Marcus Aurelius Antoninus on the intricacies of the relationship of body and soul.

Thus far I have shared texts in which the rabbis imagine conversations between Rabbi Judah the Patriarch and the philosopher emperor Marcus Aurelius Antoninus. The rabbis also quote Homer, who is not exactly a philosopher, and we have seen them mention Epicurus, who is. But the rabbis catch us all by surprise when they name Oenomaus of Gadara as one of the greatest of Roman philosophers. Oenomaus was an actual philosopher who lived in the second century in the Northeast of the province of Roman Palestine, in the town of Gadara—a Greek-speaking city. In truth, Oenomaus was quite obscure. His work is briefly quoted by the church father Eusebius, and later St. Jerome lists him in a chronicle. He apparently wrote a work titled "On Philosophy according to Homer." The rabbis list him among "the greatest philosophers," most likely because they knew him as a boy from the neighborhood.

But what about Plato, the man who truly was the greatest Greco-Roman philosopher? The rabbis never quote him by name. This may indicate that the rabbis did not study in depth the abstract thought of the Greek sages. On the other hand, they did know certain ideas from Plato. These were probably gleaned from the writings of the first-century

Alexandrian Jewish sage Philo. Philo quotes Plato in his work "On the Creation of the World."

In that book, Philo reworks ideas from Plato's *Timaeus*. Plato suggested that in order for the universe to be created, an ideal form had to be imagined first. Only afterward could the "ideal" be concretized into reality. Philo, in turn, explains Plato's philosophy by likening it to a king who hires an architect to build a great city. The architect first sketches his plan in wax, and only after that does he build. Philo goes on to suggest that this is how God created the universe.

In the fifth century CE, the rabbis comment on the creation story of Genesis with this analogy:

> The Torah says, "I was the artisanal tool of the blessed Holy One." In the way of the world, when a human king builds a palace [Greek: *palatin*], he does not build it of his own knowledge, but uses the knowledge of an artisan. And the artisan does not build it of his own knowledge, but has parchments [*diphthera*ot] and wax tablets [*pinaks*ot] to know how to make the mosaics [*psayphos*im]. Thus the blessed Holy One looked in the Torah and then created the world.

The rabbis seem to depend upon Philo and/or Plato for their analogy. God etches forms onto wax, as Philo suggests his architect might do. Indeed, the rabbis' artisan might well be an architect, although I think it more likely that it is the artist who lays down mosaic floors, and I have translated accordingly. No matter whether we translate the text as being about an architect per se or about a mosaicist, the Platonic ideal has now been "read into" the biblical creation story. Sweetest of all, the Platonic ideal for the rabbis is the Torah itself.

We've all heard about that other Platonic ideal: the so-called platonic relationship. My father, may he rest in peace, used to remind me that it was ideal, not real. Like the rabbis, my dad loved to pun; so he would say of such a romanticized notion of nonerotic platonic love between the sexes, "For him it's play, for her it's tonic."

Plato and my dad's observations are a good introduction to both Roman and rabbinic images of women. Being my father's son, I want to see if we can put the "Roman" in romantic. The rabbis certainly could imagine romance; but they were quite practical about taking a Platonic ideal and protecting it through well-grounded realities of rabbinic law. Indeed, they were in accord with Greco-Roman realism when it came to the hard-nosed negotiation of a prenuptial agreement. Both Greco-Roman and rabbinic cultures were male dominated; and women were expected to play their roles in the home (thank you very much, ladies). Men were decidedly at an advantage in contracting marriage. And men often were intemperate when it came to constructing images of their wives. After hearing the men of Late Antiquity describe their spouses, I imagine that people commented to the women, "Funny, you don't look shrewish."

Plato's teacher, Socrates, supposedly had a shrewish wife named Xanthippe. Shakespeare, in *The Taming of the Shrew*, compared his protagonist Katherina with her:

> Be she as foul as was Florentius' love,
> as old as Sibyl, and as curst and shrewd
> as Socrates' Xanthippe or a worse . . .

Just how bad was Xanthippe? In the third century CE, Diogenes Laertius recalls this anecdote or *chreia* in his *Lives of Eminent Philosophers*: "When Xanthippe first scolded him and then drenched him with water, Socrates' rejoinder was, 'Did I not say that Xanthippe's thunder would end in rain?'" Aelian, in the third century CE, reports, "Alcibiades sent Socrates a large and beautifully made cake. Xanthippe was annoyed in her usual way . . . so she emptied it out of the basket and trod on it." Or again, Diogenes Laertius:

> When Xanthippe tore his coat off his back in the market place,
> his acquaintances encouraged him to hit back; "By Zeus!" he

said, "So that while we fight you may cheer, 'Good, Socrates!' 'Well done, Xanthippe?!'"

This cavalier misogyny is fairly typical of Hellenistic literature of the period. Sadly, it is mirrored in rabbinic stories. Here is one about Rabbi Yosé of Galilee and *his* wife, told in the fifth-century Midrash Leviticus Rabbah (34:14):

> Rabbi Yosé the Galilean had a shrewish wife who used to scold him in front of his students. They said to him, "Rabbi, divorce her as she does not honor you."
>
> He said to them, "Her bride-price [*pherne*] is more than I can afford, so I cannot divorce her."
>
> Once he was studying with Rabbi Elazar ben Azariah. When they had finished their studies Rabbi Yosé said, "Would the Master attend to me by coming to my home?" He replied, "Yes."
>
> When they entered his house, she turned her face away from them and left them. Rabbi Yosé saw a pot on the stove. He asked his wife, "Is there something in the pot?"
>
> She replied, "Stewed fruit." Yet when he lifted the lid he found a chicken fricassee. Rabbi Elazar ben Azariah knew what he had heard. He asked him, "Did she not say 'stewed fruit,' yet there is chicken?"
>
> Rabbi Yosé replied, "It's a miracle!"
>
> When they had finished eating he said, "Master, divorce your wife, for she does not honor you."
>
> He replied, "Her bride-price [*pherne*] is too much and I cannot afford it."
>
> Rabbi Elazar said, "We will raise the funds for her bride-price [*pherne*] so you may divorce her."
>
> They collected the bride-price [*pherne*] and he sent her away.

Four times in this short narrative about Rabbi Yosé and his wife, her bride-price is mentioned. Each time, the Greek term *pherne* is used in place of the common Hebrew term *ketubah,* which reflects the legal situation in the time of Rabbi Yosé. In Jewish law, a woman's bride-price must be paid if her husband seeks divorce. Indeed, her dowry principal must also be restored, which gave women some bit of financial protection. The entire financial package is referred to in our Midrash by the Greek term *pherne,* which the later rabbis used to represent the two separate legal obligations: one of the bride-price given to her by her new husband as a marriage gift, the other of the dowry she brought into the marriage. Both sets of funds were hers, but her husband could benefit from any proceeds earned from their value during the marriage. Perhaps the requirement to restore the wife's capital to her control offered a woman some protection from abrupt divorce.

In rabbinic law, the right to initiate divorce remained the province of men. In Roman law, by contrast, women were granted the right to initiate divorce. The rabbis themselves recognized this difference when they wrote (Gen. Rabba 18:5): "Rabbi Yohanan says, 'Among the gentiles . . . his wife divorces him, she gives him a *repudium.*'" The Latin term, transliterated by the rabbis into Hebrew for the wife's repudiation of her husband, is attested in both Greek and Latin documents from that era. In the early 1960s, Israeli archeologists uncovered a stash of letters dating from the second century CE at Nahal Hever, a few miles south of the Dead Sea. Written on papyrus, they are mostly in Greek, with a few Aramaic and Nabatean letters thrown in for good measure. The texts, from the cleverly titled "Cave of Letters," are a treasure trove of information about the lives of Jewish women in Roman antiquity. A Jewish woman named Babatha left behind her personal archive, which dates from 120 to 132 CE. We also have papyri that document the life of her contemporary Salome Komaise. In both cases, these women rely on Greco-Roman rather than early rabbinic forms for their marriage documents. That way, they were better protected than was Rabbi Yosé's poor wife. So it is noteworthy that the rabbis use the Greek term *pherne,* even as they refer to their own rabbinic marriage stipulations.

Under both Roman and Jewish law, as indicated by the documents Babatha and Salome left behind, women were granted alimony—literally, a food allowance. In cases of Jewish law, a dead husband's estate was directed to his offspring, and so their mothers conceivably might not be provided for beyond her bride-price and dowry. In such cases courts were called upon to determine appropriate alimony. It was presumed that a woman's *pherne* provided her needs, while the children would be provided for by their father's estate. The Jerusalem Talmud (Ketubot 5:7) reports a marvelous story of a wealthy woman who came before a rabbinic court to sue for her right to continue to be provided for in "the style to which she had become accustomed."

> A case is cited regarding Martha bat Boethius. The sages ruled that she could receive two barrels of wine as daily alimony. . . .
>
> Rabbi Hezekiah quoted Rabbi Abbahu in the name of Rabbi Yohanan, "They also ruled about a daily cooked-food allowance."
>
> Despite this, she cursed the court, saying, "You should only give this to your own daughters!"
>
> Rabbi Akhah said, "We all replied to her, 'Amen!'"

I am suspicious that this story is not an actual court case but, rather, a rabbinic fiction or even a joke, given the "amen" punch line at the end of the narrative. In the papyrus documents left at Nahal Hever, we learn that Babatha, too, sued for her food allowance. Martha bat Boethius was a possibly fictional character known in rabbinic storytelling for her fabulous wealth, while Babatha was a decidedly real woman who left actual Greek court documents behind.

Although the rabbis do not like to admit it, there were plenty of real Jews like Babatha who paid little to no attention to rabbinic family law, choosing rather to take their chances in Roman courts. Indeed, many of those Jews had non-Jewish spouses, so the Roman court was a preferable venue, as the rabbis recognized only marriage between two Jews as binding under their purview. Even so, the question remained as to how the rabbis might view the offspring of a mixed union. Earlier in this book we read about an errant student who ruled in Tyre that the offspring of a Jewish father and a non-Jewish mother could be circumcised on Shabbat. This was tantamount to declaring the baby wholly Jewish, as only for a Jew could the command for circumcision on the eighth day (Gen. 17:12) take precedence over the command to observe the Sabbath (Ex. 20:10). Unfortunately, that student got rabbinic law wrong and was whipped by his rabbi.

Yet the boy had a point. The Torah consistently follows the tribal identification of the father—what is called patrilineal descent. Josephus, writing in Greek in the late first century CE, also assumes that the off-spring of a marriage between a Jewish father and a Gentile mother is Jewish. Philo, for his part (and in this he finds support from later rabbis in Babylonia), considers such a child to be illegitimate, using the Greek term *nothos*, often translated as "bastard."

It is only from the time of the Mishnah (ca. 200 CE) onward that the rabbis become zealous in their insistence that Judaism follows the religion of the mother, and not the father—what is called matrilineal descent. For the rabbis—even Orthodox and Conservative rabbis today—a child's Judaism is determined by the Judaism of its mother. We know *when* the shift occurred—sometime between the first and second centuries—but we are not at all sure *why* it shifted.

My colleague, historian Shaye J. D. Cohen, notes that in Roman law, the citizenship of a child follows that of its father, much as was the case for Jewish identity in the biblical era. But under Roman law, when a marriage does not have formal legal status, then the child's Roman identity follows that of the mother. Cohen suggests that this law, promulgated just before the editorial date of the Mishnah, is a possible source of origin for the matrilineal principle in Judaism. He suggests that this law of Roman citizenship, which was matrilineal, was transferred to the rabbis' consideration of who is a Jew. Given that Cohen's only other suggestion for the shift comes from the principles of animal husbandry, I find this a considerably more tasteful attribution.

Of course, we expect that children are cared for by both of their parents. But in the Roman and rabbinic worlds, men had stronger standing in court and so could better represent their children's legal and financial interests. A woman and child both needed a designated guardian in the absence of the *pater familias*. Such a guardian was called, in both Roman and rabbinic documents, by the Greek term *epitropos*. The term in Roman law describes the court-appointed legal guardian who is the curator of the finances and well-being of the minor. The *epitropos* can also be the estate and financial agent who cares for the property of others. This was especially important when women owned property, as they were often not legally allowed to act on their own behalf. In those instances the Roman court or the rabbis would appoint an *epitropos* to serve as business or real-estate agents on the woman's behalf. Yet the term can also refer to an imperial office, such as that of the Roman procurator. A Roman law from the beginning of the third century uses the term referring to Jews, as it tries to determine their status in serving in imperial offices and Roman court-ordered guardianships. It reads, "Jews as well shall serve as *epitropos* to non-Jews, just as they are required to perform the other services . . ." At least until the advent of Christianity, Jews held legal status on a par with other citizens of the empire.

In rabbinic literature the term *epitropos* is simply transliterated from Greek and is preserved in both the Talmuds. The Babylonian Talmud (Bava Metsia 39a) speaks of a "court-appointed *epitropos*." The Palestinian Talmud (Terumot 1:1, 40b) distinguishes between a permanent and temporary *epitropos*. The Babylonian Talmud (Shabbat 121a) also makes reference to an imperial *epitropos*. But the elasticity of the term in rabbinic literature is piquantly captured by the lament, "There is no guardian [*epitropos*] against unchastity." Apparently, even in the ancient world, when a young couple is bent on making whoopee, no chaperone can stop them.

There seems to have been a good deal of rabbinic family law, even some laws that stand in contrast to the prevailing Roman norms, such as those regarding divorce initiation. Influence is a complex phenomenon, for even as Roman legal tendencies may have penetrated rabbinic jurisprudence, the Roman rulers nevertheless may have sought to limit rabbinic jurisdiction in favor of their own imperial authority. Professor Amnon Linder suggests that "the Jewish leadership had enjoyed a considerable judicial autonomy"; but he also thinks that it all came crashing down when the Roman emperor Arcadius issued a law called an imperial *constitution* in 398 CE, limiting Jewish authorities to passing judgment only on "matters of religion." Everything else came under the purview of the Roman authorities.

Professor Jill Harries, by contrast, writing about the same exact imperial *constitution*, emphasizes the section of the law that permits two Jews to engage in "arbitration before Jews or Patriarchs . . . with the consent of both parties . . . in civil matters." In fact, the law concludes by stating that not only is this permissible, but that "the governors of the provinces shall even execute their sentences as if they were appointed arbiters by the [Roman] judges." This reading buttresses the impression we get from rabbinic literature itself: The rabbis had the ability to judge cases in family law and other civil matters, so long as both parties were Jews who were willing to submit to the rabbis' jurisdiction. According to Harries, this situation persisted even after the emperor Arcadius's ruling of 398 CE.

There were, however, severe limitations placed upon Jewish legal decisions outside of civil cases. It is generally assumed that the rabbis and other Jewish jurists were denied the possibility of carrying out executions for either capital crimes or biblical sins. This, of course, does not rule out possible mob violence; but rabbinic insistence on the rule of law certainly precluded any Jewish court from actually turning a convict over to a mob for execution. I like to think this was also true when the Second Temple was still standing. But any evidence we might have about the limitations of a Jewish court is made vastly more complicated by Christian testimony about mob violence. St. Paul claims to have taken part in a mob stoning of St. Stephen before the former's conversion to Christianity.

Christian literature also skews our understanding of early first-century Jewish law with its depiction of the complicity of the Jewish Sanhedrin with the Roman court in the trial of Jesus. To state the obvious: these accounts are tainted with religious prejudice. I confess to my own pro-Jewish and pro-rabbinic bias in this theological minefield, as well. Nevertheless, the early Christian accounts open the door to the possibility that the Jewish court may have convicted Jesus but then left it to the Roman authorities to execute him, as the New Testament reports. Given that Romans readily used crucifixion as a punishment and that Jewish courts do not permit that form of execution, this passes the test of plausibility.

I am not going to pursue this extremely complicated issue here, in part because this book is not about Jewish-Christian relations and in part because I am content to stipulate that Jewish courts, whether pre-rabbinic or those of the rabbis of Roman Palestine, did not perform executions. The rabbis did spend a great deal of time talking about capital cases. Why go to the trouble of laying out in detail the four methods of execution a Jewish court might employ? Why describe the appeals process and the use of the town crier (Greek: *kayruks*) to announce an impending execution? Why such excruciating detail if the Romans did not permit any of these hypothetical executions in the first place?

We might equally well ask why so much rabbinic literature obsesses over details of the Jerusalem Temple: its procedures, layout, and rituals. A significant proportion of the Mishnah relates to Jewish laws that apply only to the Temple—such as sacrifice, priestly purities, priestly dues such as tithing, and such—although the Jerusalem Sanctuary was destroyed in 70 CE, never to be rebuilt. One simple explanation of the rabbis' attention to things that existed only in theory—which applies both to the Temple and to the death sentence—may simply be that they had a strong penchant for Torah study. The central book of the Torah, Leviticus, is chock-full of the procedures of the Temple and priesthood that take up so much of the rabbis' exegetical concern. Which is to say: the rabbis regularly made pronouncements about the things they

studied about in Scripture. You cannot read the Pentateuch without no-
ticing that it pronounces execution as a penalty for certain sins, again
and again. Here, too, the rabbis' seeming obsession with death-penalty
proceedings may stem more from rabbinic proclivity for Midrash and
biblical interpretation than from any historic reality or theoretical desire
to execute.

In fact, the rabbis were scrupulous not only about interpretation,
but also about fulfilling the Torah's commandments regarding "justice,
justice shall you pursue" (Deut. 16:20). As the rabbis read the repeti-
tion of the word "justice" in the verse, they understood it to mean that
they were always required to use just means in their pursuit of justice.
This meant that the rabbis had great respect for what we now would
call "rule of law," and that they took care to set up courts to adjudicate
disputes in the Jewish community wherever possible. At the same time,
the Palestinian and Babylonian Talmud each offer abundant testimony
that the rabbis depended on case law, however messy and unruly such
a system might be. In this they shared a worldview with their Roman
pagan neighbors. Law as practiced in the courts and communities was
the best precedent for adjudication. It is not coincidence that the rabbinic courts (theoretically ranging in size from local tribunals of three
rabbinic judges to larger trials, which could involve twenty-three or even
seventy-one elders) were all called Sanhedrin, using the common Greek
term for a council or senate: *synhedrion*.

The historian Polybius, writing in Greek in the second century
BCE, uses the term *synhedrion* to refer to the Roman Senate—and that's
back when the Senate was still the Senate, before the advent of an emperor. Once there was an emperor, "first among equals" in the Senate,
synhedrion referred to the emperor's executive committee, which effectively stood above the Senate. The New Testament refers repeatedly to
the Jerusalem *synhedrion* as a Jewish institution. The rabbis, in turn,
styled their courts Sanhedrins. In fact, this term became so closely associated with Jewish courts that we find that the Roman legal compendium called the Theodosian code refers to "the Primates of the Jews . . .
who are nominated in the Sanhedrins of Palestine."

This Theodosian law also refers to payment to the imperial treasury of an annual tax collected by the *palatini*. From the context here it is clear that a *palatini* was some kind of treasury or tax official. A passage in Midrash Leviticus Rabbah, composed in Roman Palestine around the same time, explains a verse from Jeremiah that is still read in synagogues as the prophetic portion on the second day of Rosh HaShannah, the Jewish New Year:

> "Truly Ephraim is a dear child of mine" (Jer. 31:18). What is the meaning of "Ephraim" in this verse? Rabbi Yehoshua ben Levi said, *Palatini*. Rabbi Yehoshua b. Nehemiah said, *Eugenestatos.*

Palatini are the court officials, those of the palace. The second term, *eugenestatos*, means "very well-born," like the English term *eugenic*. The Greek word meaning "very well-born" might equally well be translated as "nobility." For each of the rabbis quoted above, to be called "Ephraim" was to have very high status in the Greek-speaking Roman East.

Sometimes rabbis found themselves in Roman courts, and not always as unbiased observers. I imagine this was no more welcome to the Jews of the Roman Empire than it would be for a member of a racial or ethnic minority today to find himself or herself in the clutches of the legal system.

In a third-century companion text to the Mishnah we read:

> The story is told that Rabbi Eliezer was once arrested for heresy and they took him to the tribunal [*bema*] for judgment. The governor [*hegemon*] asked him, "Was a grey-hair like you involved in such idle matters?"
>
> Rabbi Eliezer replied, "I put my faith in the Judge."
>
> Now that *hegemon* thought that he was referring to himself, while Rabbi Eliezer was referring to his Father in Heaven. So he said, "Since you have put your faith in me, I shall do so for you. . . . Dismissed [*dimissus*]; you are released."

When he was released from the tribunal he remained troubled that he had been arrested for heresy. . . . Rabbi Aqiba asked him, "Perhaps one of the heretics said something that pleased you?"

Rabbi Eliezer replied, "By Heavens, you have reminded me! Once I was walking on the main street [*istrata*] of Sepphoris and Jacob of Sikhnin quoted a heretical teaching of Jesus son of the Panther [*pantiri*], and it pleased me. That is why I was arrested, for I transgressed the words of Torah to "keep its ways far from you." (Prov. 5:8)

This late-first-century rabbi was arrested on suspicion of being Christian at the time when Christianity was still a proscribed religion in the Roman Empire. Hauled up to the tribunal, the governor serving as judge seeks to entrap him. Rabbi Eliezer's wily yet evasive answer is sufficient for the judge to dismiss the case. At the very same time, the younger Pliny served as the Roman emperor's representative in Asia Minor. He wrote to the emperor Trajan,

I have never been present at a trial of Christians. . . . I am not sure . . . whether a pardon ought to be granted to anyone who retracts his belief. . . . I have asked them in person if they are Christians . . . if they persist I order them to be led away for execution.

These were the stakes that Rabbi Eliezer faced. Note the incidence of Greek and Latin terminology in this rabbinic account: *bema*, *hegemon*, *dimissus*, *istrata*, *pantiri*. The happy term *dimissus*, the one Latin word among all the Greek, comes straight from Roman court pronouncements.

A brief word also is in order on the crude rabbinic nickname for Jesus, who is called here "son of the Panther." This is a double slur, as it denies both the virgin birth and the paternity of Joseph, while it imagines Jesus's parent as a Roman soldier or local tough. The nickname "Panther" is known from Roman graffiti and is a term akin to a 1950s American nickname such as "Duke" or "Rocky." Local Greek slang was used by the rabbis when they wanted to take a cheap shot at Christianity.

Another rabbinic narrative offers "a detailed and faithful portrayal of the procedure in the criminal court." For this portrayal, as well as the story of Rabbi Eliezer we have just discussed, I follow my teacher Saul Lieberman.

In the fifth-century Galilean Midrash *Pesikta DeRav Kahana* (24:10), we read:

> "For My plans are not your plans, nor are My ways your ways, proclaims the Lord" (Isa. 55:8). This is like the case of a robber [*lystes*] who is tortured by the interrogator [*questionarius*]. First he reads his deposition [*elogium*]; then he whips him; then he gives him the hook [*khamos*]; then he pronounces the sentence [*periculum*]; and then he is taken for execution.

This gruesome description is an all-too-accurate account of testimony under torture in the Roman court system. Again, the rabbinic accounting is chock-full of the Greek terms heard in the Roman courts in the East. The deposition from the original arrest record is entered into testimony, and if the defendant continues to proclaim innocence, he is tortured. First comes the flogging of the defendant's back, then the hook in his mouth. The Roman historian Tacitus offers proof of this horrific procedure when he writes that Emperor Tiberius was dragged to the Tiber River by the hook in his mouth and dumped into the river to drown. The same fate was meted out to Emperor Commodus: "The people and the senate demanded that his body be dragged with the hook and cast into the Tiber," according to the testimony of the *Scriptores Historiae Augustae*. We are left with little doubt that the rabbinic description is not a fiction but an actual horror.

The Babylonian Talmud (Shabbat 32a) promotes the spiritual value of confession of sins, especially before death. When they think of confession under that type of mortal duress, they compare it to a Roman court:

> Our Rabbis taught: if one falls sick and his life is in danger, he is told, "Make confession, for all who are sentenced to death make confession." When a man goes out into the street, let him imagine that he is given in charge of an officer [*strateitos*]; when he has a headache, let him imagine that he is put in irons [*kollarion*]; when he takes to bed, let him imagine that he ascended the scaffold [Lat. *gradum*] to be punished. For whoever ascends the scaffold to be punished, if he has great advocates [*parakletos*] he is saved, but if not he is not saved. And these are man's advocates: repentance and good deeds.

In the course of the fourth century CE, Christians went from being a persecuted minority to ruling the empire and doing so with vigor. By the fifth century, Christian Roman rulers had legislated against and subsequently persecuted those Christians whom the Catholic Church deemed to be heretics. It would not be long before imperial legislation turned toward what it saw as the problem of the Jews. Technically, this move is beyond the purview of this book, as we are more concerned about the relationships of the Jews with pagan Rome; and I am trying to avoid writing about Jewish-Christian relations. But because the Roman law codes, like rabbinic compendia of law, contain a long historical record, I will close this chapter with a brief look at how Roman law codes influenced the lives of Jews through legislation on synagogues in the Roman Empire.

Two *constitutions* from the Theodosian code, most likely promulgated in 420 and 423 CE, concern the Jewish community. The first echoes Pliny's concerns about Christians but this time applied to the Jewish communities of the empire.

> No one shall be accused and punished for merely being a Jew if they are innocent of any other crime. Nor should any religion execute him if he is but exposed to insult. Their synagogues

and homes shall not be burnt nor wrongfully damaged without reason . . . just as we provide this law for all the Jews, we offer the opinion that this warning should be given lest the Jews themselves grow insolent; and elated by their security commit some act against the reverence of Christianity.

This is an example of how one hand gives while the other takes away. The wording of this law indicates that by 420 there were mob actions against Jewish communities in the East, resulting in the torching of synagogues and beating of Jews. The law prohibited these actions, "without reason," which unfortunately left a very wide loophole. Further, it warned the Jewish community not to get too uppity, given the thinness of this cover of imperial protection.

The two-edged nature of this law was made even clearer in the subsequent law, issued two and a half years later. It directly concerned the synagogues that had been damaged or destroyed in Christian mob riots against some Jewish communities.

In the future none of the synagogues of the Jews shall be seized or put on fire. If there are some synagogues that were seized or given over to churches or consecrated to the ancient mysteries in a recent undertaking after the law [of 420, above] was passed; they shall be given new places in exchange on which to build, to the measure of the synagogues taken. . . . No synagogue shall be constructed from now on, and the old ones shall remain in their current condition.

This *constitution* marks the descent into Byzantine Christendom and what would become the ongoing degradation of Judaism and Jewish institutions throughout the Middle Ages. While synagogues that were burned were, in theory, guaranteed replacement according to the architectural footprint of the previous building, it was ruled that other synagogues remain in the state in which they existed and not be improved or repaired. Further, new building of synagogues was expressly forbidden.

Archeological remains reveal that this law was, fortunately, not enforced, as a building boom of synagogues took place throughout the Galilee and also in Asia Minor. To state what now should be expected, these Jewish buildings were designed and erected very much to the norms and influences of local Greco-Roman architecture. Let's take a look.

CHAPTER VIII

HISTORY WHERE IT HAPPENED

My wife loves New York City architecture, old and new. One year as a Hanukkah gift I bought her an architectural guide of the city, arranged by neighborhood. She has systematically walked her way through Manhattan, block by block. The practice has given her lots of exercise and a real appreciation for the built beauties of the city. In this chapter I'd like to take a similar stroll with you, touring the Roman Empire of the early centuries CE, observing the ruins of ancient Jewish buildings—their common features and the things that make one stand apart from another. I'll report what my wife and I have seen as we have visited these archeological sites together over the years, and even share a photo or two along the way.

Far and away, the best place to begin is at the greatest Jewish building ever. The Second Temple in Jerusalem was one of the "wonders of the Roman world," a magnificent structure built by King Herod, beginning in the first century BCE. A client-king of the Roman emperor Augustus, Herod was an Idumean convert to Judaism. The Greek name for the territory that was biblical Edom—Idumea—was Esau's old province, which the rabbis identified with Rome. Herod himself was thoroughly Hellenized and thoroughly bonkers. Herod was obsessed with building magnificent Greco-Roman architecture throughout his small kingdom in the Land of Israel. And in fits of paranoia, he murdered members of his immediate family. This gave rise to the *chreia* attributed to Emperor Augustus about Herod's Jewish piety in not eating pork, which ends with the punch line, "It is better to be Herod's pig than his son."

Herod spared no expense at remodeling the Second Temple, essentially rebuilding it as a classical Greco-Roman shrine. He widened the esplanade upon which it stood, adding colonnades, arches, and endless gilt, perhaps to assuage his own guilt over murdering his family. Among the Jerusalem Temple features worthy of notice—beyond the kitschy gold overlays—were the monumental ceremonial eastern gates made of Corinthian bronze. Imported from Alexandria by ship, the Nicanor gates, like the rest of the Temple, are lost to us forever. Just how amazing were the Nicanor gates? The Babylonian Talmud (Yoma 38a) reports that

> Miracles were wrought for the Nicanor gates. . . . They say that when Nicanor went to bring the gates from Alexandria, a storm arose upon his return and threatened to drown the gates. They took one of the gates and threw it overboard to lighten the load, but the sea continued to storm. When they went to throw the matching gate overboard, Nicanor wrapped himself around it and said, "Then throw me in with it!" The sea immediately became calm.
>
> He nonetheless was troubled about the one gate that had been lost. But when they came to port at Acco, there it was bobbing next to the boat! Some say a sea creature swallowed it and then spat it out onto dry land . . .
>
> When they changed all the gates of the Temple to gold, they kept the Nicanor gates untouched because of the miracle . . . but there are those who say it was because the bronze shined like gold in any case.

I assume that Mr. Nicanor was the donor of the miraculous gates. Let's give him extra credit for attentive stewardship of his naming gift. In addition to these magnificent gates, Herod's Temple featured secret passageways for the priests, grand stairways for the Levites to array themselves upon for their choral singing, and arches to buttress the entire architectural assemblage. Below is a photo of what is now called "Robinson's arch," the scant remnants of such a buttress. Note the detail of the immense ashlars—stones that are trimmed or embossed around the edges. This was a featured style of Herod's stonecutters and is still visible at the Western Wall, or Wailing Wall, in Jerusalem. The Wall, as it is now called, was part of the retaining wall holding up the enlarged plaza where Herod's Temple stood. That plaza is referred to as the Temple Mount, or, for Muslims: Haram al-Sharif, the noble sanctuary.

REMNANTS OF ROBINSON'S ARCH WITH DETAIL OF TRIMMED HERODIAN STONE

There are other monuments of the Herodian era near the Temple Mount. The so-called Tomb of Absalom is to the east, nestled in the Kidron Valley between the Temple esplanade and the Mount of Olives. You can gaze down upon it from the churches there as you look toward the fabled Jerusalem skyline of al-Aqsa and the Dome of the Rock. While the monument presumably is named after David's rebellious son Absalom (2 Sam. 18:18), the tomb is replete with Ionic columns and a Doric frieze, and so most probably was built in the first century CE, a thousand years after biblical Absalom's death.

Perhaps the most fascinating architectural works from this late Second Temple period are the building remains identified as synagogues. This is curious, since during this period the Jerusalem Temple was still standing, so one might expect it to have been the exclusive place of worship for the Jews. Yet the Babylonian Talmud (Ketubot 105a) reports that "there were 394 . . . synagogues in Jerusalem," before the destruction. Until the archeologists unearthed their finds, historians had assumed this to be another Talmudic fantasy.

Although there are no actual synagogue remains from the Second Temple period in Jerusalem, archeologists discovered what they call Theodotus's synagogue inscription. Here is an English translation from the original, which is inscribed not in Hebrew, but Greek:

> Theodotus, [son] of Vettenus, priest and leader of the synagogue [*archisynagogos*], son of an *archisynagogos*, grandson of an *archisynagogos*, built the synagogue for the reading of the law and the teaching of the commandments, and the guest-chamber and the rooms and the water installations for lodging for those needing them from abroad, which his fathers, the elders and Simonides founded.

Note that the inscription does *not* say that it was a place of prayer. Presumably, prayer went along with sacrifice in the nearby Jerusalem Temple. Or maybe it was assumed that the synagogue was so obviously a place of prayer that this function need not be recorded in the dedicatory inscription.

While there are no physical remains of the Theodotus synagogue, there is archeological evidence of other predestruction synagogues outside of Jerusalem. Herodian, a fortress built by the mad king for whom it is named, is visible from Jerusalem and is less than a day's walk away. One of the buildings within the fortress complex has been identified by archeologists as a first-century, predestruction synagogue. Even further south, near the shores of the Dead Sea, stands the famous mountain redoubt of Masada. It, too, presumably had a synagogue. The excavators of these and another site (Gamla, discussed below) identified the rectangular rooms, each with sets of columns and, most telling, benches that line the walls, as Second Temple–era synagogues.

Recently a synagogue was unearthed at Migdal/Magdala, in the north, on the shore of the Sea of Galilee—also dated to the Second Temple period. There, excavators discovered a large carved stone with a bas relief of a menorah and urns. This makes Migdal the outlier among the other so-called Second Temple–era synagogues, as it also has partial frescoes on its walls and remnants of mosaic floors. None of the other synagogues from that early period have pictorial art or decoration. Like the other presumed synagogues, Migdal has benches lining the main room.

There is general agreement that the site at Gamla in the Galilee is also a synagogue from that early period. Josephus, writing in the late first century, describes the town as a center of the rebellion against Rome in 66–70 CE:

> Gamla would not surrender, relying . . . upon the natural difficulties of its location. The high mountain descends in a ridge that rises in the middle like a hump and then descends again . . . so that it resembles a camel, from which it is named [*Gamla*=camel in Aramaic].

Although Josephus mentions the crowded city and its citadel-like defenses, he does not mention a synagogue. Indeed, with the notable exception of Migdal, aside from the benches lining the wall there is nothing that identifies this or any of these other first-century buildings as synagogues: no inscriptions, no art on the walls, no mosaics on the floors, none of the usual accoutrements of later synagogue buildings. So the question must be asked: do benches make a synagogue?

My Israeli colleague, archeologist-historian Lee Levine, in his book *Ancient Synagogues Revealed*, lists the "most frequently mentioned activities" associated with synagogues: prayer, study, meals, a repository for communal funds, court sessions, a guest house and residence for synagogue officials. Levine is clear that "benches were always a fixture in these buildings," even though none of the undertakings just listed require Jews to be seated. Prayer and study were as often as not done in standing postures; and the other functions that synagogues served likewise did not demand fixed benches.

Most Greco-Roman public and private buildings share the details we see in these early "synagogue" buildings: columns dividing the main hall, as well as benches. Dining rooms (*triclinia*), city council chambers (*bouleteria*), gathering places for all citizenry (*ecclesiasteria*), privy council rooms (*curia*), and the like are examples of essentially secular models from the Roman world that display these architectural features. Churches and pagan temple buildings also share these elements. It may be the case that Herodium, Masada, and Gamla were simply public assembly buildings.

Archeologists tend to describe Roman public buildings by the plans of the buildings or their shapes. Roman-era archeologists distinguish the colonnade (*stoa*), theater, and basilica—an oblong with its visual focus directed toward the front short wall, which may be capped by an apse or semicircular recess, and perhaps even a dome. The basilica has two rows of columns running the length of the building that serve to hold up the roof or second floor, as well as to divide the space into three aisles. Below is a photo of the Basilica of St. Ambrose in Milan. Although it has been repaired and rebuilt over the centuries, the plan and many sections date back to the original fourth- and fifth-century construction. Note the rows of arched columns that divide the church space into a center aisle and side aisles. The front of the church has a rounded apse containing the altar.

BASILICA OF ST. AMBROSE, MILAN

An alternative building plan, the broad-house, is also an oblong, but its focus is at the middle of the long wall. Synagogues and churches seem to be built with one footprint or the other: basilica or broad-house. Further, they share the fact that many of them began as private homes, which were likely donated to the religious community and then architecturally adapted for communal use over time. Excavators have discovered homes upon which were built synagogues that were later expanded or otherwise remodeled—leaving three or more layers of remains for zealous diggers to uncover.

One of the reasons I have made use of archeological terminology is to underscore the extent to which Greco-Roman structural design informs Jewish public buildings in the period. It is not all that surprising that buildings tend to be erected in the styles of the surrounding culture.

They partake of the fashion current in a particular locale. If one pauses for a moment to think of American or European synagogues from the nineteenth and twentieth centuries, the point is well illuminated. Some look like public buildings, while others look like neighboring churches. Each fits the time and era when it was built.

Before we leap ahead to examine the many different types of Jewish buildings from the later "Talmudic era" (second through seventh centuries CE), we should take a step back to situate Jewish sacred architecture within the broader context of Roman building practices. Synagogues are, to be sure, quintessentially Jewish buildings—but so are the homes and shops and assembly buildings of the Jewish community in Roman Palestine, aren't they? What makes a building Jewish, per se? Is it sufficient that it was in a Jewish town? Or inhabited by Jews? Need it have had a *mezuzah* (see Deut. 6:9) on its doorpost? Or must that building have had a rabbi in charge? This last question seems absurd on its face, since the vast majority of Jews were not, in fact, rabbis. Indeed, it may well be the case that the vast majority of *synagogues* in Late Antiquity were not related to the rabbis either, at least not to those rabbis we know from the classical rabbinic literature. With that in mind, we will take a fairly broad view of the architectural and artistic remains of Palestine and the Diaspora, counting as Jewish pretty much any remnant that bears some relationship to Jews or Judaism.

Lest we think that Jewish buildings shared common features with other Roman construction plans merely due to the limitations of engineering in that period, it is worth remembering that Roman architecture was incredibly sophisticated. Think, for example, of Roman aqueducts. These were driven by gravity, which means that for the water to run from its source to the baths or spouts of a town, great attention had to be paid to the ups and downs of local topography. Considering the lay of the land was a hallmark of all Roman construction.

Roman architecture also featured refined design. The Pantheon was built in Rome under Emperor Augustus and then rebuilt in the second century during the reign of Hadrian. It remains the largest unreinforced

Aqueduct, Caesarea Maritima

Pantheon, Rome

concrete dome in the world. Clearly, Roman architects could build pretty much any way they wished.

As I turn back to Jewish buildings, we will see that most ancient synagogues that have been discovered tend to be basilicas, which means they had columns running down the sides to hold up the roofs or upper stories. This effectively divided the main hall into a central section (nave) and two side aisles. That central hall was approached by means of doors that often opened out into an atrium or other kind of forecourt. Presumably this is where people gathered to enter and maybe to gossip about those within. The ninth-century Midrash on Proverbs captures this double doorway:

> "Waiting at the posts of my doors" (Proverbs 8:34). This refers to the gates of prayer. One is obligated to rise early and go to the synagogue every day. There he will enter through the two doorways and then stand in prayer.

This doubled entrance can be seen in synagogues all across the Roman world: in Sardis, Priene, Ostia, Dura, Delos, Aegina, Naro, and Stobi as well as among the synagogues of Roman Palestine. In a church, this area outside the main sanctuary would be called the narthex; but some of these synagogues had both a forecourt as well as a narthex-like section within the synagogue.

Some of the synagogues also had a table in the front, just where one would expect an altar in a church or the Torah-reading platform in a modern synagogue. Here is the table in the immense Sardis synagogue. Note that the upright leg has a Roman eagle and that just beyond the table is one of a pair of lions. Since most contemporary synagogues have Torah reading tables, and public reading of Scripture in synagogues is attested from the first century onward, it is tempting to assume we are looking at such a reader's table. But we don't really know what took place at this table, or whether this building had a public civic function before it was given over to the Jewish community. Maybe it came furnished, as it were.

SARDIS SYNAGOGUE STONE TABLE

Depending on the layout of the synagogue, congregants might use any of a number of inner doors to enter on the side of the main auditorium, which held what is called either the Torah-shrine or the seat of Moses, or in some cases they might enter on the side opposite these features.

The Sardis synagogue has three entry doors, with the so-called Torah shrine between the center door and the one to the right. We can see that there are steps leading up to it and that it is carved in stone but made nevertheless to look like a set of doors—symbolic either of the ark where the Torah is stored, or, perhaps, of the doors to the long-gone Jerusalem Temple. Doors like these were a common feature of synagogue art, and we cannot be sure what they were meant to symbolize. They also happen to be found in pagan and Christian Roman settings.

At some synagogues there was a "seat of Moses" in place of the "Torah shrine." The synagogue at Dura Europos offers an example from

SARDIS SYNAGOGUE ENTRYWAYS

the mid-third century. Atop the seating area at the Dura synagogue is a depiction of a large seashell. Above the shell shape there is both a menorah and a painting of a set of doors. To the right of those doors, just above the right pillar of the "shrine," is a depiction of the Binding of Isaac from Genesis 22.

Two other features are commonly found among sites identified as synagogues, as well. The first is a side room that may have been used as either a place for the synagogue officials to live or guest quarters. It was fairly common in the Roman world for observant Jews to spend Shabbat—when they would not otherwise travel or do business—within the Jewish communities where they found themselves on their journeys. The Babylonian Talmud reports that three famous rabbis, Rabbi Meir, Rabbi Judah, and Rabbi Yosé, once were traveling outside of the Land of Israel, and when they arrived at a certain town on the eve of the Sabbath, they sought hospitality there.

Dura-Europos synagogue, Torah shrine or Seat of Moses

Of course, these extra rooms attached to the synagogue could equally well have been used for storage or even served as a *geniza*—a book depository for used or worn-out sacred texts. We have evidence from the Dead Sea Scrolls, the Bar Kokhba letters, and the Cave of Letters that the storage of documents, old and current, was common among Jewish communities in the Roman world.

The second feature occasionally associated with synagogue sites was a Mikvah, or a ritual immersion pool. These small pools, which were filled with rainwater or other natural water flows, were a primary means of making ritually fit the objects and persons who had contracted unfitness—most commonly through menstruation or semen. When a Jewish community built their synagogue, it was natural for them to build these ritual baths nearby. Yet even here they mimic in some way Roman custom; as in the Hellenistic world, it was de rigueur to build public baths among the very first of the buildings erected in a town. Although ritual purity and bodily cleanliness are not the same thing, immersion was nevertheless cleansing. Neither hospitality nor cleanliness, however, was an exclusively Jewish custom within the Greco-Roman milieu.

Finally, the geographic orientation of a synagogue is notable. Ideally, at least according to rabbinic rulings, worshippers in the synagogue should be facing Jerusalem. As it is expressed in the Tosefta, a third-century companion to the Mishnah:

> Those who stand in prayer in the Diaspora should direct their hearts toward the Land of Israel, as it is said, "pray in the direction of their land" (2 Chron. 6:38).
>
> Those who stand in prayer in the Land of Israel should direct their hearts toward Jerusalem and pray, as it is said, "they pray to You in the direction of the city which you have chosen" (2 Chron. 6:34).
>
> Those who stand in prayer in the city of Jerusalem should direct their hearts toward the Temple, as it is said, "to pray towards this house" (2 Chron. 6:32).
>
> Those who stand in prayer in the Temple should direct their hearts toward the Holy of Holies and pray, as it is said, "they pray towards this place" (1 Kings 8:30).
>
> Thus those in the north face the south; those in the south face the north; those in the east face the west; and those in the west face the east. Thus all Israel prays to one place.

It might seem from this rabbinic text that the orientation of a building would be a great help to archeologists who are trying to identify whether certain architectural remains are in fact synagogues. Unfortunately, builders paid much more attention to details of the topography, such as which way the land tilted, what other buildings abutted the space, or whether there was a water source nearby, than they did to rabbinic law—assuming that they knew it or cared about it in the first place.

In truth, the most reliable means of identifying a synagogue from antiquity is the presence of a donor inscription. Of course, we cannot help but appreciate that synagogues of Late Antiquity are identified by donor plaques, much as modern-day synagogues are. A Midrash from the fifth-century Galilee (Lev. Rabbah 5:4) reminds us that nothing ever changes, at least when it comes to fund-raising:

> The story is told that Rabbi Eliezer, Rabbi Yehoshua, and Rabbi Aqiba traveled to the suburbs of Antioch to collect charity funds. There was a man there called "Father of the Jews" who gave charity generously, but he had lost his fortune. When he saw the rabbis, he went home looking ill . . . the rabbis said to him, "Even though there are others who gave more than you, we still put your name at the head of the donors' book [tomos]."

I know that you are shocked, shocked that donors got special treatment. There was a donors' list, referred to in Greek/Latin as the "tome." And just like they do at the opera or ballet today, the largest donors were listed first. In an earlier chapter we saw a Greek donor inscription from the synagogue in Hammat Tiberias. That same synagogue, dating from the third to fourth century, also has an Aramaic inscription that reads, "Peace be to all who gave charity in this Sacred Place and who will give charity in the future. May he be blessed, amen, amen, selah. And to me, amen." I just love that the guy who laid down the mosaic included himself for a blessing while he was at it.

Assuming for now that we actually can identify a synagogue in the postdestruction period by its inscriptions, art, and architecture, we should note that from the third through sixth centuries CE there was a veritable building boom. I want to discuss eight synagogues to give you a feel for their architecture, their layout, and some of their salient symbols. The number eight has no special valence but represents five Diaspora synagogues from all corners of the Roman Empire, plus three more synagogues from urban centers in the Land of Israel. Right now we will be taking a bird's-eye view. In our next chapter we will zoom in on the interior features of each and, in particular, its art.

The synagogue of Dura Europos, located on the easternmost border of the Roman Empire, is famous for its shift away from the nonfigurative art in earlier synagogues to a full flowering of biblical scenes emblazoned on wall-paintings from the top to the bottom of the sanctuary. We have yet to discover pictorial art in synagogues from before the destruction of the Jerusalem Temple, with the recently discovered synagogue at Migdal in the Galilee being the notable exception. Dura's synagogue was covered by sand when the town was destroyed in 256 CE, during the Persian invasion. Here is what archeologist Clark Hopkins wrote when he first discovered the synagogue:

> All I can remember is the sudden shock and then the aston-ishment, the disbelief, as painting after painting came into view . . . in spite of having been encased in dry dust for centu-ries, the murals retained a vivid brightness that was little short of the miraculous.

The synagogue was built in at least two stages. It originally was a private home. Dura, located on the Euphrates River, in what today is Syria, marked the border between the Roman and Sasanian-Persian empires. The synagogue was in a neighborhood that also housed temples to Roman gods, temples to Eastern gods such as Mithra, and a church. The styles of all these buildings are fairly similar. The synagogue was right up against the city's western wall. When that wall was reinforced by heaping an earthen bulwark against the invading Persians, the amazing paintings were inadvertently preserved. Once the Persians conquered the town, in 256 CE, Dura sat desolate until it was excavated in the 1920s. We will return to look more closely at Dura's art soon, but for now it is sufficient to note that the worshippers in the synagogue faced southwest—that is, they faced Jerusalem. While that may be indicative of some kind of piety, it may also simply be a function of the successive layers of building erected as the congregation grew.

I began this chapter by recounting how my wife likes to wander Manhattan observing the architecture. She also travels with me to archeological sites dotted across the former Roman Empire. We have visited locations from England to Israel. Often a dig consist of little more than a low grouping of stones that archeologists have interpreted as a given building. Sometimes there is little more on an otherwise empty plain than what appears to be a pile of rubble among the weeds. But then, with a little help from a guidebook, the outline of a former building becomes discernible. With a bit of imagination, my wife and I reconstruct the buildings in our mind's eye. My wife tolerates my appetite for visiting otherwise desolate sites because Sandy is a true believer in viewing what she aptly calls "history where it happened."

One such site is at ancient Sardis, now in modern central Turkey. The Sardis synagogue had been a public building before it was turned over to the Jewish community. It fits neatly with its surroundings, and its style—witness the eagle on the table at the front of the synagogue—is decidedly Greco-Roman. The final stage of the synagogue displays the remains of two rows of columns running parallel, creating a basilica with an atrium forecourt. At the western end of the synagogue, behind the large table, was an apse with rounded benches. Perhaps the synagogue elders sat there. The remainder of the congregation faced west-northwest—away from Jerusalem. The Sardis synagogue sits snugly in the ancient town center—there is no modern town at the site—right next to the excavated gymnasium and market.

Sandy and I have also taken the local tram to Rome's ancient port town of Ostia. The synagogue there was founded in the first or second century, and its final construction layer dates to the fourth century. During that time Ostia was still a bustling port. Since then, the waters have receded, leaving the beach of Ostia an entire tram stop farther down the line. The synagogue, in fact, was discovered when highway workers were widening the road to the beach to make it more accessible.

When we waded through the weeds, we found the scant remnant of the Ostia synagogue, with its three doorways, Torah-shrine, and forecourt. This entry court is bordered by a mini-*tetrapylon*—a monumental four-arched gate. While the architectural elegance of the structure seems out of place among the weeds today, it betokens the importance of the Ostia synagogue back when the harbor still reached the town. The inside of the synagogue covers a large area that, at least presently, is lacking interior columns. Yet it does have a curved, apse-like wall on the side opposite the entrance. If the officers of the synagogue sat on benches around the apse, they would have faced the Holy City (Jerusalem, not Rome). It is easy to imagine the synagogue's elders, shipbuilders, traders, and sailors praying heartily for a safe voyage.

The synagogue at Stobi, in Macedonia, also went through more than one phase of construction. We can gain insights into the gradual stages of a synagogue building program from this particular site. A certain Claudius Tiberius Polycharmos, described as "father of the synagogue at Stobi," repaired and expanded the building. He is mentioned in a lengthy Greek donor inscription. His name is classic Greek, and his imperial-sounding names—Claudius and Tiberius—may reflect his lineage and status. It could be that he had very impressive (and originally non-Jewish) relatives. Or, more likely, someone in his family had been taken captive in a war, become a slave to the imperial household, and eventually earned his freedom. It was the custom for freedmen to take their former owners' names, especially names as impressive as Claudius and Tiberius.

Polycharmos's private home was right next door to the synagogue he dedicated. It had those features one might expect from a wealthy donor: beautiful mosaic floors, a colonnaded court, a fancy dining room (*triclinium*) with a fountain, and another large room with a reflecting pool. I would guess that the synagogue may originally have been part of Polycharmos's house, which he subsequently donated to the community. The current archeological remains of the synagogue include a dining area, an entryway atrium, and a sacred space (labeled in Greek: *hagios topos*) arrayed as a basilica with an apse. The mosaics of the nave are still visible. The identification of the site as a synagogue is further assured by an incised menorah on a plastered wall in one of the rooms off the main hall. A church was later built atop the two layers of the synagogue, and all three building layers were subsequently excavated.

In the ancient North African town of Naro, in modern Hammam Lif, just south of Tunis, the three-door entrance to the synagogue interrupts the long wall opposite the so-called Torah shrine. This broadhouse synagogue structure has a beautiful mosaic "carpet," including a Latin inscription identifying it as *"sancta synagoga."* The art of the central mosaic includes renderings of animals, waterfowl, fruit baskets, a palm tree, and sea creatures. It is flanked by mosaics of menorahs and rather minimalist, abstract mosaics of a palm frond and citron. The latter would be unidentifiable were we not trained to expect them as symbols in synagogue art. The building is double columned and dates to the sixth or seventh century. Hammam Lif is a nice example of ancient North African synagogue construction, not far from where the remnants of the Tunis Jewish congregation still gather for weekly prayer. When my wife and I visited there, we knew we had found the right place by noting the presence of armed guards on the street outside. Such is the fragility of synagogue life, ancient and modern.

We now look toward the Holy Land and briefly describe the layouts of synagogues discovered in three ancient urban Jewish centers: Caesarea Maritima on the Mediterranean shore, Tiberias at the Sea of Galilee, and Sepphoris/Diocaesarea in central Galilee. As the names of these cities indicate, they were built as Roman towns and had a pagan and Christian, as well as Jewish, population. These Jewish communities were embedded in thoroughly Roman contexts. All three of these sites remain available for tourists to visit, as my wife and I have. Go see these ancient synagogue remains with your very own eyes.

Caesarea Maritima served as the imperial port with a major harbor complex. The city was built by Herod in the first century BCE and was named for his patron, Emperor Augustus Caesar. Early in the first century CE, it became the Roman administrative capital, and its fortunes rose and fell with the successive rebellions and quiet of the Jewish population. The synagogue at Caesarea may have been built as a broadhouse, with a door to the east. But the sanctuary of the later stratum of the building, dating to the third to fifth centuries, is a basilica with an apse, columns, and a north-south orientation. Congregants did not actually face Jerusalem as a point of worship. The inscriptions are mostly Greek and mention donors who have Greek names. This may be the synagogue where they recited the *Shema* in Greek during their prayers. Some short Hebrew and Aramaic inscriptions were found near the synagogue site. Not surprisingly, excavators also found menorahs incised or carved in relief on some of the remaining capitals.

On the shores of the Sea of Galilee lie the city of Tiberias and its suburb Hammat Tiberias. The synagogue is south of the town, near the hot springs that give the suburb its name (*Hammat* means "hot springs" in Hebrew/Aramaic). In the third and fourth centuries, Tiberias and Hammat more or less merged into one larger metropolis. The Patriarch of the Jews and the rabbinical academy held court there. The first draft of the Palestinian Talmud may have been compiled in rabbinic circles of fourth- to fifth-century Tiberias and Caesarea. This tells us that the rabbis were quite comfortable in what were thoroughly cosmopolitan Roman cities, each replete with pagan populations and imagery.

The synagogue of Tiberias's suburb Hammat has three sets of columns instead of the usual two, and so the main sanctuary is divided into four sections. Congregants faced southward, in the general if not precise direction of Jerusalem, perhaps in accordance with the dictates of the rabbinic text quoted earlier about which way to face when praying. The Greek donor inscriptions were also quoted previously, seen along with a picture of the donor plaque. That inscription is framed on either side by lions and is part of the central section of the synagogue's beautiful mosaic carpet. At the opposite end, the mosaic depicts the doors of the ark or of the Temple with menorahs on either side, and the predictable palm, citron, and shofar. The surprise is in the central panel. Here is a zodiac, complete with Greek mythical figures—including an uncircumcised boy representing the month of Tishrei (Libra). Smack in the middle of the zodiac circle is the divine figure of Zeus-Helios, riding his four-horsed quadriga. Depictions of Helios can also be found in synagogue remains at Na'aran (in the South), at Bet Alpha (also in the Galilee), and at Sepphoris. We'll discuss these unexpected mosaics in our next chapter, I promise.

Right now, we have one more synagogue to consider. The excavations at Sepphoris uncovered significant sections of the Roman-era city. The town sits midway between Caesarea Maritima on the west and Tiberias on the east. Although Jewish sources indicate that it had a majority-Jewish population, the inhabitants did not join the first-century revolt against Rome. Instead, they opened the gates of the city to General Vespasian. Yikes! Its Jewish character, however, later was assured when Rebbi Judah the Patriarch moved to Sepphoris in the early third century. It is generally thought that Rebbi completed his editing of the Mishnah there. The Palestinian Talmud says that when Rebbi Judah the Patriarch died, the Jews of the eighteen synagogues of Sepphoris turned out to mourn for him.

The city is built on a Roman plan—with a *cardo,* or north-to-south main street, bisecting the city. Many mosaics have been recovered in the excavations, including the one of Aphrodite and Eros discussed earlier. The art and architecture of Sepphoris are, in the words of its archeologists Ze'ev Weiss and Ehud Netzer, "not very different from the pagan cities of the region." The synagogue they excavated is in the northern part of town, "built on an east-west axis . . . to fit in with the topography and the alignment of the adjacent streets." Congregants entered through a single door into an antechamber, turned left, and then passed through one of two doors into the main sanctuary.

The art of the Sepphoris synagogue is fascinating, with seven rows of panels making up the central mosaic carpet. Among them there are Greek inscriptions, a depiction of the Binding of Isaac, and the zodiac we just mentioned—with a faceless Zeus-Helios depicted as the orb of the sun in the center. And then there is a menagerie of beasts; the usual menorahs, palm, and citron; and symbolic doors. Captions on these mosaics are in Greek, as are a number of the donor inscriptions. Certain of the biblical scenes are captioned in Hebrew, while some donor acknowledgements are in Aramaic. We are left with an impression of an educated congregation—at least those who liked to look at the mosaic floor.

As these eight synagogues from the Diaspora and the Holy Land demonstrate, the architecture of Jewish buildings was Roman. The cities they were built in were Roman, be they in the Diaspora or in Palestine. Town plans, inscriptions, and public buildings all provided the Greco-Roman milieu in which the Jewish community flourished. City plans were a manifestation of Hellenistic culture. Earlier, we read about poor Rabbi Eliezer's arrest. When asked why he was arrested, he reported, "Once I was walking on the main street (*istrata*) of Sepphoris . . ." I want to focus on that main street, the *istrata*.

Roman cities were planned on a grid, and the major arteries were built on a north-south axis. The main street that divided the town this way was called the *cardo*, while the east-west divide was the *decumanus*. The term Rabbi Eliezer used, *istrata*, is the same word as "street." Some of you may recall the 1954 Fellini movie *La Strada*, which was about a road trip. In any case, Rabbi Eliezer was most likely walking on the *cardo* when he met with his trouble. That very same *cardo* has been excavated by archeologists in Sepphoris. But given the size of such a main street, we might expect a *cardo* to show up in many excavations of ancient towns, and indeed it has.

At the crossroads of the *cardo* and the *decumanus*, there was often a monument marking the intersection. This was called a *tetrapylon*, or four-arched gate (mentioned above in our visit to the Ostia synagogue, which grandiosely had its own mini-*tetrapylon* on the synagogue grounds). Archeologists have uncovered many of the grander *tetrapylons* that mark city crossroads. Below is one from Aphrodisias in Asia Minor. Earlier, we discussed the lengthy inscription from the synagogue at Aphrodisias that recognized the "God fearers."

Although archeologists have not yet discovered the *tetrapylon* of the Jewish Roman city of Caesarea, it is mentioned in a third-century rabbinic source and again, poignantly, in the ninth-century Midrash on Proverbs (chapter 9), where we read how Rabbi Aqiba's disciple Yehoshua of Gerasa and the prophet Elijah accompanied the great rabbi's corpse for burial:

> They walked all night long until they reached the *tetrapylon* of Caesarea. When they arrived at the *tetrapylon* of Caesarea

TETRAPYLON OF APHRODISIAS

they first descended and then ascended some steps, and there
they found a bier prepared, a bench (*subsellium*), a table, and
candelabrum. As they placed Rabbi Aqiba on the bier, the
candelabrum lit and the table set! . . . At that moment they
said, "Blessed are you Rabbi Aqiba, who has found a good resting place at the hour of your death.

The text does not make any mention of Rabbi Aqiba having been
tortured, but instead offers a kind of dreamscape in which his disciple
Yehoshua walks with the prophet Elijah to accompany the good rabbi to
his final resting place. I can't imagine what the *tetrapylon* of Caesarea is
doing in this "dream," but might it symbolize the four-chambered heart
of the bereft Rabbi Yehoshua? I am certain that it does not describe the
actual burial of the sainted rabbi.

Let's leave Rabbi Aqiba to rest in peace, but as we do so, we should take notice of his burial place. Yehoshua and Elijah made ascents and descents until they found the appropriate chamber for his burial. Earlier we saw a Jerusalem burial monument named for Absalom that was actually from the first century. But the most significant Jewish burial finds from both Rome and the Galilee have been those in catacombs. While many tourists visit the Christian catacombs of Rome, few get to see the Jewish ones, which also date back to the second and third centuries. I described my visit to one group of Roman catacombs in the opening chapter. Another of those Roman Jewish catacombs, at Vigna Randanini, is conveniently located right across the street from the Christian catacombs, just off the famous Appian Way. Meanwhile, in the Galilee from the same era, we have catacomb complexes at Beth She'arim, associated with the family of Judah the Patriarch. This site is one of the only places where we find inscriptions bearing the names of rabbis mentioned in the Talmud.

Catacombs tended to be below-ground complexes, using either natural caves or excavated ones to hold burial chambers on the floors or in the walls. Bodies were left to decompose in these niches, called *sarcophagi* (singular: *sarcophagus*, lit. "flesh eater"). After a year, the bones usually were gathered and reburied into smaller receptacles called ossuaries. Freestanding stone sarcophagi have been discovered in the catacombs, affording more dignified burial, perhaps, than the placement of bodies into the ubiquitous wall niches. Jews no longer use catacombs or sarcophagi and ossuaries to store bones. Even so, most of the Jewish mourning customs that follow burial remain the same.

In the photo are niches in the Roman Jewish catacomb of Vigna Randanini. Once a corpse was within the niche, it was plastered over or left open until the flesh decayed. It may not be immediately clear from the palm tree photo below how these niches were carved. On close inspection we can see that the fresco had been painted, and then, at a later time, when there was need, the community returned to carve new burial sites on either side of the painting. Below it is another example of

Vigna Randanini catacomb Fig. 1

Vigna Randanini catacomb Fig. 2

how this was done. It makes the destruction of the earlier art even more apparent. Clearly, space for burial trumped the funerary art.

A great deal of information can be gleaned from the inscriptions left by the departed Roman Jews. They describe a broad Who's Who of the ancient Jewish world—one in which Greek and Roman names are very common and the Hebrew language is quite rare. We find very few pagan catacombs in the Roman world. The pagan poor were cremated. Those who could afford sepulchers followed the common practice of placing burial monuments on ground level, at the entrance routes to major Roman cities.

Indeed, the pagan sarcophagus was a ubiquitous feature of the ancient Roman landscape, as common there as they are in today's museums. Here is a sarcophagus adorned with an image of the deceased

SARCOPHAGUS—CAPITOLINE MUSEUMS, ROME

couple, now reclining at that great symposium in the sky. Notice the motif of the boar hunt, which perhaps is meant to invoke the heroism of the late departed. Boar hunting is found on a number of ancient pagan sarcophagi. Note as well the adorable *putti* (little winged angels) holding a theater mask at the top left.

In another sarcophagus, from the Naples Archeological Museum, other pagan religious motifs are displayed. The bas relief of the deceased couple depicted is wreathed with garlands held up by *putti*. On the sarcophagus's top, there is a kind of seahorse monster, or Cetus, with a corkscrew tail, being ridden, perhaps, by a nereid, or mermaid. This particular mythic animal will appear in our next chapter when we discuss Jewish art.

These types of pagan legends are common in the funerary art of Late Antiquity. Another sarcophagus from the Naples Museum depicts the mythic motif of Leda being impregnated by Zeus, who appeared to

"LEDA AND SWAN" SARCOPHAGUS—HERACLION MUSEUM

her in the form of a swan. Just above is an image of Leda and the swan from the museum in Heraclion, Crete (worth visiting if you visit the Greek islands). We will see another version of this motif, too, on a Jewish sarcophagus. Love that swan.

In our tour of synagogues, we visited the pagan world to demonstrate how thoroughly Hellenistic customs infiltrated Judaism, even its conservative burial customs. It's time for a much closer look at Jewish art in the Roman world. Let's move the tour indoors.

CHAPTER IX

THE HANDWRITING ON THE WALL (AND THE FLOOR AND CEILING): ROMAN JEWISH ART

When I visit synagogues in North America, Europe, and Israel, I am struck at the sheer ubiquity of artistic images: on the walls, in stained glass windows, in the prayer books and Bible volumes, all alongside beautiful Judaica objets d'art. If there was a time that the Jews refrained from making images, it is long, long over. In addition to displays of art, words also appear in synagogues. Clearly, you would expect words to appear in books, but words also are found on memorial and dedication plaques, on identifying inscriptions explaining the art on the walls and windows, and in listings of the names of synagogue leadership. In North America and Europe, these inscriptions are overwhelmingly recorded in Latin letters. Hebrew appears rarely, most often in biblical quotes or to identify holidays depicted in stained glass.

These combinations of pictorial art, along with the small or large inscriptions describing it, appear fairly regularly in American synagogues. For a very long time, folks who visited my boyhood synagogue in Chicago would return to New York to tell me with a smile that they had seen my Hebrew school and bar mitzvah pictures still hanging on the synagogue wall, neatly captioned with my name. Clearly, this was a high point in the history of Jewish art!

In antiquity Jews lived surrounded by artistic and idolatrous imagery also captioned with inscriptions. In bigger cities Jews were exposed to statues, mosaics, and frescoes in vivid, gaudy color. Our beautiful Aphrodite came from a mosaic floor in the banquet room of a home in Sepphoris. In Hebrew the name for Sepphoris, *Tzippori*, means "birds." The city's Greek and Latin name, Diocaesarea, means that the imperial town (*Caesar*ea) was dedicated to Zeus (in Greek inflected forms: *Dia*, *Dios*). It was a cultured city with a theater and a *tetrapylon* at the main intersection. Travel guides refer to the Aphrodite mosaic of Sepphoris as the "Mona Lisa of the Galilee"; still, the town has enough other pagan imagery to assure me that the mosaic is not just another pretty face but, indeed, depicts Aphrodite/Venus.

Among the other Greco-Roman art found in Sepphoris is a tiled floor from a private home called by its excavators "the Dionysus mosaic," named after the god it depicts. That same floor also features a Pan-like centaur and Hercules. In case there is any doubt about who he is, there is a Greek caption identifying him as Herakles, as the name is spelled in Greek. He is engaged in a drinking contest with Dionysus. The centaur, or Pan character, is on the left panel, with the accompanying Greek caption "Bacchae." The archeologists of Sepphoris also uncovered small statuettes of Pan and of Prometheus, complete with an eagle pecking at his liver. The significant polytheist population of Sepphoris enjoyed Roman-pagan artistic motifs and lived comfortably alongside the Jewish community. Given the art we have uncovered in the synagogue there, I must conclude that the Jews of Sepphoris also were comfortable living among their pagan neighbors.

The pagan images in the mosaics of Sepphoris are delightful. One mosaic shows a scene at Egypt's Nilometer, depicting the device which measured the annual rise of the famous river. Another scene shows the image of a one-breasted Amazon. Yet another Sepphoris mosaic displays the myth of Orpheus, a figure from Greek and Roman mythology who played his music to soothe the animals. Just to Orpheus's right is an array of the birds of that birdy town. To his left, a boar, a hare, and a snake in a tree are all calmed by Orpheus's music.

Of course, Jewish tradition tells of another great musician and harp player, King David. So we shouldn't be entirely surprised to see him on the mosaic floor of the early sixth-century CE synagogue on the coast at Gaza, looking remarkably like Orpheus. Just in case you might think it actually is Orpheus, the mosaic has a caption to the right of the Jewish king's head identifying him in Hebrew as "David." But he is clearly modeled on Orpheus—his harp is charming a snake, a lioness, and even a giraffe (or maybe a long-necked gazelle).

This brief detour to see King David in Gaza has brought us back from pagan gods and heroes once more to Jewish characters in synagogues. Let's return to Sepphoris now to take a closer look at the art in the synagogue excavated there. The synagogue dates from the fourth century, and its art is typical: menorahs, palm, and citron (the biblically commanded *lulav* and *etrog,* used for the holiday of Sukkot), lions, a shofar, and other biblical horns.

As we walk to the front of the main sanctuary, bordered on either side by the Jewish symbols just mentioned, there is a mosaic panel of the Temple—or maybe it's a Torah ark? In any case, the doors of that building are topped with a shell shape and bracketed by pillars. This ubiquitous depiction of doors is found in many Roman-era synagogues. But it also is found on a sarcophagus in the Naples Museum, there identified as a Christian resting place. And similar sets of doors can be found outside of religious contexts, at least Jewish or Christian ones.

We already have seen "the doorway" in funerary and synagogue contexts, but it is also found on a wall in Herculaneum, the pagan town that was covered along with Pompeii by the eruption of Mt. Vesuvius in 79 CE. The doorway is flanked by columns on both sides, with the oft-seen shell above the portal. Within the doorway is neither a Torah nor a Temple priest, but two figures: male and female. Most art historians identify them as Poseidon and his wife, Amphitrite. The shell is appropriate for the King of the Sea.

HERCULANEUM

But what can this tell me about the depiction of the shell and the doorway in synagogue art? That type of doorway may be a Torah ark or shrine, since the one depicted in Rome's Jewish catacomb at Villa Torlonia shows scrolls inside the open doors. It may symbolize God's house, as it seems to be a portal for the gods in the picture above. But the doorway also may be symbolic of the monumental gates of the Jerusalem Temple. In Jewish Roman art it may even represent the synagogue itself. There are too many options to decide with any assurance what the door is supposed to represent. I would like to think that the one thing the doorway should not represent in synagogue art, however, is a portal for pagan gods.

The god Poseidon and his wife are also depicted on a mosaic floor from a private home from Cirta, Libya, dating to the early fourth century

CE. There, they are flanked by *putti,* or little angelic figures, along with a pod of dolphins. The divine couple ride their four-horsed chariot, the quadriga, in the heart of the sea—a reasonable place for the Roman god of the waves. But given that Sisera, the enemy of the Israelites, met his end when his chariot became mired in the mud (Judges ch.4–5), and that Pharaoh and his troops drowned in the Reed Sea (Ex. 14), you have to wonder whether driving a quadriga in the water is such a good idea, god or not.

The quadriga and my mention of the Bible brings me right back to the synagogue at Sepphoris and a confusing, complex image there. The central panel of the synagogue floor's mosaic "carpet" depicts the zodiac, with Zeus-Helios riding his quadriga across the sky as the central focus. The prevalence of the zodiac in synagogue art may indicate an area of divergence between the rabbis of Talmudic circles and the Jews in the synagogue communities of Roman Palestine. The rabbis expressed their stern disapproval of the image, while the Jews in the synagogue seemed to enjoy the motif.

In fact, the zodiac occupies a significant place in the broader Jewish worldview. Each Jewish month is measured by the phases of the moon, visible over its monthly cycle. Given that this is a phenomenon observable in nature, it is not surprising that the months of the Jewish calendar correspond with other cultures' lunar calendars. Indeed, the rabbis' calendar borrows the names of its months from Babylonia; and these months are congruent with the signs of the celestial zodiac. However, the rabbis do not believe that astrology rules Jewish fate—the Talmud explicitly rejects this notion when it more than once pronounces: "The astrological signs [Hebrew: *mazal*] are not for the Jews."

Yet in Palestinian synagogue zodiac mosaics, the months are depicted by astrological signs. The roundel of synagogue zodiac wheels, even when they are captioned in Hebrew, depicts those signs. The circle of the lunar months is enclosed within a square. Each of the four corners embracing the zodiac circle has a mosaic representing one of the four seasons, while the months in the circle are most often, but not always, situated in the correct seasonal quadrant. A representative of the night sky in which the constellations of the zodiac are visible seems like an obvious choice for the center of the circle. Or a depiction of the moon and stars would be interesting. Because the book of Genesis tells us that "there was evening, there was morning," we might also expect to see a picture of the sun in its course across the sky.

Throughout the ancient world, the sun was the preeminent symbol of daily constancy. The diurnal round of the sun with its warmth and healing power was seen as a benefaction from the gods or from God. In polytheistic pagan cultures, the sun was often seen as a god, Sol Invictus, the invincible sun, also known as Zeus-Helios. Yet anyone who has read the Ten Commandments knows only too well that this is a disturbing, even forbidden, notion. Exodus 20: 3–5 commands:

> You shall have no other gods before Me. You shall not make
> any statue nor any depiction of what is in the heaven above,
> nor on the earth below, nor in the waters below on the earth.
> You shall not bow down to them nor worship them, for I, the
> LORD your God, am a jealous God . . .

When Rabbi Gamaliel made his comment about Aphrodite in the bathhouse, which I recounted to you earlier, he offered Jewish legal parameters for representation of living forms in subsequent Jewish art. We do not represent gods to be worshipped but can represent figures, even human, for aesthetic reasons. Beauty is not forbidden; it is rather encouraged, especially as an offering to God. This is how Gamaliel was able to bathe before that statue of Aphrodite. Even so, the center of the zodiac at the Sepphoris synagogue remains challenging, as it depicts the sun god Helios, riding his heavenly quadriga across the daytime sky.

In the mosaic at Sepphoris, even as the horses pulling the chariot are realistically drawn, Helios is depicted only as an orb with rays emanating to light the world. To the right of the sun-like circle, the mosaic artist also depicted the crescent moon and one star. Clearly, the community of the synagogue in Sepphoris was not too worried about the Second Commandment's prohibition against heavenly bodies, even if

Helios was depicted only symbolically. This representation might reflect a tradition in the Babylonian Talmud, where Rabbi Yehoshua ben Hannaniah likened the difficulty of looking directly at the sun to the difficulty of beholding God. So perhaps the orb of the sun in the Sepphoris synagogue mosaic is meant only to represent, but not to picture, God.

In truth, this mosaic is hardly unique. The synagogues in Huseifa and Hammat Tiberias also have zodiacs on their floors. At Hammat, Helios/Sol is not merely an orb, but incarnate. Zeus-Helios is depicted in handsome human form, holding the orb of royalty and a whip, perhaps to urge his quadriga-chariot across the sky. He is surrounded by the zodiac wheel. Each of the months has a name captioned in Hebrew, as does the four-season mosaics in each quadrant of the square that surrounds the zodiac circle. Aquarius is denoted with a Hebrew caption that is spelled backwards—perhaps indicating that the mosaic artist did not know the language and might have been a pagan who found work in the synagogue. It would be convenient to blame the floor on a non-Jewish artisan. Yet someone in that Jewish community approved the design and paid the bill.

Hammat Tiberias and even Sepphoris/Diocaesarea were Roman imperial cities. So it is possible that the Jews there were more assimilated and so were more comfortable with these pagan symbols. Perhaps the urban communities were just that much more cosmopolitan and laissez-faire about their Jewish practice. But in fact there are also zodiacs in the small town synagogues of Na'aran, near Jericho, and at Beit Alpha, in the Galilee. These are not big urban centers, and while the primitive art of Beit Alpha shows a lack of sophistication, it enthusiastically embraces the Zeus-Helios image. In the photo of Beit Alpha below, note the wheel of the zodiac and the four seasons in the corners. Zeus-Helios emanates rays of light and has a moon and stars accompanying him. Was this a case of the small town community having art envy? Or am I making too much of this apparently pagan image adorning a synagogue?

To further complicate our understanding of the images found on these synagogue floors, Helios is invoked in a Jewish prayer, recovered in a quasi-magical liturgical text from the fourth century CE among

BEIT ALPHA SYNAGOGUE MOSAIC

the manuscripts of the Cairo Geniza, the ancient used-book depository. The prayer is in a manuscript called *Sefer HaRazim*, the Book of Mysteries. We quoted this prayer above, while discussing Gamaliel's bath with Aphrodite. Here is the line of Greek, transliterated into Hebrew, which names Helios:

> I revere you HELIOS, who rises in the east, the good sailor who keeps faith, the heavenly leader who turns the great celestial wheel, who orders the holiness (of the planets), who rules over the poles, Lord, radiant ruler, who fixes the stars.

The Helios prayer gives us a peek at Greco-Roman Jewish folk religion in Roman Palestine during this period. Perhaps it also sheds light on the Zeus-Helios images on the synagogue floors. Helios, or Sol Invictus, as he was known in Latin, apparently was a revered god, at least by some. He was a pagan god who might have been identified with the One and

Only God in the minds of the Jews who beheld him riding across their community's synagogue floor.

The Helios phenomenon is even more complicated than the Jewish evidence alone allows. The last pagan emperor, Julian, who reigned from 361 to 363, wrote about Helios,

> What I am now about to say I consider to be of the greatest importance for all things "That breathe and move upon the earth" and have a share in existence and a reasoning soul and intelligence, but above all others it is of importance to myself. For I am a follower of King Helios . . . the King of the whole universe, who is the center of all things that exist. He, therefore, whether it is right to call him the Supra-Intelligible, or the Idea of Being, and by Being I mean the whole intelligible region, or the One. . . .

In Julian's "Hymn to King Helios," we see a pagan praise his god as the One. Julian defines attributes of Helios not unlike those that the rabbis attribute to their one God. To the extent that the Jews who placed the image of Zeus/Helios on the floors of their synagogues knew or agreed with Julian's theology, the image may have been a convenient pictorial stand-in for God. Some synagogue mosaics depicting biblical stories also show the hand of God reaching down from Heaven. So Helios simply might represent the Jews' God in these synagogue mosaics.

We're not quite done with Zeus-Helios, aka Solis Invictus. Julian was not the only emperor fascinated with the god. Roman emperors not only invoked Sol's assistance, but also identified themselves as incarnate manifestations of the god. The dedicatory altar to Sol, depicted below, was originally found in Palmyra, to the northeast of Roman Palestine in modern Syria. The inscription on the front of the altar, in Latin, invokes the god Sol. The Mandaic inscription on the side identifies him as King Bel. Note that Sol/Helios rides the quadriga of winged horses. Behind Sol an angel crowns him with rays of light. The small receptacle atop Sol's head—formed by the angel crowning him with a halo—likely

SOL INVICTUS—CAPITOLINE MUSEUMS, ROME

was filled with oil so that literal flames emanated from this bas relief of Sol Invictus.

The image of Sol on the chariot with angelic accompaniment may be seen mirrored in this image of Emperor Titus at his apotheosis, commemorated on the interior of the infamous arch of Titus in Rome. The other side of the arch presents the well-known relief of Roman soldiers carrying in triumph the despoiled menorah and other implements from the conquered Jerusalem Temple.

Much like Sol Invictus, Titus rides the quadriga (although his horses lack wings), and an angelic figure has his back. Titus is not the only emperor so depicted. The Roman emperor Marcus Aurelius is depicted in a bas relief riding his quadriga, again with the angelic *genius* of Rome flying at his back.

This gives me pause. These images in their various Greco-Roman guises were abundantly visible to Jews throughout the Roman Empire.

ARCH OF TITUS—ROME

MARCUS AURELIUS—CAPITOLINE MUSEUMS, ROME

Perhaps we should not read too much into the image of Zeus-Helios in the zodiacs on the synagogue floors after all, despite the *Sefer HaRazim* prayer and Emperor Julian's hymn. Romans saw this imagery everywhere. Sol Invictus might have been a god to some, but sometimes art is just art, and Sol was simply meant to represent the sun, no more. The tourists who check into the Hotel Solis Invictus in modern Rome most likely do not do so as an act of idol worship.

The images of Zeus-Helios and the zodiac often are found combined with biblical scenes as part of larger synagogue mosaic "carpets." The most frequent biblical image is of the seven-branched candelabrum, the Menorah of the Jerusalem Temple. As the Torah makes abundantly clear, God likes a nicely lit menorah. In Numbers 8:1–4, God commands Moses to tell his brother, Aaron, the High Priest, "When you mount the Menorah, let seven lamps give light at the front of the Menorah." And the passage concludes, "According to the pattern God has shown Moses, so was the Menorah made." Much more detail of the manufacture of the menorah of the desert tabernacle may be found in Exodus 25: 31–40 and again summarized in Exodus 37:17–24, where the Bible describes how the architect of the tabernacle, Bezalel, did his God-inspired work. Finally, in a set of passages dedicated to the animal offerings that were to be brought for each holiday, Leviticus 24:1–4 reports that God told Moses, "Command the Israelite folk to bring clear beaten olive oil to light and raise up an eternal flame . . . upon the pure [gold] Menorah to burn eternally before the Lord."

There are bas reliefs of a menorah on the arch of Titus in Rome, as well as at the synagogue remains in Ostia, and etched into the memorial plaque of a Roman Jewish catacomb. Note that to one side of the menorah pictured is a palm and citron (*lulav* and *etrog*), while on the other side, there is what looks like a ram's horn. Another memorial in the catacomb mentions the teacher Deutero, who is recalled as sweet (*dulcis*). He, too, is remembered with a menorah and what looks to be a citron.

The photo labeled Catacomb Fig. 3 shows one last menorah from the same catacomb. This one has been frescoed onto the wall.

CATACOMB FIG. 1—VIGNA RANDANINI, ROME

CATACOMB FIG. 2—VIGNA RANDANINI, ROME

There are dozens of images of the menorah from Jewish commu-nities in all corners of the Roman Empire. Archeologists uncovered a bronze cast of a menorah from the synagogue at Ein Gedi, to the west of the Dead Sea, while menorah images are ubiquitous on humble clay oil lamps from the period, which—if you think about it—is kind of ironic. Jewish art had a somewhat standard iconography accompanying the pagan imagery that was also in use in Roman-era and Byzantine

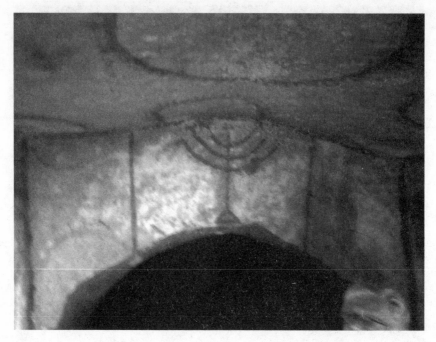

CATACOMB FIG. 3—VIGNA RANDANINI, ROME

synagogues. Some of this imagery comes from narratives in the Torah. At the synagogue in Sepphoris, among other synagogues, actual verses of Scripture in Hebrew or Greek served as captions for mosaics. I suppose this is not unlike stained glass windows found in synagogues (and churches) across North America. One of the biblical images we often see in modern houses of worship, as well as in the synagogues of Roman Palestine, is the story of the Binding of Isaac, recounted in Genesis 22. This powerful narrative was not only chanted in the synagogue when a congregation read the book of Genesis, but it was also the Torah reading for the Jewish New Year, Rosh HaShannah. The fragment that has survived in the Sepphoris synagogue depicts the two servants who accompanied Abraham and Isaac (Gen. 22:5).

The illustration of the entire story of the Binding of Isaac at the small town synagogue of Beit Alpha, on the other hand, is primitive and shocking to behold. On the left are the two servant lads; to the right is

OIL LAMP FRAGMENT WITH MENORAH—MILAN ARCHEOLOGICAL MUSEUM

the fire altar, Abraham, and a small Isaac, both of whom are identified by captions in Hebrew. In the center of the image, also with Hebrew captions, we see the ram caught in the thicket and the biblical words, "Do not put forth [your hand against the boy]" (Gen. 22:12), uttered by the angel of God in order to bring the approaching sacrifice of Isaac to a halt. The voice emanates from a dark-colored mosaic disc, with rays on either side and with a five-fingered hand extending toward Abraham. Is this the hand of God's angel or possibly even the hand of God? Either way, it is a daring depiction of the unseeable, ineffable manifestation of the Jewish God. Or perhaps, like the orb of Helios in Sepphoris, that disc is an artistic stand-in for God, rather than a physical representation of God's hand.

A conundrum is found in an archeological site in Mopsuestia, in Asia Minor. There, in a fourth- to fifth-century CE basilica building oriented east to west, is a stunning mosaic of Noah's ark, so labeled in Greek, and a series of mosaics depicting the Samson story found in the book of Judges 14–16, with fragments of quotes from the Greek translation of the biblical text. There is really only one difficulty with this site,

BEIT ALPHA SYNAGOGUE

which is otherwise a beautiful example of Roman mosaic art applied to biblical motifs: we do not know whether the building is a church or a synagogue. Scholars disagree on its role. As you might guess, Jewish archeologists identify the site as a synagogue, while Christian scholars assume it is a church.

Another site that all agree is a church—indeed, it is still in use as such—is in Madaba, in modern Jordan. On the floor of the church, roped off so that tourists and parishioners do not step on it, is a mosaic map of the world that dates to the mid-sixth century CE. It is the oldest map of the Holy Land in existence. Like most maps, it has captions that identify countries, but in the case of Madaba, the map identifies biblical sites and local ancient churches. At the center of the map—that is to say, the center of the cartographer's universe—is Jerusalem, identified in Greek as the "Holy City." Because the map is oriented with West on top, above Jerusalem sits the Mediterranean Sea, boats and all. Here is the section of the map depicting Jerusalem. You can see its columned *cardo* running left to right (south to north) across the city.

MADABA MAP, JORDAN

Let's turn now from the busy passage of the living along Jerusalem's *cardo* on the Madaba map to the equally busy precincts of the dead. I want to take a look at the art in the Jewish catacombs of Rome and of Beit She'arim in the Galilee. The menorah is ubiquitous as a symbol in these burial settings, much as it is in almost every other Jewish site. But the Jews also employed non-Jewish, even pagan, symbols in these Jewish burial places. Among the pagan symbols found is art depicting the myth of Zeus disguised as a swan raping or seducing Leda—something one would not expect in either pagan or Jewish sarcophagi, but there they are. There is a fragment of a Leda sarcophagus from the Jewish catacomb at Beit She'arim, a burial site actually containing tombs of rabbis known to us from the Talmud! We also have mentioned a pagan Leda sarcophagus, now in the Naples Museum, and seen an image of Leda and the swan from Heraclion. Still, one must ask why Leda and the swan are in a cemetery at all, and especially in a Jewish setting? In reply to this reasonable question, I translate the Yiddish expression "*Geh vays*": go figure.

In addition to the swan image in the Beth She'arim catacomb, a seahorse monster like the one I spoke about that is on the cover of a sarcophagus from the Naples Museum appears in a fresco in the Roman Jewish catacomb at Vigna Randanini.

When featured on the pagan tomb, it could reasonably be assumed to represent a nereid riding the Cetus seahorse monster of Greco-Roman mythology. But the animal is virtually the same in the Jewish catacomb, only absent the mermaid riding on its back. In fact, the lone Cetus also appears in the Christian catacombs in the same neighborhood of Rome as the Jewish Vigna Randanini catacomb. In the St. Callisto and in the Priscilla Christian catacombs, the Cetus is none other than the big fish swallowing Jonah!

For Christians, both the fish and Jonah are symbols of resurrection; the fish took Jonah down to Sheol (the underworld) but then deliv-ered him to dry land after three days and nights. For Christians this prefigures Jesus's death and resurrection. But the Cetus in the Jewish catacomb, however, depicts neither Jonah nor a nereid. We might take the hint from the Christian catacombs and suggest that in the Jewish catacombs, too, the Cetus is a symbol of resurrection. What complicates

JEWISH CATACOMB FIG. 1 AT VIGNA RANDANINI, ROME

this identification is the appearance of a Cetus seahorse monster on the base of the Menorah depicted on the Arch of Titus. Something fishy is going on here, as this might be the last place one would expect to find such an image. Most interpreters of the Menorah on the Arch assume the base was decorated by pagan Romans and is not an actual depiction of the base of the Menorah that stood in the Jerusalem Temple. I suspect that in virtually all Jewish settings, the seahorse was simply meant to depict just another creature of the deep, much as the fresco artist also depicted birds or palm trees. It's best to avoid the temptation to overinterpret.

There are still more pagan motifs in the Jewish catacomb at Vigna Randanini. On the arched dome of one of the catacomb chambers, we find what the late scholar of ancient Roman Judaism Harry Leon described as the winged goddess of victory, Nike, crowning a youth holding the palm frond of victory.

JEWISH CATACOMB FIG. 2

JEWISH CATACOMB FIG. 3

Angelic winged *putti* regularly appear in Roman funerary and other art. The Vigna Randanini Jewish catacomb shares this apparently pagan motif. Above is another fresco from that catacomb.

It is true that there were angelic figures called cherubs on the Ark of the Covenant that the Israelites carried with them in the desert. But sometimes a cherubic character means no more than the cloying little angels you might find on a Hallmark card. I suspect that the frequency of pagan images in the Roman Jewish catacombs shows us the ease with which that Jewish community assimilated the art of their neighbors. Yet for all of the artistic overlap, Jews did not adopt Roman or Christian burial customs in any wholesale fashion. The Jewish community had its own unique law and traditions for burial and mourning.

We visited the border town of Dura earlier in this book. The wall paintings of the Dura synagogue are the oldest pictorial art in the Jewish world. Dura was a Roman military installation at the far eastern end of the empire, on the bank of the Euphrates River. It served as a bulwark against the Sasanian-Parthians to the east. The synagogue of Dura originated as a private home that followed a fairly common Jewish practice when it was converted into the synagogue. The building was renovated in 244 CE, at which time the spectacular wall paintings that adorn it most likely were added to the decor. When the Parthian Empire warred against Rome in the mid-third century, Dura took the brunt of the attack. The east side of Dura was protected by the Euphrates itself. The citizens of the town shored up its walls on the west side, where the assault took place. They piled dirt up to buttress the town walls and did the same in the buildings that abutted those walls. The synagogue of Dura-Europos was among those buildings, and through this act of fortification the amazing wall paintings of the Dura synagogue were preserved. The town of Dura was overrun in 256 CE, left desolate by the Parthians, and only uncovered again in the early twentieth century.

Very few walls of art painted in Late Antiquity have been preserved. The problem of preservation is one of basic physics. Frescoes and wall paintings were painted on upright walls. Mosaic "carpets," on the other hand, were laid upon floors. Walls fall down over time, while the mosaics, already on the ground, are more likely to be preserved for archeologists to uncover. Some of the few sites that have yielded wall paintings or frescoes from the period were similarly covered over and left abandoned for centuries. Pompeii and Herculaneum were both inundated by ash when Vesuvius erupted in 79 CE.

The rabbis refer to the making of both frescoes and mosaics. For example, in commenting on the verse (Gen. 1:31) "God saw all that God had made and behold, it was very good," a fifth-century Galilean commentary on Genesis by the rabbis observes:

> Rabbi Yonatan said, "This is like a king who married off his daughter and made her a marriage-apartment, which he plastered, and then paneled or painted. When he saw it, it pleased him . . ."

Elsewhere, the same Midrash likens God creating the universe to

> a human king who builds a palace. He does not build it of his
> own knowledge, but rather the knowledge of an artisan. And
> the artisan does not build it out of his own knowledge, but
> rather uses parchment scrolls and sketch books to know how
> to lay down the mosaics.

In 1996, near Ben Gurion Airport, in Israel, in the town of Lod, or what had been ancient Diospolis (city of Zeus), archeologists uncovered an early fourth-century CE mosaic floor measuring approximately twenty-five feet by fifty feet. Recently, another, similar mosaic measuring thirty-six feet by forty-two feet was discovered near the Lod site while the archeologists were digging the foundations of a museum to display the earlier find! The well-preserved floor from the 1996 discovery, replete with tiled pictures of animals, was displayed in 2011 at the Metropolitan Museum of Art in New York, as an example of "Roman influence on local mosaic art."

Even at the far eastern edge of the empire, Rome's power is palpable. The wall paintings of the synagogue at Dura-Europos reflect Roman influence. The biblical characters in the Dura paintings by and large are shown in Roman dress. The very style of painting is Roman. In the mid-third century, in the exact era when rabbinic traditions traveled from Roman Palestine to the newly formed rabbinic academies in Sasanian-Parthian Babylonia, we find midrashic interpretations of biblical scenes among the panels of paintings on the walls of the synagogue at Dura.

The walls are covered from top to bottom with this art—a stunning display of what art historians call *horror vacui*, the tendency of certain artists to avoid leaving any empty space on their canvases or walls. This has given us all the more art to enjoy and interpret, although it does lead me to wonder if the busy walls of the synagogue at Dura might have induced feelings of claustrophobia among the worshippers. Here, I will focus on the Hellenizing aspects of these paintings rather than their artistic interpretations of Scripture.

During the 1920s and '30s, archeologist Clark Hopkins excavated the Dura synagogue, the church, and temples to traditional Roman gods, as well as to eastern gods such as Mithra. Images abounded, even those of the Zoroastrian religion of the Parthian/Persian Sasanians, Rome's enemies to the east. In the synagogue paintings of Dura-Europos, the majority of the biblical characters, including all of the "Jewish" characters, wear Roman garb. But certain eastern types, such as King Ahashverosh, are depicted in eastern clothing. Ahashverosh was king of the Persians and the Medes, and he is shown wearing a Phrygian cap and eastern clothing. He is sitting on the throne in the picture below. Next to him sits Queen Esther, his Jewish wife, bedecked with a Roman-style tiara of a city skyline—perhaps of Jerusalem. Such crowns were well known in the art of the period, and we have depictions of both women and of Tyche, the tutelary Greek goddess of given city, wearing tiaras that depict their cities.

Queen Esther is not the only woman depicted on the Dura synagogue walls. There is an entire cycle of paintings dedicated to the life of Moses. Prominent among the panels is the scene of Pharaoh's daughter lifting baby Moses out of the Nile. Appropriately for the Nile, if not a synagogue wall, the princess is naked, but for her bangles. The Esther cycle of paintings and the Pharaoh's daughter painting are on either side of the Torah shrine, or seat of Moses, which is the focal point of the Dura synagogue.

At Dura even the synagogue ceiling was covered with art. The tiles there included donor inscriptions in Aramaic, portraits—perhaps of the donors—and depictions of animals from Greco-Roman myth, such as the centaur and the now-familiar Cetus. The large portraits that are above the "seat of Moses" to either side, which would have been the central visual focus for congregants, are wearing distinctly Roman garb. Moses at the burning bush (see illustration labeled Moses at Dura) wears a Greco-Roman undergarment, the *chiton*, over which is draped the *himation*, a rectangular cloth adorned with a stripe ending in a notch. The stripes on the garments, called *clavi*, are associated with Roman patrician and military officers' garb. Note in the Moses at Dura figure below

AHASHVEROSH AND ESTHER IN DURA SYNAGOGUE

that at God's command Moses has removed his shoes (Ex. 3:5), which seem to be a shepherd's soft boots. See as well that God's hand appears in the painting (mysteriously more visible in the color plate), not unlike the hand of God in the Beit Alpha mosaic of the Binding of Isaac. This painting of Moses in Greco-Roman garb typifies the depictions of the principal Jewish males throughout most of the Dura synagogue panels. Ritual fringes for their four-cornered garments (see Num. 15:38) are absent in the Dura paintings, even though rabbinic interpretation of the biblical law might lead us to expect the male characters' clothing to be adorned with them. Perhaps the artists reasoned that biblical figures might not yet have known the law of the Torah. Or perhaps the Dura artists knew the story of the rabbinical student who had that odd adventure when his fringes smacked him, by Aphrodite!

DURA SYNAGOGUE LONG WALL

In any case, to the right of the "seat of Moses" in the Dura sanctuary is a painting of the prophet Samuel anointing David as the new King of Israel (I Sam. 16:11–13). David stands among his brothers, each in Greek *himation* with *clavi* stripes, including the garment of the prophet Samuel. David himself is wearing a gown of royal blue or, better, imperial purple, lacking *clavi*. In Rome, equestrians wore thin stripes. Senators wore broader stripes. But only the emperor could have an entire garment of purple. Roman convention indicates David's royal status.

Because I kvetched in our previous chapter about archeologists making a fuss about the presence of benches in predestruction synagogues, I am honor-bound to point out that the Dura synagogue indeed did have a row of benches around its perimeter. Maybe benches really do make a synagogue!

At Dura we find inscriptions in Hebrew, Aramaic, and Greek—languages that we now expect among Greco-Roman Jews. There are also inscriptions and graffiti in Middle Persian and Parthian at Dura-Europos. Given the locale of the synagogue, this is not all that surprising. Merchants, traders, caravaneers, and others were part of the Jewish community. But while Greek points to an eastern Roman identity, we

MOSES AT DURA

see that at the far border, Jews straddled Aramaic, Greek, and Persian/ Parthian identity. They lived comfortably among their neighbors, at home in Sasanian Parthia, or, as they might say, Jewish Babylonia. At the same time, the Jews of Dura-Europos bore their Roman citizenship proudly, ultimately dying for it when the town and its synagogue fell to the Parthian besiegers.

During the nineteenth century and the first half of the twentieth century, European art historians, particularly German-speaking ones, spoke derisively of the Jews as "an artless people." Their pun depicted Jews as awkward bumpkins and asserted that the cultural output of the

Jews did not include pictorial art. As we saw when we read about Rabbi Gamaliel and Aphrodite, there is almost no evidence of pictorial art from before the destruction of the Jerusalem Temple in 70 CE. It is not surprising that when pictorial art finally was embraced, the Jews turned to the surrounding culture for models and guidance. I have shepherded you through the explosion of Jewish art from Dura in the third century CE up to the Islamic conquest—art that belies the old canard of narrow-minded art historians. Hardly an "artless people," the Jews embraced Roman artistic principles with open arms across the entire breadth of the empire. The genius of Jewish artistic imagination was the genius of Rome.

———

CHAPTER X

FROM TEMPLE CULT TO ROMAN CULTURE

W e've traveled the Roman Empire visiting its Jewish communities. One abiding feature of the Judaism I have been showing you was, and remains, its steadfast loyalty to the Torah as a means of identifying with God's covenantal community. This focus on Torah as a text to be studied by everyone was something new. It marked a turn away from the priestly sacrificial cult of the Jerusalem Temple and their exclusive pretensions to control of the sacred text. Further, the destruction of the Temple brought an end to the animal sacrifices that are so central to the Torah's narrative.

The turn to Torah study instead of sacrifice was one more manifestation of how Hellenism reshaped Judaism in the late Second Temple period. This shift was the rabbis' way to move the power center of Judaism to their own focus on textual interpretation in the aftermath of Jerusalem's destruction. The latest of the books included in the Bible already begin to show traces of this Hellenistic bookish culture. It is not mere chance that the book of Ecclesiastes (12:9–12) closes by musing:

"Because Ecclesiastes was a sage . . . he expounded many parables [Hebrew: *meshalim*, Greek: *parabole*] . . . writing words of truth: . . . There is no end to the making of many books."

Mind you, the Bible does not say Ecclesiastes was a professor who was required to publish or perish. Rather, he is described as a sage. In Hebrew that's the same word the rabbis use to describe themselves, while in Greek the term is *sophos*, as in philo-sopher, or sophist. Writing parables and truth: these are the earmarks of Greco-Roman culture, a culture of many books.

"Many books" comes with the need to teach disciples how to interpret the canon of texts that defines the community. Even the simple idea of books and disciples was a turn away from the earlier emphasis on the dynastic kings and cultic priesthood of biblical Israelite religion. The philosophical schools of the Greeks and even the rhetorical schools of the Romans were based upon discipleship, and it was this model that the rabbis chose. The Greco-Roman educational enterprise of *paideia*, cultural instruction with its focus on Homer and other canonical texts, led directly to the rabbinic enterprise of Scriptural interpretation and then to the dialectical consideration of the rabbis' Mishnah.

At the moment that the Greco-Roman world turned from its belief in the efficacy of animal sacrifices—even as they continued to be offered—the latest books of the Bible and the rabbis, too, prepared to approach God a different way. No longer was God's banquet meal the sweet savor of animal sacrifices. After 70 CE, the rabbis imagined the covenantal meal as a very different kind of banquet. Rabbi Yohanan ben Zakkai, arguably the founder of rabbinic Judaism, is reported to have taught his disciples:

> In my dream, you and I were all reclining-at-banquet on Mt. Sinai. A heavenly voice was given to us, "Come up here, come up here! There are great banquet tables [*triclinia*] that are well spread with fine foods for you. You, your disciples, and your disciples' students are invited to the top tier!" (Babylonian Talmud Hagiga 14b)

No longer is Mt. Sinai recalled as the place from which Moses brings down instruction for the construction of the altar, which was attended by his brother Aaron's dynastic priesthood—which offered animal sacrifices to God. Instead, Rabbi Yohanan's dream, fully realized in rabbinic Judaism, is of a Sinai where masters and their disciples in the study of Torah are invited to the Hellenistic banquet. There, they recline on the most prestigious couches at God's *triclinium*. The almost casual Hellenization of Yohanan's reported dream speaks volumes about the shift to Greco-Roman culture—even Mt. Sinai is now conceived of as a Roman banquet room! As the rabbis say in Pirke Avot (ch. 4): "Prepare yourself in the ante-chamber [Hebrew: *prozdor*, Greek: *prothura*], so that you may enter the banquet hall [*triclinium*]."

I have suggested here that rabbinic Judaism is a new religion, divorced and separate from the biblical, Israelite religion of the Temple cult that preceded it. Yet my discussion of the late biblical antecedents of Hellenism, added to the evidence I quoted earlier in this book about the possibility of synagogues' existing before the destruction, should raise a flag of caution. In fact, the rabbinic obsession with Scripture, manifest in the rabbis' interpretations of every detail of biblical law, including the minute facets of the moribund Temple and its procedures, makes it clear that rabbinic Judaism is not a wholly new religion, created *ex nihilo*, out of nothingness. This shift was already under way before the time of the rabbis. On one hand, there would be no wholesale assimilation to Hellenism with a loss of Jewish identity. On the other, ancient Jewish rituals were not abandoned. Rather, there would be a measured appropriation and adaptation of Greco-Roman culture that found its expression in post-70 CE Judaism.

The ways in which I have characterized Judaism, whether as utterly new or as a remix of an old tune, are fraught with ideological significance. What characterizes the new Judaism and separates it from other emerging ideologies? Is rabbinic Judaism just one more new religion, one more flavor of many Judaisms in the Late Antique world, there to take its place alongside Christianity and other Greco-Roman religions? Or is rabbinic Judaism the one and only authentic inheritor of biblical "Judaism," genetically similar by virtue of both the performed commandments (*mitzvot*) and the constant justyfying of those *mitzvot* through tying them to their presumed Scriptural origins? Remember that in the period I am considering, *rabbinic* Judaism was not the major face of Judaism it would become for the millennium of its European ascendance, say from 940 to 1940 CE. It was only in that much later period that rabbis had the actual power to enforce their dicta. The first millennium of rabbinic Judaism resembled the Judaism we have now, in which each individual Jew chooses adherence to the commandments and how that adherence is manifested in daily behavior. To get to now, the rabbis then needed persistence, vision, and Roman Stoic stolidity to survive. The very virtues the rabbis adopted from Roman culture were among the forces that allowed Judaism to survive against oppressive odds.

The methods and biases of this book remain relevant to understanding the meaning of the journey we have taken together. However much I may see Greco-Roman culture as the context and content for rabbinic Judaism, there nevertheless remain strong ties to the biblical religion that birthed it. My bias may be as a Western university–trained scholar, but I am also a rabbi. I have been trying to keep a sense of the contexts of Judaism, particularly rabbinic Judaism, and its development within the Greco-Roman world. Early in this book I recounted a parable about a wily fox and a fish out of water. In 2005, the late author David Foster Wallace gave a commencement speech at Kenyon College. He opened with his own parable:

> There are these two young fish swimming along and they happen to meet an older fish swimming the other way, who nods at them and says "Morning, boys. How's the water?"
> And the two young fish swim on for a bit, and then eventually one of them looks over at the other and goes "What the hell is water?"

Aphrodite and the Rabbis is an attempt to answer both of the questions posed in Foster Wallace's parable. As I have suggested, it is an examination of both content and context: both "How's the water?" and "What the hell is water?" I hope I have convinced you of the extent to which the water the rabbis swam in was itself Greco-Roman culture.

The many varieties of Judaism may not all have been rabbinic, yet they shared customs, iconography, and common Hellenistic culture with the rabbis and with the other Jews in the empire. Whether it was the good relations they had with the neighbors whom they called God- or Heaven-fearers, or the overwhelming presence of the menorah as a Jewish symbol, Judaism was clearly identifiable from place to place. Pagans and Christians "knew it when they saw it." They report about certain kinds of Sabbath observance, odd dietary customs, the palm frond and citron, the ram's horn—all of these were identifiable as elements of Judaism, among the various Jewish communities as well as to non-Jewish observers. Today it might be called "dog-whistle," this subtle array of symbols and customs that united Jews one to another. They were Romans, to be sure, but also simultaneously members of their own exclusive community. This exclusivism also helped serve as a survival mechanism.

The Jews, and the rabbis in particular, carried a great deal of ambivalence about the Roman culture in which they flourished ("what the hell is water?"). I wrote of how the rabbis equated Rome with the biblical Esau/Edom. This tribe was surely deemed to be "other," yet anyone who reads the book of Genesis must acknowledge that Esau is Jacob/Israel's fraternal twin brother. There is no better symbol of rabbinic equivocation toward Rome.

The rabbis also had a "founding narrative" of their rise following the destruction of Jerusalem by Rome. In almost every version of the oft-told story about Yohanan and Vespasian, the rabbi had to sneak out of besieged Jerusalem in a casket. This story line speaks to my discussion about the creation or reinvention of Judaism. In the very legend in which Yohanan is promised Yavneh, the first home of rabbinic Judaism, Rabbi Yohanan symbolically dies—he is carried out in a coffin—and is resurrected standing before Rome, embodied by Vespasian Caesar.

As the rabbis of Yavneh and beyond focused their gaze upon the Torah and its interpretation, they showed themselves heavily indebted to the broader culture in which they read the Book. I demonstrated how the rabbis adopted the standard exercises of the Roman rhetorical schools. The rabbis also turned to a longstanding pagan literary genre, the symposium, as the skeleton for the Passover Seder. Even today, the Passover Seder is a lovely marriage of the biblical with the Greco-Roman aspects of Judaism, a banquet of East meets West.

The reach of Rome was long, and it embraced Jewish communities from one end of the empire to the other. Jews remained distinctive through their common customs, such as Sabbath observance or food laws. Even so, in their minority status they were not all that different from other subgroups of the empire. Philosophers, for example, were distinctive by their garb and deportment, and often by their food habits, as well. Christians stood outside the empire for a long period of their development before becoming the empire itself. Geographical, racial, and ethnic subgroups made up the vast expanse of an empire that stretched from England in the west to Armenia and Media in the east. The one common denominator was the Greco-Roman Hellenism that became their patrimony. This was true for the Jews in the Roman Empire as well. Like every other subgroup, they, too, were Roman.

Even as one could distinguish between the rabbis and other Jews within the Jewish world—the rabbis themselves made this distinction—nevertheless they all shared a common Judaism that was heavily inflected by their common Hellenism. The details I have surveyed in this book have made it clear that by and large, the water they swam in was very good. And when they were asked "What the hell is water?" the answer, surely, was that among the many tributaries that made up the empire—from the Atlantic to the Mediterranean, from the Euphrates to the Caspian Sea—Judaism took its place within the Roman Empire as a Roman people and religion. Its transformation from the Jerusalem-centered Temple cult to a world religion was a reinvention, a resurrection if you will, accomplished through the vivifying waters of Greco-Roman culture.

What does this all mean for modern American Judaism? If the evidence has been weighed and I can conclude with reasonable assurance that

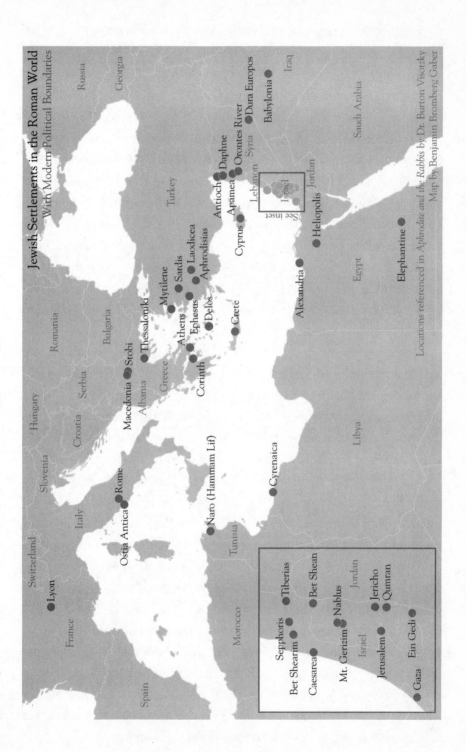

Jewish Settlements in the Roman World
With Modern Political Boundaries

Locations referenced in *Aphrodite and the Rabbis* by Dr. Burton Visotzky

Map by Benjamin Bromberg Gaber

Greco-Roman culture played a large hand in the invention of what we now call Judaism, does it make a difference? Should it matter to us?

I think it does, if for no other reason than to validate modern Judaism itself. Here, of course, bias looms large. If this book is but a defense of the lives we now live, if the Judaism I imagine in Late Antiquity is but a reflection back from the glasses I wear as a modern, if my gaze never truly penetrates through the lens to see the realities of Ancient Judaism, then I have failed in my task. It is for this reason that I have quoted so many texts and included illustrations not only from rabbinic literature but also from the other Jewish communities of the Roman Empire. I wanted to allow the testimony of antiquity its own voice to the extent possible. It is true that all of the evidence has been interpreted by me in support of the theory that Greco-Roman culture served as the midwife for the birth of Judaism as we know it. But still, the evidence is here to be read one way or another.

If the rabbis and other Jews took the best of their Roman culture and heartily imbibed Hellenistic civilization as they invented a Judaism to survive the destruction of the Jerusalem cult, then it can be an encouragement for us to do the same. Almost two centuries ago, the German-Jewish movement called *Wissenschaft des Judentums,* "the scientific study of Judaism," appropriated Western methods and traditions. It created a Judaism that was consonant with the intellectual, university life of European culture. It allowed for the academic study of Judaism, German Jewish Reform, and other forms of modern Judaism. Even after World War II and the horrors of the Holocaust, acculturation to the West remained the norm with the emergence of American Judaism. Jewish leadership in modernity both observed and celebrated the choices rabbinic Jews made long ago in the Roman Empire.

Much as they swam in the waters of Greco-Roman culture, so we flourish in American society, transforming Judaism as we go. Jews are in very large measure university-educated, schooled in the culture of the Western world. Jews have imbibed those values as, for example, we welcome forms of women's equality into our Jewish life. I, a rabbi, am comfortable living in the multifaith, pluralistic country that has given the Jewish community unprecedented opportunities. Jews today mediate among their heritage of European Jewry, the legacy of Talmudic, Greco-Roman Judaism, the history of biblical covenantal religion, and the ethos of liberal democracy. In this Jewish adaptation of the broader culture, the Jewish community stands as a direct inheritor of the Judaism of the Greco-Roman world. God willing, our legacy will be as rich and long-lasting as was theirs.

Earlier in this book I noted that when the Roman emperor arrived in a town, his *advent* was celebrated by citizens lining the streets to loudly greet him with shouts in Greek of *Ho Kalos,* "This one is The Good one!" This expression was accompanied by a gesture: pointing the index finger on the raised, outstretched right arm. This pointing was not considered impolite but, rather, the appropriate gesture acknowledging the emperor's, the Good One's, sovereignty.

FROM A COLOSSUS OF THE EMPEROR CONSTANTINE—
CAPITOLINE MUSEUMS, ROME

The gesture was adopted by the rabbis as a way of acknowledging God's rule, and it still is reflected in synagogues today when Jews point to the Torah as they sing, VeZot HaTorah, "This is the Torah which Moses put before the people Israel." It is the demonstrative pronoun, the word "this," in Hebrew feminine zot (or, in the masculine, zeh), that provokes the pointing. How appropriate that the very gesture by which Jews still acknowledge God and Torah is itself a legacy of Roman culture!

The Babylonian Talmud tractate Taanit ends with a reference to this custom of pointing to God. I quote it here as a closing benediction:

> In the Future, the Blessed Holy One will host a circle-dance for the righteous in the Garden of Eden. God will sit in the middle of them. Each and every one will point to God with their finger, as it is said (Isa. 25:9), "On that day they shall say: This [zeh] is our God; we looked to God and God delivered us. This is the Lord to Whom we look, let us delight and rejoice in God's deliverance."

Timeline

132–135 CE	Bar Kokhba Jewish rebellion against Roman emperor Hadrian
200 CE	Compilation of the Mishnah
220–250 CE	Rabbinic Tannaitic (early) works edited
224–651 CE	Sasanian Empire in Iraq (Jewish Babylonia)
225 CE	Beginnings of rabbinic Judaism in Babylonia
312 CE	Roman emperor Constantine converts to Christianity
325 CE	Christianity declared a licit religion in Roman Empire
330 CE	Constantinople founded
361–363 CE	Emperor Julian attempts to revive "paganism," tries to rebuild Jerusalem Temple
363 CE	Julian killed in battle against Persia/Sasanians
375–425 CE	Editing of Palestinian ("Jerusalem") Talmud, rabbinic Midrash on Genesis, Leviticus, Lamentations, Song of Songs
410 CE	City of Rome sacked by Visigoth king Alaric
450–550 CE	Redaction and compilation of Babylonian Talmud
570–632 CE	Mohammed flourishes
637–640 CE	Fall of Sasanian Empire
637 CE	Muslim conquest of Jerusalem

ACKNOWLEDGMENTS

My first reader and life editor is my wife, Sandra Edelman. She is the ideal reader for whom I write—smart, committed to her Jewish identity, willing to be educated. As my in-house counsel, she is not shy about telling me what to add, delete, or change. I also heartily thank my research assistant Madeline, whose bibliographic help, keen comments, and careful editing made the book so much richer. Sandy and Maddie read and reread an earlier draft of this work. My editor extraordinaire at St. Martin's Press, Elisabeth Dyssegaard, pushed me to revise, and then re-revise, and then revise yet again. In every instance she was correct. Any readability this book may have is thanks to her. I am blessed to have her as an editor. *Merci beaucoup* as well to Laura Apperson, Alan Bradshaw, Clifford Thompson, Josh Evans, and the incredible crew at St. Martin's for so ably seeing the book through press. To my champions at Levine, Greenberg, Rostan, I offer two decades worth of appreciation.

My gratitude is extended to Professors Lee I. Levine (Hebrew University), Seth Schwartz (Columbia), and Shaye J. D. Cohen (Harvard) for their comments on an early draft of chapter 3. My warm thanks to

Prof. Steven Fine (Yeshiva University) for his careful reading of the bulk of the chapters of an earlier draft. His acute comments saved me from both errors and omissions. I deeply appreciate these professors' collegiality and comments. Any errors that remain are my responsibility.

Thanks to the Russell Berrie Foundation (Angelica Berrie and Ruth Salzman), the Institute of International Education (especially Borcsa Barnahazi), Rabbi Jack Bemporad, Prof. Adam Afterman, and the John Paul II Center at the Pontifical University of St. Thomas Aquinas (Angelicum) in Rome, for my appointment there as Distinguished Visiting Professor of Jewish Studies in spring, 2014; and to Prof. Father James Puglisi and A. J. Boyd for their good care while I was in their house. Many of the photos in the book were shot during my time at the Angelicum.

I am grateful to Agnes Vajda and Noemi Csabay (both of the Institute of International Education) and Dr. Irle Goldman for being my catacomb companions, and to Dr. Laura Supino for twice now guiding me through the Jewish catacombs of Rome. Warm thanks to my old friend Dr. Joseph Sievers for setting both visits in motion and for his graciously hosting me as Master Visiting Professor of Jewish Studies at the Cardinal Bea Center of the Pontifical Gregorian University in Rome back in 2007.

My academic home for forty-five years has been the Jewish Theological Seminary (JTS). Every page of this book displays my debt to my beloved teachers Professors Saul Lieberman and Elias Bickermann, *requiescant in pace,* who taught me about the Greco-Roman world, each in his own brilliant, earthy, inimitable fashion. My thanks, too, goes to current JTS Chancellor Arnold Eisen and JTS Provost Alan Cooper as well as my colleagues and students for their collegiality, support, and friendship.

My appreciation to Dr. Jacob Wisse of the Yeshiva University Museum for his graciousness in allowing me to photograph their replicas of the synagogues of Dura Europos and Beit Alpha. I am especially grateful to Steven Fine (yet again), Robin Jensen, and Alisa Doctoroff, who graciously and generously shared their own photos with me for this volume.

I am most grateful to Nanette Stahl, Susan Matheson, and Megan Doyon of Yale University for making available a hard-to-get image of the Esther painting from the synagogue of Dura Europos. Special thanks to my long-time student Ben Bromberg Gaber, for his expert map-making. Thanks to Letty Cottin Pogrebin for a timely tweak to the subtitle of the book. And to my old friend and consummate reader Tom Cahill: *grazie mille.*

PHOTO CREDITS

*(IN ORDER OF APPEARANCE;
BOLDED NAMES ALSO IN PHOTO SECTION)*

Alexander the Great mosaic: Carole Raddato (https://commons.wikimedia.org
/wiki/File:Detail_of_the_Alexander_Mosaic_depicting_the_Battle_of_Issus
_between_Alexander_the_Great_%26_Darius_III_of_Persia,_from_the
_House_of_the_Faun_in_Pompeii,_Naples_Archaeological_Museum
_(14859288847).jpg)

Map: Ben Bromberg Gaber

Ostia Antica synagogue: Burton Visotzky

Catacomb inscription with Menorah: Burton Visotzky

Map: Ben Bromberg Gaber

Sardis synagogue: Burton Visotzky

Beit Alpha synagogue mosaic: J. Schweig

Berlin Brandenburg Gate: JoJan (https://commons.wikimedia.org/wiki/File:Berlin
.Brandenburger_Tor_006.jpg)

Dura synagogue, long wall: Sodabottle (https://commons.wikimedia.org/wiki
/File:Dara_Europos_replica.jpg)

Alexander the Great mosaic: Carole Raddato (https://commons.wikimedia.org
/wiki/File:Detail_of_the_Alexander_Mosaic_depicting_the_Battle_of_Issus

_between_Alexander_the_Great_%26_Darius_III_of_Persia,_from_the
_House_of_the_Faun_in_Pompeii,_Naples_Archaeological_Museum
_(14859288847).jpg)

Arch of Titus: José Luiz Bernardes Ribeiro (https://commons.wikimedia.org/wiki
/File:Spoils_from_Jerusalem_-_Arch_of_Titus_-_Rome_2008.jpg)

Hadrian equestrian statue: Burton Visotzky

Student bearing letter: Burton Visotzky

Equestrian Marcus Antoninus: Burton Visotzky

Mosaic Aphrodite in Sepphoris: © Dea Achivio J. Lange/Getty Images

Crates the Philosopher: Museo della Terme, Rome (https://commons.wikimedia.org
/wiki/File:Crates_of_Thebes_Villa_Farnesina.jpg)

Remnants of Robinson's arch with detail of trimmed Herodian stone: Brian
Jeffrey Beggerly (https://commons.wikimedia.org/wiki/File:The_remains_of
_Robinson%27s_Arch_on_the_western_side_of_the_Temple_Mount.jpg)

Basilica of St. Ambrose, Milan: Burton Visotzky

Aqueduct, Caesarea Maritima: Carole Raddato: https://commons.wikimedia.org
/wiki/File:The_high_level_aqueduct_of_Caesarea_built_by_Herod_(37BC
_to_4BC),_Caesarea_Maritima,_Israel_(15154565604).jpg)

Pantheon, Rome: Marcus Obal (https://commons.wikimedia.org/wiki/File:Roman
_Pantheon_Dome.JPG)

Sardis synagogue stone table: Burton Visotzky

Sardis synagogue entryways: Burton Visotzky

Dura-Europos synagogue, Torah shrine or Seat of Moses: Marsyas (https://
commons.wikimedia.org/wiki/File:Dura_Synagogue_ciborium.jpg)

Tetrapylon of Aphrodisias: Burton Visotzky

Vigna Randanini catacomb fig. 1: Robin Jensen

Vigna Randanini catacomb fig. 2: Burton Visotzky

Sarcophagus—Capitoline Museums, Rome: Burton Visotzky

"Leda and Swan" sarcophagus—Heraclion Museum Jebulon (https://commons
.wikimedia.org/wiki/File:Leda_and_the_Swan_archmus_Heraklion.jpg)

Herculaneum: Wolfgang Rieger (https://commons.wikimedia.org/wiki
/File:Herculaneum_-_Casa_di_Nettuno_ed_Anfitrite_-_Mosaic.jpg)

Beit Alpha synagogue mosaic: J. Schweig

Sol Invictus—Capitoline Museums, Rome: Burton Visotzky

Arch of Titus: Sailko (https://commons.wikimedia.org/wiki/File:Arch_of_titus
_-_imperial_cortege.jpg)

Marcus Aurelius—Capitoline Museums, Rome: Burton Visotzky

Catacomb fig. 1—Vigna Randanini, Rome: Burton Visotzky

Catacomb fig. 2—Vigna Randanini, Rome: Burton Visotzky

Catacomb fig. 3—Vigna Randanini, Rome: Burton Visotzky

Oil lamp fragment with menorah—Milan Archeological Museum: Burton Visotzky

Beit Alpha synagogue: J. Schweig

Madaba Map, Jordan: Jean Housen (https://commons.wikimedia.org/wiki /File:20100924_madaba57a.jpg)

Jewish catacombs fig. 1 at Vigna Randanini, Rome: Robin Jensen

Jewish catacombs fig. 2: Burton Visotzky

Jewish catacombs fig. 3: Burton Visotzky

Ahashverosh and Esther in Dura synagogue: Yale University Art Gallery, Dura Europos Archives

Dura Synagogue, long wall: Sodabottle (https://commons.wikimedia.org/wiki /File:Dara_Europos_replica.jpg)

Moses at Dura: Dura Europos (https://commons.wikimedia.org/wiki/File:Moses _Dura_Europos.jpg)

Map: Ben Bromberg Gaber

From a colossus of the emperor Constantine—Capitoline Museums, Rome: Burton Visotzky

FOR FURTHER READING

Fine, Steven, *Art and Judaism in the Greco-Roman World: Towards a New Jewish Archaeology,* New York: Cambridge University Press (2005, revised 2010)

Fischel, Henry, *Essays in Graeco-Roman and Related Talmudic Literature,* New York: Ktav Publishing House (1977)

Hengel, Martin, *Judaism and Hellenism: Studies in their Encounter in Palestine during the Early Hellenistic Period* (English translation), Philadelphia: Fortress Press (1974)

Hezser, Catherine, ed., *Rabbinic Law in its Roman and Near Eastern Context,* Tübingen: Mohr/Siebeck (2003)

Hezser, Catherine, ed., *The Oxford Handbook of Jewish Daily Life in Roman Palestine,* Oxford: Oxford University Press (2010)

Hopkins, Clark, *The Discovery of Dura-Europos,* New Haven: Yale University Press (1979)

Leon, Harry, *The Jews of Ancient Rome,* Philadelphia: Jewish Publication Society of America (1960)

Levine, Lee, ed., *Ancient Synagogues Revealed,* Jerusalem: Exploration Society (1981)

Levine, Lee, *The Ancient Synagogue,* New Haven: Yale University Press (2000)

Levine, Lee, *Visual Judaism in Late Antiquity: Historical Contexts of Jewish Art,* New Haven: Yale University Press (2012)

Rutgers, Leonard, *The Jews in Late Ancient Rome: Evidence of Cultural Interaction in the Roman Diaspora,* Leiden; New York: E. J. Brill (1995)

Rutgers, Leonard, *The Hidden Heritage of Diaspora Judaism,* Leuven: Peeters (1998)

Shanks, Herschel, *Judaism in Stone: The Archaeology of Ancient Synagogues,* New York: Harper & Row (1979)

Sperber, Daniel, *Greek in Talmudic Palestine,* Tel Aviv: Bar Ilan University Press (2012).

Weiss, Zev and E. Netzer, *Promise and Redemption: A Synagogue Mosaic from Sepphoris,* Jerusalem: Israel Museum (1996)

INDEX

"True enough. But I tortured a man once and bear the guilt. I vowed to God I would never be party to such again, and I'll not break that vow here."

Carefully Erling stood, set his helmet back on his head, took up his shield and walked toward the mob, drawing his sword as he walked.

Quietly we all went after him. I, being unarmored and unarmed, kept close to Erling, as did Freydis.

We felt the black eyes of our hosts on us as we went.

When we reached them Erling yelled, "Give me cover, men!" and began to swat the women away with the flat of his blade while our warriors moved in to form a shield wall between him (and me and Freydis) and them.

"A prayer would not come amiss just now, Father," said Erling as he carved with his sword blade at the rawhide thongs that bound the victim.

One of the advantages of having been a monk, or even a novitiate, is that you always have the psalms handy at need. I lifted my voice above the screams of the offended copper people and began to shout:

"*Let God arise, let His enemies be scattered: let them also that hate Him flee before Him.*

"*As smoke is driven away, so drive them away: as wax melteth before the fire, so let the wicked perish at the presence of God.*"

Erling got the fellow free at last, and the wretch fell into his arms. The copper men had come to join their women now, and were all around us shouting and waving their arms. I saw some stone clubs waving, too. Our men formed a circle with Erling, Freydis and me inside.

"*But let the righteous be glad; let them rejoice before God: let them exceedingly rejoice.*

"*Sing unto God, sing praises to His name: extol Him that*

rideth upon the heavens by His name Jehovah, and rejoice before Him."

"Father, I think you'll have to carry him," said Erling.

"Carry him!" roared Steinulf. "The dog's as good as gone. Make a quick end of him and let's be off."

"Carry him, Father!" cried Erling. I took the man by his arms and hoisted him on my back like a pack. Erling joined the shield wall.

The shields began to rattle as weapons fell on them, like hailstones on an awning.

"A father to the fatherless, and a judge of the widows, is God in His holy habitation.

"God setteth the solitary in families; He bringeth out those which are bound with chains: but the rebellious dwell in a dry land."

"We move as one!" cried Erling. "Keep the shields tight. Do no harm to these folk so long as possible, for we've eaten their meat!"

Carefully we began to move toward the forest path, back the way we'd come.

"Will we be able to find the way?" asked Bergthor.

"I can find the way, I think," said Steinulf. "I marked it with my axe, coming.

"By the way," he added, "this is utter madness."

"O God, when thou wentest forth before Thy people, when Thou didst march through the wilderness; the earth shook, the heavens also dropped at the presence of God; even Sinai itself was moved at the presence of God, the God of Israel."

We went, as fast as we might. You can't move so very fast while maintaining a tight shield-wall, so our former friends had no trouble keeping up with us. The rattling on the shields grew louder and the shouts more outraged. The man I carried was heavy and he was getting blood and grease all over my best priestly robe.

At one point I saw Thorlak break the shield-wall for one second. He reached out to grab something and thrust it into his shirt before raising his shield once more and taking his sword again from its sheath.

Stupid boy, I thought. *This is no time for plunder.*

Steinulf cursed him.

"The chariots of God are twenty thousand, even thousands of angels: The Lord is among them, as in Sinai, in the holy place."

We made our crawling way along the path. Steinulf faced ahead, to look for his marks and guide us.

No shield-wall is perfectly tight. Round shields leave chinks. A spear with a flint head was suddenly thrust in among us. Fortunately it struck a man's *brynje* and did no harm, but it passed just by Freydis' cheek.

With a roar Lemming dropped his shield and leaped out among the copper men. He lifted the spearman as if he'd been a puppy and threw him hard and far.

Our attackers took fright, as most men do when they see Lemming in a rage, and ran a good distance off. Lemming re-joined the shield-wall.

"Do you think they've decided to let us go?" asked Thorlak.

"No," said Erling, watching them. "They're getting enough distance to shoot arrows."

And sure enough the flint arrows began to strike our shields. They sounded just like the iron-tipped kind we knew from home.

"It won't be long before they think to shoot at our legs," said Erling. "We'll have to make the shield-fort."

The shield-fort is a formation where some men hold their shields at ground-level all around, and others hold them at breast-level, and others hold them up to make a roof overhead. The men were well-drilled and did it without wasted motion, but it was tight inside for Freydis and me and my burden.

We made even slower progress now. I thought we'd be all

night getting back, except that it would be dark soon – it was darkening already – and we'd be lost when that happened.

"The good thing is that they've no iron weapons to break our fort," said Erling. "Just keep at it, men. As long as Steinulf can find the way…."

"I think I've lost the way," said Steinulf.

We halted, feeling chill under our coats of grease.

"Look hard!" said Erling.

"It's uneasy to see in the shadows," said Steinulf.

I peered over Steinulf's shoulder, between the chinks in the shield-fort.

And I saw a figure before us. It looked like my sister Maeve. She beckoned to me and pointed to our right.

"I know the way!" I cried. "That way – toward the gnarly oak!"

"No!" said Steinulf. "I've got it now. Straight on, the way we've been going!"

"You're wrong!" I cried. "I see it with my Sight! This is the way! Go where I tell you!"

"Your Sight has led you wrong before!" cried Steinulf. "I'm sure of the way now! I see my mark!"

"Listen, Erling!" said I. "You must trust me. Our lives depend on it!"

Erling did not answer for just one moment.

Then he said, "Lead the way, Steinulf."

"No, no, no, no, no –" I cried, but I must needs go with the others – to certain doom, I was sure.

It seemed all night we went – it grew darker and darker. I knew Steinulf was leading us blindly. I could see the figure of Maeve, pointing ever more to our right as we went farther and farther off the course.

And our enemies howled and made a hedgehog of our shields with their arrows.

And I wondered how it would end. How long could the men

endure to keep the shield-fort tight, upholding shields heavy with arrows?

I waited for the arrow that must inevitably come through the widening chinks and strike me dead.

Perhaps I'd be but wounded, and taken prisoner.

I'd seen what these folk did to their prisoners.

God, have mercy. Send Your angels to protect us here, at the ends of the earth, I prayed.

"WE MADE IT!" Steinulf cried.

And I looked and we stood at the brow of the hill, and there before us was the beach with our men and our towboat, and the inlet and our ship.

"Sing unto God, ye kingdoms of the earth; O sing praises unto the Lord: To Him that rideth upon the heavens of heavens, which were of old; lo, he doth send out His voice, and that a mighty voice," I cried in relief.

"Fast as you can go, men!" cried Erling.

We made our ungainly way down the hill, and our men on guard by the shore, who had bows, gave us a covering fire and our enemies fell back. We all piled into the boat and pulled hard for the ship, and we hoisted the broken copper man over the rail, then went up the side one by one.

Konnall set men rowing. It was too dark for proper navigation, but he steered by memory in the light of the sunset, and by God's grace we got out with only one scrape over a shoal.

And then we were safe, back on God's blessed sea.

I was weary and wanted nothing more than to curl up in my sleeping bag.

But I borrowed an axe from one of the men and went to the rail.

"What are you doing, Father?" Erling asked me.

"I do what must be done," said I. I took the axe in my left hand and laid my right forearm on the rail. "I've believed in the

Sight that this thing has given me, but it only brought confusion and deception. It near killed me once, and if you'd listened to me it would have killed us all tonight. 'Tis true what my abbot once said – 'If God gave men a new sense, they'd just use it to fool themselves in a fresh way.' The Eye must go where I was told to send it – to the bottom of the remotest sea."

I raised the axe to strike my hand off.

And if thy right hand offend thee, cut it off, and cast it from thee; for it is profitable for thee that one of thy members should perish, and not that thy whole body should be cast into Hell.

But just as I steeled myself to strike, a stabbing pain pierced my palm and the Eye hopped out into the sea of its own accord, as if it were a toad I'd palmed.

Chapter 19

"WELL that was as much fright as I've ever taken for the least profit," said Steinulf the next morning at breakfast. "One thrall gained."

"Not a thrall," said Erling.

Steinulf sputtered, "Not a thrall?"

"I didn't rescue this man to take his freedom from him."

"I'll speak plain, Erling. If you want to play the hero and be kinder than God, that's your affair, but you're wrong to ask your men to put their lives at risk with you. Not for thralls and outlanders."

"I have a reason," said Erling.

"I'd be pleased to hear it."

"What think you of this land?"

"Barring the mosquitoes I'd call it among the best I've seen."

"My thought as well. What would you say to a Norse settlement here?"

Steinulf scratched his beard below the chin. "It's a long pull from Norway," he said.

"I don't think we'd fare to Norway much. But we could sail

to Greenland. There's much here that the Greenlanders would want."

"But what do they have that we'd need? The Greenlanders export walrus rope and walrus ivory. Fine things in their place, but we'd need iron and meal."

"We'd have to get our iron from Norway by way of the Greenlanders. Grain we'd grow ourselves, and make our own meal. And I'll wager there's iron in this land somewhere, if we look in the right places. Where there are mosquitoes there are marshes, and where there are marshes there's often iron."

"It's a gamble..." said Steinulf. "But look here. We've made enemies of the locals. And you've seen what they do to enemies."

"That's where our friend here comes in. You said it yourself. These people know the ways of war. There are nations here, or clans, at least. We've one clan for an enemy, but perhaps we can make this man's clan our friends."

"He might be just a felon of some kind."

"I don't think so," I put in. "He isn't tonsured like the men there."

"This man's clan may be as bloodthirsty as that other. Maybe that's why they treated him so hard – because his people are even crueler."

"Well, we won't know until we go see, will we?" said Erling. "I never knew you for a cautious man, Steinulf."

"I'm bold enough on ground I know. But I hate not knowing the rules. Norsemen should make the rules, not have to learn them."

"New places, new lessons," said Erling.

"New ways to die."

Konnall came to squat by us. "How long do we lie to here?" he asked Erling.

"Until the copper man is able to show us the way to his home."

"Humph. How's he doing?"

"He's sleeping. Astrid says she doesn't think it's a deadly sleep."

"How long will this sleep last?"

"Who can say?"

Konnall shook his head. "We've a fair wind," he said. "I'd like to be on our way."

"Let's give it some time. It's not so bad waiting out here. We're far from our enemies and far from the mosquitoes. And the fishing's good."

And so we waited, rocking on the waters. I'd been so long at sea that I'd come to take seasickness for a way of life. Everything I ate I cast up, and so I grew thinner and thinner. I elected to call it a fast, and spent a lot of time in prayer, thanking God in particular for getting us out of that last mess, and for letting me be rid of the Eye without maiming myself. I hoped this land would not take much hurt from being washed by a sea with the Eye in it.

I still saw spirits from time to time, but they appeared less and less often, and I did not miss them.

It was the third day when Astrid told us that the copper man had awakened. I went to see this wonder. He was not a handsome sight, torn and bruised and burned as he was. Astrid had sewn his worst wounds up while he'd slept.

He'd a face like those of all the other copper men we'd seen – flattish and broad-cheeked, with a large nose and black eyes that slanted a bit.

The first thing that face showed when he looked up at us was terror. You can hardly blame him. If I'd awoken to find myself surrounded by a shipload of his people I'd have been kidney-struck too. He made to run off and two of the men had to hold him down.

Erling was ready to demonstrate good will. He offered him chunk of cheese.

The man looked uncertain. Erling took a bite, just to prove he was on the up and up.

The man smiled then and took the cheese, clearly famished after his long slumber. He seemed to find the first bite surprising, but warmed quickly to the taste.

Once he'd finished the cheese he took fright again, and again the men had to hold him, this time to keep him from jumping the rail and trying to swim back to the shore, a distant shadow to the west. They had a hard time keeping a grip on his grease-covered body.

"Get him something to wear," said Erling. "It'll make him easier to hold onto if nothing else." Someone rooted out a yellow shirt from a chest and with some difficulty they got it onto him. Once they were done he seemed fascinated by the cloth. He stroked it and smiled. The men laughed at him.

"Hush!" said Erling. "Whatever else this man may be, he's a warrior and brave. You saw how he stood under torture. Pray God you're as hardy if it ever comes to that."

"Now is the hard part," he said then, calling for some dried fish for the man. "Figuring how to ask the way to take him home."

"Not so hard," said Konnall. "I'll bring us in nearer shore, where he can see the lay of the land. Then we follow his face like the polestar."

We did this and Konnall, as usual, was right. We came close in to the inlet we'd left, trusting that our enemies were no longer watching for us, and confident we could easily outrun them if they were.

"We need to call him something," said Erling. "He ought to have a name."

"He looks a little like a Lapp – a Finn," said Bergthor. I hadn't thought of the likeness before, but now that it was said I could see it. Though the Lapps are mostly shorter and broader than these folk.

"Finn it is, then."

The closer we drew, the more "Finn" turned his gaze northward. Konnall set the sail (something that made Finn's eyes go wide) and took us along the shoreline, east of north.

It was only a short sail before Finn grew excited and began to point and jabber. He grasped Erling's arm, trying to tell him something and pointing to a wide river mouth.

Erling smiled. "I take your meaning, friend," he said. "Konnall, what think you of that river for a road inland?"

"I like the color of the water," said Konnall. "I think we needn't put out a boat, if we go carefully and take our soundings."

And so we did, and we rowed into the broad river mouth in the stately fashion of a king.

Now that he knew where he was going, Finn grinned like a boy and puffed his chest out, clearly proud of the impression he'd be making on the home folks.

The oarsmen stroked us up the wide river, Konnall keeping an eye on the color of the water to know where the channel was deepest.

We traveled some distance on a broad blue road between wood-covered hills and stony beaches. The sun was past its height when we came in sight of a palisade very like the one we'd visited before. The palisade was down by the riverbank, and there were a number of copper people on the stony bank and in the water. There were also a number of long and narrow boats lying bottom-up at the river edge. Finn began to jump up and down, grinning and chattering and pointing to the people. The folk on the bank were behaving in much the same way, pointing back at us. Erling gave Konnall a look and Konnall turned our head that way. He took us as close in as he thought prudent, then bade the anchor be dropped.

Erling told off Steinulf, Thorlak, and eight other men to board the boat with him and go ashore to meet Finn's people. He told them to bring weapons and their *brynjes*, to be donned when they were ashore (no use putting them on before the boat ride, risking certain drowning if it should tip).

"Let me come too," said I.

"The boat will be heavy laden."

"The hand of the Lord will hold us up. And I don't weigh much after a sea voyage."

I think Erling guessed that my real reason was my wish to get some earth under my feet; that, and my curiosity. But he said, "I suppose it's fitting to have God's messenger with us when we greet a new people. Come along, Father."

"I'd give much for some of that stink-grease now," said Steinulf, as he came back from his sea-chest with his arms and his brynje.

"You've only to ask," said Thorlak, who was coming from his own chest. He bore a pot of the stink-grease in one hand.

"Where'd you get that?"

"I picked it up on my way out of the copper men's camp. I was thinking of Thorliv at the time, but we haven't needed it since we put out to sea again."

"Well we need it now," said Thorliv, coming up beside him. We'd already explained the use of the stuff and, indeed, the mosquitoes were swarming now. Thorliv quickly covered her face and hands, and even anointed her hair.

The pot went around to all of us then, and soon we were shining and stinking, but happy.

We of the shore party, along with Finn, then clambered down the rope to our boat (a job made harder, at least for me, by my greasy hands) and had our gear passed down to us. The men put out their oars and began to row, and we were soon ashore.

I'd like to just stop and tell you once again the joy I felt on touching land, but I suppose I've sung that song before.

Finn was out among his kinsfolk in a moment, jabbering to them in their tongue and strutting a bit in his fine yellow shirt. When I remembered how little healed were his wounds, including many on his feet, I wondered at his hardiness.

As the men armed themselves, we submitted patiently to the same kind of poking and fingering we'd undergone in the first village. Erling cautioned the men to let them have their way.

"It's a little galling," said Thorlak, as a young girl tugged on his beard to see if it was real. "We're supposed to be frightening."

"Yes. Now take the Irish," said Steinulf, putting his hand firmly on his belt knife's handle so that no one could draw it out, "the Irish know how to show a fighting man proper respect."

"I thank you on behalf of all the Irish," said I.

An old woman was feeling my chest, apparently to find out whether I was a woman or not. This is my gift – wherever I go, even to the ends of the earth, I am a monster.

These people were dressed much like the first copper folk, except that the men mostly wore their hair long like Finn, though some were tonsured.

A few of the younger men set out running for the gate of the palisade and after a bit a small group of older men and women came out and spoke to Finn.

Finn answered them in great excitement and we could follow what he said, for the most part, for he acted the story as he told it. The older people looked back and forth from him to us and whispered to one another.

When he was finished, they made a circle and took counsel together.

While they conferred, I joined Steinulf in examining the long boats lying beached by the riverbank.

"Leather boats!" said Steinulf. "Can you credit it?"

I bent and lifted one a little. "They're very light," I said.

"Eggshells."

"I suppose it's all in how you handle them, as with any kind of boat. Irishmen have taken leather coracles near everywhere you Norsemen have fared in great ships. That includes Iceland. This land, too, perhaps."

Steinulf laughed. "Irishmen sail anywhere in leather boats because they don't care if they get home again. I suppose I wouldn't either, if all I had to go home to was Ireland."

I lost interest in the subject and walked over to the garden patch, where Erling was examining the plants and the soil.

"This is good crop-land," said he. "We could grow wheat here to feed the Greenlanders. It's better soil than any in Norway; better than Jaeder, better than the Vik. I'd compare it to England."

By now the elders of the copper folk had made a decision, and the eldest was saying something to Finn. Finn turned to us with a broad smile and spoke in words we could not understand but gestures that were plain. We were welcome to enter the palisade.

These folk did not live in a few longhouses like the first group we'd met, but instead in many small, mound-shaped houses covered over with leather, which looked to be of a size for single families. But, like the other village, there was an open place at the center of the compound where we were invited to sit on fur robes.

"Look at these furs," said Erling. "We could trade for such furs and sell them to the Greenlanders for export."

"You'll give me first chance to be your middleman, won't you?" asked Konnall.

Erling said of course, smiling to know his dream was making way.

Our hosts saw to our entertainment while our noses told us a feast was being prepared. There was dancing by men and by women. I've never understood dancing, but I had the idea that theirs celebrated victories in war and stories of their gods, whatever their gods were.

At last the food came, and I, whose stomach had been empty for days, fell to with relish. It was very much the same sort of food we'd had before, and I decided I liked it well.

I do not know if these folk treated their prisoners in the manner of the first we'd met, but I can say that they tortured no one that day, and nothing happened to hinder the flowering of our fellowship. We talked with signs, understanding about a quarter of what was said, and we all laughed a great deal.

We went back to our ship that night and slept there, then returned with the whole company to feast with our hosts a second day. Erling set his mind to making clear the idea that he would like to trade wool cloth for furs, and found that the principle of trade was not foreign to them. The following day we combined feasting with bargaining and got a very handsome pile of fur robes in return for some of the *wadmal* cloth we'd acquired in Iceland. We also traded a few extra knives, but we'd not brought knives for trading purposes and the raw iron in our hold would have been no use to them.

Our hosts insisted we sleep among them that night. Trustful of their goodwill, we agreed. Two families moved out of their houses and we all slept close-packed inside one or the other. The houses had a smokehole above, and fur robes covered the floors. From the inside we could see that they were built of many saplings set in a circle, bent inward to form a bowl-shape, then covered over with leather.

I slept my land-sleep, a good sleep, and my dreams ranged far.

I thought I was in a house, but a house of a kind I'd never seen or imagined. The walls were of beautifully finished wood that shone like polished marble. The floor was of the same sort of wood, with a few tapestries strewn about – as if they were meant to be walked on! Dim light came in from three enormous windows of the finest, clearest, colorless glass I'd ever seen. It was evening without and all I could see was the sky. The room was lit by a lamp shielded by a clever glass globe.

And there were books! So many books I'd never seen. Shelves and shelves of them, covering one wall from floor to ceiling. There were other objects sitting about on tables and chests, whose uses I could only guess at.

Dimly, as if at a distance, I could hear noise that sounded something like a storm, but not quite.

Head-first to one of the walls stood a bed, wide but low, where a man lay under blankets with his head propped on several cushions. The cushions were of fine white cloth like linen, but much stained with use. The whole place looked as if it had been a rich man's dwelling once, but had not been kept up.

The man himself looked deadly ill. On coming nearer, I could see that his fine blue blanket was wet with blood.

He was a brown-skinned man, with a long face and darkish curling hair. He wore no beard but needed a shave.

He looked at me and his dark eyes widened.

"You have blue eyes!" he said.

"Many folk do," said I.

"Not anymore. Not anywhere. I asked God to comfort me in my last night, and he sent me a blue-eyed angel. I've always wanted to see someone with blue eyes."

"I'm no angel," said I. "I'm just a priest and I'm dreaming."

"You're mistaken," said the dying man. "I am dreaming you."

"Perhaps we're each dreaming the other, meeting in the world of dreams."

"Perhaps." His head fell back against the cushions as if the labor of speech had used him up. He was wet with sweat, but when I touched his hand it was cold.

"Are you a bishop, or an abbot?" I asked. "You've the finest library I've ever seen."

"What, my books? It's just an ordinary private library, or it was ordinary not long ago."

"Ordinary? So many books as this must have cost a fortune!"

"A fortune? Haven't you ever seen – wait. You're not dressed like modern man. Where do you come from?"

"I'm an Irishman, but my home has been Norway. I suppose I don't have a proper home now."

"What year?"

"The Year of Our Lord 1002."

"1002." He sighed the words. "Tell me more," he said. "Tell me how you came to be here."

So I told him the whole story – my own tale in short, and the tale of our voyage more fully.

"Incredible," he said when I was done. "You say your friend Erling had a dream of free land in this country?"

"If this be the same country we were visiting," said I. "Though I never saw aught like this fine house where we fared."

"Your friend's dream came true, in time," said the man. "There was such a land as he dreamed of; one where there was no king and every person had equal say."

"In truth? How do you know this?"

"Because I'm not of your time. I come from far in the future – more than a thousand years."

"Truly?"

"As truly as I live – which is not much longer, I fear."

"Every person had equal say? What of the thralls? The slaves?"

"We ended slavery."

My knees went weak and I knelt by his bed. "No more slavery? God be praised!"

"It didn't come easily. It took war and much blood, but we did it. And we had schools for all the children. Not only the rich, but every one. They didn't all wish to learn, and some could not, but they all had the chance."

I bowed my head. "Now I understand. You say a library such

as yours is common. I see why. God, who is just, must have blessed this good land with riches beyond compare. Truly these are the Blessed Isles!"

The man coughed a while then, and his face showed his pain. I looked about for some way to help him, but could see nothing that looked useful to me. So I moved up beside his head and held him about the shoulders, thinking that might ease him a bit.

"Thank you, friend," he said. "It was never quite the Blessed Isles, if I recall the legend correctly. We did great deeds here. We built houses tall as mountains, and learned to send messages around the world in a moment. We even sent a ship to the moon. But men are still men, and there is no Heaven on earth. These books are not a sign of wealth. We made books cheaply, and in great numbers."

"Is that not uncommon wealth in itself?"

The man smiled. "Now that you mention it, I suppose it is. It is, indeed."

"But how is that you lie here alone?" I asked. "Surely your good neighbors can help you."

The man's smile turned down on one side. "There was a time when that would have been true," he said. "But I'm afraid you've missed the good days. All I told you of – it's over now. Gone. I lie here alone because I've been wounded to death. If my neighbors break in here before I die – and they will surely break in, in time – they will kill me."

"How did such a thing come to pass?"

"We started well. We started with the idea that all men were equal."

"A sweet thought."

"Then we went on to hold that all thoughts were equal."

"What kind of asses could believe a thing like that?"

"Asses with too much gold and too much safety, who understood nothing of real life or of their own natures. First we held all men equal, then all thoughts, and finally we came to believe that all deeds were equal."

"All deeds? Murder equal to acts of charity? Rape equal to marriage?"

"That is what we came to believe. I say 'we' as a man of this land. I myself never believed such rot."

"But – but how do you keep order when you cannot judge an evil deed?"

"You cannot. And that is why I lie here wounded and dying. Do you hear that noise outside?"

"The storm?"

"That is no storm. That is the sound of weapons. A particular weapon that we have. No need to describe it to you. Enough to say it makes that noise. Men and women are killing one another out there. Children too."

"Aren't there men strong and good to build order?"

"There are men who wish to build order, and no doubt they will when the people have had their fill of blood. But I do not think they are good men. Remember, we no longer believe in good in this land."

I bowed my head. "I am sorry to hear this. You are too excellent a man, I think, to die alone this way."

"But I'm not alone. God sent you. He never lets His children die alone – surely you know that."

"Sometimes I forget. But what of the Church? Surely the Church would not tolerate such thoughts and deeds!"

"Much of the Church did. Have you read the Book of Revelation? Of the great apostasy, the Whore of Babylon? These are the days of the Whore. The Church committed many crimes in its history, and was guilty of much corruption. But it was only in this last age that she abandoned the Faith itself, preaching the fashions of the crowd instead of unwelcome truth."

"Surely the Church can't be gone altogether!"

"No. There is always a remnant. But we must gather in secret, and we are hunted. That is how I came to be wounded. Enemies broke into one of our house meetings and began to kill. I got away, but not whole, and I crawled home to die." His voice had grown very faint.

I felt my cheeks wet with tears. "You are a martyr, Brother," I said to him. "This day you shall be with the Beloved in Paradise."

He rambled at the end – some nonsense about blue eyes, and how no one dared speak against the killing, lest they be called bad names. Senseless ravings, poor man.

He died in my arms. I woke and it was morning in the copper folks' village.

* * *

On the fourth day, we tore ourselves away from our new friends' hospitality and sailed off on a northerly course, furs and timbers in our hold. We promised to come back, but I'm not sure they understood.

And that's as well.

Chapter 20

E were the next six days at sea, sailing before a light southeast breeze that kept trying to nudge us into land. Land was most times to be seen to port, though Konnall kept clear of it. I was glad of that. I wanted no more exploring. I wanted to go to Greenland and find Maeve. I had all I could do to keep from asking Konnall, "Are we soon there?" like a child, several times a day.

Erling, for his part, spent much time at the port rail gazing landward. I knew he was spying into the future. I was happy to leave the future to him. I'd had my fill of the future, too. I was seeing almost no spirits at all now.

We saw birds of many kinds. We saw porpoises from time to time, and other fish. They interested me not at all, except as dinner.

The boredom of our sea-time was relieved somewhat by the scrapping of Thorlak and Bergthor. When you've got above thirty men cooped up in a ship with nothing to do, you can't avoid some stepping on tails back and forth. It's not so bad in foul weather, or when you have to row or bail, but fair sailing is always chancy – being becalmed is worse.

In any case, Bergthor had taken it into his head that Fingal ought to be his personal thrall. The first few times Bergthor bade him "Wash out my bowl for me, Fingal, there's a good fellow," or "Tie my shoelace, Fingal, I seem to have trouble reaching it these days," Fingal had gone ahead and obeyed out of respect for an elder, and no doubt out of the prudence always needed by a freedman dealing with a free man. But one morning when Bergthor bade him rinse out his socks for him, Fingal lost his head, grabbed the socks and cast them into the sea, telling Bergthor where he and the socks could both go.

Bergthor slapped him across the face and soon we had to hold both of them back, mostly to protect Bergthor who hadn't looked for such impertinence.

"Leave the man alone, Bergthor!" shouted Thorlak, who was helping to subdue Fingal. "He's not your thrall! You've no call to bid him wipe your nose and your backside for you!"

"The trolls take you, you pup, don't talk to me!" Bergthor spat back. "The times have come to this, that thralls strike their betters, and rag-ass vagabonds think they can marry lords' daughters! If I were twenty years younger – ten years younger! – I'd slice your ears off and serve them to you toasted!"

Thorlak went bright red then and moved to strike Bergthor himself. Erling stepped in and caught his hand, speaking to Bergthor.

"If you've aught to say about the way I provide for my sister, say it to me," he said.

Bergthor shook himself loose from his crewmates' hands. "What use would it be?" he said, slumping off toward the prow. "I'm only ballast on this ship. No one cares what an old man thinks."

Erling followed and spoke to him quietly, but Bergthor was not soothed. He treated Fingal thereafter as if he did not see him, but Thorlak he belittled whenever he got the chance. He called him "Jarl Rag-ass," and I had to speak to Thorlak more than once to keep him pegged down. I also begged Thorliv to speak to him, lest he kill the old man.

Which is not to say the old man didn't deserve it. I'd seen Bergthor testy often – more often than not, to speak the truth. But I'd never before seen him mean.

I tried to draw him out, but he shut his mouth when I spoke of it. That, too, was unlike him.

The wind freshened on the sixth day and the land which had been our constant companion to port fell away. We then sighted a new land to the north.

"Greenland?" I asked Konnall.

"Nothing like," he said.

He steered us eastward along the shore, sailing close to the wind and making slow time. The land fell away at last so that we rounded a point and were able to make better time northering. The country was wooded, with low hills.

"It's getting cooler," I said to Konnall. "I think the nights are shorter, too. We must be getting near to Greenland."

"Not cool enough; not short enough," said Konnall. I think he got pleasure from saying it.

We spent that night at anchor. The next day we passed another point and there was an inlet there, like a fjord. We saw a large island before us, and a distant, misty shore beyond that was the far side of the fjord.

"A boat!" cried someone in the prow.

"One of the copper men's leather boats?" asked Erling, who was playing with Aslak.

"No! A Norse boat!" the man replied. "A proper Norse boat of wood, with men in it!"

Erling gave Aslak over to Astrid and hurried to the rail. By then, our men were shouting and waving and the men in the boat were shouting back.

"Who are you?" Erling cried, once he'd got the men quieted so that he could be heard.

"We're Greenlanders!" cried one of the boatmen. "Who are you?"

"I'm Erling Skjalgsson of Sola! We were bound from Norway to Greenland to see Leif Eriksson, but were blown off course! Do you know Leif Eriksson?"

"I'd think we do! Leif is chief man of Greenland! We sail under his brother Thorvald!"

"In that boat?"

"No, we're just out fishing! Our ship is in harbor at Leif's Booths!"

"And is that far?"

"No! Just around the point there! If you're friends of Leif's, you're welcome!"

"Are you done fishing? We'll give you a tow home!"

"Thanks for that! It doesn't take long to catch your fill in Vinland!"

"*Vinland?*" I asked Konnall. "Wine-land?"

"A good name," said Konnall. "I'm fond of wine."

Chapter 21

THEY directed us around the point, past some islands into a sheltered bay. We had to down sail and row in, and Konnall had to fight the rudder, the currents there being strong. At anchor in the bay lay a workaday Norse knarr, like enough to our own to be her sister. Even I, who have no fondness for knarrs, felt an easing in my heart at the sight of something so homely after all our outland wanderings. It was as if we'd grasped a string we knew to be tied at its other end to Norway, be it never so long.

We anchored near the other ship and I went ashore in the first boatload with Erling. We rowed into the mouth of a brook on the eastern shore, and above us on a ridge stood a house very like the ones we'd known in Iceland – all of turf. The fishermen beached their boat and ran up to announce us, then came back to say that Thorvald Eriksson bade us welcome.

Before leaving the ship we'd taken counsel about what gifts to bring. "We brought goods meant for Greenland's needs," said Erling. "But this is not Greenland. There's plenty of wood here. Meal might have done, but we used ours up in Iceland. Pitch we have none, and they could likely make their own here. I doubt they'll be needing wadmal or furs."

"Some of our wrought iron might be welcome," said Konnall, frowning. "Beyond that, I'd say just ask them what they need. In my experience, you're bound to run out of something you can't do without on any long voyage."

We climbed the bank. On the landward side the country was covered by a tangle of small trees and brush.

The house, like many in Iceland, was of an irregular shape, several rooms being huddled into one building for warmth – though this place was nothing so cold as Iceland. Not to say it wasn't windy – it was – but this wind was as different from Iceland's as a down pillow is from an axehead.

We passed a small, turf hut, which I took for thrall quarters, and entered the house through a door near the south end of its eastern side.

We found ourselves in an empty room that was meant for people but clearly doubled as a storage room, and passed through a second door into the great room, where something above thirty men – the ship's whole crew – waited to greet us. Most of the walls were turf, though it looked as if someone had begun paneling. In the high seat sat a man who was not hard to name. His face and red hair were very like his brother Leif's, though the features were blunter and his hair fairer.

"Greetings, Erling Skjalgsson of Sola," said Thorvald Eriksson. "You are welcome and well met. When I was a boy I learned to think of Thoralf Skjalg and his kin as enemies, but you dealt generously with my brother Leif, and we've had good profit from trade with you since. Sit, all of you, and drink with us, and tell us how you came to be on the wrong side of the ocean."

"What can they have to offer for drinking?" muttered Berg-thor as we sat on benches along the walls. "Have they learned to grow barley out here?"

"They're drinking something," said I. "Look at them. Red faced and grinning, every one. If they're not drunk, I'm a Cornishman."

Thorvald grinned like a boy with a secret as thralls came through the northern door with stoups. One of them filled a horn and carried it to Erling.

Erling looked at the contents. "Wine!" he said. "You have wine!" He took a deep drink, smiled, and passed the horn to Astrid. The thralls filled other horns and the wine began to go around from drinker to drinker.

"We've more wine than the king of England," laughed Thorvald, and his men laughed with him. "We've more wine than the Emperor of Constantinople – or we can get it. This is Leif's Vinland – Wineland the Good."

"I'd have thought us a little far north for grapes," said Konnall.

"No grapes grow just here, that's true. The grapes come from Hop, a land to the south where Leif voyaged and where we'll be going next summer. But Leif and his crew made more wine than they could carry in the ship, so they left barrels behind in this house." He leaned forward as if imparting news. "It gets better when it sits awhile."

"Wine is a rare pleasure," said Erling, "and that was true even when I sat at Sola. My esteem for this good land grows by the day."

"Aye, it's a rich land; a fat land," said Thorvald. "I think I may never go back to Greenland." He mused a moment. "But I forget my guests. Tell us how you came to be here of all places, Erling of Sola."

Erling asked Bergthor, as our eldest and our skald, to tell the story, which Bergthor did after asking for and getting another drink.

"I'd thought of seeking land in Greenland," said Erling when Bergthor had finished. "I've been told there's still land for the taking there. But now that I've seen... Vinland, I've had other thoughts. Do you think your father Erik would grant me land in Vinland? I'd thought we'd discovered this land, but it seems you got here first."

Thorvald said, "It might have been chancy with my father Erik. He hated Christians and priests. But Father died in a pestilence last winter. Leif is chief man now, and I think he'll be glad to do it. If you don't mind paying tribute."

"I grieve to hear of your father's death. I paid tribute to Olaf, and to Jarl Haakon before him. I've no objection to it, as long as I'm not meddled with overmuch."

"Thorvald Eriksson and Erling Skjalgsson, lords of Vinland," said Thorvald. "It makes the odds better. I like it."

"The odds?"

"Look about you – we're thirty-four men in our crew, thralls included. That's nearly one of every ten men in all Greenland. There's much to be gained in this land – but there are few of us. More men for Vinland; that's what we need."

"There are others in Norway who chafe under Jarl Erik," said Erling. "Perhaps we can entice them here, with prospects so fine."

The horn came back to Erling and he drank. "We weren't sure what to bring you as a gift," he went on. "What we carry was meant for Greenland, and it's mostly things you possess here already. Do you need iron? We can offer you iron."

"You've brought us something we need more," said Thorvald with a grin.

"What's that?"

"Women."

Erling's face fell, and on his cheekbones appeared the familiar red spots that meant he was ready to do murder. "I must have misunderstood you, friend," he said in that quiet voice that was more alarming than a roar.

"Oh – don't mistake me!" said Thorvald, raising a hand. "I meant nothing improper. What I meant is, we made the mistake of going off on this journey without women. We miss having women to cook, but worse than that is the sewing. When a garment gets ripped we have to do the best we can to repair it ourselves, but if you look carefully you'll note that we're ill-clothed one and all. If some of your ladies could do some mending for us, and cook a bit while you're here, we'd be mightily grateful."

Erling unstiffened, and Astrid made a pretty speech about her willingness to help, and how she was certain Thorliv and Freydis would feel the same. Thorliv said so too, as did Freydis, though I thought Freydis looked a tad disappointed.

"I've a sister named Freydis," said Thorvald, giving our Freydis a long look. "Well, a half-sister. Back in Greenland."

"I'm sure she misses you sorely," said Freydis, giving him the same look back with usury.

"Tell me about Leif and his exploring," Erling asked.

"'Twasn't so great a matter in itself," said Thorvald. "'Twas Bjarni Herjulfsson of Herjulfsness who saw the land first, fifteen or so years since. He was sailing from Iceland to Greenland and got sea-bewildered, much as you did. He sailed for his northering, like you, and beheld three different lands. As best I can reckon, the first land he saw must have been somewhere hereabouts. Further north he found a land with rich forests but no tillable land. Further on again there was a land with great flat rock-slabs and glaciers, no use to anyone. Soon after he was able to make east and find his way to his father's farm in Greenland.

"Leif, as you doubtless know, came back from Norway with a Christian priest. Father spat iron-slag about it. He went on and on about how Leif was ruining the land, bringing shysters in. Half the reason he'd left Iceland was to get free of the Christians, he said – which was a lie. He left Iceland because he'd made the place too hot for himself.

"For my part, I was happy to be baptized. The latest fashion from Nidaros, you know. And Mother took to it right off. She forsook Father's bed, declaring that she would sleep no more with a heathen. That did not improve his humor.

"So Leif sat down to ponder the problem. 'I asked myself, when was Father happiest?' he said to me. I said to him, 'That's easy. He was happiest when he was getting his own way.'

"Leif said, 'No. Father was happiest when he was exploring, when he was flying in the mouth of the unknown. When we set out for Greenland on the chance that it might be a place where men could build – that was when his eyes shone. That was when life tasted sweet to him.'

"So Leif proposed a voyage to take a closer look at Bjarni Herjulfsson's land. Father grumped and muttered about how he was too old for such capers, but you could tell he liked the idea, much as he tried to hold his grudge against Leif. It was only a matter of time before Leif talked him round.

"Unfortunately, as they were riding down to the jetty on the day they were to embark, Father's pony threw him and he fell and hurt his leg. As they helped him up he said that was it, his exploring days were over; the gods did not mean him to see new lands. Leif feared to lose the wind; he didn't have time to talk him around. So Father rode home and Leif sailed west. And we had to put up with Father at home."

"Your father was ever a proud man," said Bergthor. "I knew him in his youth – as a foe. He had the worst battle-luck, for one who got out alive, of any man I ever knew. But his sailing luck was good."

"And Leif wanted that luck with him," said Thorvald. "But as it turned out, he had plenty of his own.

"He crossed the water westward and came to Bjarni's stone-slab land, which he named just that – *Helluland*. He sailed southward and found the forest land, too, and of course called it forest-land – *Markland*.

"Then he arrived here, and he liked the place and built booths here. Later he built a house, the one we're sitting in. But we still call the place 'Leif's Booths.'

"He and his men wintered here and explored further south in the spring. They found a place they called Hop, where there was self-sown grain of an unfamiliar sort and where our old house-thrall, Tyrkir, found grapes. He's a German – he comes from a place where grapes grow. He was a happy man, and he made the others happy, too. Leif gave him his freedom. And he called this whole southern land Vinland.

"In the spring, he sailed home with a shipload of timber and wine. On the way, he spied something in the distance no one else saw – Leif has remarkable eyesight. Everyone wondered why he was steering close to the wind, but when they got nearer they could see a crowd of people on a skerry, waving with all their might. Leif was cautious, since Vikings have been known to entrap sailors by feigning such need, but he got near enough to talk to the people and learned that they'd been sailing to Greenland with a load of timber and had been shipwrecked there. Leif took them aboard with their possessions and brought them safe home to Brattahlid. Later, he went back and got the timber, which was his by right of salvage. So he made a double profit and piled up good works in Heaven, to boot. That's why they've taken to calling him Leif the Lucky.

"But then Father died last winter and Leif inherited the lordship. He longs to come back here, but has much on his mind at home. So I asked for the use of the ship and got it, and sailed out myself. But I got a late start because Leif had to collect his salvage.

"And here we are, drinking wine in Vinland. Come spring we'll explore."

When evening came, the thralls served us dinner – indifferently cooked, I'm afraid, but we filled our bellies and enjoyed "the blood of the daughter of the vine" as Bergthor named wine in the poem he made.

And we laughed a great deal, and somehow Freydis came to be sitting next to Thorvald.

And the next day, we had headaches of unusual intensity and found that when we drank water to ease our throats, we grew drunken again.

We felt better on the third day and Astrid, Thorliv and Freydis set about the mending they'd promised, which was no small labor. They took over the cooking, too, to shouts of loud thanksgiving. Erling and the others helped Thorvald and his men with paneling the walls.

"We've time to build another house, Erling," said Thorvald. "Why not winter with me here? We'd be glad of the company and you could join our exploring in the spring."

My heart stopped a moment as I watched Erling consider it.

Great was my relief when he glanced at me and smiled wryly. "I've promised Father Aillil we'd make Greenland this summer. He's waited long, and I fear he'll shed his skin if I hold him back another winter."

That night we feasted again, and as the conversation grew more and more disjointed, we somehow got to speaking of Africa.

"This is Africa, or a part of it," said Thorvald.

"Never Africa," said Konnall.

"Have you ever been to Africa?"

"No, but I've spoken to men who've seen it. Have you?"

"No, but my father taught me about the world. The sea is like a great bowl, is it not?"

"Everyone knows that."

"Well, what's at the south rim of the bowl? Africa."

"We're very far west of where men say Africa lies."

"But that's the bottom of the bowl, don't you see? It curves around till it gets here."

Steinulf put in, "It's still a far distance. There could be many lands in such a distance."

"But look at the *skraelings*!"

"*Skraelings*? Screamers?" asked Erling.

"The people of this land."

"The copper men?"

"Yes, you could call them that, I suppose. They have dark skin and dark hair. What do Africans look like?"

"Dark skin and dark hair," said Erling, "but –"

"Clearly these are Africans and this is Africa."

"I've seen the men from Africa in markets, and done business with them," said Erling. "They are tall and they wear long garments of woven cloth. They all wear beards. The copper men have no beards. I don't think they can grow them."

"That's in the east part of Africa. This is the west."

"East and west are just what I'm talking about."

They went on in that vein for a while, and then passed on into a discussion about the biggest fish they'd ever caught. Later, in a very drunken state, Thorvald asked Lemming for Freydis's hand in marriage. Lemming looked favorably inclined, but Freydis only laughed, which made Thorvald dejected, and he buried his nose in his wine-horn. Lemming looked dejected as well.

We had a hangover day the next day. The day after was Sunday and I said mass. And the day that followed, we sailed away.

"I liked Thorvald," I said to Erling as Leif's Booths dropped from our sight.

"So did I," said Erling. "But he won't make a lord, I think."

"Why do you say that?"

"He cares more for being liked than for being obeyed. There was no order in his camp. Did you see the paneling-work? Nothing had been done on it for weeks. The men preferred wine to work, and Thorvald let them have their heads. No doubt he meant to take control again at a later time, but a real lord knows that once you let it go, you never get it back."

As it happened, Thorvald never got a chance to learn. We would not hear of it for years, but he would die of a copper man's arrow the following summer and find his last bed in his new land.

Part Four

Greenland

Chapter 22

*T*o *Greenland at last!* The thought buzzed in my blood. I could not sleep nights. I had no taste for food. I almost forgot to be seasick.

To Greenland, where Maeve is.

I will do…everything for her. I will make it right. Whatever she has suffered, I'll make it right. I'll wipe the tears from her eyes. I'll smooth the lines of care from her brow. I'll teach her to walk straight again, a free woman. I swear it before God.

I beg you, Lord of Heaven – aid me to keep my vow. Holy Mother of God, watch over her. Keep her safe until I come. Not long now. Not long.

But it was long. The winds were contrary as often as not, and over-gentle when they were fair. For three whole days we sat becalmed in fog, floating like herring in a barrel. I thought I'd go mad.

We passed the two lands Thorvald had told us to look for – the wooded one and the slab-rock one with the mountains behind – and at last came the blessed day when Konnall judged our northering right, and he swung our head eastward.

And the next morning, we saw the ice-blink off the white mountains.

"*Greenland?*" I asked Konnall as the frozen peaks hove into view. "They call this *Greenland*? White-land, maybe, or blue-land. Iceland would be the truest name."

"Iceland was already taken," said Konnall.

"Compared to this place, Iceland is the Garden of Paradise. I think it's poor business to trade with the kin of a man who'd call this place Greenland. If a man tried to bring me to settle here calling it Greenland, I'd burn him in his house." It made me ill to think that Maeve had been wasting in such a comfortless country.

"Be patient a little," said Konnall, whose manner had eased now that he knew he'd gotten us safe to our destination. "Erik the Red wasn't wholly a scoundrel."

We drew near the coast, passing the odd iceberg and giving it wide berth, and entered a maze of islands. Konnall steered us through them, sure of his way now, and we anchored for the night in a small harborage near the mouth of the Eriksfjord, which is flanked by a pair of tall crags. The night-sun painted the mountains rich shades of blue and I watched them through the night, for I could not sleep.

"We won't sail up the fjord," said Konnall the next morning after breakfast. "The westerly winds mean you'd have to tack forever to get out again, and sometimes you run into ice. We'll walk to Brattahlid. It's not a long road." We used the oars as he steered us to a jetty where a headland sloped down from the foot of the mountain, on the north side of the fjord mouth.

"How far from Brattahlid to Gardar?" I asked him. Gardar farm, he'd told me, was where he thought he'd seen the girl I was sure was Maeve.

"Just a short row across the fjord and a short walk across the ness."

I was nearly the first onto the jetty, hopping on one foot or the other while the rest disembarked. By now, local folk had come to see who we were and we sent them ahead to tell the Brattahlid people we were coming.

We left a few men to watch the boat, and the rest of us headed along the path that followed the fjord. The water below us on our right hand was glacier-melt, milky-blue and sparkling. It would be a fair place to live if one didn't have to eat.

But, before long, we reached kinder country, where scrub birch belted the hills as in Iceland and there were meadows and buttercups and beds of osier.

Perhaps parts of Greenland aren't wholly bad, I thought.

In time the fjord bent northward and the land grew even fairer. The meadow-lands on the slopes were rich and green, the birches taller, the flowers thicker. A stream wound its way down to the fjord. We saw horses and cattle and grazing sheep, and turf buildings after the Iceland pattern.

"Brattahlid!" said Konnall. "And this – *this* – is Erik's Greenland. It's the heads of the fjords where the living is good."

I granted that it might not be the utter backside of the world.

We passed a couple of smaller farms where the folk waved and called out welcomes, crossed the stream and proceeded into the farmstead.

A small crowd awaited us, led by a fair-haired, round-faced woman in a rich green overdress. At her side stood a tall, stoop-shouldered man whose tonsure marked him as a priest.

"I am Thorhalla, wife of Leif Eriksson," the woman said. "Welcome to Brattahlid, and welcome to Greenland." She extended a horn to Erling. "I regret we cannot offer you ale. It's scarce here."

"We can remedy that, and better," said Erling, motioning to two of the men who carried between them a cask. "Vinland wine, sent by Thorvald Eriksson."

"You've been to Vinland?" asked the priest. He introduced

himself as Father Andrew. I almost remembered him. He'd come with Leif when they visited us at Sola.

"We've had a long and muddled journey," said Erling.

"Come in," said Thorhalla. "Travelers with a tale to tell are doubly welcome."

The house was a simple longhouse, with one door in a side wall. Inside was a single room with two rows of pillars and benches along the sides. Once our eyes grew accustomed to the dark, we saw that the man in the high seat was one we knew. It was the same young Leif we'd met before, only not so young. In truth he looked as if he'd aged ten years. He held a babe in his arms.

"Welcome, Erling Skjalgsson and company. We are honored to have you in the lands west oversea," he said. "You've met my wife, Thorhalla, and this…" he lifted the child for us to see, "is my son Thorkel."

Erling said how glad he was to be there, and Leif bade us take seats. And then there was a weary time while we told our story. Thorvald's wine flowed and all were merry but me. I felt like a man stuck in a meeting with the king from which he cannot excuse himself, sorely needing to use the privy.

At last I thought we'd covered the main points, and I made bold to shove my oar in. "There's a farm hereabouts called Gardar, I'm told," I said.

"Aye," said Leif. "Thorvard Einarsson lives there."

"'Twould be a great kindness to me if you'd send to him for a thrall called Maeve whom I believe to be there."

"And what would you want with a thrall?"

"She is my sister. I've come of a purpose to buy her free."

"You've come far to do a good deed. You should not have to wait longer. Guttorm! Send someone to Gardar. See if they have a thrall named Maeve there! If so, ask Thorvard and Freydis to bring her."

When the messenger was gone Leif said, "I'd have sent to Thorvard ere long in any case, since he's married to my half-sister Freydis."

"I was sorry to hear of your father's death," said Erling. "I'd looked forward to meeting him. They still tell tales of him in Jaeder."

"I doubt it not," said Leif, "since most of those tales involve your kin thrashing mine. No! Peace! I'll not prod old wounds. Those days are over, but Father had a long memory. It's as well he's not here today, if only for our digestions."

"And for his," said Thorstein Eriksson, another brother of Leif's. "Especially as you brought a priest."

"I fear the *paterfamilias* never really grasped the truths I tried to teach him," said Father Andrew.

"'Twas the same with my father," said Erling.

"He took it ill that I became King Olaf's man and accepted baptism," said Leif. "He said Christianity was for women and thralls. Tell me of Olaf. Tell me how he came to die."

So there was that saga to tell, and it filled the time while I waited. It was a long saga, remarkably long for a man who went under as young as Olaf did.

As the story went on, Freydis (our Freydis – the other one hadn't arrived yet) moved over to sit near Thorstein Eriksson and engage him in whispered conversation. Lemming sat watching her, with the eyes of a mother bear nosing her dead cub.

One pities a beast that suffers, for it cannot name its grief. Lemming, I thought, merited just such pity.

When Erling's telling was done, Leif rose and took a sheathed sword down from a peg on the wall. "Olaf gave me this sword," he said. "It may be the best sword in Greenland. But it's never been in a battle."

"Better to have a sword and not need it, than to need a sword and not have it," said Steinulf.

"I tried to give it to Father," Leif went on. "I thought the gift might cool his anger at my christening. But he said he was Thor's man and if he took a damned Christian sword, Thor would strike him dead, and rightly. But once, when he did not know, I looked and saw him draw it out to admire it."

Leif drew the sword and we all called it a beautiful piece of work.

"I think 'twas the same with the Faith," said Leif. "I think he admired it in secret, but was too proud to own he might have been wrong."

"'Tis hard for proud men," said Erling.

"Pride is the cardinal sin," said Father Andrew. "It was the undoing of Satan himself, and of Adam and Eve."

"Yet Erik had much to be proud of," said old Bergthor. "I knew him, you know. When men like he are gone from middle earth, a thing of worth will be lost."

We sat silent for a moment until Erling said, "I think pride is in no near danger of vanishing from middle earth."

We laughed. Bergthor rose suddenly, his face red. "'Tis no joking matter to me, that men like Erik and I are passing." He strode out the door.

I rose to follow him, but Erling said, "Let him be, Father. He gets these moods; we've all seen it before. He'll walk it off and forget it by morning."

"Besides, your sister is coming," said Leif. "You must be here to greet her."

"Aye," said I. I'd nearly forgot for a moment.

Erling told the tale of how we'd come to make this voyage. Leif was as surprised by it as Snorri had been, I think, but unlike Snorri he seemed to have no problem believing it.

"So this is what I wish to do," said Erling. "I've seen Vinland. I like it. It has all a man needs. It's better than Jaeder. It's better than England.

"I need not step on your rights. The land we visited was well south of your place, Hop, if I understood Thorvald's description rightly. I want to work with you. We'll bring men from Norway. We'll bring Norsemen from Scotland and Ireland and Orkney. There're always dispossessed Vikings and younger sons hungry for land. We'll build a proper colony.

"And it won't be like Norway. It won't be like anyplace in Christendom. It'll be more like Iceland. No king but the law. A land of free men.

"In fact, I've been thinking about it. We'll have no thralls. Once a man steps onto my land, he'll be free."

"No thralls?" asked Leif.

"No thralls."

"There'll always be thralls. You can't do without thralls."

"Why?"

"Who's to do the scut work? Who's to dung the fields, cut the peat?"

"There'll always be the poor. We'll pay them to do it."

"Perhaps we can make thralls of the Skraelings...."

"*No*," said Erling. "They're the people of the land and more in number than we. If we make enemies of them, we're doomed."

Leif leaned back in his seat and pondered. "If all men in your land are free, all our thralls would run to your land. Unneighborly of you, to lure our thralls away."

"I hadn't thought of that."

"Damned bothersome, having saintly neighbors. I begin to see my father's point of view." He called for more wine. "It's early days yet," he said. "We'll work something out."

I saw Bergthor come back in at about that time, and he took his place on the bench.

We feasted richly. There was pork and reindeer and three kinds of fish, and cheese, and butter but no bread. We spread the butter on the fish. We drank wine. The weary time dragged on and I glanced at the door again and again, listening for footsteps in the entry, for little was to be heard through those thick turf walls.

The wine went to my head, and I dozed and woke, and dozed again.

And then someone was shaking my shoulder, and I looked up into Erling's face. "They're here," he said with a smile. "Best pull yourself together."

I heard the voices and the footsteps in the doorway, which in a turf house is a sort of passageway. I heard men's voices, and I heard a woman's voice.

I stepped off the bench. I ran my fingers through my hair, hoping I didn't look overmuch like a drunkard disturbed.

And they came – two men I did not know, and two women. It wasn't hard to tell the thrall – she wore an undyed garment and her hair was cropped, just as in Norway.

It is as I feared, I thought. *The years and the labor have changed her beyond knowing.*

"Maeve?" I said.

"That is my name, Father," said the girl.

Even her voice is changed! I thought. *How is it that her voice has grown higher?*

And how can it be that her nose has grown shorter? And her eyes – they're brown. Can thralldom change a person's eye color?

The truth settled on me like a load of snow off a hill-slope.

"You're not from Connaught, are you, Daughter?" I asked, choking the words out of a throat as dry as old flax.

"Nay, Father. I come of Munster stock"

I sat on the bench then and leaned my head on my arms. "'Tis the wrong Maeve," I said. "I've crossed the great sea for the wrong Maeve."

Chapter 23

"Forgive me for not being your sister," said the girl to me. The words were so pitiful, they broke my heart. Her voice was indeed sweet, as Konnall had told me, and she was an innocent soul, I thought.

I looked into her face. "'Tis but a small sin to not be my sister," I said. Then I said, "I came all this way to buy you free and, before God, I'll do it. He must have His purposes, even if they cross mine."

The look of joy that came over her face was almost worth the disappointment.

The business with Thorvard was quickly done; and when I'd paid my silver over, I made a bed on the bench and rolled up in my blanket and gave myself to sleep.

* * *

I woke to the sound of men's voices louder than they ought to be in the morning. I saw men milling about in the house. My head hurt.

"What's the matter?" I asked Steinulf, who was nearby on the bench doing up his leg-wrappers.

"The night is past and Bergthor hasn't returned," he said.

"Of course he returned," I said sleepily. "He came back in during the feasting last night."

Steinulf looked at me. "He did not," he said.

"But I saw him—" I began, and then it hit me. I sat bolt upright and began to pull on my shoes. I'd not seen Bergthor the night before. I'd seen his fetch.

The appearance of a man's fetch means he's doomed to die.

A hasty fish breakfast was brought in, and we bolted it down before going out to search. Every man took a spear.

Erling stood in the yard with Leif. Leif was saying, "Let's send five men that way, and five men up the slope, and five to search the fjord—" when Thorlak knelt and looked at the ground.

"Bear," he said.

"*Bear?*" asked Leif.

"I've hunted bear many a time in Norway. I know bear tracks. And these lie atop the tracks of a man. The bear was chasing him."

Leif looked unconvinced. "What kind of bear goes after a man when there are cattle and pigs and sheep about?"

"A bear with a white mark over one eye," said I, going cold in the belly.

"A white mark?" asked Leif. "Greenland bears are white all over."

"A happy chance for Ulf Lodinsson," I said.

"Ulf Lodinsson?" asked Erling. "What has Ulf to do with anything?"

"All this journey I've been seeing beasts with white marks over their eyes, like Ulf's eyebrow. I saw Ulf in his own shape at Helgafell. I did not speak of it to you because...because there was little to be done about it, and I feared he was after the child, and I didn't wish to frighten you."

"I'm the child's father," said Erling. "'Tis my business to be frightened for him."

"Put it down to my pride. I like to fight the spiritual battles alone. No need to tell me I'm a fool."

"If Ulf indeed seeks the child, we must not let him lure us out leaving Aslak unguarded. You must stay here, Father, and watch over him and his mother."

"Father Andrew is here. I'm sure he can pray as well as I."

"You said it yourself. 'Tis a spiritual battle."

"I also said I'm a proud fool."

"Then humble yourself and do as you're bidden."

Sometimes I used to think that because I read Latin I must be smarter than Erling. I never was, but I was slow to learn the lesson.

"My father would never let a bear be hunted here," said Leif, hefting his spear. "He said one of our ancestors was a bear."

"If I have my way, this bear will never be anyone's ancestor," said Erling, and they were gone. They did not divide their force. They all followed the bear-trail.

I went back into the house. There was Leif's wife Thorhalla with little Thorkel, and Astrid with Aslak. There were Thorliv and Freydis, as well as Freydis the sister of Leif. There also was Maeve the thrall.

"Poor Bergthor," said Astrid, giving Aslak a breast and making me look away. "I fear for him. He's been so odd of late. When men get that way...."

I knew what she meant. We all knew that when men grew fey as Bergthor had, it often forebode their death. And Bergthor himself had spoken to me of death.

"I'm sorry about your friend," said Maeve. "I pray God will spare him."

"Thank you, Daughter."

"May I ask, what are your plans for me?"

"Plans for you?"

"Now that I'll belong to you."

"You won't belong to me. I bought you free. You can go home to Ireland – or anywhere you like."

"How? I've no wealth. I've no way to earn my bread. If you free a thrall, begging your pardon, you make yourself answerable for his living. That's the law. You must know it."

"Yes, of course. I hadn't thought about that. I'd had…other plans. Don't trouble yourself. I'll see to you."

"You might ask her if she has any thoughts of her own on the subject," said Astrid.

I blinked at her. "You're right, as usual," I said, and I turned to Maeve. "I beg your pardon, Daughter, I'm dull as a lead spoon this morning. What would you? Would you go home to Ireland? Come with me to Norway? Remain here?"

"I've never been to Ireland; my parents were thralls in Iceland. I'd as soon stay here as anything, I think, though I've no idea what I'd do. And it would make it difficult for you to look after me. So I suppose I'd best go where you go."

"We'll think on it and come to a plan in the end," said I.

"I hate this waiting about," said Freydis Eriksdatter. "I hate it that the men always go out and do things, while the women stay home fretting." She was red-haired like all Erik's offspring, graceful of form, with a nose that turned up.

"I rather like it," said Freydis Sotisdatter. "The men face the hardships – suffer the cold and the heat and the wounds and the broken bones – and in the end they come home to us to lay their little prizes at our feet, like a cat with a dead mole."

"There's no reason for you to be idle," said Thorhalla. "Astrid and the baby are to stay in the house, as I understand it, but there's plenty of work for strong young women on the farm."

Freydis Eriksdatter was immediately up and heading for the door. Freydis Sotisdatter followed with lesser joy. Thorliv and Maeve went with them.

That left me with the two mothers and their babes. They

straightway fell into shop-talk, discussing tonics for colic and what to do about rashes; I sat idle, feeling useless. Someone ignorant had once told me a priest was neither a man nor a woman. I did indeed feel like some monster of nature, good for nothing useful, and useful for things no one wanted.

I should have been praying. I'm certain that's what Erling expected of me. But I was cast down. My great dream had come apart in my hands like an ill-fired pot. I'd dragged my friends across the great sea in pursuit of my will, and done no good in the world. Bergthor, indeed, might be dead. For naught.

I wallowed in the sin of Sloth, a backhand form of Pride. I knew it well enough to give it its name, but did not care enough to fight it as a Christian ought.

And so I was ill prepared when Ulf Lodinsson walked in through the door. He had a knife in his teeth. He took it out and held it in his hand.

"You!" I cried, jumping to my feet. "I thought you – I thought you were a bear."

"A bear I was," he said with a mocking smile. He stood in front of the door, blocking it. "And no doubt will be again. I like being a bear. Everything eats something, but a bear eats everything."

"But they chased you. You chased Bergthor, and the men chased you."

"Even so. But it's no hard matter for a shape-changer to kill an old man and double back on his pursuers unmarked in another form."

"You killed Bergthor?" My mouth was dry. It took me a couple tries to get the words out.

"He made a good death, you'll be glad to know, though not a very Christian one, if I understand what that means. He cursed me to my face as he hung from the cliff-edge. 'Twas no easy task, driving him up the mountain. He kept trying to circle back, to return to the farm for help. But I had all night. I got him there at last, as a farmer drives a pig to slaughter."

"Do you take pride in that – in killing an old man?"

"It's a matter of no concern. If it were not he it would have been another. My vengeance was the point. The lives of men are but a means."

"Then face Erling. Give him a fight, man to man, if you must have revenge. Why bother with all this smoke-craft?"

"Kill Erling? Why would I kill Erling? Would he suffer as I've suffered? I, who saw my father killed, who watched my mother enter the burning hall, who heard my brother's screams as they put him to death? Erling will suffer as I have. Erling will lose what he loves most and walk this earth in pain so long as the Norns choose to prolong his suffering."

"You cannot harm Astrid and Aslak. Astrid bears the holy cross on her breast. They are both under God's protection, never to be touched by your devilish powers."

"One need not always touch," said Ulf pleasantly.

And before my eyes he became a great white bear. I did not know then how big a Greenland bear might be, but I thought (rightly) that no natural bear could be as large as that one. His head overtopped the cross-trees of the roof when he stood like a man.

I fell back on the bench in terror, but he was not concerned with me. He turned to Astrid and Thorhalla, where they shielded their babes with their bodies. His angry roar rolled up the blankets left behind by the last night's sleepers and raised dust from the rushes on the floor. Both women tried to flee for the door, but Ulf deftly cut Astrid off while letting Thorhalla go.

Astrid looked desperately around for some other way of escape.

And a door that had not been there before opened in the gable wall, behind the women's bench.

Astrid ran for it.

"No!" I cried. *"He cannot hurt you if you stay!"*

But it was more than one could ask of the bravest woman, to keep her child in harm's way when a bolthole was in sight.

She ran through the door. She paused on the other side and tried to close it against the bear. It would not budge.

So she disappeared into the darkness beyond.

The bear followed, suddenly small enough to pass through.

I followed the bear.

Chapter 24

*I*T was like one of those houses in Iceland with one room after another, divided by doorways.

But the rooms went on and on. There was always another. The house had no end.

I heard the bear roaring ahead of me, but I did not see him again. I only followed the sound, in the half-darkness, in the hall without a gable-end.

"Oh God," I prayed. *"I've brought naught but evil and disaster with this mad hunt of mine. Let this final evil not come to pass. Preserve the mother and child, You who inhabit the heights of Heaven and the depths of the sea. If someone must die or be lost in the Other World, let it be me."*

But the bear's roaring grew fainter and fainter and, at last, I heard it not at all. My wind was gone, sapped by long weeks at sea. I slowed to a walk. I went forward only because I already knew what lay behind.

I pushed through the next door, stepping over the threshold, and pulled up short because the room was not like the others. Or rather, it was like the others, but by way of another door.

This was not like Ulf's witchcraft door through the gable wall, but like the true door in the side-wall. I walked through the passage of turf, and into something like the same room. But now there was a man there. It wasn't Ulf. It was a man I didn't know, tonsured and dressed in a brown shirt.

He looked up at me as I approached him. His face looked familiar. I thought for a moment he was my father, dead these many years.

But he was younger than my father. I knew the face then. It was my own, as I'd seen it reflected in water.

He looked at me and said, *"You're not from Connaught, are you?"*

"Yes," I said. "I'm Aillil son of Douglagh, from Connaught."

"No. You think you're Aillil. But you're not. I've been looking long for Aillil. I fear there is no such man."

"I am Aillil, I promise you," I said, but as I spoke I heard a step behind me and turned to see another man enter the hall. This man was also dressed in a brown shirt, and he also had my face.

He walked to the Aillil who sat on the bench and that Aillil said, "You're not from Connaught, are you?"

And the new Aillil tried to say he was, but by then another Aillil was coming in.

And so we came, one after another – ten Aillil's – twenty – a hundred – so that the hall was crammed with us. We weren't all the same. One Aillil was blind. One had a single leg and hobbled on a crutch. Some were boys, some were old, and one coughed and coughed, clearly dying of some wasting disease. One was a dwarf.

I'd had enough of Aillil. I was sick of the sight of me. I elbowed my way through the press to the door through which I'd entered. At least I'd be able to get away from myself and be alone with...myself.

Instead of finding myself in another room as I expected, I found myself in the steading, outside Leif Eriksson's house.

I quickly turned back in, but found the house empty. All the Aillils were gone. I was in the Other World no longer.

I went out again. The other women were there, waiting for me.

"What of Astrid and Aslak?" asked Thorliv.

"I don't know. I couldn't keep up."

"You must go back!"

"I tried. You can't just go in and out of the Other World at will. When the door closes on you, it's closed."

"But we have to do something!"

"I agree. What?"

I saw the two Freydises exchange a look. They were sisters under the skin, those two.

"What are you thinking?" I asked.

"If we cannot hunt the bear, there are other ways…" said Freydis Eriksdatter.

"Speak!" said I. "I'll listen."

"You say this Ulf followed you all the way from Norway, taking the shapes of one beast after another?" she asked.

"Aye. So it seems to me."

"Such magic is not easily come by."

"Yes?"

Freydis Sotisdatter put in then, and said, "It takes many years to learn such magic. Years of study and bitter self-mastery. A great warlock is most often a very old man, like Eyvind Kellda. But Ulf is not so old, from what Erling says."

"Which means…?"

"He must have taken the second way."

"The second way?"

"There is a short road to the powers of a great warlock. Short but costly."

"All right…."

"There's a price to be paid. The Old Ones who grant such

powers want something in return – something not just valuable, but without price. They demand one's life."

"How do you mean?"

"They demand something from your body. Something you can't live without. Sometimes they'll settle for a liver or the lungs, but most times they demand the heart."

"You think Ulf gave up his heart?"

"Very likely."

"Then how does he live?"

"He'd have been given a spirit friend – a bogey beast to carry with him wherever he goes. He draws his life from it. Its heart beats for his."

"And he carries this about with him always?"

"No. He carries it when he must – when he's traveling across the sea, for instance, for he dare not go far from it. But it's too dangerous to carry it about. Most often he'll find some safe place to keep it, and hide it there."

I frowned. "Then it might be possible to find it."

"There are…ways…."

"Don't make mystery, girl. Astrid and the babe are in the Other World, and the longer there the harder it is to come home."

"I hesitate because I know you won't like it."

"Just say it. Let me say what I like."

"If you can learn the bogey's name and call it, it must answer you. When it answers, you can find it. Once you find it, you have the warlock's life in your hands and can make him do your bidding."

"And how are we to learn the bogey's name?"

"That's what you won't like."

"Say it, girl. You can say it, at least."

"Someone must perform a *seith*, a spirit-journey."

"I know what a *seith* is. I was there at the Great Summer Sacrifice."

"Where my mother was killed." Freydis' eyes were cold as she said it. "But the *seith* was only part of what happened that night. We can do it without sacrifices. All we need is a wise woman."

"Like you."

"I know how to perform a *seith*."

I rubbed my chin. She was right. I didn't like it one bit.

"All these years I've tried to keep you from such things," I said.

"I'm a woman grown. You can't shield me forever."

"I'd hoped you'd learn to shield yourself."

"Perhaps I don't need shielding."

"When you're young you think you're the master of whatever you touch. As you grow older, you find that too often those things master you."

"You said it yourself, Father, the time is short. You think my heart cold, but I care for Astrid just as you do. Let me do her this service."

I ground my teeth. With every finger-width the sun moved, we had less chance of getting the mother and child free. I'd striven for Freydis' soul for years, though, and had no wish to see her backslidden.

She took my silence for agreement and moved toward the house, telling Thorhalla and the other Freydis how to prepare the high seat she needed, and to cook a dish of beasts' hearts for her to eat.

"Wait!" I said. "This name – the bogey's name. Does it choose its own or does the warlock name it?"

"The warlock gives it its name."

"Then let me try something."

I cupped my hands around my mouth and shouted, "LODIN!"

Nothing happened.

I shouted, "GYDA!"

Still nothing.

I tried once more. "RAGNVALD!"

Nothing for a moment, and I bowed my head.

Then the voice came, high and brazen— *"Who calls for Ragnvald?"*

"You did it, Father!" said Thorliv.

Freydis Sotisdatter looked, I thought, a tad disappointed.

"Which way was the sound?" I asked.

"Up the slope, that way!" said Thorhalla.

"How'll we know where to find it?" I asked Freydis.

"Most often they bury it and pile a cairn of stones over it."

"Look for a cairn," I told the women, and we fanned out over the hillside.

"RAGNVALD!" I called again. Again the voice came, *"Who calls for Ragnvald?"*

We tightened our search.

"RAGNVALD!"

"Who calls for Ragnvald?"

"Here's a cairn!" cried Thorliv.

We ran to her. It was but a small thing, not knee high.

"Have you seen this before?" I asked Thorhalla.

"No. And I've dried wool on this slope many times."

I bent my back and began to shift stones. The women helped me.

At the bottom lay a flat stone. Once we'd uncovered it I tipped it up, and in a hollow beneath lay a pouch of oiled leather. Something within it moved.

I took it up and said, "Ragnvald?"

The voice from inside said, *"Who calls for Ragnvald?"*

I did not open the pouch. I carried it back to the steading, the women following me.

Before we'd gotten there Freydis Eriksdatter said, "Look! The men are coming!" We turned to see them trooping down the slope behind us. They walked with the bent backs and shambling steps of men whose hunt has been luckless.

"What news of Bergthor and the bear?" I called.

Erling answered, "Bergthor is dead. The bear we lost."

I saw then that four of them bore a litter made from spears and a cloak. An unmoving body lay on it.

"Bergthor, old friend," I whispered. "I'll say you a mass."

When they came to us, Erling said, "We followed the tracks to the edge of a cliff. There the bear tracks vanished. All that was left was Bergthor's fingers."

"His fingers?"

"Cut off neat, as by a knife, lying on the cliff-edge. His body lay on the rocks below."

"No bear did that."

"Nor did any bear leave that place. The tracks went up, and did not return."

"Ulf most likely left as a bird."

"That was my thought. But no man can track a bird. Our labors went for naught." He looked about him. "Where's Astrid?"

"The answer to that is ill and good." I told him of how they'd been lost, and I told him of what I held in the pouch.

"Then we can command Ulf?" he asked, his eyes blazing.

"If Freydis knows whereof she speaks."

"Then let's lose no more time."

He took the pouch from me and shouted so that it rang from the mountain-slopes, "ULF! ULF, COME TO ME OR I'LL CRUSH YOUR HEART IN MY HAND!"

And across the yard a wolf loped, a black wolf with a white mark over one eye, to crouch growling before Erling. All but Erling moved back, and those with weapons drew them.

"A wolf," said Erling. "In the end, you're true to your name, Ulf."

"I come as I must," growled the wolf. "Once my family's lives lay in your father's hand as mine does now in yours."

"My father did you evil. Name a price; I'll pay it. Let this thing end."

"I have my price. I've taken your woman and your whelp. I'm satisfied."

"I hold your heart. Give me my wife and child back and I'll let you live."

"Living has brought me small joy. To have injured Erling Skjalgsson is the sole sweetness I've known. So slay me now – I'll die gladly."

I opened my mouth and said, "Is that all your life is worth, Ulf? To throw it away on vengeance? Life is a gift! You're young! You've time to love a woman, raise a family, see your grandchildren! You'll throw these treasures away for a cinder like vengeance?"

"Thorolf Skjalg burned my life to a cinder. I was left with naught but vengeance. Is it not a great thing, god-man, to make the most of what little you've been given?"

"Is there nothing I can offer you?" asked Erling.

"You can offer," Ulf snarled. "Offer me gold. Offer me lands and power. Offer me your life. Offer your honor. Perhaps I'll give you your family back if you get down on your hands and knees and beg for mercy. Or perhaps not. There's but one way to know."

I watched Erling's face, and I knew that he was giving real thought to taking the chance. I was terrified. I did not want to see Erling abase himself to this beast.

I tried to think of something to say. I was as empty of words as a beehive is of cats.

It seemed as if time stopped then. We stood, all around that hell-wolf, wondering what would happen next.

What happened next was that the door of the house opened and Astrid came out, carrying Aslak in her arms.

The moment Erling turned his head to look at her, Ulf made a leap for his throat. As Erling swung back to fend him off, the heart-pouch went flying from his hand.

Ulf was big and heavy and strong, full of purpose to rip Erling's throat out. Erling struggled against him and got his arm between Ulf's jaws, and a dozen men leaped forward to prise the beast off him. But it was as if they were not there. The same power that had shaped Ulf into a giant bear kept him in the place he wanted to be, doing the murder he meant to do. His growls, and Erling's cries, and the grunting of the men and the screams of the women rose in a clamor that hammered the sky.

And then a howl rose like a damned soul screaming, and the grappling men were thrown aside, and I could see Ulf, his whole wolf-body stiff, with his face turned up to heaven in a rictus like death six days gone.

And I saw Freydis Eriksdatter stamping her foot again and again on Ulf's heart-pouch.

* * *

They skinned Ulf out and made a rug of his pelt. Leif Eriksson gave it to me, and I knelt on it for years when I said masses.

When I asked Astrid how she'd escaped the Other World, she looked at me as if surprised I should ask. "I went toward the light," she said. "We've been through this before."

We buried Bergthor in the churchyard at Brattahlid. It struck me that he'd been like a monk, in a way. No, he wasn't celibate and he didn't keep the fasts well, but he'd chosen to live in Skjalg's household and Erling's afterwards, with no family other than the men of the bodyguard. He left no sons or daughters to mourn him. We mourned him there, west oversea, and he lies under the sunset. Perhaps it's a comfort to him to keep company with Erik the Red, a good enemy from his youth.

We were feasting in Bergthor's honor when a battered ship from Norway dropped anchor at the mouth of the fjord. They'd had bad winds and storms, and had beaten upwind most of the season, they said. Leif invited them to feast with us.

When the skipper, a man named Ketil, was introduced to Erling, he said, "I'm not sure I care to share a bench with a man whose name is cursed up and down the Westland."

Erling stood up, his face white and red. "I'll overlook those words out of respect to our host, but I warn you not to say them again."

"Wait," said Astrid, putting a hand on his arm. "If people are saying such things, it would be good to know why. Tell us, sir, what do folk say about my husband in Westland?"

"I did not come here to fight anyone," said Ketil.

"My wife is wise," said Erling. "I must hear this. I'll not hold you to account for other men's words."

Ketil said, "It is told in Norway that you left the Westland in the hands of your brother Kaari, who is like no man that ever lived and is driving the people to revolt. They say he takes the jarl's taxes and then takes as much tax for himself, leaving the people beggared. He hangs any man who opposes him, and makes thralls of the family. You even left your mother in his care, and he's put her out of her home and left her to the charity of friends."

Erling's face was still white, but the red spots on the cheekbones had gone.

"Leif," he said, "we must finish our trading quickly, so I can make sail for Norway."

Chapter 25

LEIF got some bargains by Greenland standards, for Erling's mind was set on home. But still we got a shipload of wares – Greenland bearskins, wool, walrus ivory – it was a very white cargo. And a falcon, a gift from Leif that Erling meant to keep. Also white.

"I suppose we can fit it all in, somewhere," said Konnall in the hall one night. He knew as well as we that what we took home would be less bulky than what we'd brought.

"I'll make space for you," said a voice, and Fingal the thrall stepped toward the bench where Erling and I sat.

"What's that?" Konnall asked.

Fingal looked at Erling. "Erling Skjalgsson," he said. "I am a freedman in your care, bound to you by law. I ask now to be loosed by you and allowed to go my own way."

"This is unusual," said Erling, who was favoring his bandaged arm. "Most freedmen wish a protector."

"And I make no complaint of you. But Leif Eriksson tells me he'll take me on if you release me, and he's offered me land here in Greenland."

"Greenland?" I put in. "I thought you meant to go home to Ireland!"

"Things change. Men change. I'm not the boy I was in Ireland, and if I went back, no doubt it'd not be the place I remember."

"So you wish to stay in Greenland?"

"Where else could I get land of my own? And there's one other thing...." He looked to his side and Maeve the thrall stepped out of the shadows. She moved to Fingal and took his hand.

"Father Aillil," she said to me. "I, too, beg to be loosed from the protections due a freedwoman."

I looked back and forth from one of them to the other.

"We mean to be wed," said Fingal. "We'd be pleased if you'd marry us, Father."

I looked to Erling.

"No time for the banns before we sail," he said.

"Then Father Andrew will have to do," said Fingal. He did not seem heartbroken about it.

We did as they asked, of course. I'd been wondering how to provide for the woman anyway. We left them with gifts and, from what I've heard since, they did well.

Later I said to Erling, "Do you suppose that was what all this was about?"

"What 'that'? What 'this'?" he asked.

"All the sailing and adventures and dangers and death – was it all so two thralls could find each other and be wed?"

"Why not?"

"It seems a small birth to come from such great labor pains."

Erling smiled. "Small things are not always small. Do you know the tale of Baldur?"

"He was a god, wasn't he?"

"Some say a god; others say a half-god, the son of Odin and a mortal woman.

"He was something of a bad lot, Baldur. He bullied people, and none could hurt him, for Odin had gotten an oath from every thing under the sky not to do him harm.

"But there was a hero in Denmark, a prince called Hodur. Baldur had assaulted Hodur's wife. Hodur learned that there was one small, feeble plant, the mistletoe, that had never given its oath. He made an arrow of mistletoe and shot it at Baldur, killing him."

"The point being?"

"Sometimes the smallest, feeblest thing does the greatest work."

I thought a moment. "I can't believe I'm sitting here listening to Norse parables."

"I thought I was going west to find a new home," said Erling. "Instead, the whole voyage made a road back to Norway again. My destiny is there."

"You're certain of success?"

"Not at all. I may die. But it's there I'll die. I know that now, in my heart."

We sat over our *skyr* (the wine had been drunk up) and pondered the matter.

"'Tis a pity about Vinland, though," he said.

"How so?"

"My new land. The land with no king but the law, and no thralldom. I suppose it'll never happen."

"I suppose not," said I. I could have told him of my dream about the dying man, but only fools put stock in dreams.

Part Five

Norway

Chapter 26

*T*HE winds and storms that had bedeviled Ketil's voyage served us as foul-weather friends. We fairly flew eastward with the tempest on our tail and sighted the snow-topped mountains almost before I'd had time to be properly miserable.

"Home," I thought, as I watched them rise over the sea-brim. Then I thought how strange it was to look at Norway as a home rather than a place of exile.

Having got back, we were left with the question of where to make our harbor. Erling was all for heading straight into Hafrsfjord to beard Kaari at Sola.

"Madness," said Steinulf. "You'd as well set your throat in a wolf's mouth. We're one knarr's crew. Kaari has his bodyguard, plus the whole Gula-Thing levy, with Jarl Erik to back him up, if that weren't enough."

"The men of the west will come if Erling Skjalgsson sends out the war arrow."

"Perhaps. We've only this Ketil's word for the way Kaari has borne himself and the enemies he's made. You don't just charge in to such things. You send spies first, learn your enemy's strengths and weaknesses. Don't let your heart lead you, Erling! You're a hersir. You must use your head."

Erling frowned but could not deny Steinulf's sense. "I must get my mother free at least," he said. "I can't leave her Kaari's hostage."

Steinulf nodded. "Now you're thinking like a warlord."

Erling sat on a cask and drummed his fingers on his knee. "We need to go to someone we can trust not to betray us, but far enough from Sola that we'll not greatly risk running into Kaari's people."

"One of the freedmen," I said. "Someone you set up on a farm further out. They'll know the gossip, and the great folk barely see them."

"Good," said Erling, nodding with vigor. "I'd best wear poor man's clothing, so I won't be known."

"Let me go instead," said I. "The freedmen are shy of you, for all your help to them. They're easier with me. Besides, it'll get me onto dry land."

"She's my mother. Her rescue is my business."

"Then do your business when we know where to find her. But let me handle this spying job. With all respect, you'd make a poor spy. You walk too tall, and you look folk fair in the eye."

"And your tonsure and shaven face are known all over Jaeder. How do you think to go unremarked?"

"I'll wear a muffler to cover my jaw, and a cap to hide my tonsure. The weather's cool enough."

Thorlak Gudbrandsson broke in. "I'm least known in these parts of any in the crew. Let me come along."

Erling gave him a long look and said, "Very well. But don't take too long with this thing."

"We still don't know where we're going," said I.

Erling slapped his knee. "Upper Sande farm," he said. "I set up Copar, Turlough's widow, there, with her new husband Brian."

"Aye," said I. "That's a good choice. Not too far to go, but out of the Sola neighborhood. And surely they'll help all they can."

"We could put in at Randaberg bay and let you take the boat to shore…" said Erling.

"No," said Steinulf. "Poor harborage for a ship at Randaberg bay, and the great folk at Randaberg would notice. They might support you or they might not – we'd best not take the chance."

"Dusavik, you think?"

"Aye a larger harbor, and no one will mark a knarr putting in for the night. It'll be a farther walk for the spies, but that's all to the good. No one at the harbor will know where they went, unless they take the trouble to follow."

We rounded Tunge and sailed south past Randaberg bay, making Dusavik by sunset. I donned a woolen cap and wrapped a muffler about my face, and Thorlak and I rowed the towboat ashore.

We tied up at the pier and got our feet on dry land (I love that weak-kneed, rocky feeling). The half-moon gave us light enough to find our way along the road that took us up the peninsula between the low hills. After spending time in Iceland and in Greenland, it seemed to me a tame country indeed.

"Perhaps Erling's mother is kept somewhere hereabouts," said Thorlak to me.

"'Tis possible."

"A man who rescued Erling's mother might be thought to have done him good service."

"Don't outrun yourself, lad. If we barge in undermanned and underthought, we're like to make a bad case worse."

"Well, there's no harm in planning out what a fellow might do were a chance to come his way. Isn't that how one readies oneself for whatever the Norns send?"

"I don't believe in the Norns. God, however, sends chances, too, from time to time. Just don't go seeing them where they're not. Do you know what they call a rash man's companion?"

"What?"

"Raven's food. That would be me."

"Ah, well, it likely won't come to anything. We're cursed, Father. We live in dull times. It's not like the great days of old that they tell of in the tales."

It was a fair walk to Upper Sande, but not a weary one. We passed between the hill at Randaberg on our right hand and Bo Pond on our left, then went down a slope to the low farm that faced a broad, surf-beaten bay on the west.

"There's a Sande farm and an Upper Sande farm, north and south," I told Thorlak. "Both belong to Erling. As often as not they've been worked as one farm, since Upper Sande has never prospered much. But Erling thought it worth trying to set up a freedman there."

We reached the small steading and I knocked on the door, hoping Copar and her man were not abed yet. My knock brought a muttering from within, and the door opened a crack.

"Wha'yoowant?" said a man I could not see for the shadows. His breath smelled of ale.

"Brian?" I asked.

"Who's askin'?"

"Father Aillil."

"Father Aillil's gone to chase whales in the west."

"He's back. Can he come in?"

"I suppose there's no help for it."

He moved back and we stepped in over the threshold. It was a common hearth-house with a hearth-way dug into the floor, leaving an earthen bench along the walls on either side. Copar knelt on one bench. She greeted me with her head bowed. I couldn't be sure in the hearth-light, but I thought she had a black eye.

"Light a lamp, Copar," said Brian. "Who's this pup?"

"This is Thorlak."

"Is he anybody that matters?"

"I will be," said Thorlak.

Brian laughed. "Every young buck thinks he's going to be somebody."

"This one is promised to Erling's daughter," said I.

"Erling's daughter?" asked Brian. "I spit on Erling and his daughter."

Thorlak half drew his sword. "Is this how the thralls in Jaeder speak of their betters?"

"Betters!" snorted Brian. "Erling may have been my better once. But now he's just another grasping, blood-sucking landlord. He may have rank, but I call him no honest man."

Thorlak drew his sword fully and Brian took up a cudgel. I stepped between them.

"Peace!" I said. "There's no good in this for either of you. You, Thorlak, would get no honor from killing a thrall, and you, Brian, would get only a rope for killing Thorlak." (Well, that's the sense of what I said. It came out somewhat more ragged, as I was thinking it out as I went).

Fortunately Brian had only ale-courage to back him up. He stepped back, muttering dark threats we all knew to be worth less than his shoe-soles. Thorlak put his sword back where it belonged.

"Listen to me, Brian," said I. "You know me and you know whether I'm like to lie. Erling is back from the western seas, and he'll know the name of anyone who does him ill – or good. He gave way to Kaari out of honor, and Kaari showed his mettle. Now he'll deal out of honor again. We've put ourselves in your hands in coming here. There's naught to stop you running to Kaari with the news of Erling's return, and perhaps he'd give you some reward if he's in a giving mood. But if you help us, Erling will know of it. So judge for yourself whether you want to be his friend or not."

Brian peered at me through squinting eyes. "What's this about

Erling being back? Hasn't he been back these three months?"

"Three months?" said Thorlak. "We only sailed in this night."

"Haven't we all seen him, big as life? He's been back three months, I say!"

"I swear to you by the rood," I said, "we only made land today. We've been to Iceland and Greenland and lands further west, and Erling was with us every moment."

Brian sat and scratched the back of his neck. "You can't expect a man to speak well of a lord who promises his help, runs off to the end of earth, then comes back and shows himself a worse leech than his bad brother. We've suffered under Kaari, all of us, and under Erling worse since his return, and the freedmen most of all."

I looked the tosspot close in the face, leaning forward across the hearth-way. "It's these things we've come to learn about, Brian. Of all the folk in Jaeder, we've come to you for the true story."

The flattery pleased him. He sat back with a satisfied grin and said, "Copar, I think there's some ale left. Bring it for our guests."

Copar dipped ale from the stoup and brought it to us in cracked wooden bowls. Closer up I saw clearly that one of her eyes was purpled.

Brian said, "First of all, there was the rents. We all pay rents, of course, who live on Erling's farms, but Kaari doubled them all. Twice the fish or butter, twice the labor. When we complained that we'd little left to live on, Kaari answered us that the land was his – why should such as we get wealthy on it?

"Then there were Jarl Erik's taxes. That touched us freedmen less than the rents, but it was the talk of the country. Merchants' tolls, fines from the Thing, tributes from the lords, the bargain is that the hersir takes the tribute, sends the jarl what is due to him, and keeps the rest for his own. It works well as long as the hersir isn't too greedy. Kaari is greedy. The jarl was getting what he expected to get, but Kaari was getting fully as much. Everyone knew it. One of the lords set off to complain to the jarl. He was seen no more by sun or starlight.

"But worse was to come. One day the word went round — 'Erling Skjalgsson has returned.' Men shouted it along the roads. The thralls and freedmen wept in thanks to God.

"But what happened? Along came Erling, and he demanded the same rents and tributes already collected by Kaari! Where there had been want, now there would be plain famine. Say Erling Skjalgsson's name anywhere in Jaeder, and you'll get no other response than the one I gave you."

"Lies!" said Thorlak. "Damned lies, and if you say more I'll —"

"Peace," said I. "I begin to guess what's been going on." I leaned forward again. "Brian, Copar," I said. "Listen to me. Have I or Astrid or Steinulf or any of Erling's household been seen when Erling has gone about these last months?"

"Not that I've heard."

"And how have they explained that?"

"The saying is that he came back in a ship of the jarl's, and the rest of you lingered with his kin in the Faeroes."

"Do you believe that? Look at me. Am I not Father Aillil? I say to you that I have been voyaging with Erling these months."

Brian struggled with an effort to think, clearly work he was unused to. "Then who came and demanded the double rents?" he said at last.

"Who do you think? Who looks like Erling?"

Brian's eyes went wide as he caught my reasoning. "Kaari!" he said.

"Aye. Kaari presented himself as Erling."

Brian shook his head. "I'd have figured that out myself in time," he said.

"No doubt," said I. "But Erling is back in truth now, and

we'll be about setting things right. For a start, we need to know where Ragna is – Erling's mother. We must have her free and safe before we can do aught else."

Brian's face split in a grin. "Nothing easier than that," he said. "You'll find her at Rygg farm."

"How is she guarded? Do you know that?"

"There are no guards."

"No guards? Kaari doesn't care if she flees?"

"Where would she go?"

"Kinsmen, friends of Erling's. There are many places she could go."

"She wouldn't do it."

"She's a brave woman. I can't see her staying in Kaari's power when there's a way out."

Brian still grinned. "Just go to Rygg and see her. You'll understand then."

Thorlak put his hand on his sword again. "If this is some kind of trap –"

"You'd not believe me if I told you. You must go and look for yourselves."

We got no more from him, so we left shortly. Out in the night Thorlak said, "Imagine living like that. He beats that woman, doesn't he?"

"I'm sure of it."

"Poor creature."

"Indeed. The saddest thing is that her first husband used her the same."

"And she went and wed another like him?"

"You'd be surprised how often it happens."

"I'll never understand thralls."

"'Tisn't only thralls. You should try being a priest sometime. You'd never believe what you'd learn."

"So where's this Rygg farm?"

"It's near the harbor where we started. That ridge we crossed — Rygg gets its name from that."

"So we go back the way we came."

"Yes, but more carefully this time. Brian says there are no guards, but that makes no sense to me."

"Nor to me."

We walked in silence for a time. As we neared Rygg, a tall figure came along the path to meet us. We'd met few folk that night, but those we'd met had taken little note of us so far as we could tell. I pulled my muffler up to my nose and went on, trying to carry myself like a man on commonplace business, benighted on his way.

As the man drew nearer, the moonlight revealed familiar features.

"Erling!" said Thorlak, rushing ahead.

The man did not answer, but continued to approach us.

"Erling! We know where your mother is —" said Thorlak.

"Hush lad," said I. "This isn't Erling."

I wish I could say some spiritual insight or wisdom had warned me. The truth is that the man wasn't acting as Erling would, and that left but one possibility.

"Kaari!" said Thorlak. He went on his guard, sword at the ready.

"Welcome home," said Kaari.

I looked about for his bodyguard, but so far as I could tell he was alone.

"You're a bold one," said I. "To meet us here naked of supporters."

"A fellow's in no danger from such as you," said Kaari. "What brings you out in the night on an unpeopled road?"

We said nothing.

Kaari smiled. "You need not answer," he said. "One guesses your errand. Would you like to be shown the house you seek?"

We stared at him open-mouthed.

"Why should a fellow keep secrets?" said Kaari. "You'll not get the woman away."

"Don't tell us what we will and will not do," said Thorlak.

"See for yourselves," said Kaari. "Do you spy that small house somewhat apart from the steading there?" He turned and pointed along our way toward Rygg farm. I saw the house he meant, dimly in the moonlight.

"Ragna is there. Go see her. Try and take her with you if you will." Kaari wrapped his cloak about him and continued on his way.

Thorlak turned and watched him go. "I do not like this," he said.

"Nor I. But I can't think what to do other than go look."

"Perhaps she's dead. Perhaps that's what Kaari meant."

"I pray not. Let us hurry."

We hurried. We reached the little cottage quickly. It was near ruined, its turf roof sagging.

I put my hand on the door latch and opened it. I held my breath as I stepped over the threshold, steeling myself for whatever horror awaited me.

A fish-oil lamp burned on a small table within. In the light of the lamp I saw a fair young girl.

"Father Aillil!" the girl said. There was some emotion in her wide blue eyes, fear or ecstasy, I could not tell.

"Greetings, daughter. You seem to know my name, though I do not know yours."

"'Tis I," she said. "'Tis Ragna."

I sat on the bench, speechless.

Thorlak had entered by this time. "What's this?" he asked.

"You I do not know," said the girl.

"You're not Ragna," said I. "I know Ragna. She's a woman in her fifth ten of years."

She stared at me, and I knew the emotion I saw in her eyes. She was terrified.

"I *am* Ragna," she said. "Believe me, Father Aillil. I am Ragna. Kaari did this for me. To me. For me."

"He made you young?"

"Aye."

"I don't understand," said Thorlak, "but it seems to me it's all to the good. You can come more quickly with us back to the ship."

"No!" she cried, curling her feet up under her and scuttling back over the bench away from us.

"Why not?" I asked.

"'Tis Kaari's spell. I stay young just so long as I remain in this house."

"Then you must be old again," said Thorlak. "Let's make haste."

"No!" she said. "I can't bear it. Do you understand, Father? I'm young! I'm fair! There is health in my flesh and no aching in my bones! If I walk out that door I'll never feel this way again." She began to sob. "I'm sorry," she said.

We sat and watched her weep a moment.

Finally I stood. "Come, Ragna," I said. "We must go to the ship."

She shook her head so that her thick golden hair flew from side to side. "I can't! Don't you understand?"

"I do understand. You look eighteen summers, but you are not eighteen summers. You are Ragna, wife of Thorolf and mother of Erling. Ragna is a woman of courage. I know. I've seen her courage. You're not afraid of losing your youth again. You're afraid because you know you're going to walk out that door, and you fear your own bravery."

"You mock me!"

"I do not. I speak what I know. You know it too."

She buried her face in her hands and shuddered with her weeping.

"Come, Ragna," I said, putting my hand on her shoulder. She looked up at me, tears streaming down her soft cheeks.

"Tell me I'm fair, Father," she said.

"You are very fair, Ragna."

"Would you kiss me?"

"That I dare not."

She turned to Thorlak. "Would you kiss me, young man?" she asked.

Thorlak widened his eyes. "With pleasure," he said. He put his face to hers and they kissed.

I felt compelled to say, "Ragna, you should know that this boy is likely to be your son-in-law."

They broke the kiss off with laughter.

"I bind you to silence on this, Father," Ragna said with a light laugh. "And you, young man —"

"I'm Thorlak Gudbrandsson."

"You, Thorlak — if you say naught about it, neither will I."

Thorlak, to my surprise, was blushing. He nodded his agreement.

Then Ragna straightened her back and blew out the lamp, and we all went out of the house.

And it was as she had said. The moment we were out of doors, Ragna curled in on herself like a fallen leaf, and was an old woman again.

"I don't understand," said Thorlak. "Kaari was so sure Ragna would never leave."

"I don't know quite what the matter is with Kaari," said I, "but he doesn't understand people. I'm guessing he thinks he's beginning to. But he's wrong."

"You talk as if Kaari isn't a person himself."

I made no answer to that.

We made our way to the harbor and rowed out to the ship. We told it all to Erling.

"Kaari frightens me, Erling," said Ragna. "A woman should feel some bond with her child, but when I'm with him I feel only the kind of fear I'd feel when facing a serpent.

"Have you heard about Bjorn Reidarsson and his son Vigleik?" she asked.

We said we hadn't.

"Bjorn and his son were caught trying to burn Gorm Anleifsson in his house."

"It doesn't surprise me a great deal," said Erling. "Bjorn was always a hothead. I never knew Vigleik to make trouble, though."

"That's what the witnesses said when Kaari and his men captured them. So Kaari punished them differently."

"That sounds fair."

"Not the way Kaari did it. He made Bjorn pay a fine and hanged Vigleik. He said it was right to hang the better man, because he'd go to Heaven, and it would give the worse man time to mend his ways."

We all sat and thought about that.

"It's plain Kaari has turned all Jaeder against us," said Steinulf. "The sooner we get away, the better. I say let's winter with Sigurd and Sigrid and Thorir up north."

"No," said Erling. "We end it now."

"Now? With every man our foe?"

"Things aren't always as they appear, and even men are not always what they think. There'll be famine in Jaeder if Kaari is not put out. I believe I know how to do it. Sleep, all of you, and I'll make plans."

Chapter 27

"THIS is what you'll say to Kaari," said Erling the next
morning to the farmer at Rygg. We'd gone ashore after
breakfast and called on the man, bidding he be our messenger
in return for a stout walrus-hide rope from Greenland. "Tell
him Erling Skjalgsson will meet him tomorrow morning on the
neck of land between Leikvold and Sunde farms to settle our
rights by trial of arms. Tell him I hope he's not overawed by my
greater force."

"Greater force?" said Steinulf. "He has his bodyguard plus
the farmers' levy. We've but one ship's crew."

"Perhaps," said Erling with a smile.

"It makes no sense."

"I am counting on that."

Steinulf grumbled over the matter all day. At last, toward
evening, the farmer returned with word that Kaari looked forward to the meeting.

We slept that night and set off southward, before dawn, for
the battleground. There are two lakes, Haaland Lake and Stokke
Lake, that lie east and west of one another, divided by a ridge of
high ground. It was on a hill on that ridge that Erling proposed
to array our force, facing another hill to the south.

"One could have a worse battleground, I suppose," said Steinulf as he stood in the red heather surveying our position. It was an unusually still morning in Jaeder, and the sky was milky. "We've got high ground if we stay on the defense, and we can't be flanked."

"Unless Kaari's raised men in the north to take us from behind," said Konnall, who'd come along. He had told Erling, *"Blood or seawater, we're partners till you get home; and the way I see it, you're not home till you're hersir at Sola again."*

The women would be watching from the hilltop, above the battle-line, and I as usual would be with them. But I'd shriven the men and said mass before we left the ship.

The sun rode high before Kaari and his army came to face us, making their own shield-wall on the hill-face opposite. They were not over-careful about it, knowing they'd be doing the attacking. But I reckoned their shields at 200 or so.

"Dear God, it must be ten to one odds," said Astrid beside me. Her face was as white as if the babe at her breast were sucking out her very life's blood.

"What can Erling be thinking?" asked Ragna.

"He's not confided in me," said I. "But he seems tolerably sure of himself."

"He's taken risks before and forced the Norns to dance to his tune," said Ragna. "But how many times can he make water run uphill?"

"Well, he's likely to make men run uphill, at least," said I.

Kaari's voice rang out across the dell. "Good morning, Brother Erling! One trusts you slept well!"

"An honest man sleeps the sleep of the just. I tell you that, Kaari, as I'm sure it's a thing you did not know."

"A fellow must confess his disappointment, Brother! You promised a battle. It looks to be but a short butchery – little sport in that."

"I hope I can offer you better," Erling cried.

"How? With that handful of men?"

"No, with my own men."

"And what men are those?"

"Those men arrayed about you."

A laugh went up from Kaari's army. Kaari did not join in it.

"You think these men will come to your side?" Kaari asked. "Pick out a man! Some man you think your friend here!"

"Ogmund Bodvarsson!" cried Erling.

"I am here!" said a tall, fair-haired man.

Kaari said, "Tell Erling what you think of him, Ogmund!"

"I held you in honor once, Erling Skjalgsson!" said Ogmund. "But that was before you came and robbed me of rents I'd paid already to your brother! If my family makes it through the winter it'll be no fault of yours!"

"I swear to you, Ogmund, as I am a Christian man, that whoever robbed you was not Erling Skjalgsson."

"I know you when I see you!"

"I swear – and Father Aillil and this whole crew will swear – that I was at sea up until the day before yesterday."

"Tell it to my hungry children!"

"Listen to me!" Erling cried. "Not long since, all men knew what Erling's word meant! I have lived among you all my life! You know me! You know my deeds! Though you've known Kaari but a year or so, you've had time to learn his words and deeds!

"Take a moment and think! Think of your life when I was at Sola. Think what it's been since Kaari came! Whom do you trust?"

He stepped out through the shield-wall. He threw off his helmet and cast his shield to the ground. He dropped his sword-belt and bent double to let his *brynje* slide from his body of its own weight.

He straightened and spread his arms cross-wise. "I come

before you naked of iron!" he shouted. He walked down the hill toward them. "I offer myself to your arrows and your spears! If you believe me to be the man Kaari says I am, then slay me now!"

"No!" came the voice of Kaari. "It makes no sense to a fellow!"

With a shout, the whole crowd of Jaeder men rushed forward in a wave to raise Erling onto their shoulders and bear him home to Sola.

From my vantage on the hilltop, I could see Kaari, alone now, turning and walking away. He walked up the southern hill. It had begun snowing, and the light flakes fell on him like a grace, unmarked.

As he walked, his appearance was changed. He ceased to look like Erling, or like any man at all.

His legs elongated and grew thin, and they bent backwards like a crane's.

His body grew small, the back bent, and when he glanced back over his shoulder, I could see that his nose was long as a stork's beak. Pointed ears grew high on either side of his head.

When he neared the summit, the hilltop raised itself up like the lid of a pot and stood on six red pillars to let whatever he was in.

What tale will you tell to those who sent you, Kaari? I wondered.

And then I shouted, "Form the shield-wall!" for a multitude of misbegotten bogeys was vomiting out of the place where Kaari had just gone.

I saw a giant hairy beast with the head and horns of a bull. There was something like a woman with the head of a dog and feet that turned backwards. There was a horse with a cock's beak and the front feet of a bear. There were a hundred or two unnatural things out of nightmares, screaming and waving, brandishing claws and hooves and horns, and gnashing their teeth. They massed at the hilltop, becoming a host, as more and yet more monsters emerged.

Our men looked upward and came near to fleeing, though Erling managed to rally them with a few shouted words. The men of Kaari's force fell back to join our line.

Erling had no time to don his brynje again. It would not be a far run for the bogeys. He shouted for the men to lock shields as he strapped his helmet under his chin and took up sword and shield.

The bogeys raised a cry like souls damned and beasts tormented. I tried to reckon the odds. They were still pouring out of the hilltop.

"Play the man, lads!" cried Erling.

A man can face an army, can face an arrow-storm and a charging pig's snout of spears because, in the end, for most men, there are things he fears more than death in battle. One of these things is to be known by the name of coward.

But what, I wondered, will make a man stand when all the things he *does* fear most have gathered together to assault him? Whatever a man's nightmares might be – whatever he fears in the secret cellars of his soul – must surely have been found in that army that massed against us on the neck between the lakes.

I wanted to join Erling's line. Against such an enemy as this, a priest ought to stand. Lack of arms would mean nothing in this defense.

I could not move. I who have faced the Old Ones and the gods themselves, who have battled witchcraft and demons, I stood there with knees shaking and a shameful swampiness in my trousers. I wanted to flee. I wanted to run until I reached the sea, and then drown myself in it. If I could just get my legs to move, I'd do just that.

And then I heard a voice, singing.

At first I thought it must be Bergthor, for he was a skald. But Bergthor was dead.

It was Erling. I'd never heard Erling singing by himself before. His voice was not the most musical, but it was strong.

He sang the *Bjarkamal*, the Lay of Bjarki, an ancient battle hymn from Denmark, though its author is said to be Norwegian. *Bjarkamal* is a psalm to the Norsemen – a song every man knows and carries in his kit for use at greatest need:

> *Day has come; the cock stirs his feathers;*
> *The thralls must trudge the path to the workplace.*
> *Awake, good friends, be ware and watchful.*
> *Lords and chieftains in Athil's hall!*

> *Har the Grasper, Hrolf the Bowman,*
> *High-born men who scorn base flight,*
> *I rouse you not to drink or dalliance*
> *But to Hild's game – the warrior's sport!*

Voices joined Erling's. One by one, the warriors took up the song their fathers and grandfathers had sung.

> *War is a chapman who weighs men's value*
> *And pays them in glory for blood in the balance.*
> *Each man may choose the proof of his silver;*
> *The height of his place in Valhalla's high hall.*

> *So let true warriors doff sleep's warm blanket;*
> *Cast comfort aside; take steel for a leman;*
> *Trade feasting for fighting and mattress for mail-coat;*
> *Give worth to you lord for the gifts he has made you!*

I hate Norse lays. They're crude and artless and even Norsemen need to have them translated.

But as the song blossomed from more and more throats I thought I found a place somewhere in my belly where I did not want to run – where I wanted to stand and face the enemy and see what would happen – where I was a man who did not shame me.

Stir up the fire to warm our hands!
Make supple the fingers that handle the sword-grip!
Remember the helmets, the brynjes and Frankish blades!
Your lord gave you arm-rings – now give him return!

Once in the hall we guzzled the brown ale
And bragged of our arms and our keen battle weapons;
Now Odin watches from Hlidksjalf above
To see how men's deeds give worth to their boasting.

I found I had the strength to walk, with great difficulty, down to a place near Erling, behind the shield-wall.

Brynjes on backs! Tie helm under jaw!
Grasp the shield-grip and bare the white blade!
The sight of our backs no foeman shall look on!
Breast to breast the eagles claw –

And then the Underground Army came at us, like a swarm of insects, like a herd of horses, like the sea-hedge of the Great Ocean that sweeps away all ships and leaves shattered floating splinters behind.

The song went on. I did not know it, but I picked out a psalm and fit the words to the tune. What came to my mind – like one of the visions the Eye had given me – was not a warrior girding for battle, but a lone man, bloody and beaten and swollen, carrying a beam of black wood up a barren hill.

Then Erling cried, "ATTACK!"

Every man turned to look at him, to see if he'd been head-wounded.

"Uphill?" shouted Steinulf.

"Why wait?" Erling cried. He began to run, breaking the shield wall and leaving it behind, reaching the foot of the hill and sweeping on up onto the other.

We all ran after him. It was not an attack of arms. It was just men running toward their fear, rejoicing in the freedom that comes when you've made peace with your death.

And it was as if the sun had come out from behind a cloud. All that ugliness, those ungainly beast- and man-forms – of a sudden they seemed merely silly. They looked like toy beasts shaped from mud by children. They looked like the idols of the heathen, intended to terrify but worthy only of pity. They looked like nothing in the world that a grownup need fear.

And our whole army burst into laughter as it ran. The hills rang with robust, wholesome, holy laughter – God's comfortable gift to fallen Adam's sons.

And the host from under the hill faded out of our sight like dew in the morning, leaving not a spoor behind. We came to the place where they'd been and stopped and laughed there, while God's snow fell on our heads. We laughed at them, we laughed at ourselves, and we laughed at the whole foolish, glorious enterprise of the kingdoms of the earth.

The last sign of them was a shout from the hill – "IT MAKES NO SENSE TO A FELLOW!"

Chapter 28

"So what do you make of Kaari after all?" Erling asked Eystein a few nights later, as we feasted at home at Sola. *At home* – yes, by St. Margaret, even for me. I'd been abroad too long not to know my home by now. I may not be a Jaederer, but Jaeder is my home.

"I make nothing of him," said Eystein, his eyes narrowing at the memory. "He was the worst lord and the worst man I ever knew. If you hadn't come home, I'd have set out west to find you ere long, to bring you back or share your exile. I wasn't fooled when he played at being you. What do you make of him?"

"He went into the hill in the end. I'd wager he came out of the hill in the first place. My brother Kaari is dead, I think, or if he lives, he's a prisoner of the Old Ones, his mind wasted. This Kaari was a changeling, an Old One sent in his shape to take his place."

"But why?" asked Steinulf. "Do the Underground Folk care who's hersir in Jaeder?"

"They say Jarl Erik is less than a zealous Christian. I think it wouldn't trouble him overmuch to strike a deal with them."

"What could he offer that they'd want?"

"I've no idea. I understand the Old Ones no better than Kaari understood us."

"Since we're on the subject of Erik, what *are* we going to do about him?" asked Steinulf. "Our standing here has weakened sorely under Kaari, and you'll have to earn the Westmen's loyalty again, I fear."

"I'll be sending messengers out tomorrow. Anyone with a claim against Sola can have whatever he asks in repayment. I won't ask for witnesses; I'll just give them what they say Kaari took."

Eystein sneezed in his ale. "This'll cost you, Erling. Not all men's words are trustworthy."

"It's a price I must pay, even if we go hungry at Sola this winter. Steinulf was right; I must earn back their loyalty."

"It may not be enough, not if Jarl Erik comes with ships before winter."

"I'll have Father Aillil pray for the snow to keep coming."

I don't know if my prayers had aught to do with it, but the snow did continue. The dusting that fell on the ground the day of our battle with Kaari had continued through one white day after another, the wind gaining strength, and winter came and stayed. Erling's messengers traveled by ski and sleigh and nail-shod horse where they could, and by ship where they must, and when the claims grew too heavy to hear one by one, he just sent loaded knarrs out and told the folk to take what they needed.

"You're mad," said Steinulf. "You've got to feed your household too! Winter won't guard us forever, and in the spring you'll need a healthy bodyguard!"

"We'll tighten our belts one winter," said Erling. "There'll be other years, God willing."

"Hmmph," said Steinulf. "At least we've got our cargo from the western seas. Perhaps we can learn to eat wool and walrus hide. Or maybe you can pay Danegeld to Jarl Erik and King Svein like an Englishman, so they'll leave you alone come spring."

But in the event, the matter was decided by a mightier hand than either Erik's or Svein's. I don't mean God's. I mean that of the royal witling, King Ethelred of England. For when spring had come and Erling had called up his ship-levies to defend his Westland, no fleet appeared against us. Week after week passed with no cloud of sails breaking the horizon to the south. We waited and we wondered. What was keeping Erik?

The answer came at last in the form of a merchant from York, a man with trading ties to Erling's friend Thorbjorg Lambisdatter, who liked to put in at Stavanger. One of Erling's ships waylaid him and brought him to Sola.

"They've all sailed to England," he told us. "Svein and all the Danish host, and Erik with them."

"Why?" asked Erling.

The man shook his head. "A bad business," he said. "Who'd have looked for it? It happened last November, on St. Brice's Day. Ethelred tried to massacre all the Danes in England."

A hundred men said, "*What?*" and I crossed myself.

"Among the dead, it's said, was Svein's sister. Svein has put everything out of his head now save vengeance. He'll be King of England or die trying, they say."

I heard Astrid saying, "Ethelred, Ethelred, how massively stupid can you be?"

Erling sent the levies home, and we returned to life as we'd known it. He gave rich gifts to Konnall and sent him to England to do business and, incidentally, to learn what he could and keep him posted.

* * *

It was to Stavanger that a man named Geirodd Thorbardsson came one day in summer. Erling was building a warehouse there, and Geirodd, a large, red-faced fellow whose arms were loaded with silver rings, came in at the head of a troop of bullyboys and said, "All right, Erling Skjalgsson, what have you done with my sons?"

"Your sons?"

"Thorbrand and Thorlak Geiroddsson. I'm told they went west oversea with you. I'm a man with responsibilities; I've no time for larks."

"I know no Thorbrand or Thorlak Geirrodsson. I had two crewmen named Thorbrand and Thorlak *Gudbrandsson.*"

"My brother and I," said Thorlak, coming toward us brushing wood shavings off his shirt. "Greetings, Father."

"Why the false names?" asked Erling.

Geirodd snorted. "Boys' calf-capers. Hot heads and weak minds."

"You said we were nobodies, Father. You said that without your wealth behind us we'd never amount to anything," said Thorlak.

"Ale-talk. You baited me and I answered in kind. You shouldn't have taken it so near."

"We made up our minds to go into the world without our names and prove ourselves," said Thorlak. "How better to do that than to seek adventure with Erling Skjalgsson?"

"Well I hope you've got it out of your blood," said Geirodd. "Where's Thorbrand? Is he well?"

We all exchanged looks. "Thorbrand is dead, Father," said Thorlak. "He lies in Iceland."

Geirodd's face took on that icy mask you see on Norsemen when they get bad news. One of his bullyboys who must have known him well quickly shifted a wood-stump for him to sit on.

"How was his end?" he asked, when he was seated.

"He died well," said Erling. "He fell in honorable fight against bad odds, his wounds to the front."

Geirodd nodded his head. "It is well," he said. "Fate rules all. I have no complaints."

"He was shriven and lies in holy ground," said I.

"Thank you, Father. It is well."

He sat wordless for a while.

"You're my only heir now, Thorlak," he said at last. "Erling Skjalgsson, I'd ask you to release my son from any oaths he's sworn you. I need him at home."

"By all means, if he wishes it."

"I've a marriage in mind for you, too, Thorlak."

Thorlak smiled. "As for that, I'm already promised."

Geirodd put his head up at that. "Promised? To whom? I'll not wed my son to some tenant's daughter."

"Thorlak is promised to my sister Thorliv," said Erling. "I trust she's a good enough match for you."

Geirodd grinned a wide grin. "It will do, it will do," he said.

"Of course," said Thorlak, "the match depends on my making my fortune in the world."

"I think that'll be no problem," said Geirodd.

* * *

We had a little church in our market of Stavanger, and I was in it when an Orkneying merchant named Oddketil came in to see me.

He genuflected, then said to me, "Did you see the girl? Was she the one?"

This confused me, because I couldn't recall ever telling him about Maeve in Greenland.

"No, the voyage was for naught, for my part. There was a Maeve there, but not the one I sought."

He looked at me cross-eyed. "What are you talking about?" he asked.

"The thrall girl I went to Greenland to find. She wasn't my sister."

"Greenland? I was speaking of the girl here in Stavanger."

"Here?"

"Aye. I found a girl named Maeve in Kaupang who matched

the description you'd given me. Everyone knows it – you keep catechizing all the merchants about her. She told me she had a brother Aillil, and that she'd been sold in Gotland. When I brought her here, I found you'd sailed off to the west. I knew not what to do, but I went to Kaari Skjalgsson and he bought her from me."

I took him by the shoulders. *"What did Kaari do with her?"* I asked.

"I know not. He said he'd see to the matter. I trusted him – he was Erling's brother and all. Except that now they say he wasn't Erling's brother. I know naught of that. But I did try, Father Aillil."

I asked about, but no man recalled Kaari buying a thrall girl, or had any inkling what he'd done with her.

I hope the crabs had a meal out of Odin's Eye, for I got no good from it. All soothsayers may go North-under, me among them.

I found an Irish thrall who knew stone-cutting, and bought him his freedom in return for his carving a proper Irish high cross. I set it up by the christening pool at the Gula-Thingstead to stand forever to the glory of God, in honor of Maeve, and to beg her pardon.

The End

Afterword

I owe an apology to the town of Sola.

During a trip to Norway in 2001, I had the privilege of being interviewed by a reporter from the Stavanger *Aftenblad* newspaper. The reporter, out of consideration for my weak Norwegian, interviewed me in English, which was not her strong suit.

In all my research about Erling Skjalgsson, I had missed one point I should have been aware of. Sola and Stavanger have been engaged in a tug of war over Erling Skjalgsson for a number of years. The people of Stavanger like to believe that Erling was the founder of their city (a view I have taken up in these novels, though I have it on the authority of an archaeologist at the Stavanger Archaeological Museum that no shred of evidence for that contention has so far been found). The same view holds that when history speaks of "Erling Skjalgsson of Sola," the word "Sola" refers not to the town (then a farm) of that name but to a larger region that (theoretically) included Stavanger. They theorize that Erling's home in his heyday was not Sola Farm but someplace in Stavanger, perhaps the old Royal Farm (*Kongsgaard*).

The reporter and photographer escorted me around the Stavanger Museum (where Erling's ancient stone memorial cross stands) and the Kongsgaard, and took my picture in both places. While at Kongsgaard I said, in a speculative way, "I *could* move Erling to Stavanger."

The next day my picture appeared on the front page of the *Aftenblad* next to the headline, "WILLING TO MOVE ERLING SKJALGSSON TO STAVANGER."

A planned interview with the Sola paper the next day was abruptly cancelled.

I can't accuse the Stavanger reporter of misquoting me. I said more or less what she thought I said, but she didn't catch the nuances of a language not her own. And I learned a lesson about how one ought to talk in the presence of the press.

But, for the record, I have no plans to move Erling to Stavanger. His market there will flourish and he will reside there from time to time, but he will remain Erling of Sola (farm) in these romances.

Special thanks are due to Mari Anne Naesheim Hall and Arne Sivertson of Stavanger. Mari Anne and her family hosted me, and Arne provided transportation while I was in the city. More thoughtful tour guides will never be found this side of Ragnarok. Special thanks are also due to Marit Egaas of the Sola *Folkebibliotek*, who overlooked the ignominy that covered my name in her community to make the resources of their Erling collection available to me. Thanks to my numerous cousins on Karmøy island, and (posthumously) to Cousin Oddvar Rygg of Kolbotn.

I also want to thank Torgrim Titlestad for his books (in one of which, *Norge Blir et Rike,* he reproduces the cover of *Erling's Word* as an example of Vikings in English-language popular literature). Although I disagree with Titlestad on some points, it would be false and ungracious to deny that many of his ideas have found their way into Erling's political philosophy as I imagine it. It was also Titlestad who suggested that Erling might have visited Greenland at some time, which was the germ of this book.

Thanks to Dale Nelson of Mayville State University in North Dakota and to David Alpern, for their comments and suggestions on the manuscript. Dale also lent me his copies of William Morris' *Icelandic Journals* and Lord Dufferin's *Letters from High Latitudes,* both invaluable resources. Thanks, too, to my editors at Nordskog Publishing, Desta Garrett and Kimberley Winters Woods, for their careful eyes. Thanks also to Ben Nelson for vetting the text from a sailor's point of view.

Anyone who wishes to know more about Snorri the Chieftain may read *Eyrbyggja Saga,* and those who'd like to find out what happened to Kjartan, Bolli, and Gudrun should read *Laxdaela Saga.*

Lars Walker

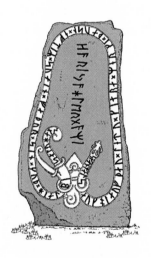

About the Author

PHOTO BY RUTH GUNDERSON

Lars **Walker** is a native of Kenyon, Minnesota, and lives in Minneapolis. He has worked as a crabmeat packer in Alaska, a radio announcer, a church secretary and an administrative assistant, and is presently librarian and bookstore manager for the schools of the Association of Free Lutheran Congregations in Plymouth, Minnesota.

He is the author of four previously published novels, and is the editor of the journal of the Georg Sverdrup Society. Walker says, "I never believed that God gave me whatever gifts I have in order to entertain fellow Christians. I want to confront the world with the claims of Jesus Christ."

His Website address is www.larswalker.com. He blogs at www.brandywinebooks.net.

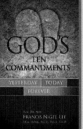